Ruining Mr. Perfect
What to Do with a Bad Boy

Body Shop Bad Boys
Test Drive
Roadside Assistance
Zero to Sixty
Collision Course

The Donnigans
A Sure Thing
Just the Thing
The Only Thing

Veteran Movers
The Whole Package
Smooth Moves
Handle with Care

All I Want for Halloween

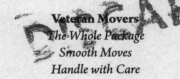

Handle with Care

MARIE HARTE

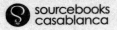

sourcebooks
casablanca

*To DT and RC, I love you guys. I figure if I dedicate
enough books to you, you might one day crack the spine
of one and even, perhaps, read it. Willingly. But not this
one, of course, because it has too many kissy parts.*

Published by Sourcebooks Casablanca, an imprint of Sourcebooks
P.O. Box 4410, Naperville, Illinois 60567-4410
(630) 961-3900
sourcebooks.com

Printed and bound in the United States of America.
OPM 10 9 8 7 6 5 4 3 2 1

CHAPTER 1

THE SIGHT THAT MET EVAN'S EYES HAD HIM STARING, unsure of what to do. Though he owned part of his and his cousins' local moving company, he'd only been doing the grunt work of actually moving people for the past two weeks. With one of his cousins temporarily out due to an injury, Evan had willingly stepped in to take up the slack.

At first, being able to get out from behind a desk, away from a past life of accounting, had seemed a blessing. Sure, he was still sore, taxing his muscles on a daily basis doing manual labor, but he considered the physical exertion to be just the thing to kick-start his new life.

No one had mentioned what to do when the client got into a free-for-all in the middle of the living room.

The client, Rachel Kim, a petite Korean woman with a soft demeanor and a cute dimple, was wrapped around a tall, statuesque black woman. Rachel had her in a headlock, clinging to her like a koala on a tree.

"I'm taking it!" she shrieked and refused to let go. "It's a memory, and it's mine!"

"Idiot, it's not yours," the other woman managed, gripping at the forearm across her neck. "It's *ours*! Ask Kenzie. Rachel, get off!" She swung around, and the two did an odd dance as the poor woman tried to shake her human burr. "Besides, you don't deserve it! Leaving me for a man? Way to idolize a penis, love slave."

O-kay. That was more than he wanted to hear. Evan had

been hired to move Rachel's things, not involve himself in her private life.

"Shut up, Lila. You're just jealous! Backstabbing *bitch*." Rachel started going off in what sounded like Korean.

Lila choked, and Evan stepped forward. Then he realized she was laughing. Well, as much as one could laugh while gasping for oxygen. She continued to struggle for freedom, to no avail.

Evan decided he should probably get involved before Lila passed out. But just as he took another step to separate the two women, sunlight beamed through the front windows, illuminating the avenging angel who stormed through the front door, her brown eyes blazing.

His world stopped. As if the woman had been bathed in radiance, she made everything around her pale in comparison. He found it difficult to breathe.

Long, light-brown hair floated around her shoulders, framing an attractive face full of life and emotion. She looked to be about his age, and she moved with grace and energy. "You two are being ridiculous," she huffed as she tried to pull Rachel and Lila apart. Dressed in ripped khaki shorts, a *Drink Local* T-shirt, and flip-flops, she shouldn't have appeared so impressive. But she did.

Evan just stood there, staring, trying to figure out what the hell was happening as his heart raced, his focus narrowed to this one incredibly arresting woman.

"Well?" the angel snapped at him. "You going to help me with these two or what?"

He started. "Oh, right." But he hadn't taken a breath before Rachel shifted to the new arrival, latching onto her and including her in the weird three-person tango.

"Nooo," Rachel moaned. "Everything is changing too fast."

Evan blinked, and the three women dissolved into tears, crumpled to the floor, and hugged one another. No one made any sense as emotions and a jumble of words, everyone talking over everyone, filled the air.

He cleared his throat. "Ah, you guys need help?"

They continued to wail, ignoring him, so he left them to their emotional crisis while he tried to figure out why he'd... panicked? Frozen? Lost his mind?

He'd once done the Heimlich on a choking man in a crowded restaurant while everyone else watched in shock. He'd prevented a young lance corporal from shooting his instructor at the rifle range during training back in his Marine Corps days. And he'd more than once talked down his oldest cousin from a fight, saving him from jail time and accompanying fines. Evan didn't panic, and he *always* knew what to do.

So why the hell had the sight of that woman frazzled him?

He walked out to the moving van, grabbed his water, and guzzled it. August in Seattle typically proved to be hot, but temps had been higher than normal, and the current heat wave had his shirt plastered to his back. The sun continued to blaze overhead, spotlighting the charming home he'd parked in front of. A small Craftsman-style cottage with a surprisingly wide doorway, thank God. Getting furniture through some of the older homes in the city took real work, and Evan always wondered how the people had gotten their furniture in to begin with because not everything came in pieces from IKEA.

He held the cold bottle against the back of his neck and studied the front walkway. The front door remained open, and he could see and hear the three women crying, laughing, and talking together.

Talk about weird.

"Yeah, they can be a bit much to take."

Evan spun around to see a lanky teenager approach. "Huh?"

The boy nodded to the home. "Chicks. Can't live with 'em, can't live without 'em."

"Wise words from one so young." Evan grinned.

The boy smiled back. "I live down the block, but this area is usually pretty loud. I think the women who live here had some kind of party pad. Lots of guys coming over, to both places." The boy nodded to the home next door as well. "My mom told me to steer clear, but maybe now that the crazy lady is moving soon too, I can swing by more."

"Crazy lady?"

"Yeah." The boy peered at the doorway. "See that woman with the long brown hair? Not Lila, the African goddess— she makes everyone call her that. She's kind of mean. I'm talking about the crazy one."

"Rachel?"

"Nah, she's just hyper. The other one is batshit nuts."

His angel. "Ah. How crazy, exactly?"

The boy sighed. "I'm not supposed to tell anyone because my mom says it's bad to spread gossip, but I'd be careful if I were you. She tried to stab some guy who broke up with her a month ago. At least I saw her screaming and waving a knife at some dude. Then *another* guy calmed her down, and her wacko friends stepped in." He shrugged. "I don't know, but it was a mess. Had the cops down here."

Considering what Evan had just witnessed, the scene didn't seem so far-fetched. "Thanks."

"Sure. Just like to help." The boy looked at the truck.

"Vets on the Go!? You some kind of animal doctor or the military kind of vet?"

"Military kind. Our company employs veterans to help people move."

The boy glanced around. "Just you?"

"Yeah. I'm helping one of the ladies move out. And she mostly only has smaller stuff. Though I'm supposed to have some help on the larger furniture. But her boyfriend hasn't arrived yet."

"Well, if you need help, let me know. Got a phone?"

Evan frowned, wondering if this was part of a scam to steal cell phones, which had become a citywide problem recently.

"Whoa." The boy raised his hands, appearing harmless. "Easy. I'm not gonna take it or anything. I'm just gonna give you my number. You can text me if the boyfriend doesn't show."

Not that Evan would. He could just see the boy getting hurt and the company being liable for a lawsuit. "I'm good, kid. But thanks anyway."

"Your loss." The boy smiled to take the sting out of his words. More shouting from inside the house turned them both in that direction once more. "Well, I'd better leave. If my mom catches me around here, she'll ground me." The boy turned and tripped, and Evan caught him before he hit the pavement.

The kid quickly righted himself, a flush on his cheeks. "Nice catch."

"Thanks."

"Well, if you change your mind, I'm the red two-story four houses down. Good luck with the crazy ladies." The boy waved goodbye.

Evan waved then turned to the job at hand. He'd given the women enough time to get it together. He had a schedule to keep, and this house had to be moved *today*. Time to load the rest of the boxes from the bedroom.

Skirting the drama in the living room, he emptied what remained into the truck, leaving room for a few larger pieces, like an armoire, desk, chair, and bed. Rachel didn't actually have that much to move, so she'd only requested one mover and a smaller truck.

He stared at the armoire and frowned, wondering how he might heft it out himself. Even with the dolly, it would take some doing. Fortunately, Rachel's boyfriend arrived, and they muscled it and the other big pieces into the truck. The women had vanished. Though Evan would have liked to have seen the "batshit nuts" looker again, he thought it for the best that he didn't.

"Thanks, man." Will, Rachel's boyfriend, tried to tip him as he locked up the back of the vehicle.

"Nah. This is such a small move. It's no biggie." It wasn't as if Evan needed the money. And Will had been a big help; he had a good amount of strength behind those wide shoulders.

"Take it," Will insisted, and Evan reluctantly pocketed twenty bucks. "Trust me. You doing this saved me a lot of hassle." Will wiped a hand over his face and asked in a lower voice after glancing around, "Did she freak out?"

"Uh, yeah. You could say that. Wrapped herself around her friend Lila like a boa constrictor and was choking her over something she insisted on taking with her. Apparently they disagreed over the thing."

Will sighed. "That stupid trophy."

"I don't know what the fight was about. I just know it got a little ugly. Then some other woman arrived, got sucked into the group brawl, and they collapsed into tears. Then laughter, then tears again. It was scary."

Will laughed. "Better you than me."

Evan wanted to ask about the sexy chick, but he stopped himself. "I'd better get going. Got to get this unloaded before traffic gets too bad." Traffic was always bad in the city, but there were degrees of road rage Evan could handle.

"Gotcha. My brother's waiting for you at my place, and you can just unload it all into my garage. He'll help with the bigger things."

"Great." Evan reached into his back pocket to verify the address on his phone. And found it empty. "Shit." He double-checked the vehicle to make sure he hadn't left it inside. Nope. Not there either.

"What's up?"

"My phone's missing." The same phone he'd had in his back pocket when he'd helped the boy who'd tripped over his own feet.

That freakin' kid.

"What color is it? I'll check the house."

"It's a red iPhone." Evan went with him. Nothing turned up.

"Man. That sucks." Will shook his head.

Evan would strangle the boy when he found him. "You ever see a tall teenager hanging around here? Light-brown hair, brown—maybe hazel—eyes?" He frowned. "Good-looking kid, seems friendly. Lives a few blocks down in a red house."

Will shook his head. "Red house? Never seen him."

"Well, he apparently knows all about the crazy lady who lives next door."

"Kenzie?"

"I don't know, but I need my phone. My life is on that thing." At least he'd password-protected it.

"I know what you mean." Will shrugged. "Might as well see."

They walked next door and knocked at the back entrance. Will shouted to be heard over raised voices, "Yo, Kenzie. I got a problem."

The door opened, and Evan's angel appeared…holding a knife.

Evan gaped. "Holy shit. The kid wasn't kidding."

She stared from them to the knife in her hand and blushed. "I was just making a salad. Cutting vegetables."

"With a *butcher knife*?" Evan had a tough time believing that. Then he met her striking gaze, that color in her eyes an intriguing mix of green and brown that seemed to change as he watched her. All thought left his mind.

Her blush intensified. "All the other knives are dirty…" She threw over her shoulder, "Since someone hasn't done the dishes like he was supposed to!"

No one answered, though Evan heard Rachel and Lila talking in another room.

Kenzie stepped back. "Come on in."

Evan knew it wasn't smart, but drawn to Kenzie and needing his phone, he followed her into the kitchen, Will behind him. Rachel and Lila joined them.

"Hey, babe." Rachel gave Will a kiss, the petite woman comfortably enfolded by the larger man hugging her so tightly.

"Lunatic." Will grinned. "Oh, and Lila. Didn't see you there, Lunatic Junior."

Lila flipped him off.

"What's going on?" Kenzie asked Will while studying Evan with an odd look on her face. He couldn't tell if it was fear, disdain, or curiosity because the expressions flashed by so fast and she refused to meet his gaze. Probably a good thing, considering a smart guy shouldn't want to be on this woman's radar. No matter how fine she might be.

He couldn't help noticing her long, slender legs or the curves under the thin cotton of her T-shirt. Or that she must be reacting to the cool breeze that suddenly blew through the room because her nipples had turned to hard little points.

Forcing himself to glance away before he embarrassed himself by leering, Evan saw a surprisingly neat and orderly kitchen, something he wouldn't have expected of the supposedly unstable woman.

Will explained, "Someone took Evan's cell phone. Some teenager who lives a few doors down in the red house."

Rachel frowned. "Red house? That's Tom McCall's place, and he's eighty-four. His grandkids live in Vegas, and they're in their thirties."

Kenzie's eyes widened. "He did not."

Lila blew out a breath. "Oh boy."

"What's going on?" Evan had a schedule these people were destroying minute by minute. "Look, I really have to get going. And I need my phone. So if you have any idea where this kid is, I'd appreciate you telling me."

Kenzie gripped the knife in her hand even tighter, Evan noticed. "Ah, maybe you should put down the weapon, Kenzie." Saying her name gave him an odd thrill, and he chalked it up to adrenaline.

"Knife? What?" She looked confused.

Lila answered, "I think he means the potential murder weapon in your hand. Put it down before you stab someone."

Will took a step back, and Rachel planted herself in front of him. "Not the face, Kenzie. You can stab him anywhere else, but I like my men pretty."

"Jesus, Rachel, it was one time and an accident," Kenzie snapped.

"That I'll never forget." Will showed Evan his forearm, where a large scar bisected his arm. "Almost took my arm off."

Lila and Rachel erupted into laughter.

"If you could see your face." Will grinned. "Kidding, man. This is from a car accident years ago. Kenzie only stabbed me with a paring knife when I got too close to her cucumbers."

Kenzie chimed in, looking furious, "That I was in the middle of cutting. *Daniel*," she shouted. "Get your ass down here!"

"We can never be truly sure it was an accident," Rachel added in a loud whisper.

Will nodded. "I still have the emotional scars."

Evan felt as if he'd fallen down the rabbit hole. "You people are giving me a headache. Do you or do you not know where my phone is?" He stared at the knife still clutched in Kenzie's hand.

She dropped it in the sink and stomped into the living room.

Everyone followed her, so Evan did as well. He couldn't help seeing a fairly neat and eclectically decorated house full of color. Rich hardwoods and handcrafted moldings gave the house an upscale feel, but the furniture appeared worn and comfortable. No sign of clutter except for some gaming magazines, a pair of large sneakers by the couch, and an opened bag of chips on the coffee table.

They continued up the stairs and passed two bedrooms and a bathroom then paused at the doorway to the last bedroom down the hall.

"He's not here," Kenzie fumed. She spun around and moved so quickly she knocked into Evan.

He gripped her shoulders to stop her from moving *through* him. The contact startled him, once more shocking him into immobility.

Kenzie stared back, her lips full, rosy, and begging for a kiss.

Someone cleared her throat.

Evan immediately dropped his hands and stepped back. "Sorry." *Shit.* His voice sounded thick, gravelly.

"S-sure. I just… It's my…"

"Mom! I'm home," a familiar voice called from downstairs.

Evan stared into Kenzie's face, putting the pieces of the puzzle together. Now that he thought about it, the boy did look a lot like his mother. Yet their ages seemed a little close for her to be a mom. Unless she'd had him as a teenager herself.

Her eyes darkened. "*Mom?*" She stormed past Evan.

He noted the caution on the others' faces. "This can't be good."

Rachel sighed. "You got that right."

Then he followed the group once more, aware he was losing time, his focus, his phone…and wondered when crazy had become contagious.

CHAPTER 2

KENZIE SYKES RUSHED DOWNSTAIRS TO SEE HER "SON" smiling like an angel.

Ha. More like the devil in disguise. She must have been very bad in a past life to be saddled with such a little punk. One not so little anymore. The boy had surpassed her own five-seven frame years ago and now took great delight in looking down on her. Literally.

"What's up, Mom?"

"Look, bozo, we're not doing this again. Give him back his phone."

"What? Whose phone?"

"And quit calling me Mom." Her cheeks blazed, and she wondered why today of all days she had to meet Evan—Adonis personified.

When she'd spied the hottie moving Rachel's things, she'd peered through the window, catching every glimpse she could. Tall, muscular, great cheekbones. And that ass… She sighed.

So *of course* Daniel had to ruin it for her. Because no way sexy mover guy would want to go out with a woman surrounded by so much nuttiness. Not that she'd ask him out or anything, but a girl could dream.

First, he'd seen her break down with her best friends. Then her thief of a brother had stolen his cell phone. And Daniel had been doing so well lately.

Mr. Not-So-Innocent blinked. "Why are you so mad?"

She knew that look, the one that said Daniel had done *exactly* what he'd been accused of.

"Buddy, where's my phone?" Evan's deep voice sounded calm, but she knew he had to be furious.

"Buddy?" Daniel raised a brow and in a lofty tone added, "My name is—"

"Daniel. Thomas. Sykes," she answered for him in precise, clipped words. "You give the man his phone back *right now*."

"But Mom…"

"And quit calling me Mom!"

Behind her, Rachel snickered. Will coughed to stifle a laugh.

"It's not funny."

"It kind of is," Lila muttered.

"Hey, I don't have his phone. Frisk me." Daniel held up his hands.

Evan sighed. "I'm so behind." She noticed him glancing at the clock on the wall. "Look, kid, I have a job to do. Just give me the phone, and I'll let this go."

Daniel shrugged. "I saw it on the ground, so I picked it up and put it on the hood of your truck. If it's not there now, it's not my fault."

Evan stormed out the door, and Kenzie rushed past her brother with the others. She saw Evan reach for a phone on the hood of his truck.

Suddenly she felt bad, that she might have accused her brother of something he for once hadn't done.

"Told you," Daniel said.

Evan glared at him. "Neat trick. Especially because it was in my back pocket until you bumped into me. But whatever."

He turned, speared Kenzie with a frustrated expression—
how is this my fault?—then got into the truck and left.

"Well, that's a potential love slave down the drain," Lila
said. "Too bad. He had a nice ass."

"True." Rachel and Lila bumped knuckles.

Will rolled his eyes.

Daniel gagged.

Kenzie turned and yanked her brother into the house.
She didn't yell at him, just stared, giving him her guilt-heavy
"I'm so disappointed" look because she knew how much he
hated it.

He tried to outlast her, but as usual, he failed. "I hate
my life!" He rushed away, heading upstairs. A door slammed.

She turned to see her friends pitying her. "Oh, screw
off."

They started laughing, and she couldn't help a sigh.
"That was terrible, wasn't it? That guy is never going to
help any of us move ever again." Sad, but since a relationship didn't seem to be in the cards for her anyway, losing the
moving god before she'd had a chance to screw up their first
date could only be expected.

"That poor guy. A twenty-buck tip wasn't enough." Will
shook his head. "Daniel is such an ass." He chuckled. "I love
that kid."

"Shh. Don't let him hear you," Rachel admonished, and
in a lower voice added, "Not in front of Kenzie."

She wished her friends would discourage her brother
from his illegal antics. But since Daniel had been banished
from anything computer-related for the next few weeks until
school started, he'd taken to "acquiring" electronic devices
from friends to reach the internet. Now, how to make him

stop behaving like a jackass and turn back into the responsible teenager he'd once been, back before the evil entity called puberty had entered his body and turned him into a conniving monster?

"Still, too bad you didn't get a shot at being Moving Man's love slave," Lila said. "Because he was giving you the eye. We all saw it."

"I did," Will agreed.

"And he was sex-eee. With three e's." Trust Lila not to let it go.

"So *you* date him." Kenzie shrugged, pretending the potential loss didn't annoy her. Which told her she'd better start putting in overtime at the job. If she had time to think about dating, she had enough time to take on that pain-in-the-ass client she'd told herself not to take.

"I'm not into white guys." Lila grinned, lying through her teeth.

Even Rachel snorted at that.

Lila frowned. "And you hush. You got your own white guy."

"I'm a quarter Hispanic, actually," Will cut in. "And my uncle is—"

"Besides, Moving Man wasn't looking at me like he wanted to do me. Which is too bad because I could teach him some things…"

Kenzie groaned. "Can we please not talk about him anymore? Why don't we focus on what's really bothering all of us?"

"The fact that no one has commented about how fine *I* am?" Will asked. "Because I'm much better looking than Evan."

Rachel nodded solemnly and patted Will on the arm.

"No, what's really bothering us is the fact that you're stealing Rachel," Lila answered. "I mean, I know you're not. Not really. You're all in love and stuff, but I'm going to miss my roomie." Lila teared up.

Damn it. Kenzie thought she'd expended enough tears for the day. "I'm going to miss you too."

"I feel it, right here." Rachel put a hand over her heart. "But we'll always be sisters from other misters."

"Oh my God." Will let out a loud breath. "We're just moving eight blocks over. You still work together all the time, and we're within walking distance."

"I feel it," Rachel repeated. "Not the same."

Will groaned. "I need a drink. I'll talk to you drama queens later." He gave Rachel a peck on the lips. "I've gotta get back to work. See you soon, Meryl Streep."

They watched him leave.

"Yep. Thrown over for a penis." Lila shook her head.

Daniel froze behind her, having come into the kitchen. He turned around and stomped back the way he'd come, throwing over his shoulder, "Have I mentioned how much I hate my life?"

Evan dropped off the furniture with some help from Will's brother and returned to the office three hours later. A traffic accident, combined with the five o'clock rush, had pushed him into a bad time to be on the road.

He checked the truck back in to the large warehouse space they shared with a local bakery's delivery vehicles.

The original office, which used to exist on the ground floor near the front of the building, had been under repair since Vets on the Go! had opened. It was supposed to be fixed at some point, but his cousins had decided to make the upstairs space the central point of the company. With all the business they'd had recently, no one had the time or energy to redo what had already been done.

Taking the stairs to the second floor, Evan walked down the long hallway, passing a watch repair shop and phone/computer repair store on his right and a clothing boutique on the left. "Clothing boutique" was being kind. Miriam, an older woman who equated female empowerment with sexual awareness, sold clothes when not running her workshops where women got naked and explored themselves.

As the new guy, he'd been pranked not long ago into dealing with her on behalf of his poor, beleaguered cousin Reid.

Evan still couldn't believe he'd fallen for it. Especially since Reid had claimed not to be able to handle the woman himself. As if. Reid could and did handle everything that came at him. He'd been the one to come up with the idea of tailoring a moving company to employ veterans, making a future for his rough-talking older brother, Cash.

Added to that, they now employed more than a dozen veterans and had made a name for themselves as trustworthy and professional. Being a part of Vets on the Go! with his family made Evan proud and helped him feel included. As part of a larger family.

Too bad that like all families, this one had its share of dysfunction.

And speaking of which…

"Oh, there you are, Mr. Suave," a deep voice growled from the main office at the end of the hall. "Reid was looking for you." A large man with large muscles and an even bigger mouth stood in the doorway, looking like a mountain of irritability under that scowl.

"And now my day is complete." Evan glared at Smith, the old new guy. Smith had only been with the company for a few weeks longer than Evan.

Smith Ramsey—Cash and Reid's secret brother, who wasn't so secret considering Smith and Cash resembled each other way too much to be a coincidence. But only family and Cash's girlfriend knew the truth. Evan still wondered if Smith knew of the connection, but he'd leave that to his cousins to sort out.

"What's wrong, Griffith? Not used to working up a sweat?" Smith smirked.

Evan resisted the urge to wipe that smirk off his face because one, the guy was huge, and two, the punch might be satisfying but the resultant mess they'd make of the office would be a nightmare. Evan preferred a peaceful resolution over a physical one, and he really didn't want Smith rearranging his face. Ever.

Evan ignored him, not giving Smith the reaction he wanted, and stepped past him toward Reid's office.

Vets on the Go! was situated at the end of the long hallway, a suite of four rooms, the main lobby being the largest. Behind the welcome desk sat Finley, a prior Navy guy, typing into a computer. No one waited in the seating area, and the other two offices looked dark behind the glass doors. Beyond the desk, Reid's voice carried past his open door.

Finley glanced up from the computer, stopped typing,

and picked up the quarter lying next to the keyboard. "Reid wants you."

"I heard."

Finley flipped the coin over his knuckles with a dexterity best left to thieves and magicians. He said he had magic in his blood, but Evan wouldn't put it past the guy to also have a shady history. Like most of the colorful staff at Vets on the Go!, Finley had served his country and had an entertaining past. Because God forbid his cousins hire normal people.

The thought popped into his head: *As if* you're *normal?* He had adjusted to the motley crew pretty fast.

He walked into Reid's office and was waved into a seat. As usual, his cousin had a full cup of coffee by a stack of invoices and paper piles neatly organized on his desk. The demand for their services continued to skyrocket, and Evan couldn't be happier. He usually downplayed his excitement, though he watched every single Vets on the Go! commercial on TV, getting a huge kick out of seeing his and his cousins' faces flashing across the screen.

Reid hung up the phone and groaned. "Man, I need a break. Is it Friday yet?"

"Try Tuesday, five-ish. Want to go grab a cold one while we chat?"

"Hell yeah." They left Reid's office after Reid had gathered his things. "Finley, lock up and go home."

"Roger that."

Smith must have already left because Evan saw no sign of the gruff man. As he and Reid walked down the stairs and made small talk, Evan filled him in on his day and had Reid in tears by the time they reached their cars.

"Seriously? You got taken by a teenager?"

"Laugh it up. The kid was good. Smoother than Finley, and I—" His phone buzzed in his back pocket, and unfortunately his ring tone…was not what it should have been.

Reid blinked. "Your ring tone is 'Dancing Queen'? ABBA, Evan? Really?"

Evan flushed. "That freakin' kid."

Reid burst into more laughter. Great. Evan would be hearing about this for days.

They planned to meet at their usual hangout, a bar a short drive away. Ringo's Bar had great appetizers and killer dark ales. More than ready to sit down and eat, Evan entered and found Cash and his girlfriend, Jordan, sitting at a table, arguing over something.

"Man, he and Smith really do look alike," Evan said once Reid had joined him by the entrance.

Reid nodded. "We're still not sure how to handle it. I mean, it's weird enough Smith is my half brother. But to know Cash is too? That Dad wasn't Cash's dad? Weird. Weirder to think Smith and Cash are actually full-on siblings."

Evan had learned, along with his cousins, that his aunt Angela had been unfaithful. So while Uncle Charles was Reid's dad, the man didn't have any blood relation to Cash, which would explain the ugly family dynamics from years past.

"Sometimes it's good to be an only child," Evan said, meaning it, wondering if that was why Daniel, the phone thief, had acted out. Evan had done his share of rebellion growing up, though never to the extent of thievery. Or breaking the law. Or getting a detention. *Man, I guess I am as boring as Sheila accused me of being.*

But what could he do? Evan had responsibilities, a

mother who needed him, and a career he cared about. Blowing it all off to spend a spur-of-the-moment getaway in Hawaii with Sheila, on his tab, didn't make much sense. The sex would have been nice, but not when it came with so much attached. Ending it with her months ago had been a no-brainer, but now he had to consider her insults might have had merit.

Cash looked up and waved them over.

Reid tugged Evan with him. "No talking about Smith, okay?"

"You don't have to tell me twice. Guy gets on my last damn nerve."

Reid chuckled. "Yeah, he's just like Cash."

They reached the table, and Jordan scooted over in the booth. Before Reid could sit with her, Evan nudged him out of the way. "Let me sit next to the hot chick. You sit next to Conan."

"Funny guy." Cash grinned. He smiled a lot more now that he'd hooked up with Jordan, another veteran and fellow Vets on the Go! employee. With Cash and Jordan now living and working together, the jokes at work had been flying fast and free. And mostly by Smith, come to think of it.

Evan asked, "So when are you coming back to work? The cast comes off, what, in four more weeks?"

Cash nodded and held up his left arm, still in a cast.

Jordan frowned. "No, the doctor said eight weeks."

"Actually, he said six to eight weeks. It's been two weeks since I got the cast. So doing the math," Cash said slowly, as if speaking to someone not so bright, "that's four more weeks."

Jordan's scowl spoke volumes.

Evan and Reid shared a grin. Cash had a habit of trying

to boss everyone around. At six foot four and armed with muscles and the know-how to use them, he normally won. But with Jordan, the outcome of any argument was sixty–forty…in her favor. An Army vet and prior military police, Jordan didn't take crap. From anyone.

"So before you two get into a slapfest, how about pretzel bites on me?" The frowns Evan received for "slapfest" disappeared at the mention of free food.

"Fine." Jordan huffed.

"Good." Cash nodded.

Evan left to order and returned to his seat to hear Cash ask Reid, "Where's Naomi?"

"Had a late meeting with a new client. And no, I'm not worried. I trust her," Reid said before Cash could tease him. "Naomi's doing some PR work for Jennings Tech. You remember Chris Jennings, Evan?"

"Chris Jennings. That geek who's now a millionaire? Man, I knew Chris's brother in the Corps. Hell, I set up logistics for his platoon for a few exercises. He's a good guy and still in that I know of." Out in the field, Marines needed supplies, and Evan's job had been to coordinate and oversee logistical support. "I remember Matt talking about Chris, surprised his little brother had joined."

Reid smiled. "I know. Small world. Cash and I both knew him overseas, and we're still renting his house."

"You mean you're renting until you officially move in with Naomi," Jordan cut in, "and Cash moves the rest of his stuff into your mom's house. I mean, your house."

"*Our* house," Cash corrected her, warmth in his eyes.

Wow. Had his oldest cousin changed. Still a hard-ass, but now Cash showed his affection. Funny what love could do to a guy. "Speaking of moms," Evan said, "my mother is demanding a family dinner. So don't even think of putting her off again."

Reid flinched. "I know, I know. I'm sorry. I've just been so busy…"

"She wants you two over for dinner this Friday. No more excuses." He glared at Cash, who raised his hands in surrender.

"Fine by me. I love to eat, and Aunt Jane can *cook*." He took Jordan's hand across the table and kissed the back of it. "But not better than you, honey."

"Because I was so worried." Jordan rolled her eyes.

"Not to exclude you or Naomi, Jordan," Evan hurried to say, "but Mom has some things to tell these two she doesn't want to share outside of family just yet."

"Oh, sounds like you two are in for it." Jordan's eyes brightened. "No problem."

Cash groaned. "Aunt Jane always had a way of making you feel two inches tall. But only when you did something bad."

"Which for Cash was about all the time," Evan said.

Reid nodded. "I was the good one. But not as good as Evan."

Evan ignored the knowing smirks they shot him. "Not my fault I can do no wrong."

Cash and Reid shared a glance.

Jordan patted his shoulder. "Ignore them, Evan. They just wish they could pull off manly, handsome, and sophisticated like you do."

He beamed. "For that, I forgive you for setting me up with Miriam." Because Reid and Cash had definitely been behind it, but Jordan had suckered him into that awful prank.

Jordan laughed. "Thanks. But you know, I'd do it again.

So worth it to hear the horror in your voice when you saw what the ladies in her self-awareness class were up to."

He felt himself blushing. They laughed, and talk turned to the varied personalities in the Vets on the Go! building.

After Evan and the others had eaten and drunk their fill, Reid explained his original reason for their meeting. Budget concerns.

Evan and Reid, once again, argued over where to direct their funds. Marketing and publicity continued to take priority in Evan's eyes. But Reid thought they'd done enough, even though his girlfriend was their PR liaison.

Reid frowned. "I'm not saying fire her or anything. I just want to keep our amount the same. Let's funnel our increased revenue into more trucks."

"And maintenance?" Evan knew all about the headaches associated with keeping an organization running. "No. We have a set amount put aside for this. I told you that already."

"Here we go." Cash sighed. "The eggheads talk money and tax breaks. My head hurts."

"Neanderthal," Evan said in as insulting a tone as he could manage.

"He got you on that one." Jordan nudged at Evan to move, so he slid out of the booth. To Cash she said, "Come on, love muffin. Let's let the big kids talk while you and I take a hike. This is beyond my pay grade."

"Mine too." Cash shoved Reid, who almost fell onto the floor, and stepped around him.

Reid caught himself and muttered under his breath.

Once Cash and Jordan had left, Evan turned to Reid. "Okay, we hashed this out days ago. Why did you want them gone?"

Reid sighed. "I thought you should know."

"Know what?"

"Your mom."

"What about her?" Evan had been making up any time away from work on those days he had to take his mom to the doctor. Or grocery shopping, or to anywhere she needed to go. Several months ago they'd learned she might be sick. Now Evan needed to spend as much time as he could with her.

Reid cringed. "I, ah, saw her kissing some guy at the market a few days ago. Thought you might want to know."

Evan blinked. "My mother? My seventy-one-year-old does crochet and has bingo night with her friends every Thursday mother? That mother? Jane Griffith?"

"Yeah. Her. She looked happy, though."

"Mom was kissing some guy." Evan couldn't believe it. Mom, with a guy? And she hadn't told him? They told each other *everything*.

"Hey, I think it's great she's dating again. I mean, your dad's been gone for six years. She should live a little."

"She'll have a coronary if he goes for second base," Evan growled, uncomfortable just thinking about it. "I mean, Mom's older. She should be—"

"Cuddling her grandchildren?" Reid raised a brow. "Spending her golden years smiling and laughing instead of trying to match up her socially awkward, annoyingly clever only son?"

"*Most* of that sounds like it came from her mouth."

"Well, I added the socially awkward and annoyingly clever parts myself."

"Thanks a lot."

"Hey, I told her I'd mention it." Reid pointed a finger at him. "Get married and give her grandkids because she's not getting any younger. Those *are* her exact words, by the way. And she'd already called me to remind me about dinner this Friday, but thanks for nagging us about it."

"If she talked to you, why did she tell me to tell you?"

"Covering all her bases, most likely." Reid put down some money for the bill. "Now I have a date with a beautiful redhead, and you can bet your ass I'll be talking about her at our dinner Friday. Get a life, Evan. You're no longer working all the time, so you have no excuse."

An image of the knife-wielding angel from earlier in the day surfaced. "I'm not interested in dating. Besides, my last girlfriend called me boring."

"You are boring. But I hear desperate single women aren't so choosy."

Evan flipped him off.

Reid laughed. "Right. And have I mentioned that Smith will be your moving partner for the next two weeks? The Hillford job starts tomorrow. Magnolia, big project. Don't be late."

Evan's phone rang, and ABBA sounded loud and proud from his back pocket.

Reid laughed his ass off. Evan plunked his head down on the table and groaned.

CHAPTER 3

THURSDAY AFTERNOON, DANIEL SYKES COVERTLY STARED at his sister, currently moping with Lila about missing Rachel, who sat next to them chattering about how wonderful her boyfriend was about moving in together—all while the three of them sketched new ideas for some job they'd contracted.

Girls. He shook his head and quietly left his crouched position at the top of the basement stairs. Sykes Design, his sister's graphic design business, had done a lot for his life. It allowed Kenzie to be around if he needed something, provided her with awesome friends he'd grown up loving like his own family, and gave them an income so they didn't lose the house their parents had willed to them.

But while he appreciated being around his sister, whom he loved like crazy, it was also kind of annoying to have her hovering all the time. Especially when he had crap to do she likely wouldn't approve of.

Stealthily, he snuck to the kitchen, dropped a note on the counter, and left the house for the nearest bus stop. Twenty minutes later, he found his friend hanging at a local coffee place that made the best soft pretzels. And for cheap.

He bought two pretzels and two sodas and met Rafi in the back. Cha-ching. The awesome guy had brought his laptop.

"Payment." Rafi held out a hand. An upcoming junior who stood a few inches shorter than Daniel, Rafi was supposedly a cute guy in demand, according to all the girls last year. Daniel didn't know about that, but he did like the fact they played the same video games. Plus they had bossy older sisters in common. He still couldn't remember how they'd become friends, but he treasured hanging out with the guy. Rafi was cool, older, and he treated Daniel like an equal.

Daniel handed him a pretzel and a drink. In return, Rafi pushed his laptop Daniel's way.

When Rafi noticed Daniel Googling Vets on the Go!, he snorted. "Man, those guys are everywhere."

"Huh?"

"Why are you looking at that? My sister works for them."

Daniel glanced at his friend. "Really? Because they helped my mom's—my sister's—friend move a few days ago." He inwardly winced. He usually did much better at calling Kenzie his sister. But he'd been calling her Mom forever, and sometimes he relapsed.

"Cool."

"Yeah. But the moving guy was giving my sister looks." Daniel had stopped *that* right away. His "crazy chick" stories usually worked in his favor. Kenzie didn't need more crying jags or a man treating her like dirt. Why deal with that nonsense when you could stop it before it began?

But Kenzie's actions had been…strange, even for his sister. She hadn't so much as looked at a guy since jackhole Bryce. Yet she'd seemed seriously interested in the moving dude. Daniel knew her tells, the way she worked so hard not to show that she liked a guy. He decided it wouldn't hurt to get more information about the "hunky mover with the nice ass."

God, if he had to hear Lila say that one more time he'd puke.

"What kind of looks?" Rafi's eyes widened, then he nodded and sighed. "Oh, right. *Kenzie.*"

"Ew."

Rafi grinned. "Come on, man, she's hot. And she's not your mom, so it's normal she have a life, right?"

"You like to think of *your* sister with some guy?"

"I have two sisters. One's engaged to a jerk, and the other's in love with some huge, badass Marine." Rafi snorted. "Some guy? Jordan just moved in with 'some guy.' But he's not so bad, really. He took care of Juan for me and beat up some gangbangers."

"Really?" Daniel frowned. Evan hadn't seemed all that badass, but he was big. And driving that truck, he had to be some kind of service member. Maybe a Marine. How great would it be if he was the guy actually shacking up with Jordan? Then Daniel could tell his sister what a loser Evan was. "What's the guy's name your sister's living with?"

"Cash Griffith."

Bummer. But Griffith was Evan's last name, according to his cell phone. "The guy checking out Kenzie was Evan Griffith. Is Cash his brother?"

"Cousin, I think. Reid is Cash's brother."

Daniel smirked. "I swiped his phone and set him up."

"Nice." Rafi slurped his soda. "You want me to see what I can find on the guy? I'll talk to Jordan, but all casual-like."

"Yeah." Daniel moved his fingers over the keys, never as at home as he was when typing on a keyboard. While Rafi messed with his phone, Daniel pulled up Evan's name, found out a few particulars, then did a more detailed search.

In seconds he had Evan's address, phone number, and places of business at hand. Kenzie had been a little too emphatic about how much she didn't like the guy. Unfortunately, Daniel had seen her looking pretty hard at Evan when the guy had been bitching about his phone.

Kenzie hadn't so much as looked at a man since she'd broken up with Bryce over a year ago. As usual, thoughts about Bryce hurt. Made Daniel feel that same old guilt for ruining his sister's life.

So he did what made him feel good and tapped into a locked system—the school's admin server.

"What schedule do you want for this upcoming year?"

Rafi put his phone down and said through a mouth of pretzel, "I registered last term."

"Yeah, but we can make sure you get what you wanted."

Rafi swallowed and leaned closer. "Well, I know I don't want French with Mathison. Can you hook me up with Mr. Charbeau instead?"

"Don't you mean Monsieur Charbeau?" Daniel asked as he made some changes, rearranging Rafi's schedule so he had more classes with friends. Then he did the same for himself.

Some time later, he checked his phone and saw a few messages from Kenzie. "Shoot. Gotta go."

Rafi nodded, pleased. The guy had been a lot happier lately since moving back home with his folks. Rafi didn't seem to realize how lucky he was to have a choice. Daniel had one home, no parents, no other family to stay with but Kenzie. If he didn't include Lila, Rachel, and now Will.

And who knew how long Will would last with Rachel? Bryce had said he loved Kenzie. He'd lived with them, had hung out with Daniel like a best friend. Then he'd left and hadn't come back.

Daniel hated thinking about Bryce. "See you tomorrow?"

Rafi nodded. "After my tutor. Got math and science to make up."

"Summer school's gotta suck."

Rafi sighed. "Yeah. But at least I don't have Simpson to worry about. What a tool."

Daniel stood and left, but before going home, he made a decision he hoped wouldn't have negative consequences.

———————————————

Evan counted to ten in his head. Then out loud. Smith truly had a superpower because it took a lot to get on Evan's last nerve.

"You like numbers, eh?" Smith pulled the truck into the warehouse garage, where they'd keep it overnight before offloading the next morning into the Hillfords' *first* storage facility. The customer had three different storage lots to contain the possessions filling the nine-thousand-square-foot home they'd recently put up for sale.

"I love numbers," Evan muttered. "I can't stand know-it-alls who don't know when to shut up. I thought you didn't talk."

"I don't. Normally." Smith gave him a wicked smile. "But then, I had no idea you had an alter ego... Nice ass." He snickered for the millionth time that day.

Not only had that Daniel kid given Evan a new ringtone, he'd also made it so that anytime Evan's number appeared on anyone's contact list, it now read *Sexy Movin' Man with a Nice Ass*. And Smith had been all over that all day long.

In fact, everyone had something to say about it. They'd been brutal. And his mother... He flushed. She'd laughed and laughed, so hard he thought she'd choke. He had to get his phone fixed, stat.

He slammed out of the truck and checked the back to make sure it remained locked. And then he heard that voice. The bane of his existence.

"Um, is Evan Griffith here? I need to talk to him."

Smith said, "Who wants to know?"

"Look, no-neck. Is he here or not?" Daniel Sykes didn't have a lick of sense.

Silence.

Evan moved around the truck and saw Daniel Sykes nervously studying Smith, who stood propped against the front of the truck, his huge arms crossed over his chest.

"Yo, Evan, somebody here looking for you." Smith didn't move. "And he's got a big mouth."

Daniel blinked at Smith, in awe. "Are you Cash Griffith?"

Smith straightened, and Evan saw the fury in his face. Even Daniel took a step back.

"Fuck no. That asshole's not here today. Instead *I'm* stuck with him." He nodded to Evan then left, fiddling with something in the back of the truck.

Daniel seemed to sag in relief then stiffened when he realized Evan was watching him.

Evan adopted Smith's pose, waiting for the boy to speak. He wanted to ring the kid's neck…then slap him on the back and congratulate him for a prank well done. Hey, Evan might be annoyed, but he had a sense of humor. ABBA had been bad enough, but the new moniker was inspired…as long as someone else became the butt of the joke. Evan actually couldn't wait to try it on his fellow vets.

"I, uh, I'm sorry." Daniel let out in a rush, "About before. I can fix your phone if you want."

Evan just watched him.

The kid fidgeted. "It was just a prank, okay? And you started it."

"How did I start it?"

"You were eye-fucking my sister."

"You mean your mother?"

"Don't be a dick. You know what I mean."

Evan blinked. "First of all, nice mouth. Second, I was more interested in your sister wielding a knife and getting my phone back than anything else." A total lie, but he couldn't admit he found her attractive after the kid had caught him checking her out. "Besides, *someone* told me she was crazy."

"I was protecting her from a perv."

Evan sighed. "Is this an apology you worked on, or are you winging it?"

Daniel flushed. "I'm sorry I screwed with your phone. So are you into my sister or not?"

"Sorry, kid. I have too much on my plate to be dating." Like a mother who needed help to doctors' appointments and pharmacies when she wasn't making out with some stranger in public. "Even someone as amazing as your sister surely is."

Daniel seemed to relax. "Oh. Okay then. Give me your phone, and I'll put it back the way it was."

Evan knew he'd be a fool to trust the boy again, but what worse thing could the kid do? Besides, he wanted it fixed before he had to check in with his old job at Peterman & Campbell Accounting for some consulting work they wanted done. While Evan did have a nice ass, he didn't think it professional to announce it to his old firm or his remaining clients.

He handed over his phone and watched Daniel. "So do you screw with all your sister's guys the way you messed with me? And before you get started, I don't mean anything by 'guy' in my case. I was just there to do a job, and I did it."

So remember that the next time you fantasize about kissing her, he ordered himself. *Don't be a leering hypocrite.*

"Maybe I do. But they aren't her guys, just wannabes." A pause. "Kenzie, guys? Right." The boy's lips thinned, and he handed back the phone. Then he hit a button and showed Evan his proper screen name and played back his normal ringtone.

"Where the hell did you get ABBA, anyway? Isn't that before your time?"

"Kenzie, Rachel, and Lila have odd tastes in music." Daniel looked around. "So you're a mover? Like, you do this for a living?"

"Yeah. It's not bad. Hard work, but it's brainless." Evan realized how that sounded. "I mean, I use my brain of course. But it's less mentally taxing than accounting."

Daniel frowned. "You're an accountant?"

Evan's growing headache killed his desire to prolong the conversation. "It's late, and I'm getting ready to call it a day. Is there something else you needed?"

"Ah, no." The boy looked disappointed.

Great. Now Evan felt like an ogre. "Do you have a ride home?"

"I took the bus."

"Come on. I'll drive you."

"Nah. I'm good."

"Jesus, kid. I'm not going to jump your sister. I'm just going to give you a ride home then leave and never come back."

Daniel narrowed his eyes. "You swear?"

Evan blew out a breath. "Does crazy run in the family?"

At that, Daniel grinned. "Had you going though, didn't I?"

Evan smiled back. "Yeah, you little punk. You did."

"Kenzie calls me that sometimes. A little punk."

"Well, it's better than a little shit. That didn't sound so nice the first time I thought about you that way."

"Daniel! You'd better be here, you little punk."

Daniel's laugh turned into a groan at the sound of his sister's voice. "See?" He covered his eyes with his hand. "She found me."

Kenzie Sykes stormed into the bay, looking as fine as she had two days ago. Sadly, Evan had committed her features to memory, and he hadn't been wrong. For a woman with brown hair and brown eyes, average in height and build, she should have been, well, average.

Yet she fascinated him. Even her voice, husky, sensual... Hell. *Not interested,* he kept reminding himself.

She spotted him and stopped in her tracks.

Daniel stared from Kenzie to Evan and frowned. "How did you find me?"

"The finder app. I snuck it onto that phone I told you not to take out of the house. You know, the one you're not supposed to be using?"

He blushed. "I was hanging with a friend. I took it for emergency only. Didn't even use it."

"Uh-huh." She held out her hand and waited for him to give it back. Then she turned to Evan, stared, and said nothing.

He stared back, waiting.

"What the hell is this?" Smith boomed and took in the scene. He gave the woman what passed for a smile on his grim face. "Well, hi there."

"H-hello." She cleared her throat and focused on Evan once more. "Evan? That's your name, right?"

Evan nodded.

"I just wanted to apologize for that scene the other day. My brother can be a little much sometimes." She smacked Daniel in the back of the head.

"Ow."

"Apologize," she ordered between gritted teeth.

"I did already—ow," he said again when she smacked him once more. "Okay, okay. Sorry, Evan. My bad."

"No problem." He bit back a grin, having himself been smacked in the back of the head once or twice by his mom. "So is Rachel all moved out, then?"

Kenzie nodded. "Yeah. It's weird. She's lived next to us for the past seven years. We miss her."

He felt an irresistible pull to comfort her. A woman he didn't know, whose brother had actively asked him to stay away from. "Oh, well, that happens." He shoved his hands in his pockets, nervous and not sure what else to say. A first for him.

"So...yeah." Kenzie shuffled her feet. "I guess we should get going. I just wanted to... Can I buy you coffee or something? To apologize, I mean?"

As soon as she said it, her cheeks blazed with color.

Her brother stared at her, looking horrified.

"Forget him. You can buy me a beer," Smith offered with a laugh.

Evan ignored him. "No apologies needed. Don't worry about Daniel. Younger brothers are like that." He glanced at Smith, the epitome of all younger brothers. "Or so I've heard."

Smith shot him a wary glance.

Kenzie tugged on her brother's arm. "Well then. We'll

be on our way. I wish he hadn't bothered you before. But he's very sorry."

"I'm right here, Kenzie." Daniel tried to tug his arm free. She wouldn't let him.

Evan didn't want her to go, but he had no reason to keep her near. Well, not that didn't sound strange. *No, stay. Let me stare into your beautiful eyes for the rest of my life. Yeah, because that's not creepy at all.*

Hell, where were these thoughts coming from? He hadn't wanted to do anything more with a woman than take in a movie or enjoy dinner for months. In a dry slump, as Reid had called it. But Evan didn't want superficial dating and meaningless sex. Then again, had he ever?

Rita's image sat hazy in his mind's eye, her loss growing more distant with each passing day. Guilt rode him for not remembering the way he used to, but he pushed it aside. Rita would want him to be happy. Maybe he *should* try again, start fresh with a woman looking for a meaningful relationship. Not Sheila though. Maybe…Kenzie.

But she was halfway to her car, Daniel in tow.

Evan had missed his opportunity. "Not meant to be."

"You know what else isn't meant to be? You and me as partners," Smith said, his hands tucked into his pockets.

"You got that right," Evan agreed, out of sorts. Tired of dealing with Smith's attitude, he let go of the filters normally guarding his mouth. "You're a huge pain to work with. I'm stuck with you because no one else wants to work with you."

"Bull." Was that a flash of hurt in Smith's green eyes? "Jordan likes me. Hector's okay."

"Jordan is tired of your negative attitude. And so is Saint Hector." Hector tolerated everyone and had a smile that warmed the frostiest of attitudes. And lately even he'd wanted a pass when it came to partnering with Smith. "You don't like it here? Quit. But stop complaining all the time." Then feeling bad for kicking at Smith, even if the truth did hurt, he added, "You work hard. You do the job. You're a Marine. That alone makes you better than most everyone I know. Now act like it."

Always the pacifier, that was Evan. He sighed, even as he accepted that about himself. But being a nice guy only went so far. He turned and left before he said something he'd regret.

Like asking Smith to join him for a beer after work.

Kenzie couldn't believe she'd asked Evan on a date. For coffee, but still. And in front of everyone! The invitation had slipped out. Lost in that sexy face and body, she'd been unable to look away. Or to think.

God. I really need to get busier at work. Or get laid. No, work harder. It's easier in the long run and much more profitable.

Daniel remained strangely silent for most of the ride home until he said, "So you like this guy."

"*What?*" She swallowed. "I do not. I feel bad for the way we treated him. Frankly, I don't know him well enough to like or not like him."

"But you'd like to get to know him better. You asked him to coffee, Kenzie."

"So what?"

"So you never ask guys to coffee. Not since Bryce."

The name still had the power to hurt. "Bryce is gone." She pretended to be more carefree than she felt. "It wasn't meant to be and wouldn't have worked anyway."

"Because of me."

"Because he and I wanted different things from life," she corrected. "With or without you, Daniel, I don't want to travel the world by backpack, train, or horseback. That's something you do when you're in college, not as a grown adult. At least, not for me."

"So if you found out he was engaged, it wouldn't matter?"

She felt sick and tightened her hands on the wheel. "Bryce is engaged?"

"No, but the fact you look like you want to cry isn't good. He's a loser who dumped us. Who needs him?"

Everything her brother said was true, mostly. But Bryce had never been a loser. He'd been a kind man, one she'd loved with her whole heart. He'd done his best, but he'd never signed on to help raise a teenager not his own. Life with Kenzie would never be just the two of them, not when she was all Daniel had left in the world. She'd explained that up front, and Bryce had tried. But the reality of her life hadn't worked for him.

And though she knew she and Bryce were both better off, she still missed his kindness, his laughter. And the intimacy of being with a man to call her own.

She hated that a tear escaped and could only be glad Daniel didn't see it.

She held her sniffles in on the ride home. Only after her brother had left the car did she allow herself to wipe her senseless tears and blow her nose.

She dialed Lila.

"Yo."

"I'm Brycing again."

Lila sighed. "Say it."

"He's gone. I've moved on."

"And?"

"And I will date again. Someday." *Nope. Never.* She never wanted to experience the pain of rejection from a lover, a true love. It sucked so hard. And especially because those same wounds that scarred her had imprinted on Daniel, possibly messing him up on relationships for life. She needed to talk to him about it, had been planning to for some time. Maybe. If she could do it without tearing up.

Lila cleared her throat.

"Yes?"

"Now repeat after me. Lila is a goddess."

"Lila is a goddess."

"She is always right."

Kenzie smiled. "She is always right."

"And I will spring for pizza tonight to show her how much I care."

"And I will spring for pizza tonight because I love her. Come over in an hour."

Lila hung up, and Kenzie knew sharing a meal would help her friend deal with the loss of her roommate as much as it would keep Kenzie focused on a happy, man-free existence.

She had more important things to worry about than the cool gray eyes that had so mesmerized her earlier. After fixing herself in the rearview mirror, she left and locked the car. A deep breath later, she felt more herself as she went inside and yelled at her brother to take out the trash. Because broken hearts sucked, but someone still had to take out the garbage.

CHAPTER 4

KENZIE DIDN'T APPRECIATE BEING GRILLED BY HER brother and Lila over dinner and having to lie her ass off. No, she did *not* have a crush on Evan. No, she did *not* miss Bryce. Yes, she did have plans to date again in the near future. And her one truth: yes, she would one day be Lila's maid of honor when Lila met and married her own MMFA—Moving Man with a Fine Ass.

Apparently fine asses had their own title now.

Thursday night blurred into Friday. Kenzie spent the day with the girls working on their newest account. Though Rachel had moved out, Will had been right when he'd said everything would pretty much stay the same. The girls and she still ran Sykes Design. The graphic design studio pulled in enough money to keep the three of them busy and the bills paid.

And being self-employed allowed Kenzie the flexibility to deal with her too-smart-for-his-own-good brother. Daniel should have been a grade below his current status as an upcoming sophomore. He was a prodigy when it came to computers, and his hacking skills threatened to get him into real trouble.

Raising a mini genius wasn't easy. Though Kenzie was smart, having gotten a degree while raising her brother all on her own, the mothering part hadn't come naturally. She'd had to study up on that as well, and she'd made her share of mistakes during those first years. Grieving after her parents' deaths, she hadn't had time to do anything but suck it up and deal. She'd dated sporadically, not having energy for a man in her life, not with so much else going on.

Years had passed, and Daniel had grown up. Her boyfriends had never lasted, and none of them had ever been serious contenders for her heart. Until a few years go. When she'd met Bryce. Her one and only.

She knew now that they wouldn't have lasted, not when she looked back and saw how many ways they'd been incompatible. But her emotions were taking longer to heal, the betrayal of loving and losing taking its toll.

So it surprised her to feel so intrigued by Evan, Rachel's MMFA. Kenzie had seen good-looking men before, been asked out plenty by men with great bodies and entertaining personalities. She didn't know Evan, but something about him stayed with her. Maybe it was the way he'd first looked at her, with an intensity she'd never before felt. Or that he fit all her perceptions of what she'd consider just her type. Well, apart from the blue-collar job. Not that she had anything against his work, but she'd always been more attracted to academic types.

Whatever the case, she hadn't meant to ask him to coffee. His easy dismissal had been polite, kind. And annoying, because she'd wanted to at least get him out of her system. Now she'd wonder.

"Hello? Earth to Kenzie?"

Kenzie glanced at Rachel staring at her. Rachel and Lila exchanged a look.

"What?"

Lila said, "Daniel told me you guys apologized to *Evan* yesterday."

Daniel and his big mouth. "I thought it was the right thing to do."

"Uh-huh." Lila paused. "I also heard you asked him out, and he said no."

"I did not ask him out." She flushed. "I would have treated him to a coffee, with Daniel, just to say we're sorry. He could have called the cops on us, and Daniel's been in enough trouble with them as it is. I was just being nice."

"Sure you were." Rachel smiled. "Will thought he was cool."

"Are you always going to mention him now?" Lila asked.

"Well, she used to mention him all the time before." Kenzie shrugged. "Don't think it matters much."

"I guess not." Lila sighed. "I need to rent out your room, but I don't want to."

Rachel grew teary-eyed. "Aw, that's so sweet."

"It's nice having the house all to myself."

"Oh?" Rachel's eyes narrowed.

"Yeah, there are no weird noises or smells. And I can use your room as my love nest so I don't contaminate my bed with boy germs."

"Love nest?" Kenzie did her best not to laugh as she sketched ideas for a local organic food company's new branding logo.

"Well, I could call it my harem. Did you know in the romance books, reverse harems are now a thing?"

"Wait. What?" Rachel leaned forward. "What's a reverse harem? Have I read any of those?" Rachel and Lila, being huge book nerds, regularly swapped and shared books.

"Yeah, they just called them something else before. Reverse harems are when there's a group togetherness, but the woman is in the center of it instead of the guy."

"So polyandry instead of polygamy," Kenzie explained.

"Well, yeah, but not everyone's about getting married. Just about getting a little some-some. Right?" Lila winked.

Rachel snorted. "Oh please. If you got as much action as you talk about, you'd be nothing more than a glossy toilet seat getting so much ass."

"That is beyond gross." Kenzie grimaced, thinking the logo needed more curve, more pop.

"And sadly true." Lila sighed. "I need a man, ladies. We need to go out and find me one. Oh, and one for Kenzie goes without saying if she's not going to go after your MMFA, Rach."

"Um, no. I don't think—"

Lila talked over her. "Come on, Rachel. Doesn't Will have one decent friend for me or Kenzie?"

"Oh no." Rachel shook her head. "The last time we tried to set you up, you scared the guy. Will told me he only has so many friends."

Kenzie stifled laughter when Lila glared.

"Bull. That guy wasn't scared. He was an asshole, trying to play me while having two other ladies on the side. So sorry I'm not willing to be a stand-in while he tries to do better on his weekends with someone else. And let's be honest, no one can do better than *moi*—the Lila Richards."

Kenzie nodded. "Will's friend was clearly deluded."

"He's not Will's friend anymore. Just a coworker. Thought I should clear that up." Rachel took the sheet Kenzie handed her and started working on it. "But back to my MMFA…"

"Stop! Look, I know you guys mean well, but—"

"But you called me just yesterday Brycing," Lila said bluntly. "And you haven't done that in months."

Rachel glanced at Lila. "She did?"

Lila nodded and made a face. "Yep. Bryce. Bryce. Bryce." She walked over and smacked Kenzie on the arm.

"Hey. What was that for?" Kenzie rubbed her shoulder.

"This is called aversion therapy." She started smacking Kenzie again. "Bryce." Smack. "Bryce." Smack. "Bryce." Smack.

"Would you stop?" Kenzie slapped her hand away.

Rachel laughed like a loon.

"Well, it's working, isn't it? Now when you hear the name Bryce"—Lila tried to punch Kenzie on the shoulder again, but she dodged out of the way—"you'll think of how much you hated me punching you instead of how much you miss that dickhead."

"He was such a tool." Rachel shook her head.

"A power tool." Lila swung wide again. "Like, a tiny drill with tiny bits that do nothing and go nowhere."

"Oh yeah."

Kenzie had to admit that as annoying as Lila was, she had a point. Kenzie needed to stop avoiding the subject of Bryce, because not thinking or talking about him had made him fester inside, so that anytime his name came up, a well of sadness pooled and filled her with depression. "You make sense, surprisingly. I'm not ready to talk about him right now." Though she'd shared buckets of tears with her friends for a solid month after the fact. "But I will soon. I promise."

"Good." Lila smiled.

"But I'm still not going out with Evan. Let me ease back into the dating scene, okay?" She had no intention of making a mistake that would cost Daniel so much. Not again. And her odd fascination with the sexy moving man warned her to be wary.

"Perfect. We're here to help."

Kenzie stared at their overly innocent expressions and couldn't help laughing. "You guys look eee-vil. Yes, Lila, with three e's. Excuse me if I'm not feeling better about your offer."

"That's just because you have no idea when a good thing hits you. But we do. We'll provide assistance when needed." Lila's shark-like grin didn't inspire confidence.

"Oh man. Please don't."

"Enough of this." Rachel waved a royal hand. "Now, minions, we must return to the work at hand. And I for one am not calling Ellie Ruger until we nail down our concept. Because, Kenzie, your interpretation of a loaf of kale with legs needs work." Rachel pointed to the monitor in front of her.

"It's not a loaf." Kenzie rolled her eyes.

"A head, then."

"Nope. I looked it up. Lettuce have heads, kale have leaves."

"Whatever." Rachel shrugged. "Your drawing sucks."

"So does your face."

"I hate kale," Lila muttered, and they buckled down to make kale look appetizing, a new shoe account appealing, and Lila not so pathetic on her dating profile.

Friday evening, Evan made up his mind, tired of dithering. Tired of being "boring." And frankly, tired of dealing with Smith and his bitching, though, for Smith, complaining about Cash or Reid only twice a day was a marked improvement.

Sitting in the front room of his mother's house, waiting for his cousins to show, Evan decided to call Rachel Kim. He drew a deep breath and focused, telling himself to word his request correctly so she couldn't call him unprofessional. Which he was totally being.

But he couldn't stop thinking about Kenzie.

"Honey, are the boys here yet?" his mother called from the kitchen.

He and his mother had always been so close, talking, laughing. But lately, she'd been breaking their mother–son dates, going off without him, not telling him about doctor appointments unless he interrogated her about them. He didn't understand what he'd done to upset her, and if he tried asking about it, she snapped at him. Hell, last week he'd shown up to do some maintenance on the sprinkler system, and she'd griped at him to leave well enough alone. A chore he'd always taken care of no longer needed attention.

Then again, he'd been visiting on a Friday night to deal with his mother's sprinklers. Not barhopping, trying to score a date, or hanging with friends. Hell, he couldn't remember the last time he'd done that.

His cousins were right. He needed a life.

"Not yet, Mom," he yelled back. "They're coming though."

"Huh. About time."

While his mom went back to her meal prep, Evan bit the bullet and dialed.

"Hello?"

"Hi, Rachel?"

"Yeah. Who's this?" She sounded suspicious. Not that he could blame her with all the telemarketing calls he received on any given day. *No-call list, my ass.*

"Well, I'm not a telemarketer, so you can relax. It's Evan, the moving guy from—"

"Vets on the Go!" Her voice warmed. "Hi. How are you?" she seemed to purr.

He thought he heard Will in the background.

"Fine. Um, I just wanted to ask a favor, but I don't want to put you out or anything."

"Oh, no problem, sweetie. What do you need?"

"*Who the hell is that?*" definitely came from Will.

Evan said, "Your friend, Kenzie."

"You want the knife-wielder, not the African goddess, right?"

"Ah, yeah." He coughed, feeling the laughter build. Something about her, Lila, and Kenzie made him want to smile. "I wanted to talk to her about Daniel. Nothing bad, but—"

Rachel rattled off a phone number so fast it took him a moment to jot it down.

"And in case you didn't get that, I'll text you her contact info. Okay? Uh-oh. Gotta go. Bye, Evan!"

She disconnected in a blink. But sure enough, Kenzie Sykes's phone number popped up in a text.

Now unsure what to do with his victory, call her before he chickened out or put her number aside to think on it, Evan decided to go big. He took another deep breath, let it out, and called.

She answered on the third ring before he had to leave a message, thank God. He loathed voicemail.

"Hello?"

Just like her friend, she sounded untrusting.

"Hi, Kenzie. It's Evan, the guy who helped Rachel move? You know, Daniel's phone guy?"

"Oh, uh, hello."

Great, now she sounded even more hesitant.

He put some energy into sounding nice, pleasant, but not boring. "Well, I was hoping I could take you up on that offer of coffee."

Silence.

He waited a few more seconds then wondered if maybe she hadn't heard him. "I—"

"Coffee is good. Nice, I mean. It's good. I like coffee." Her words came faster. "But I just got a new contract, and I'm super busy right now. Maybe I could get back to you?"

The brush-off. He swallowed a sigh. His own fault for not jumping on her invitation right away. "Oh, sure. Sorry to have bothered you but—"

"*Greatgottagobye.*" She hung up.

He swore. Talk about the perfect ending to his day.

As if being rejected by a woman he couldn't stop thinking about wasn't bad enough, the rest of his day had been awful. The Hillfords had a grown daughter who'd started hanging around to help them, and Smith had shoved Evan toward the chatty woman, hiding in the garage with the excuse of having to move the heavy stuff so their token lightweight could charm the customers.

So not cool. Especially since the woman had been *too helpful* all damn afternoon.

The doorbell rang, and he left his phone in his mom's reading room, despondent and needing to get past the feeling. Going out with Kenzie would probably have been a mistake anyway. He didn't really need a woman in his life. With his accounting work, the moving business, and taking care of his mom, he'd been too busy to do more than fall into bed the moment he got home.

Now with the accounting aspect of his life slowing

down, he had time to relax. But his mother still took precedence in his life. He loved her, and he'd care for her until he took his last breath—with or without the promise he'd made to his father on Evan Senior's deathbed.

His mom loved him, supported him, and always tried to give him space. That's when she wasn't hammering him to get married and give her grandkids.

The front door opened before Evan could get to it.

"Yo, Aunt Jane. We're here!" Cash had arrived.

Evan joined the family in the kitchen, where good smells filled the air.

Reid appeared a moment later looking annoyed. "Thanks for waiting, bonehead."

"Hey, you snooze, you lose. I want some of that, Aunt Jane. I'm starved."

Evan's mother smiled, doting on Cash as she always had.

Growing up the single child of two older parents, Evan had always longed for playmates. Though his cousins had lived close by, Aunt Angela and Uncle Charles had been distant from relatives, an isolated family unit Evan used to envy. Especially since he'd idolized the boys. Though they hadn't spent a lot of time together, their few get-togethers had always been fun. Cash and Reid had never had to be reminded to include Evan in their play and never treated him as if he didn't belong.

His cousins had been everything he'd wanted in a sibling whom, sadly, his parents couldn't provide. Probably why he'd been so gung ho to join the USMC after seeing his cousins enlist, following in their footsteps. His concession to his parents had been to get a degree in accounting first and thus a commission as an officer.

Evan had liked the Marine Corps, but he hadn't loved it. Politics had soured him, and his assignments in the States hadn't satisfied. Hearing how Cash had been treated had only reinforced that his notion to separate had been a good one. Six years and an honorable discharge later, Evan rejoined his cousins stateside. And he'd taken advanced accounting classes, gotten a kickass job in a prestigious accounting firm, then burned out from too much work.

Somehow he'd come full circle, investing in his family, making the most of a new job, and feeling like he had the brothers he'd always wanted. So why, then, did he feel so empty? As if he was missing something crucial to his own happiness? Because even after leaving his stressful job, that zest for life had yet to appear.

"Hey, you're blocking the guacamole. Move, Evan." Cash gently nudged him out of the way of the kitchen island, where Evan's mom had placed plates of munchies.

"Seriously. You know better than to get between Cash and food," Reid told him. "Thanks for having us, Aunt Jane. I'm sorry it's taken us so long to come over."

"No worries, honey." She smiled, still beautiful and vibrant in her seventh decade. Evan thought she looked years younger, but he never said so. She'd more than once lectured him on accepting one's age and feeling beautiful no matter what year you were born. "Just make sure you don't eat so much you ruin your appetite. I made a mean chicken teriyaki for tonight."

"Yum." Cash continued to eat. Reid took a seat at the island next to him and dug in. But Evan felt too unsettled after the call with Kenzie to do more than stand by the others.

"But boys…" She paused. They drew closer, and she slapped them both on the head.

Yep, he'd definitely been seeing a lot of moms in action lately. The thought of Kenzie chastising Daniel made his smile widen.

"Hey, Aunt Jane," Cash whined, rubbing his head. At her expression, he quieted. Fast.

"This has been a long time coming, so you listen good. You boys had crappy parents. I'm sorry to say it, but it's true. You know it, and I know it. I've tried to tell you this before, but you've both done a pretty good job avoiding it." She pierced Reid with a stare.

He squirmed. "I, well, I didn't..."

"Just accept the blame and move on," Evan murmured, keeping well out of reach of his mother's surprisingly strong hands.

"Sorry."

"Me too, Aunt Jane," Cash offered.

"Good. You two are idiots." At her insult, they blinked, and Evan couldn't help a chuckle. "You're special, and you always have been. Yes, Angela made mistakes. And yes, she put you last in her affections. I tried once to adopt you, you know, but Charles got so mad we never brought it up again."

Evan hadn't known that.

"Despite the way you were raised, you both grew up to be men I'm proud to call family. Put the past in the past."

"I'd like to," Cash said, his voice gruff. "But we kind of have a situation we can't ignore."

"Smith Ramsey," Evan reminded his mother. They'd talked about Smith, and she'd wanted to embrace him. Probably because she hadn't met him and didn't believe he could be as coarse as Evan had described.

The stubborn tilt of Jane Griffith's chin told Evan they

wouldn't like what she had to say. "The boy is your brother, Cash. And yours too, Reid. Half, full, a quarter, whatever. None of that matters. Evan, he's your cousin. No matter how much you complain about Smith, he's blood. That means you stop avoiding what makes you uncomfortable and deal with it. Family's all we've got in the end, you know." She paused, her eyes shiny. "You boys will always have me. I'm only sorry I didn't do more when you were younger."

"Aunt Jane—" Cash tried.

She waved him off. "But I can make up for it now. I know you're grown, but you still need love. And I have plenty to give. Since this one"—she pointed to Evan—"is so clueless when it comes to his future, you'll have to help him. Honey, Rita died years ago. But you didn't. Move on."

If only it were that easy. Sure, Evan missed Rita. But he didn't suffer from some kind of survivor's guilt or a heart frozen in grief. He swallowed but didn't speak.

"There now." She closed her eyes and smiled then opened them to stare at them with love. "I've finally said my piece. I can die happy now."

"Aunt Jane?" Reid frowned.

Cash blinked and around his food, mumbled, "Huh?"

Evan groaned. Not this again. "Mom."

She laughed. "Oh relax. I'm fine. I've been to a bazillion doctor's appointments. I know my ticker is good, so I have that."

Then why are you so tired and wan all the time?

"And I'm on birth control, so you all don't need to worry about that either."

Evan gaped. So did his cousins. His mother laughed harder, snorting when she could catch a breath. "Oh, that felt good. I'm kidding, you knuckleheads. But I might as well confess I found myself a nice man friend. We're dating. And, well, it could get serious."

Reid shot him a look.

Evan needed to sit on the stool he'd been standing in front of. "What? Serious?"

Cash paused, glanced from him to his aunt, and quirked a brow. "So, what? You getting Evan a new daddy?"

Reid choked on his food. "Cash."

"Oh my God. Mom, what's going on with you?" A second wind in life at seventy-one?

"You heard me." She thrust out her chin. "But my love life is nowhere near as exciting as yours apparently is. Why don't you explain just why you're a 'sexy moving man with a fine ass'? Because this I have to hear."

Cash and Reid grinned, and Reid, that sly bastard, said, "Yes, Evan. Why don't you tell us all about the woman with the knife, your phone, and 'Dancing Queen'? Inquiring minds want to know."

CHAPTER 5

Kenzie stared at the phone, half expecting it to bite her. Had she really said no to a date with Evan? Yes, yes, she had, because she didn't need complications right now. And the way he made her feel certainly qualified as difficult, perplexing, and chaotic.

"Who was that?"

She jumped, not having heard her brother return to the living room. "Um, no one."

"Really? Because it sounded like you were saying no to coffee, and the only guy you've talked to about a coffee date was Evan. I was there, remember?"

She didn't need lectures on honesty from a thirteen-year-old juvenile delinquent. "Shouldn't you be heading to bed?"

"Kenzie, it's seven thirty on a Friday night."

"And? You're a growing boy."

He rolled his eyes in the way only an adolescent could, sneering without sneering. "Admit you like the guy."

"I admit he was nice. So what? I'll probably never see him again, unless there's something you're not telling me. Did you steal his phone again? Will he be a character witness for the feds when they come to take you away or raid our house for some illegal mess you've once again gotten yourself into?"

He flushed. "No. And quit changing the subject."

"There is no subject. Now go watch TV or something. I have more work to do."

He stared at her, his brows drawn, then headed back upstairs. She felt bad about chasing him away...for all of three seconds. Her brother loved Netflix, and she really did have work to do. Especially since she'd spent much of the afternoon trying to ignore thoughts of Evan while the girls continued to talk about him.

If only he weren't so attractive and polite. If only he hadn't asked her out after she'd already put him in the "must try to forget" pile.

The little demon perched on her shoulder, an amalgamation of Lila and Rachel with its nonstop yammering, whispered: *What would really be the harm in going out with him?*

She tromped downstairs to her office and fired up her computer. The harm, she thought, would be in getting involved, liking him as a friend. Then a boyfriend. Then dating, having him interact with Daniel. They'd hang at his place, then her place. More and more, until she would grow attached. Then she'd fall in love with him, and he'd leave.

Just like Bryce.

To torture herself a little more, she dug up an old picture of the three of them from happier times, the one she kept hidden in a bottom desk drawer. She tried to see the flaws in her relationship, but the picture only showed a woman and man in love and a young boy ecstatic about going to a fall festival.

Kenzie gripped the frame, wishing she could go back and undo...what? She hadn't stepped a foot wrong. She'd always put Daniel first, had checked out Bryce before their first date, and thought long and hard on it before living together. Bryce had never been anything but loving and fun—until the end, of course.

How could she have known things might change?

Before she could cry, she smacked herself on the arm and laughed, not a little hysterically. Holy crap, Lila's aversion therapy kind of worked. Because instead of crying, all she could think about was Lila's silly "Bryce." Smack. Rinse and repeat.

Kenzie tucked the photo away and, smiling now, concentrated on her work, liking the new idea for their footwear client though still not sold on the walking, talking kale for the organic food business.

Friday rolled into the weekend, her "free days" filled with cleaning, a few chores, more work, and ignoring Lila's invitation to hang out with Rachel and Will.

The three girlfriends were tight, family, but sometimes Kenzie needed a break.

Fortunately, the girls understood, having fought over this in the past.

Before Kenzie knew it, Monday had come once more.

It should have been a perfect weekend. She loved nothing more than getting things done, checking tasks off her ever-growing to-do list.

Unfortunately, a good night's sleep continued to remain at the top of her list. Why? Because images of Evan haunted her, her subconscious bringing him back to visit each night wearing less and less clothing. Friday night he'd been in jeans and an unbuttoned shirt. Saturday night in shorts with *I Want You, Kenzie* tattooed across his glorious chest. And last night, his jeans had been parted, revealing an incredible set of abs and a trail of dark hair leading down his belly and beneath those jeans. He'd watched her with a smile as he'd slowly peeled said jeans and leaned over her in bed, his mouth hot, his eyes so bright they glowed.

He'd whispered her name as he'd drawn closer, and her body had tightened up all over, so hungry to feel him against her. She'd tossed. She'd turned. And every time she'd closed her eyes, she'd imagined Evan making love to her.

The snooze she'd turned off twice this morning hadn't helped. If she didn't hustle, she'd miss her morning appointment downtown. And they *needed* this new job because some unexpected expenses thanks to a shitty bookkeeper had recently come to her attention.

Needless to say, Kenzie's week wasn't starting out well. Her eyes felt gritty, and her mouth tasted like something had died in it. The shower nearly shocked her into a coronary when the water turned ice-cold.

"Daniel," she screeched as she tried to dodge pinpricks of ice turning her goose bumps into icicles. Quickly rinsing the conditioner out of her hair, she cursed and danced to avoid more ice as she shed the soap running down her body. After turning the water off and wrapping herself in a towel, she stepped out of the shower, shivering. "Daniel Thomas Sykes!"

"It wasn't me," he yelled through her door.

She opened it to see him draped in three towels, huddling for warmth. "I had cold water too. I think the water heater is busted or something."

Great. She'd need to call someone about the hot water heater. *Again.* And no, that hadn't been part of the monthly budget.

A quick check at a weather app showed the temperature

cooling today, so she dressed in a pair of jeans and a sleeveless tank she layered with a long-sleeved floral-print pullover. Good enough to show an artsy flair while also being business casual thanks to her killer heels—a mere two inches of height disguised as something grander by the rockin' leather pattern. The shoes were courtesy of an early client that had exploded into a big business.

"Daniel, I have to go. What are you up to today?" she yelled as she snagged an energy bar and threw it in her purse. She grabbed her portfolio and laptop case and waited for the shaggy teenager to appear.

Daniel had two and a half more weeks until school began, but some early activities started soon, including soccer, which he'd expressed interest in playing. Extracurricular activities would help him be more involved in school and hopefully keep him out of trouble. A good thing since he claimed he intended to go to college upon graduation...*in two more years*.

That she even thought about her little brother in conjunction with life after high school scared the crap out of her and made her feel old. At thirty-one, she was the youngest of her friends. But raising a teenager was turning her hair gray. She'd never tell Lila or Rachel, but she swore she'd seen a rebel strand of silver in the mirror this morning.

Her brother ambled down the stairs, dressed in athletic shorts and an ancient Asteroids T-shirt with holes in it. Funny and appropriate, though the holes had appeared due to too many washings.

She could have sworn she'd thrown that away last week.

"I'm just hanging around the house today. Probably play some video games, watch movies."

"How about getting out in the sun and taking in the vitamin D?"

He rolled his eyes. "Sure, Doc. Any other pseudoscience you have for me?"

"It's not fake science, it's—never mind. Just get outside for a while, okay? I'll be in meetings this morning since Jinny apparently screwed up our books." She growled, ready to tear into something. "I told Rachel we shouldn't hire her. And now look."

Daniel frowned. "What did Jinny do?"

"More like what *didn't* she do. File our monthly state and quarterly taxes for the past six months. And that makes me think maybe our accountant isn't doing what I pay him to do either."

"I think Paul was waiting for you to call him for help so he could get into your pants."

"*Daniel.*"

"What? You know your accountant's a douche."

"Yes, but he's a cheap douche who's usually pretty good at his job." She didn't have time for this.

Daniel watched her scramble to find her keys then pulled them out of the silverware drawer.

"What were they doing in there?"

"You put them in there yesterday, staring into space. I wanted to see how long it would take you to remember."

"Jerk."

Her brother grinned. "Yeah, so I'll just be here, wasting my brain. And yes, I will weed the back garden like I was supposed to do Saturday. If you'll give me five bucks for coffee."

"Fine. There's a little cash left in the jar."

A monster cookie jar that never held any cookies

because her brother ate them straight from the bag before she could fill the monster's mouth.

"Right. So, uh, where are you going today, exactly?" At her raised brow, he said, "In case I have an emergency, I like to know where you are."

He looked defensive, and young. She softened. "I'm meeting Ellie in the university district at her office to go over the kale designs in half an hour. Oh man, I have to move," she muttered to herself, noticing the time. "Then I'm meeting with a potential new client at Storyville, the Pike Place one, at noon. After that, Lila and I might do lunch, and then I'll be back, probably around two thirty-ish."

"Gotcha. Break a leg."

"Something else we can't afford, not with the water heater on the fritz."

Hustling to her first meeting, she made it with minutes to spare.

Ellie Ruger, a budding foodie expert who'd made a huge splash with her organic kale chips, had decided to branch into nutrient-dense superfoods, making them more accessible to regular people who usually put the word *super* in front of *man*. She'd picked the right city because Seattle was known for growing smaller businesses into big ones, and everyone loved an entrepreneur.

Personally, Kenzie thought the food tasted like crap, but Rachel swore by it. Lila refused to take sides.

"Hey, Ellie. I've brought you some samples to look at." Though Kenzie could easily have emailed her the ideas they'd tossed around, she found that a more personal encounter helped flesh out new ideas and identify problems early in the process.

Fortunately, Ellie, though a millionaire on her way to

earning twice what she'd earned last year, didn't buy into her own hype. She'd been working with Kenzie before she'd hit it big, and she believed in loyalty earned.

"Oh, good. Hey, I saved you some carrot-and-guava balls." The cute blond smiled and pushed a plate of sample foods toward her. "Tell me what you think."

Hell. Kenzie should have sent Rachel, but with Rachel and Lila working on a deadline for a local moving company, oddly not Vets on the Go!—*and there I go thinking about Evan again*—she'd been the only one to do the job.

An hour later, and feeling the need to down a few Snickers to stem the rush of vitamins heading down her gullet, Kenzie hurried downtown to find a place to park. Half an hour later, the queasy feeling had left her, and she headed toward Storyville, one of her favorite coffee shops. A caffeine junkie, Kenzie liked a good bean, and the smooth taste of freshly roasted coffee always hit the spot.

Especially after broccoli-cheddar-onion bites and chia-filled whatever.

Once inside, she sought Rob Talon, her future dream client, and sat with him. He pushed a cup of coffee toward her.

"Oh, I was planning to buy *you* coffee," she said with a smile.

Rob smiled back, his teeth slightly crooked and oddly charming in a face that looked sculpted from marble. He had Nordic good looks: styled blond hair, bright-blue eyes, and a tall frame filled with muscle. Plus he headed the marketing arm of an up-and-coming tech firm. Something to do with nanotechnology. Daniel had tried to explain it then stopped after she'd complained of a nerd-induced headache. He'd then accused her of being an unenlightened redshirt and left her with even more questions.

"Okay, Kenzie. I'm happy to see what you've got for us today."

Was it her imagination, or did he give her an interested once-over? She was terrible when it came to knowing what men thought. Damn. She really should have had Lila and Rachel handle the meetings today, leaving her in her happy place, surrounded by alternative rock and her bright basement filled with creativity and ideas. And no people.

"Oh, ah, well, let me break out my laptop."

"Outstanding." He checked his phone. "I hate to do this, but we'll need to cut this short. An unexpected meeting with some shareholders popped up, and my sister wants me there. But hey, if all goes well, we'll have to do this again soon, right?"

Rob and Kayla, partners in their business, were said to divide their responsibilities evenly. The vibe she'd gotten from a friend who'd recommended her was that this would be a terrific company to get in on early before its stock really took off. Because it would.

That he needed to end their meeting early didn't bode well. Especially because he didn't seem too keen on rescheduling. Despite his "do this again soon" spiel, she heard his noncommitment clear as day.

Kenzie pasted a smile on her face and showed him on her laptop what she'd been thinking about for his company. From her research, she'd pieced together some key concepts that had him nodding.

A good sign.

He'd barely said anything when he lit up, looking over her shoulder. "Evan?"

Kenzie blinked. That name. It was like her sexy mover was haunting her.

She turned and *bam*. There he was, looking better than any man should in jeans and a plain blue polo.

He and Rob shook hands, though she saw Evan's eyes widen upon seeing her.

As the two caught up on old times, Kenzie waited, her opportunity to impress Rob shrinking. And her irritation with Evan Griffith growing. Bad enough he'd been invading her dreams, now he was affecting her work.

"Hell. I have to go." Rob sent a guilty look Kenzie's way. "I'm so sorry, Kenzie. Call my secretary and let's schedule a meeting in a few weeks. I do want to see your designs."

"Sure." She smiled, doing her best not to shoot Evan any death glares that Rob might see. She'd be sure to save them until Rob left.

"Oh, are you thinking of hiring Kenzie?" Evan said.

Great. Now what?

"Sykes Design has a great reputation," Rob said, surprising her. "Our company needs to rebrand before we go bigger. Something techie yet intimate so that the regular guy won't think us too highbrow. Kayla's interested in working with someone local in particular."

"Good idea." Evan nodded, avoiding her gaze. "Some of my old clients have used Kenzie, and they can't say enough about her. You really should schedule that meeting before she's overbooked and can't fit you in."

Kenzie frowned. Old clients? What was he talking about? Overbooked? Please. They needed all the help they could get. When she saw Rob looking at her, she cleared her frown and nodded. "He's got a point. But I know you have a meeting to get to, so—"

"No, no. Evan's right. I don't want to miss out on working

with you." Rob brushed a hand through his hair and smiled. "Besides, it's not often you get to talk business with someone as attractive and capable as a woman like Kenzie. Plus my sister can't say enough good things about Rachel, and Kayla doesn't like many people."

When the hell had Rachel met Kayla? Wait. Rob had called her attractive?

Evan slapped Rob on the back. A little hard, by the way Rob teetered before catching himself.

"Well, I'd best be off," Rob said. "Talk to you soon, Kenzie. I'll make sure to get back to you later today on a new time to meet." Rob left.

Evan turned, and Kenzie trapped him in her death glare.

"Oh, ah, funny meeting you here."

Funny, he'd said. Evan had been set up. *Again*. Daniel Sykes needed some discipline, something the Corps, or a foot up his butt, might just provide. Then again, should Evan be upset at another opportunity to see Kenzie up close?

Damn, but even angry she turned him on. Yeah, that was it. He wanted her. Physical desire. That he understood. And if he ignored the quickening of his heart and the need to sigh just looking at her, he'd believe his own bullshit. Because falling for a woman he didn't even know made no sense. And Evan was nothing if not rational.

"What are you doing here?" she asked, biting out each word.

"I'm supposed to meet your brother to discuss financial matters. He had a legitimate question about tax penalties, and since I was already in the area, I told him I'd meet him."

Kenzie clenched her jaw.

"So he was lying?"

"No. I am having some issues with my books, but I'm not sure why Rachel's moving guy is qualified to help us."

Evan smiled. "I'm an accountant. I was, I mean. Well, I still am. I'm just working for myself now."

"Why?"

"So much suspicion." He grinned, not telling her how adorable she looked in her pique. Women didn't like hearing that they were cute when trying to appear serious. "I wasn't fired for any wrongdoing. I left the firm because I couldn't handle the hours. But I'm still consulting for them, and I have a few clients staying with me who left Peterman & Campbell Accounting when I did."

She blinked. "I know that firm. One of my clients uses them. They're big money."

"Yep." Evan wanted to stroke her cheek, to see if she felt as soft as she looked. So he tucked his hands in his pockets.

"What was with lying to Rob about your clients using me? Or me being overbooked?"

He shrugged. "I know Rob. He's competitive. The thought of him not getting to use your services because *you* don't have time for *him* would annoy the crap out of him. Plus it never hurts to make people think you're more than you are. Perception is everything, and before you know it, you will be overbooked."

"Oh." She gave him a tentative smile. "Thanks."

"Mind if I grab a coffee and wait with you for your brother? It's getting crowded in here."

She nodded, her gaze thoughtful.

Evan picked up a coffee and a few pastries and returned

to Kenzie. "How about some sweets as a peace offering? I had no idea I was interrupting a meeting."

She accepted an apricot Danish. "Thanks. It's not your fault I couldn't snare Rob Talon on my own."

He didn't know about that. Rob had seemed pretty smitten when Evan had seen the pair sitting together.

"How do you know him, anyway?" Kenzie asked.

"I knew his sister from a long time ago. She and I dated briefly in college. Rob is a good guy, and he and I became friends after Kayla and I broke up."

"Really? Kayla is amazing."

"She is. But I was the problem." *I was too boring for Kayla. And I really hate that word.* "She wanted to see the world, and I had responsibilities." He sipped his coffee, remembering the past and wondering where the time had gone. "Well, actually she wanted to go to India for some technology conference, and I wanted to go to Miami for a wild spring break. We parted ways after I joined the Marine Corps and she moved to Bangalore."

"You were a Marine?"

"*Am* a Marine." He smiled with pride. "You're never an ex. You become a 'prior' or 'former' Marine. It's always with you." Even though he hadn't enjoyed many aspects of the military, he missed the camaraderie, which explained why he loved working with the gang at Vets on the Go! It felt like a mini-Corps of likeminded individuals.

"So if you don't mind me asking, why are you moving furniture for a living? Because you burned out doing accounting?" She sounded disbelieving.

He couldn't blame her. "Actually, I'm a partner in our moving business. My cousins and I own Vets on the Go!, and one of our guys is out due to a broken arm. So I'm helping out until he's back. But to be honest, it's been enjoyable using my muscles more than my brains for a while. I got tired working eighty-hour weeks for Peterman & Campbell."

Her eyes softened. "That makes sense. I love my job, but I get tired too. I worked all weekend in between cleaning my house and running errands." She sighed. "And today was a bust."

"Sorry to hear that. I'll make sure Rob calls you back since I interrupted you."

"No, please don't. I can handle my business myself."

He sensed a little bit of tension there, but he understood the need for independence. "No problem. At least finish the Danish."

She shoved half the pastry in her mouth and grinned at him. "Happy now?" she asked, her mouth full, and he laughed.

"You know, I can see where your brother gets that attitude."

She managed to swallow the ball of dough and groaned. "Now I should be apologizing to you. I can't believe he tricked you into coming here."

"So you're not having a problem with your taxes?"

"Yes, but—" The buzz of her phone interrupted her. She read a text and blinked. "Daniel just told me he's on his way here to meet with you and not to be freaked out if I see you because you're not stalking me, you're doing him a favor."

"Wow. He texted all that?"

"Mostly in abbreviations and emojis, but I understand teen-speak."

Evan laughed. "Better you than me. I couldn't even figure out how to change my name back."

"What did he change your name to?"

"Well, my ringtone became 'Dancing Queen.' And my name became Sexy Moving Man with a Fine Ass."

She couldn't stifle her mirth, and he saw it.

Instead of looking angry, he grinned. "Oh yeah, laugh it up."

"That's not your fault. My brother is a genius with electronics."

"Good to know it's not me. I know how to work my phone, but after he messed with it, nothing I did made a difference."

She groaned. "Yeah. That's Daniel."

The two of them sipped their coffee, watching each other. "So if you really do need some accounting help, why not let me take a crack at it? I'm sure I can make things better."

CHAPTER 6

MAKE THINGS BETTER? JUST SITTING NEAR HIM WAS making everything *hotter*. Her temperature, the coffee, her lungs as she studied his firm chest and broad shoulders, those light-gray eyes… She could almost hear herself panting.

Kenzie cleared her throat. "Well, I hate to bother you, and I doubt I could afford you."

He shrugged. "Nah. Consider it a freebie for earlier."

She would be foolish to turn down advice from someone who'd worked for Peterman & Campbell Accounting. Heck, Ellie did her business there. Kenzie had once overheard her mention what a terrific job the firm had done handling her taxes.

"Well…" She felt Evan's attention like a beam of sunlight, warming her from her toes to the top of her head, and decided to take a chance.

It couldn't hurt just to talk to the guy. She hadn't noticed a ring on his finger. Then again, he'd asked her out, kind of, so she wouldn't have expected him to be attached to anyone. But maybe he had a bunch of girls on the side?

"Well?" Evan prodded.

She blushed, realizing she'd been staring at him while he waited to hear about her problem.

Kenzie filled him in on all her bookkeeper had and hadn't done then mentioned a few worries she had about her accountant.

He listened, his expression serious, and she had a sudden thought: What would he look like after a kiss?

She took a sip of coffee to hide her nerves.

"That's a problem, but one I could help you with. Or I could recommend someone to help you," he offered.

She groaned, not wanting to add on another cost.

"What's wrong?"

Kenzie met his gaze, and something inside her snapped. "What's *not* wrong? I'm in trouble with the IRS. My brother is on his way to becoming a criminal hacker. My water heater broke today. The big client we really need to nab to stave off the financial wolves had more to say to you than to me. And you're really good-looking, and it's throwing me off."

His slow grin annoyed her even more because it drew her like a magnet.

She lowered her head to the table and banged her forehead a few times, needing to knock some sense into herself. "I can't believe I just said that."

Evan laughed. "You think you have problems? A beautiful woman asked me to coffee, and I froze. By the time I'd recovered enough sense to say yes, she'd left with her brother. Then when I got the stones to ask her out, she rejected me. Even worse, now she thinks I'm stalking her because her brother once again set me up. Oh, and don't forget I probably ruined her huge business deal. So I think I'm winning in the 'I can't believe I did that' contest."

She raised her head, taken by his charm. "Oh yeah? I'm trying to sell walking, talking kale for a superfood company. And every time I sample their food, I want to puke."

"That's nothing. I'm filling in on the moving gig for my idiot cousin, who broke his arm while fighting a gang. Yeah, a gang. And he won. I couldn't even save Lila from Rachel."

She laughed then coughed and tried to look sad. "At

least you have a cousin. I might have stopped Rachel from choking Lila, but I don't have any cousins, a mom, or a dad. Just a criminally aspiring younger brother."

"My dad is dead, my mom is forty years older than I am, and I sadly wish my cousins were my brothers because I always wanted a big family."

"Hmm. That's a good one." She tapped her fingers on the table, mesmerized by Evan's bright-gray eyes and sexy lips curled in a grin. "You're as pathetic as I am in the family department. But my idea of fun is working and organizing my pantry, which I did twice on Saturday." She started to enjoy the odd conversation.

"I do nothing but fix up my mom's house and take her to doctors' appointments when not working all the time."

"I work with women who use words like *love slave* and *penis worshipper* and have been known to wrestle in front of moving men."

He laughed. "Yeah? I'm forced to work with a guy who just happens to be the secret son of my aunt, who's now dead. Which makes him another cousin, but I'm not sure he knows we're related, and I can't ask."

She gaped. "Seriously? That's soap-opera worthy."

They smiled at each other.

She started laughing. "You win. That takes the cake."

"Did someone say *cake*?" her brother asked as he sat next to her. "Hey, Evan."

"Daniel." He pushed his uneaten pastry at her brother, who gobbled it up with a muffled thanks.

The gesture touched her.

"So is the tax problem a huge deal?" Daniel asked.

"It can be if it's not handled right. But not really, no,"

Evan answered. He said to her, "How would you feel about a trade?"

"What do you mean?" *A kiss for a kiss? You're on. Oh my God, I need to stop thinking with my ovaries!*

"I fix your accounting problems. You design me a logo and help me with branding for my side business. I'm still doing accounting but on a much smaller scale, and I should probably have a more professional presence on the web. Word of mouth will only travel so far."

"Um, that sounds…workable."

"On top of that, I'll throw in fixing the water heater. I'm a handy guy, always fixing stuff for my mom. So, do we have a deal?"

Before Kenzie could say yes, Daniel stuck out his hand.

"Heck yeah. I can't do cold showers. And that's not a sex reference. I just hate being cold in the water."

"Daniel, ugh." Kenzie wanted to sink through the floor. Bad enough her brother even knew about sex. She didn't need to hear him referencing it.

"Nobody likes a cold shower." Evan shook Daniel's hand then let go and held his out to Kenzie. "Sound good?"

Though she knew better than to get involved with Evan, she reached out. The contact sent waves of desire to every point of her body. Her heart raced, and her senses went on overload.

Evan seemed to stiffen, as if affected. Or that could just be wishful thinking—Kenzie not wanting to be the only one weirded out by such chemistry.

Am I that hard up that a simple handshake makes me sweat? Sadly, yes.

She disengaged with a smile, ignoring Daniel's watchful

gaze. "When do you think you might be able to fix the water heater? Because honestly, that's my new priority."

"Yeah." Daniel gave a heartfelt sigh. "This morning was brutal."

Kenzie ran a hand through her hair. "He's not wrong."

Evan sipped his coffee, his gaze intent. "How about now?"

Kenzie frowned. "What about now?"

"I think he means he wants to fix the water heater now," Daniel explained. "Sounds good. Let's go."

"Hold on." Kenzie frantically tried to remember what state she'd left the house in. Had she put her dirty clothes in the hamper, or were her bra and panties still lying on the rug in her bathroom? And did she really want Evan in her home again when it was all she could do not to think of him?

"Kenzie, what's to think about? I can take him home. Go do whatever you have to. I want hot water," Daniel said.

"No, it's fine. I mean, we can go now." She gathered her things, still unsure how Evan had gotten an invitation to her house when she'd planned on never seeing him again. "Lila and I will do lunch later in the week." Or so she texted her friend.

"I'll ride with Evan to show him where to go," Daniel offered.

Evan cleared his throat. "I was there just a few days ago, remember?"

"Oh, right." Daniel grinned. "But I'll still ride with you. Kenzie drives like a blind nun."

She scowled. "What's that supposed to mean?"

Daniel snorted. "If you went any slower, we'd be going back in time."

Evan coughed to muffle a laugh, but she saw it.

"Ha. You think that's funny? You get to drive Daniel, and he gives the term *running at the mouth* all new meaning."

"Ha ha." Daniel made a face.

She automatically made one back then realized what she'd done.

Evan laughed and tugged Daniel to follow him. "Feel free to chatter on the way. Anything's gotta be better than Smith whining about work all day."

Daniel did talk, and talk and talk, on purpose to feel Evan out. Different from the first time they'd met, this Evan seemed cool and collected. And far from a moving guy. He drove a Lexus. And not an old-guy kind of luxury car but an RC F sport coupe. The dude looked really polished, even in jeans and a polo shirt. Knowing Evan had worked at a prestigious accounting firm explained a few things.

And seeing him with Kenzie had been…interesting.

"So."

Evan glanced at him before looking back at the road. "So." He drove with cool competence, not speeding but taking the turns smoothly. Daniel would love to see what the car could do if Evan opened it up.

"This is, like, a really great car. It's got high-backed seats, Wi-Fi, and Bluetooth?"

"Hell yeah." Evan grinned, his teeth straight and white, his sandy-brown hair a lot like Daniel's but styled. "This baby can move. Five-liter, V8 engine, 467 horsepower. It's sleek, designed for speed, and really hugs the roads."

Daniel glanced around, noted how clean the thing was—it even had that new-car smell—and studied Evan. "You don't have kids, do you?"

"Not yet. Unless you count this baby."

"Is it new?"

"Got it two years ago."

"But…gray? Didn't they have red or black?"

"I like gray. Black shows dirt. Red stands out. So does the blue. I don't need to be flashy, and I'd much rather run under the radar on the highways."

"Good point." Daniel ran his hands over the red-leather interior, wanting a car like this someday. He couldn't fault Evan for his taste. "Hey, I just wanted you to know I wasn't trying to play you or anything by meeting up at the coffee shop."

"So the fact your pretty sister happened to be there had nothing to do with anything?"

"No. I thought she'd be done with her meeting." Not really, but Daniel had wanted to see them together. Kenzie had that look when she stared at Evan. A look Daniel dreaded seeing, yet he liked his sister happy all the same. She was into Evan, no matter how much she tried to deny it.

And the guy liked Kenzie just as much. Daniel had watched Evan do his best not to stare too hard, but Evan had it bad.

Daniel decided to let it play out but keep a close eye on things. Besides, he, Rachel, and Lila had discussed it, and they all agreed. Kenzie and Evan sparked when near each other. And Bryce hadn't been like that with his sister. They'd been comfortable and happy, but not…whatever Kenzie was with Evan. Not that Daniel remembered.

He didn't know how to feel about that exactly.

"Seriously, Evan. How bad is Kenzie's accounting

problem?" Daniel forced himself to sound calm. "Like, we're not going to lose our house or anything, or have Kenzie go to jail for tax evasion, right?" He'd learned a few things in school last year. And no two ways about it, taxes sucked.

Evan shot him a look. "Nothing like that. Your sister is smart enough to fix things while the problems are small. She might have a little fine to pay, but that's it. Although I haven't looked at her books, from what she's told me, that's probably all there is to it."

But if there wasn't, Daniel knew how to shift money around, to look as if they'd paid the right people and departments, then to shift it back. He'd gotten in big trouble for doing that once. He wouldn't do it again...unless he had to.

"So, um, that's good," he said when Evan let the silence build.

After a moment, Evan asked, "What's up with your sister? She's single, right?"

"Yeah."

"And you don't want me going out with her. I got that."

Daniel shifted in his seat. "Well, I mean, you could go to dinner or something if you weren't planning to use her for sex then dump her."

Evan's lips thinned. "That happen before?"

"Not like that. A little, but different."

"That's not cool. Real men don't use women for anything."

Daniel liked the sentiment, but he'd learned the hard way people said what they thought you wanted to hear.

"And I don't kiss and tell." Evan gave Daniel a look. "That's so high school."

Daniel shot him the finger, and Evan laughed.

"You shouldn't kiss and tell in high school either.

Girls don't like it," Evan said. "And besides, it's stupid and immature."

"Thanks for the life lesson, Dad." Daniel gave Evan a wide, insincere smile.

"Wow. You really are a smart-ass." Evan didn't seem to mind. "So the phone pranks, could you show me how to do it? I really want to get my cousins and some of the guys I work with."

"Sure." Good to know Evan had a sense of humor. "But I have to know. Do you like my sister or what? 'Cause with you, it's hard to tell."

Like seemed too tame a word for it. Considering he'd barely spoken to Kenzie before today, Evan had no way to classify his feelings. He didn't *know* the woman. He found her beautiful and funny, but his emotions concerning her didn't make sense. Evan didn't do superficial relationships, and what did he and Kenzie really have but a few conversations, a knife, and a missing phone between them? Yet his entire mind and body buzzed when around the woman.

Daniel waited for his answer.

"I don't know your sister, but she seems nice and intelligent. And she's beyond beautiful."

Daniel grunted in response, and Evan wondered how exactly he'd been put on the spot by a thirteen-year-old boy.

He distracted the kid by pointing out the different satellite radio channels and letting him fiddle until he found a techno station he liked. Evan didn't mind it, though he preferred classic rock.

They pulled up to Kenzie's.

"You should park in the driveway. You don't want anyone messing with your car."

"It's not safe here?" Evan didn't like the thought of Kenzie and Daniel living in a dangerous area. Though he wouldn't have pegged the neighborhood to be anything close to seedy.

"Nah. But Lila isn't the best driver, and we have a lot of super-old people on this block."

"Really? I saw a bunch of families the last time I was here."

"Todd a few doors down is forty-two. Mr. McCally is eighty-four, but his grandkids drive him around. And they're probably Todd's age."

"Right. Old." Evan bit back a laugh. "So I'm not considered old yet."

"Oh no. You're old. Just not super-old."

Good to know. He followed Daniel inside and saw the same clean counters and picked-up house he'd seen on his last visit. "You have tools?"

"I'll go get them. Hold on." Daniel went through a door into the garage.

Evan absorbed the feel of the place, seeing hints of Kenzie in everything. Light and airy, with bright colors and a fresh feel, her house felt like a home. The place charmed and was beyond clean.

So, Kenzie was a neat freak.

She had a ton of cookbooks, many on dessert making. No doodads or frippery. Everything seemed to have a purpose, but what she possessed had touches of whimsy. An octopus egg timer. A cartoony dishtowel. Scooby Doo magnets on the fridge and anime figurines sitting in the corner of the kitchen window. They might have belonged to Daniel, but he had a feeling Kenzie could claim her share.

Colorful stoneware plates and flat, silver utensils sat in the dish drainboard. Even her glasses went with her décor, fun and funky but practical all the same.

A short walk through her living room showed him pictures of her and Daniel, with more of Rachel and Lila scattered around. He noticed an older photo of a young Kenzie and her parents but nothing of Daniel with them. He wondered about that, about what had happened to leave her in charge of a teenager, but he didn't feel at a place in their sudden relationship to ask.

He still couldn't believe he'd actually gotten to talk to her, let alone been invited to come to her house. He found himself counting their coffee date as a real date and felt foolish for being so happy about it. So they'd had coffee. So what?

Kenzie blew through the door, the woman always in perpetual motion. Even at the coffee shop she'd seemed too energetic to be truly still.

"Oh good. You're here." She blew a strand of hair out of her eyes. "Nice car."

"Thanks." He couldn't stop himself from staring at her, wondering if she'd get mad if he tucked that strand behind her ear. "Daniel's in the garage getting the tools."

She blinked back at him and flushed. Had he been staring too hard? Giving her an odd look? "Oh. Okay. Come on. I'll show you the water heater."

They walked downstairs into an airy basement.

"Wow. This place is great." It wasn't at all dark. Daylight streamed through several high-set windows, and the walls were painted a warm, buttery yellow, accented with white built-ins and colorful pillows and throws. Facing each other in a loose triangle, three standing desks with large monitors occupied a far corner yet didn't detract from the roominess of the space.

"It's home, and it's work." She sighed. "I love working from home, don't get me wrong. But I always feel guilty when I'm not at my desk."

"I feel the same now that I'm working from a home office." One he really needed to get organized. Though he had much less than half the workload he'd had at Peterson & Campbell, he had enough to keep an office full of paper stacks and in- and out-boxes.

She led him past a full bathroom down a dark hall toward a large closet. Inside, the water heater labored. He pulled on the chain of an overhead light inside, and she flicked on the hall light, which still didn't illuminate much.

"Here." She handed him a flashlight. "Daniel should be coming with those tools."

She stood close, and Evan did his best to ignore her proximity. But it was as if his every cell was attuned to Kenzie, and he didn't know how to handle it, having never been so attracted to anyone before. Even Rita had been a slow, steady build toward love. He'd thought her pretty, but his body hadn't tried to turn itself inside out when near her.

There was something to be said for physical chemistry, he guessed, wondering if Kenzie felt it too.

He turned and tripped over her, of all things. "Oof."

She stopped him from braining himself on the door-jamb, the two of them standing way too close for his peace of mind. His body started to respond, the feel of warm woman, the scent of lavender and female overriding all else.

"Oh." Her hands spread on his chest, and she had to be feeling his racing heart. "S-sorry, I didn't mean to get so close."

"It's not a problem." *Unless my heart jumps out of my chest.* "Can I ask you something?" His voice sounded impossibly deep, even to him.

"Sure," she breathed, and the scent of chocolate and mint wafted over him. His favorite combination.

"Is it just me, or are you feeling this too?" He cupped her cheek, knowing he shouldn't but unable to stop himself. Damn. She *was* as soft as he'd imagined.

She drew in a breath. "This weird kind of attraction?"

He rubbed his thumb over her jawline, staring at her full lips that appeared to darken under the moving shadow of the swaying overhead light. "Yeah."

"It is different, isn't it?"

"Why are you whispering?" he asked as he leaned closer, intent on tasting her.

"Why are you?"

His lips ghosted the edge of her mouth. Her fingers clenched on his shirt, digging into his chest, and his body went rock-hard in an instant, a fact she couldn't possibly miss.

"Kenzie?" Daniel's voice grew louder as the sound of his feet on the stairs rebounded.

"Ack!" Kenzie shoved Evan back so hard he bumped his head on the doorframe.

"Shit."

"Sorry," she mumbled and darted away, leaving him frustrated, aching, and annoyed with himself for starting something he couldn't possibly finish.

Not now, and not with her brother around.

CHAPTER 7

KENZIE DIDN'T KNOW WHAT SHE'D BEEN THINKING. Kissing Evan Griffith with Daniel just upstairs? Was she *insane?* She hurried to get as far away from Evan as possible, standing by the stairwell leading up to the kitchen as Daniel brushed past her with the toolbox.

God, just a breath from kissing Evan and her body had done a complete meltdown. She ached in all the wrong places and had to cross her arms over her chest and pretend a sudden chill to hide the effect that blasted man had on her.

Did he have to exude such sex appeal? Did he have to smell so freakin' good? He wore a subtle cologne, nothing overpowering, but it made her want to sniff him all over. Then nibble, lick, kiss…

And his chest. *Momma.* Kenzie had a thing for a firm upper body, and Evan's promised to be ripped with muscle. Not bodybuilder huge, but that of a powerful man who could lift her easily. Lay her down just so and—

Stop. It.

Fortunately, Lila came over, providing the perfect distraction. "Yo. Anyone home?" she yelled from the kitchen.

"Down here."

Lila had a key and normally let herself in to work through a separate door and stairwell that led from the backyard. Just past the water heater, that door remained closed, or Lila would have seen Kenzie about to kiss Evan.

Lila walked down the stairs from the kitchen and filled

her in. "Rachel's still working but making real progress on Milo's Brakes."

"Great." Kenzie smiled.

"What's with the wattage?" Lila's eyes narrowed. "You're hiding something."

The tinkering sound of tools behind her alerted Lila to men working.

"Who's back there? *Please* tell me it's the—"

"Just Daniel and Evan," Kenzie said to hopefully cover whatever inappropriate thing came out of Lila's mouth.

"—Moving Man with the Fine Ass. Is it him? Wait. He's *here?*" Lila gurgled with enjoyment.

"Oh my God. Could you be any more embarrassing?" Kenzie hissed as Daniel and Evan stuck their heads out of the closet.

Daniel shook his head and said something to Evan that had him laughing.

"Hi, Lila. I'm just the hired help." Evan went back to working on the heater, sending Daniel back and forth to the garage a few times.

Lila dragged Kenzie toward her and in a low voice asked, "What is he doing here?"

"He's fixing my pipes," Kenzie deadpanned.

Lila hooted. "Man, you wish."

I so wish.

"Really, what's up?"

Kenzie explained about the water heater and about almost losing the Talon account before they could try selling it.

"That would have hurt," Lila agreed. "So let the cutie help. I like your plan." She whispered, "Did you do him yet?"

"Are you insane? Daniel's here!"

Probably not the smartest thing she might have said. Her denial would be more believable if she'd expressed not being attracted or ready to date. Using her brother as the only excuse was too close to the truth and totally lame.

"I see."

"I'm scared about what you think you see." Kenzie groaned. "Come on. Let them work and help me fix this issue with the kale."

"Loaves or leaves?"

"Lila."

"Can't you convince her to go with something strong and GMO-y? A logo, something natural, not cartoon kale with legs."

Kenzie sighed, relieved to be talking about work and not Evan. "I'm trying, but Ellie is stuck on her first product that went national, and she's afraid if we change her initial brand we'll confuse people. So we need to incorporate the leaf with the new logo you were working on. I think your idea is closest to what she'll really want, especially after talking to her earlier. But next time, *you* talk to her. You're more aggressive, and you seem nice. So you can intimidate her into a good idea."

"I love how you insult and compliment me at the same time. I'm never sure if I should insult you back or say thank you."

"You're welcome."

Lila muttered, "Bitch."

Kenzie grinned.

"Kenzie, can you come here?" Daniel shouted.

Evan continued to talk to Daniel, but Kenzie couldn't make out more than his deep, sexy voice.

The man gave her the shivers, and she was all too aware of Lila following, watching her.

"Yes?"

"Okay, so I think I see your problem." Evan pointed to some open square on the heater. "You have no hot water, which was what happened to my mom's tank a few months ago. In her case, the heating element failed. We checked it over, and it ended up needing to be replaced, so we called a plumber. If you need them, McSons Plumbing is great. I'd highly recommend them. But here, see this?"

She leaned closer, Lila's head right next to hers.

"Oh, he smells good," Lila whispered way too loudly.

"Lila, not now," Daniel complained. "I'm learning manly stuff."

Evan chuckled. "Every time I'm here it's like I'm living in a sitcom."

"Try living next to it," Lila said. "It's real. But honey, I'm not lying. You smell amazing."

"Thanks. Lucky for you, Monday is shower day."

Kenzie grinned, and even Daniel laughed.

"Anyway, what I'm trying to tell you is that sometimes it's not the heating element. First you'd check the breaker to make sure that's not the problem, which it isn't, because Daniel checked."

"Yeah, that happened before."

"So look here. The limit switch might need to be reset. Sometimes it can trip if the water is too hot. Or the switch can fail and need to be replaced. We'll reset it and see what happens." He had Daniel cut the power and Kenzie hold the flashlight for him. Then he removed some insulation from inside the heater and pressed a button. "Daniel, put the power back on."

"On it." Daniel raced away, and the light in the closet came back on.

"It'll take about twenty to thirty minutes before you'll know if it worked," Evan said, stopping her in her tracks before she could go to check the water.

"Oh, okay."

They stared at each other before Lila cleared her throat. "So, we getting back to work or what?" she asked, a wide smile on her face as she stared from Evan to Kenzie.

Daniel returned and watched as Evan put the insulation and switch plate back, screwing the plate back in, and showed the boy what to do, again instructing him about cutting the power first. Daniel nodded then left when the house phone rang, yelling, "Sorry, that might be Rafi."

"Teenagers." Kenzie sighed.

Evan smiled, his gaze warming the cool gray of his eyes. "How about I text you that number for the plumber? That way if it doesn't heat up, you'll have someone reputable to call. And they're reasonably priced."

"That's a great idea." Kenzie tried not to look at his eyes, afraid he might see how much she liked him right now. And not just because of the heater, but because having him in her house, helping her out of a jam, felt so darn good.

She was tired of always having to be everything for everyone. Lila and Rachel's friend, boss, confidant. Daniel's mom, sister, caregiver. The one who paid for everything and fretted when checks just barely covered their debts.

"Don't you need her number first?" Lila asked oh so innocently.

"Rachel gave it to me," he admitted.

Lila stared at him. "Well, isn't she free with our personal information."

Kenzie didn't comment, not sure if she should scold or thank her friend.

A contact pinged through a text, and Kenzie read the number. "Thanks."

"You ever need them, tell them Vanessa sent you and ask for the family discount."

Kenzie immediately wondered who Vanessa might be.

"Who's Vanessa?" Lila asked.

Thank you, Lila.

"My old boss, who's married to the plumbers' brother. Man, you want to talk about a dragon. Vanessa could work me under the table, and I'm a pretty hardworking guy."

Daniel announced moments later from the top of the stairs, "It was Rafi, and he's coming over. Oh, and the shower's still cold."

"You have to wait to let the tank heat up," Evan reminded him. "Give it a little time. And speaking of time, I'm sorry, but I have to go. I've got a client I have to handle before I go back to work tomorrow. Old job, then new job."

Kenzie understood, but Lila looked confused.

"Walk me out?" Evan asked, glancing at Kenzie.

Daniel started to follow, so Lila latched onto him. "Bye, Evan. See you soon!"

"Why can't I go too?" Kenzie heard Daniel asking.

"Because I saw a spider near my table and I am not going near it, that's why."

"Lila, you're such a girl."

"Thank you, Captain Obvious."

Kenzie preceded Evan up the stairs, but he stopped her in the kitchen. She looked up at him. "What's wrong?"

"I just need to know. The mint chocolate. Where did that come from?"

"Huh?"

He slid his thumb over her lower lip, and her heart rate shot into overdrive. "When we nearly kissed downstairs, I tasted chocolate and mint on your breath."

"You want some?" she asked, frazzled. Had she finished off the candy bar in her car? Did she have another in her secret candy drawer? And did any of that matter with Evan's face drawing closer?

"Yeah. I want a taste."

"O-kay," she breathed, meaning okay to anything he wanted. And hallelujah, he wanted the same thing she did.

He kissed her, the pressure soft then firmer as he seduced her with a simple press of his lips. He gently drew her closer, but he didn't have to pull. She shot forward and hugged him tight, like a heat-seeking missile savoring the warmth of her target.

The man was hot, built, and aroused. She could tell by the generous swelling against her belly. He gave a small groan, and she forgot everything but Evan. The urge to feel him even closer surged, and she drew him by the neck to seal them tighter then penetrated his mouth with her tongue.

He froze for a moment before pushing her back against the wall. Before she knew it, he had his hands on her ass, holding her up with little effort, while she automatically wrapped her legs around his back.

The kiss turned ravenous, the hunger inside her growing.

He pulled his mouth away on a swear, his erection riding between her legs *just right*.

"Christ. I want you." He kissed her again, and she ran

her hands through his hair, taken with such softness. The scent of man and cologne made her dizzy. Or maybe that was a lack of air.

He tried to pull back twice, but she wouldn't let him go.

"Kenzie," he moaned. "Sweetheart, if you don't let me go, I'm going to fuck you right now."

That should have been a bad thing, but feeling such strength holding her close, she couldn't for the life of her understand why. She blinked up at him, enraptured by the desire on his face. "God, you're handsome."

He kissed her, this time his lips softer, the connection less intense. "And you're gorgeous. And sweet." He pulled back and nuzzled her neck, kissing her there. "And your brother's downstairs."

That served to bank the embers smothering her remaining brain cells. Kenzie groaned. "I'm sorry."

She slid down his body and saw him wince when she grazed his erection.

"I'm not. Well, maybe that we aren't somewhere a little more private." Evan smiled at her, and the embarrassment she'd started to feel vanished as if it had never been. "So do you think if I asked you out for coffee, you might say yes this time?" He ran a hand through her hair, and she wanted to purr.

"Um, no." She turned her head and kissed the palm of his hand. When he tensed, she added with a smile, "I think we should go to dinner instead."

"That's a terrific idea." He kissed her again, with a tenderness that gave her all the feels. "I hate to do this, but I need to go before someone comes up here and sees how excited I am to be near you."

She grinned. "Sometimes it's good to be a girl."

"Yeah." He pulled away then turned and left without another word.

She heard his car start and looked out the front window. His car didn't move, but she heard a text arrive. Dinner Friday night, my treat. Can I pick you up at six?

Happiness bubbled up through her. She sent back a few smiling emojis.

He finally drove away after a beep goodbye. Still too revved up to return to her brother and Lila, she decided to test out the shower.

And found that the hot water had come back on.

A pity because she could have used a spray of cold to shock her back down to earth.

She'd made out with Evan Griffith, had humped him in her kitchen, for God's sake, and agreed to go out on a dinner date with the man Friday night.

What the hell was wrong with her?

Apparently nothing a little Evan couldn't cure.

She turned the spray to cold and shivered until common sense returned.

Evan had no idea what had come over him. For the next three days, he drifted in a daze at the Hillford house, unsure if his experience with Kenzie had really been so awe-inducing. Had the sexy nature of the woman been exaggerated due to either his lack of a love life or hers?

Sometimes sex could seem earth-shattering in the moment, especially coming off a long dry spell. From what he gathered, Kenzie hadn't been with anyone in a while. And he hadn't either, not since Sheila more than six months ago. Just thinking about her made him cringe.

He didn't like to judge anyone, but Sheila had done enough judging, trying to "fix" him, for them both.

Kenzie, though... He sighed.

"Oh my God, Evan. What is wrong with you?" Hector Jackson propped his hands on his hips, the ex-Navy sailor built like a brick house. They stood in the Hillfords' crowded garage that teemed with massive furniture prepped to be moved. "You've been sighing and, I'm sorry to say, dreamy-eyed since Tuesday. It's like your first teenage crush except you're a dude and you're thirty."

"Thirty-one," Evan said, his mood still buoyant. "Hector, I met someone. We hit it off right away."

"Good for you, man." Hector smiled, a slash of white in his dark face. Hector was easily the heart of the company. The man had served in the Navy alongside his twin brother. He had a work ethic that never quit, and he got along with everyone. Even Smith, most days. Women seemed to love him. He was a gentleman, strong, and humble. Dependable as the sun rising and a genuinely nice guy.

"Hector, how come you don't have a wife or girlfriend?"

"You proposing, handsome?" Lafayette asked as he dropped off a small computer desk that had to weigh a hundred pounds at least. Evan had lifted it earlier and winced.

Hector laughed. "Easy, bro. Or I'll tell Simon you're flirting on the job."

"I was just teasing, though I will say Evan's been looking fine as shit lately. Must be love." Hector's identical twin, Lafayette, had the same good-natured vibe as his brother, and he could lift mountains without trying.

Evan smiled. "Thanks, Lafayette. You always know what to say."

"That I do." Lafayette grinned and went back for more.

Smith groaned as he dropped off two forty-five-pound plates with ease, emptying out the Hillfords' exercise room. "For fuck's sake, can we just move shit and stop all the chitchat?"

Evan and Hector exchanged a look as Smith left to grab more from the house.

"Is he serious?" Hector asked and shifted a few things in the back of the open truck. This would make load number three to be dropped off. They'd spent the week packing and prepping to move the family. "This from the same man who's been complaining twenty-four seven about Cash not being here? I think he misses the big guy."

Honestly, Evan thought the same. "Yeah, I know."

"So who's this mystery woman that's got your panties in a bunch?"

"Nice imagery."

Hector grinned. "I try."

Evan tried to put it into words that made sense. "I met this woman, and she's... I... It's weird. I can't explain it. The first time I saw her, time seemed to stand still. It's the damnedest thing."

"Nice." Hector bumped fists with him. "She got any friends?"

Evan laughed. "As a matter of fact, she—" His phone chimed, and his heart raced. Anytime he got a text, he wondered if it was from Kenzie. He kept praying she wouldn't cancel their date. He'd been so blown over by their connection, he figured she'd be a little freaked out by it. Or at least, he hoped she was. Because he was seriously enamored, and that should have worried him.

Forcing himself to be slow about it, Evan checked his text and felt as if a rock had dropped in his stomach, landing hard and hurting.

Hector frowned. "What's up?"

"I think she's trying to ditch me." He read the note. "She says she forgot she'd promised to go to a birthday dinner with her friend Lila. She's really sorry but said I was invited if I wanted to come with them. Otherwise we can reschedule." And why did he feel like her idea of rescheduling was a lot like getting blown off?

"Maybe it's legit," Hector offered.

"Maybe." But Evan felt in his gut it wasn't.

"Then again, who forgets a birthday dinner? They have cake and singing," Hector joked.

"Yeah. But maybe it would be easier if she and I did ease back a little. Just being with her is intense, for sure."

"This could also be a test, to see how you do with a little disappointment. Are you a man who can handle that? Or are you gonna throw a tantrum and show your true colors?"

"Huh. Dating is a lot more complex than it used to be."

"What? You mean back in the nineteen hundreds when you last went out?"

"Screw you."

Hector gave him a wide smile.

Evan's reluctant laugh started his friend chuckling. And then he had a thought. "Hey, you want to do me a solid?"

Hector's smile dimmed. "No. Nope. No favors."

"Oh, come on. You asked if Kenzie had a friend."

"I didn't mean it."

"Well, she does. Lila is funny, stacked, and fine."

"What's wrong with her?"

"Besides being a little neurotic? Nothing. I'd have asked her out if Kenzie hadn't caught my eye." Not a lie. Lila was pretty, just not as awe-inspiring as Kenzie. But Evan liked what he knew of Lila, and he thought Hector would too. And that had nothing to do with skin color and everything to do with Hector finding a woman who could handle him. Evan had a feeling nothing much scared Lila.

"So she's high-maintenance, eh? What the hell. Not like I have anything better to do now that Lafayette is always too busy to hang, cozying up with his new boyfriend."

Lafayette popped his head out from behind a large ceramic pot he'd hefted into the garage. "How many times do I have to tell you? Simon prefers being labeled my boy toy. Get it right, Bro."

"Nobody wants to hear about you and your 'boy toy,' Lafayette. And we especially don't want to hear your adventures at night. You guys have been keeping me up," Hector complained. "Can't you just move on from being into each other to an old married couple who never gets any?"

"Bitch, please. With all this to love, Simon would have to be insane to say no. And you want me to stop talking about dick, maybe you should stop spinning stories about tits and ass."

Hector growled, "I *never*—"

"Christ. What the ever-loving fuck are you girls talking about now?" Smith scowled, enraged as he dropped off a large ottoman, and lowered his voice a fraction. "There's a kid inside, damn it."

"Oh, my bad. I'll keep it down." Lafayette had the grace

to look embarrassed. "Thought the kids were at the playground," he said as he went back inside.

"Mrs. Hillford just brought them back." Smith used two fingers to point at his eyes then at Evan and Hector before he walked back inside.

"He points at me again, I'm gonna shove that finger up his ass," Hector murmured.

"Can I film it?"

"Please do." Hector helped Evan move two large hope chests into the truck. Panting, he managed, "So, date night. Just text me when and where."

"You're the best, Hector."

"Yeah, yeah. Just remember, you owe me."

"Invite me to your wedding, and we'll call it even."

Hector made a sour face. "You're hilarious. Now go help Smith before Finley finds him. Last I heard, Finley was ready to make Smith disappear. Permanently. And you know if he tries, Smith will bend him into a pretzel."

"Good point. With Cash out, Heidi training for her next Ironman, and the rest of the gang maxed out, we need every man on deck."

Hector nodded. "Yep. And you don't want to be working more hours just because Finley pushed Smith too hard."

"There is that." Finley was a master at making a quarter disappear. But he had a habit of running his mouth. And Smith only had so much patience.

Now in a much better mood since outmaneuvering Kenzie, though she didn't yet know it, Evan decided to be generous.

Inside, after a few minutes spent hunting Smith down, he found the huge man sitting next to a sobbing five-year-old in a pink bedroom draped with white lace. Smith sat cross-legged on the floor before a tiny table covered with play tea-cups and fudge-stripe cookies.

"Look, kid. It's okay. Sometimes moms and dads split. They still love you. And your big brother is just being a pain 'cause he's sad. But he loves you a ton. I heard him say so earlier."

"Really?" The *r* sounded more like a *w*, so Evan heard "Weally?"

It was enough to break a guy's heart.

Smith nodded and wiped the girl's tears. "Really. So you have to forgive Billy. Sometimes parents are dumb and don't know how to tell their kids the truth. But it's never a kid's fault. Only stupidhead parents."

"Okay." She let out a sigh, her lower lip trembling. "My mommy thinks you're pwetty."

"They all do, kid." Smith gently patted the little girl on the shoulder, and her pigtailed braids swung.

Evan wasn't surprised by Smith's ego, but he was enchanted by the sight of the large man being so careful about a little girl's feelings.

Smith cleared his throat. "Now can you pour me some more tea? I'm really thirsty. I needed this break, but I don't want to get in trouble for slacking. After I move your night-stand, I'll sneak back in, and you, me, and Mr. Bumpers can talk some more, okay?" Mr. Bumpers being the oversized stuffed gorilla sitting at the table, half leaning on it.

The little girl nodded, solemn, and poured a pretend cup of tea that Smith drank, the tiny teacup pinched between his thick fingers.

"Mmm. Delicious." He gave her back the cup then stood.

She held out her arms.

"Uh, what?" Smith swallowed, looking nervous.

"One hug, pwease. For the tea."

Smith glanced around, saw Evan, and froze.

Caught by the tender scene, Evan nodded to the girl with a smile then watched as Smith gathered her in his arms and stood tall. Her legs dangled, and she laughed as he swung her around.

He quickly set her down and put a finger over his lips.

Evan moved back so the little girl wouldn't see him watching.

"I'll be back soon. And I want a cookie next time." Smith and the girl locked pinkie fingers, then Smith took her nightstand outside.

Before Smith could say anything and ruin the moment, Evan clapped him on the back. "Truck's getting full soon. Hurry up and we'll finish the day with a beer at Ringo's. I'm buying."

He took Smith's grunt as a yes and wondered what else the gruff guy might be hiding behind that surly nature. Because he certainly had a big heart, and Evan never would have guessed.

And maybe that little girl wasn't the only one needing a friend.

CHAPTER 8

"So. You got a thing for high tea and fudge stripes, eh?" Evan teased.

They sat in a fairly crowded Ringo's Bar, hanging by themselves while Hector and his brother teased Reid and Naomi, who'd shown up for some relaxation time. Evan didn't know if the others realized why they felt so comfortable together, but he thought they functioned more like family than coworkers.

Reid made sure they all had what they needed, and Cash was usually right by his side. Evan filled in when necessary, and the others liked spending time together. No one forced them to hang out after work. They *chose* to, laughing and enjoying themselves, because that familiar sense of solidarity abounded at Vets on the Go!

Smith, for once, didn't focus on a Griffith brother. Instead he watched Evan with caution.

"What? I don't bite."

Smith grunted and swigged his beer. "Waiting for another smart-ass comment about my teatime."

Evan grinned. "Aw, come on. It was cute. And what you did for that little girl was nice."

Smith flushed, seeming disconcerted by the praise. "She's only five. Has no idea why her old man isn't around or why her mom keeps crying or flirting every two seconds with anyone swinging a dick."

"Poor kid."

"Yeah. Divorce isn't fun, and it's the kids who suffer the most."

"Is that what happened to you?"

"Nah. I just had a shitty mom. No dad. Then I joined the Corps, and that was all she wrote."

Evan nodded. "My parents had me later in life. Just me, no other kids. They meant well, and they loved me, but they could be a little much with the protection and hovering."

"Better too much than not enough."

"I guess." Evan knew he'd been luckier than most, and he truly loved his mother. "So your mom, is she still around?"

Smith tensed for a brief moment. Had Evan not been watching him so closely, he might not have noticed. "She's dead."

"Sorry, man."

Smith finished his beer. "It is what it is."

"Any other family?" Evan asked carefully, not acting as if the answer meant anything. "Brother or sisters? Aunts, uncles?"

"Nah, just me." Smith watched him.

Evan felt as if in a gunfight, waiting to fire an unloaded pistol at a man with dead-center aim. "So, ah, you ever miss not having anyone else?" He paused as a thought struck. "You're not married, are you?"

Smith grinned. "Married? Me? Please." He chuckled. "What is this, twenty questions?"

"We're a team. Even me, the FNG." Fucking new guy. "Pretty much everyone knows a little about everyone else's past. Except for you."

"And you," Smith pointed out, and then he ordered another beer from a passing waitress. "What's your story, Captain Griffith?"

Evan grimaced. "Yeah, I loved the Corps, but the politics sucked. Not much to tell, really. I went to school, got a bachelor's in accounting. Joined the Marine Corps as a logistics officer. Did six years and came home. More school, joined a posh accounting firm, and worked myself almost into an ulcer. So I quit. Now I'm filling in for Cash while he heals. Then I'll go back to some part-time clients."

"You can afford that?"

Now who's asking personal questions, Smith? But hell, Evan had nothing to hide. "I made some smart investments years ago that are paying off. And I'll keep working on the accounting side. Well, it's either that or eat bread and water every day. And I like my beer." He tilted his drink at Smith, who took his from the passing waitress and held it up in a toast.

"What about chicks?" Smith asked. "Never married?"

"Engaged once." He kept his tone lighthearted, still sad about Rita, but his heavy grief had left him long ago.

"What, did she leave for someone prettier?" Smith teased.

"Nah. But she should have."

Smith's smile faded. "Why aren't you married to her then?"

"Cancer came on fast. She was gone within a year. It was brutal."

Smith frowned. "Sorry, man."

"It happened. It's over, and she's at peace." *And she'd want you to move on.* Evan put his past in the past. "So how come you're not dating?"

"Who says I'm not?"

"The fact that you're here with me on a Thursday night,"

Evan said dryly. "Look. Reid brought Naomi. Lafayette brought Simon. And is that…Finley and a girl?"

"Damn." Smith leaned closer. "She's not bad looking. Maybe she's drunk."

Evan grinned. "Maybe." He'd told himself he wouldn't, but he planted a seed anyway. "Hey, I gotta know."

"What?" He'd never heard Smith so laid-back before.

"What's with you and Cash? You guys look enough alike to be brothers."

Smith stiffened. He didn't answer, and Evan wondered if he'd pushed too hard too fast.

"You think we look alike?" Smith asked, quiet, staring down at his beer.

"Yes. But maybe it's just me. I don't think Reid and I look that much alike, but I guess we do. Our dads were brothers, after all."

"Yeah. Blood will tell, huh?"

"I guess. But that doesn't make sense with you and Cash."

Smith lifted his head, his eyes full of rage and pain. "Doesn't it, Evan?" He finished his beer, never looking away. Then he stood. "Thanks for the drinks. See you tomorrow." He left without another word, and Evan let out the breath he'd been holding.

Shit. Smith in a rage was as bad as Cash in a rage. Evan had gotten lucky. He crossed the room to his cousin. Naomi stood at the bar talking to the Jackson twins and Simon while Reid nursed a beer at their table.

"What's up with you and Smith being all chummy?" Reid asked. "Slumming?"

"Ha ha."

"I'm kidding. I don't mind Smith. I just wish he'd ease up on Cash."

"He knows."

Reid paused. "Come again?"

"I said he knows. I think." Evan relayed the conversation. "Look, you three keep dancing around it. Just talk to each other. Life is short, Reid. You have the chance to add to your happiness."

"With *Smith?*"

"Okay, he isn't the easiest person to deal with. But today he sat with a little girl and drank pretend tea, all to save her from getting her feelings hurt. There's more to Smith than an obnoxious pain in the ass. And I hate to say it, but that could be said about Cash too, couldn't it?"

Reid wiped a hand down his face. "I *know* we need to talk about it. I've been trying, but Cash is getting cozy with Jordan, and he's got a broken arm he's dealing with. I don't want to mess with him right now."

"Smith is all alone."

Reid brightened. "No, he's not. He's got you."

"Wait. What?"

"Yep. You're good for him. You keep him grounded. Look out for the big bastard. Before you know it, we'll get him to sit down with Aunt Jane and have a huge talk about life and coincidence, because we all know he didn't look us up by chance and sign on because he loves moving furniture."

"Hell, Reid. That's a lot to ask."

"But you'll do it because you're you."

"What does that mean?"

Reid smiled. "It means your parents raised you to be responsible. To put family first and always do the right thing."

"You mean to not rock the boat and get along." Dull. Predictable. Boring. "I'm the family peacemaker."

"Yep, and you're good at it."

Too good at it. Evan had rarely rebelled, joining the Marine Corps only after he'd gone to college to make his parents proud. He did what he was told, and he was still doing what he was told, he realized. Because he *would* try to be there for Smith, who likely didn't realize how lonely he really was.

"You're annoying."

"I know. Evan, you're a good guy. Hell, you're the best of us. Smart, intelligent. Got a few degrees, were an officer."

"Quit blowing smoke up my ass," Evan said, fighting a blush. "I said I'd look after him."

"And that's good because I don't know what will come of all this. One thing I do know is I'm not losing my brother over Smith." Reid paused. "That sounds harsh, and I don't want to be cruel, but the plain truth is we might never be a close family. With Smith, I mean. You, me, Cash, and Aunt Jane are solid. Maybe even your mom's Jerome guy. Smith is an unknown. And Cash has been through a lot. He doesn't need Smith shitting all over him every chance he gets."

Evan frowned. "You mentioned Jerome."

"I mentioned a lot of things. Jerome is all you heard?"

"Have you met him?"

Reid huffed and shook his head. "One-track mind. No, Evan, I haven't met him yet." In that moment, Evan realized he and Reid did look alike, except that Reid had darker hair. Same gray eyes, same stubborn chin. They were family, like Cash. Like Smith, no matter what the big bastard had to say. "But we're going to dinner with Jerome and Aunt Jane next week."

Evan still hadn't met the guy, and he didn't understand his mother hiding him. He and his mom used to share everything. But now with her being sick, her symptoms just like Rita's had been, he worried about her. *And why the hell is she introducing him to Reid first?*

"Let me know what you think."

"I will. But, Cuz, maybe you should be asking your mom why she hasn't introduced you two. Because from what I saw of them kissing and the way Aunt Jane talks about him, it's a lot more serious than her getting a piece of tail."

"Jesus, Reid."

Reid laughed. "Yeah, Aunt Jane's my hero. And so are you if you keep an eye on Smith."

"I'm giving myself a bonus," he grumbled, his thoughts all over the place. Smith, his mom, Kenzie…

"You've more than earned it. Now come talk to Naomi and remind her how great I am. I don't want her to forget."

"As if you and your ego would let her."

Reid put him all too easily in a headlock and dragged him over to the others, who laughed. "Say it. Come on, Evan. Say it."

"Jackass."

Reid's arms squeezed harder. "Say it…"

"Reid is great." His cousin let him go, and Evan rubbed his neck, scowling. "A great big asshole."

"Reid!" Naomi laughed and gave Evan a hug. "Oh, you poor thing. Let me help you make it better."

"A kiss might help," Evan said, sounding weak, and met Reid's narrowed gaze with a smiling one of his own.

"Get your own girl," Reid growled and pulled Naomi

to him then whispered something in her ear that had her blushing.

"You heard the man," Hector said. "Just text me when and where."

"Will do." Evan nodded, wanting what his cousin had.

A woman in his arms, surrounded by friends and family.

Friday evening, Kenzie sat with Lila and twisted the napkin in her lap.

"Nervous much?" Lila teased. "Though it serves you right, involving me in your sex games."

The young server, who'd dropped by to take their drink order, stuttered that she'd be right back with more water.

Lila whooped with laughter, and Kenzie grimaced, staring at the already full water glasses on their table. "Great. There goes our service for the night. You scared away our waitress."

"Worth it." Lila glanced around. "So Evan's coming?"

"He said he was. Should I be glad or afraid that you being here didn't scare him off?"

"I'm impressed, to be honest." Lila looked gorgeous as usual. She wore a buttercream tank top that showed off her toned arms and curvy figure, as did the tight jeans and strappy sandals.

Kenzie had done her best to look as if she hadn't dressed with Evan in mind while second- and third-guessing every decision she made, from what shoes to what shade of eyeliner to wear. She'd settled on a cute linen skirt, flat sandals, and a cropped pink top.

"I should have just gone out with him myself, huh?"

"Yep." Lila never pulled her punches. "You look like a total loser bringing your girlfriend along. No way he believes it's my birthday dinner." Lila grunted. "But you can bet your ass I want cake."

"I told you I'd get you some." Kenzie let go of her napkin to worry at her bracelet, a silver-and-turquoise piece that had been her mother's favorite. "Now I feel silly."

"Good. Can I just say I told you so? Hell, girl, who brings a buddy on a dinner date…that isn't a teenager, I mean? Do you want me to drive you to the movies too? Make sure he stays at least six inches away from you at all times?"

Kenzie cringed. "No. And we're not going to the movies."

"I was making a point." Lila sipped her water. Her eyes widened, caught on the area by the bar.

Kenzie glanced over and saw Evan dressed in jeans and a button-down blue shirt that made his eyes look amazing. God, he was handsome, turning more than a few heads as he smiled and made his way to the table.

She blinked up at him. "H-hi, Evan." She sounded weak, even to her own ears.

"Hey, Kenzie." He took her hand and kissed the back of it. Then moved to Lila and did the same to her. "Lovely Lila."

"Well, hel-lo, handsome." Then she smiled widely over his shoulder. "And who's your friend?"

Kenzie hadn't noticed anyone but Evan. The handsome man giving Lila a subtle but approving once-over smiled. Muscular, a little bit shorter than Evan, and sexy, the man had a smile that made her want to smile back. His eyes crinkled as he studied her. "You must be Kenzie."

Evan prodded his friend to move into one of the chairs

across from theirs. "This is my buddy, Hector. I hope you don't mind me bringing him." The too-bright smile he shot her raised her suspicion. About what, she didn't yet know.

"Not at all," Kenzie said, keeping her voice even. "Hi, Hector."

"Great to meet you." Hector smiled and turned his gaze to Lila. "And Lila, it's a real pleasure."

"Oh," Lila said. "Is it *your* birthday *too*, Hector?" Obviously not making any attempt to go along with Kenzie's cover story.

Kenzie wanted to hide behind her menu.

"Ah, I…" Hector paused.

"Why *yes*, Lila, it is," Evan said, his eyes gleaming. He smirked at Kenzie. "Can you believe that? What a great idea to celebrate at dinner, am I right?"

Hector shot Evan a cautious glance before looking back at Kenzie. "Sure. I'm always game for a meal, and what could be better than dinner with two beautiful ladies?"

Lila grinned. "I like this one. So how old are you, handsome?"

"Thirty. You?"

"You're not supposed to ask a woman how old she is. How old do you think I look?"

Hector laughed and shook his head, then he waved at a passing server. "We need drinks over here."

They laughed and ordered, and Kenzie started to feel at ease. Small talk centered around how everyone knew everyone.

"Yeah, Evan's the new guy at the job," Hector said. "He wasn't man enough to be in the Navy, but hey, the Marines took him, so it's all good."

Evan scoffed. "Please."

"But he also keeps us rolling in legit money and the IRS off our back, so that's good."

"Legit money as opposed to the billions we're cleaning for the mob, you mean?" Evan said dryly. "Just because taxes intimidate most people doesn't mean they're actually that hard to do. Or that men in black suits will break your legs if you miss a deadline."

"If you're an accountant, they're not hard to do. They frustrate the crap out of me." Lila sighed. "I hear you're going to help Kenzie iron out a few problems. So thanks in advance, unless you get her arrested for tax evasion. Then I'll kill you."

Kenzie groaned. "Lila, relax on the death threats. At least until we have wine." The waiter finally dropped off their drinks, and she took a hefty sip of her chardonnay.

"Lila sounds a lot like Daniel." Evan chuckled. "Why does everyone think a problem with the IRS equals jail time?"

"What?" Kenzie frowned. What had Daniel been saying?

"Before you scoff at my death threats, I have to say I think they're an important part of any beginning relationship." Lila nodded.

Kenzie thought, *Kill me now.* To her relief, Evan didn't seem offended. He looked to be biting back a grin.

Lila wouldn't stop talking. "Hey, if he scares off this easily, he's not the guy for you."

"Exactly," Hector agreed.

Lila drank her beer. "Great. Threats have been delivered. Now let's talk about you being in the Navy, Hector. Because I love a man with guns." She waggled her brows, staring at his thickly muscled arms.

Evan groaned. "Don't get him started."

Mirth and good fun filled the table, as well as good food. Hector talked about life in the Navy with his twin then goaded Evan into a discussion about the Marine Corps, which Kenzie found fascinating. She could see how that kind of structure would suit what she knew of Evan, though he seemed a little too easygoing to have survived in such a regimented field.

"How did you and Kenzie meet?" Evan asked Lila. "And when did Rachel come into the group?"

Lila grinned. "We all met at the same time, believe it or not. Eleven years ago in school. Kenzie was struggling, so Rachel and I helped her out."

"Design school," Kenzie elaborated, wishing Lila didn't make her sound so helpless. "And yes, I was struggling. I was twenty years old trying to navigate college with a two-year-old."

Hector nodded. "Being a full-time mom at that age must have been hard. Didn't you have any help?"

"Oh, the baby wasn't Kenzie's," Lila said. "He's her little brother. Kenzie's folks died in a car accident, and Kenzie became Daniel's guardian."

"He loves calling me Mom to throw people off." Kenzie didn't feel the pain of her parents' passing the way she used to. She'd become numb to it, experiencing only a small sense of loss at their mention.

"I'm sorry." Evan's eyes expressed his sincerity. "That had to be tough." Then he gave her a sly smile. "I've met your brother."

The heavy mood lightened, and she could have kissed him for not making the date that wasn't a date awkward.

She hadn't realized she'd been staring at him, and he at her, until Hector cleared his throat.

"Well, I don't know about you guys, but I'm ready for dessert."

Lila patted her slender stomach. "Yeah, me too. For my birthday cake. Because it's not every day a girl turns twenty-four."

Hector raised a brow. "Now that's funny, because I would have pegged you as twenty-three, tops."

"Really?" Evan scratched his head. "I was thinking thirty-two."

"Nah," Kenzie said, looking at an amused Lila. "With that beautiful skin? Forty-five, max."

"You're an ass," Lila said to her. "Evan, you were close, but not as close as Hector." Lila batted her eyelashes at him, and Kenzie did her best not to laugh out loud.

Hector looked entranced. *Another one bites the dust.*

Evan ordered the pair slices of birthday cake and a brownie sundae to share with Kenzie.

"Ordering for me, Evan? That's a little high-handed, don't you think?" Kenzie's breathy tone sounded playful. *Oh my God. I'm flirting. Maybe hell really has frozen over.* Even Lila raised a brow.

Kenzie tried again, trying to sound more normal. "Maybe I don't like chocolate."

"Really? Because I remember you liking chocolate and mint pretty well."

She blushed to the roots of her hair, the memory of their explosive kiss impossible to forget.

"Oh, now that's a response that demands an explanation," Lila said, bringing attention to Kenzie's red face.

"I'll be right back." Kenzie shot out of her seat for the bathroom, but not before seeing Evan's satisfied smile.

She used the facilities and took a good minute to study herself in the mirror, doing her best to calm both her raging hormones and her nerves.

Lila entered, saw her, and laughed. "He got you good."

"Shut up." She left Lila to her amusement and returned to see Evan and Hector arguing about something.

When they spotted her, they stopped.

"You okay?" Evan asked with all due solicitousness.

"Oh, I'm fine. Just dandy."

He smiled.

She smiled wider.

Hector mumbled something about Evan being an idiot, which she found funny.

When Lila returned, they celebrated two fake birthdays, and she shared a decadent dessert with Evan. Every time their spoons brushed or their eyes met, she fought a shiver of arousal, so she was not herself when she agreed to meet the next night for bowling.

"And bring friends. Hector and I plan on trouncing you."

"Oh, it's on, big man," Lila taunted with a wink at Hector. "We'll bring Rachel and Will. Oh, and Daniel. He's pretty good for a skinny teen."

Evan shrugged. "Bring whoever you want. We'll still kick your pretty butts all over the place. Military guys know how to throw down."

"Nice trash talk, Evan." Hector approved.

"Thanks, I've been practicing."

The pair stood, joking with each other, and waited for Lila and Kenzie to leave with them. Before Kenzie could mention the bill, Evan told her it had been taken care of.

"Tell him thanks," Lila prodded, not so softly.

"Thanks"—she glared at Lila—"that was nice of you."

"I aim to please." Evan put a hand at the small of her back and walked her to her car, while Hector did the same with Lila.

"I had a great time," Kenzie told Evan, sincere and surprised she meant it.

"Me too." He smiled, brushed a finger over her cheek, then stepped back. "I look forward to beating you tomorrow night. That's if someone else doesn't have a birthday, anniversary, or celebration that pulls you away. But hey, no problem. Just bring them with you."

She flushed, not sure if she should stick to her story or not. "Well, heck. You flustered me, okay? I'm not used to kisses like that."

His look turned tender. "If it makes you feel any better, I'm not either. It's been a while since I've even been out on a date, to be honest."

"Oh. Really?" Why did that brighten her night?

"Yeah. My mom's been sick. Work has been crazy. And I just... I haven't wanted to see anyone, I guess. Until you." He stepped close and gave her a soft kiss on the lips. He took a quick step back. "Crap. I still feel it."

She had to laugh, liking the fact he looked shaken. "Me too."

He stuffed his hands in his pockets, a sure sign of nerves she found adorable—a word she never would have thought to use with sexy Evan Griffith.

"Are you really okay with me bringing my friends and Daniel tomorrow?"

"I am. I like you, Kenzie. And I'd like to get to know you better. No pressure about anything else."

Though that should have made her feel better, he somehow made it worse. Because everything about Evan made her like him more. "Great. Tomorrow night. And don't be surprised when I bring my own ball."

"Oh, a ringer. I can't wait." He looked as if he might step close again, but he turned around with a wave and left.

She watched him leave, her lips still tingling.

CHAPTER 9

EVAN WASN'T PROUD OF IT, BUT BEING AROUND KENZIE had stirred him up so much he'd had to return home and take himself in hand to get some sleep.

Upon waking, he had the same problem.

Thoughts of how sweet she'd been, how fascinating, a contradiction of shyness yet the strength to tease him as well, had only enhanced everything he found attractive about her.

On one hand, he wanted to sit and listen to her husky voice for hours while he stared into her eyes—not brown but a subtle blend of green and amber whose color constantly shifted. On the other, he too easily imagined watching those eyes close with passion as he drove inside her, feeling all those soft curves hinted at under her pretty pink shirt.

God, the woman was a walking wet dream. Even Hector had mentioned how beautiful she was…when not gushing over Lila. That had been a treat: Hector thunderstruck by the Amazon that was Lila.

That evening at the bowling alley while he waited with Hector at their lanes, he joked, "Remember, I get an invite to the wedding."

"Ass." Hector glanced away, embarrassed and trying to hide it.

Especially when Evan laughed at him.

"Say what you want, but you have it bad for Kenzie. She's fine, man. Can't fault your taste. But she's no Lila." Hector smiled. "That woman is funny, sexy, and she likes me. I can tell."

"I thought they all liked you."

"Well, they usually do," Hector said with very little modesty. "But there's something about Lila that's so real. I can't explain it."

Join the club. The first time Evan had seen Kenzie, he'd been shaken. Shattered. And time spent with her only reinforced the fact she was special. Tonight he'd get to see her with her friends and Daniel.

Oddly enough, he looked forward to spending time with the teenager. Daniel reminded him a little of himself, smart and itching to rebel. But while Daniel clearly tangled with authority, Evan had been more subtle.

And speaking of authority… He frowned, wondering why his mother was ducking his calls. He'd planned to take her to a doctor's appointment this morning, but she'd gone on her own, claiming she didn't need his help.

Was she upset over something he'd done? Hadn't done?

Evan didn't consider himself a mama's boy, but he loved his mom. Her illness felt so much like Rita's it scared him. Though he knew they'd caught his mother's symptoms way earlier than they'd caught Rita's. He'd left a message on her phone but planned to head over for Sunday breakfast to clear the air. Thinking that made him feel better. He didn't like conflict with family. Hell, he didn't like conflict at all.

Will and Rachel arrived, and he waved at them. After he made the introductions, Lila showed up with Kenzie and Daniel. The boy looked as if he'd rather be anywhere but there until he spotted Evan.

He left his sister and Lila behind as they grabbed rental shoes and trotted over. "Hey."

"Hi, Daniel. This is my friend Hector."

Daniel nodded. "Hello."

Hector held out a hand, and Daniel's eyes widened as he took it. Evan masked a grin. Hector had a grip like a human vise.

"Nice to meet you." Hector grinned. "So are you the mastermind behind 'Dancing Queen'?"

Daniel flushed. "Ah, yeah."

Hector slapped him on the back, and Daniel nearly toppled over. "Awesome."

Will told them all to get ready to lose, badly. Rachel made a face, then Daniel told her to dream on. Evan tried to plug into the conversation as everyone started trash-talking everyone else. But he couldn't stop looking over at Kenzie.

"Relax, Evan," Rachel murmured, taking no pity on him. "She's coming."

"Shush."

She laughed and patted him on the shoulder. "So how are we doing this?"

"Guys against girls seems only fair," Evan said.

"What about me?" Daniel frowned.

"Um, you're a guy, aren't you?" Evan made himself focus on Daniel even though Lila and Kenzie approached in colorful bowling shoes.

Kenzie held a large pair out to her brother. "Here. Be prepared for the slaughter." She held up a bowling bag.

Daniel shrugged. "Fine by me. It's guys against girls. But you're short one chick, unless you count Rachel twice because she talks so much."

Will laughed until Rachel elbowed him in the gut. "Oh, ah, be nice, Daniel."

"That's it. We're wiping the floor with you losers." Rachel glared.

While Evan and the guys got ready, Hector took food requests then hustled to the counter to place their orders.

"I get beer too? This is awesome." Daniel put his shoes on and grabbed a second bag from Lila. He withdrew a glittery blue ball. "Who goes first?"

Evan rubbed his hands together with glee. "Great. Another pro on our side—that's in addition to me. I can't speak for Hector. Navy guys typically suck at sports."

Hector returned in time to hear him and frowned. "Ass."

Evan ignored him. "We can go by age, I guess. You first."

"Sounds good. I'll put us in." Daniel sat and entered their names into the console. "Oh, and don't worry, man. I won't let you look weak in front of my sister."

"Thanks, Daniel. I was worried."

Daniel didn't seem to catch Evan's sarcasm, but Will and Lila grinned.

"We need to bet something." Lila frowned in thought. "It's not as much fun unless you can rub someone's face in their defeat."

Hector grinned. "Man, Lila, you're brutal. I love that in a woman."

Lila smacked him on the arm and pretended she'd hurt her hand.

Will and Rachel bandied insults, and Daniel tried to pretend to be above it all, though Evan saw him biting back laughter.

Then he noticed Kenzie studying him, and Evan wondered if she knew how much he liked her.

She didn't look nervous tonight. She looked focused, intense. "You're going down, buddy."

Immediately Evan's mind filled with thoughts of going down…on her. He couldn't help it. He laughed and leaned closer to whisper, "Sounds good to me."

"Why is that funny?" Daniel asked.

Kenzie held up three fingers. "Peel the banana." Which would leave him with her middle finger standing straight and tall.

"Just meeting your sister's pitiful challenge, Daniel. That's all." Evan flexed his arms, pleased when Kenzie's eyes widened. "Yeah, that's right, little woman. My manly team will crush your pretty, pathetic efforts."

"You need to work on your trash talk, bro." Hector shook his head. "So lame. He means we're gonna kick your asses. Losers buy the beer."

"And a soda for Daniel," Evan said before Kenzie could protest.

Daniel glared at him, but Kenzie clearly approved.

Then the game was on.

Halfway through their first match, Evan left to use the restroom and returned to see Kenzie and Daniel still dominating the board. Kenzie hadn't been kidding about being good. And her brother consistently bowled either strikes or spares. Wow.

"Daniel, quit taking it easy on your sister. We play to win," he reminded the kid.

"I'd probably do much better if I wasn't so hungry. When is the pizza coming?"

Considering the boy had already downed half the nachos and a hot dog, he shouldn't have been hungry.

Kenzie sighed. "You see now why we need more clients? This kid is eating me out of the house."

Lila laughed. "My brothers used to eat everything not

nailed down. So I'd hide my snacks in my room. Then we got mice." She shuddered. "But that was also an excuse to get a cat." She turned to Hector, a sly look on her face. "Do you like cats, Hector?"

Hector paused and glanced at Evan and Will, all of them apparently thinking the same thing.

"Do you?" Evan asked. "I do. I *love* cats."

Will nodded, smirking. "Oh yeah. Me too. Love 'em."

"I like dogs better," Daniel said, the innuendo going right over his head.

Kenzie's cheeks were pink, but he saw the laughter in her eyes.

Hector's embarrassment was awesome to behold. "I do like cats. And dogs. I like all animals, really."

"Way to be smooth, man," Evan murmured.

"Dick."

Evan poured himself another beer and sat back, enjoying himself immensely. When was the last time he'd had so much fun? Being with Kenzie and her friends felt good. Natural. He wasn't forcing anything. He liked her friends and enjoyed the competition. He hadn't been bowling since his Marine Corps days, but damn if he wouldn't do this again. With any luck, he'd get Kenzie to join him.

He stood up on his turn, ignored the mockery behind him, and almost missed a step when Kenzie, in a loud voice, said how nice he looked from behind. He stopped mid-stride, turned, and took in the ladies' jeers and Daniel's disgust. Which had him laughing.

Then he turned back, tuned everything out, and bowled a strike.

"Man. That was nice." Daniel nodded.

He slapped the guys' hands and winked at Kenzie. "For you, lovely lady."

"Oh, kiss off." She stomped to her lane and bowled a spare.

A voice called out, "Evan?"

He turned to the see his old boss staring at him in surprise from a few lanes away. "Hey, Vanessa." The cool blond wore jeans and a T-shirt that said "Go Vegan" and looked like a runway model. She had the mind of a computer and the tenacity of a bull shark. He liked her, especially now that he wasn't working for her. "Hey guys, be right back," he said to his friends.

Vanessa met him in the middle and held out a hand. A no-nonsense boss, she'd been the professional anchor he'd enjoyed when putting his advanced accounting skills to good use. But when the hours grew too demanding, he'd known it had been the right time to leave.

She shocked him by pulling him closer, her grip tight, the other hand on his shoulder, standing much closer than he'd ever been to her. After a split second, she let go of him and stepped back. "Sorry. I'm supposed to work on my personal development skills with coworkers. Thought I'd try it with you since we're more than passing acquaintances. I don't think it worked."

He stepped back with a laugh. Same old Vanessa, dissecting everything, even a simple greeting. He wasn't surprised to see her husband frowning at her. Evan waved. "Hey, Cam."

Cameron nodded, his arms full with their toddler. Behind him sat his rowdy brothers, part of Vanessa's loud, extended family. "Cam, you going to let him get away with that?" one of them yelled.

"Ignore the cretins," Vanessa said, both dismissive and cold. Her family laughed, apparently used to being dissed.

"So how's business?" he asked, itching to get back to Kenzie.

"I'm glad you asked." Vanessa started in on a few clients she wanted him to consult for, and he tried to figure out when he could fit them in and why the Danvers were having problems working with Harry, who'd been newly promoted at the firm, when Daniel tapped him on the shoulder.

"Dude, it's been like fifteen minutes. You're up." He looked at Vanessa, nearly straight in the eye she was so tall. "Who's the babe?"

Vanessa narrowed her gaze on him, but before she could say anything, her little girl tugged at her leg.

"Mama, up."

"She got big," Evan said, though he'd seen her daughter a few months ago. He had a special affection for the small girl, named Jane like his own mother.

Vanessa picked her up and smiled, and the look softened her. "Yes. My little genius is now running and getting into everything, aren't you, Jane?"

Her daughter looked just like her, a blossoming beauty. But though Evan had always considered Vanessa pretty, she did nothing for him. Not like Kenzie could without trying.

The toddler held out her arms to Daniel. "Pretty," she told her mother.

Daniel took a healthy step back.

Vanessa shook her head. "Just like her father, flirting already. I'll let you go. But call me this week."

"Sure, sure." Evan waved and walked back with Daniel. "*Not* a babe, that was my old boss. She's surprisingly human today. Who would have thought?"

Daniel gave him a sharp look then shrugged. "Whatever.

But if you don't get us another ten points, we might not be able to make a comeback."

"What? We're losing? When did this happen?" Evan gaped at the score as he rejoined the group.

"When you were flirting with the tall blond," Will explained.

"I wasn't flirting. Vanessa used to be my boss."

Kenzie didn't look too thrilled with him, but Evan had no idea why. He'd been far from flirting, and Vanessa's entire family had been right there along with her little girl.

Wait. Was Kenzie *jealous*?

"Your boss sure is pur-ty," Rachel said. "Isn't she, Lila?"

Lila nodded and around a mouthful of chips said, "Yep. Just stunning. Gorgeous, even. Right, Hector?"

Hector sat, his chin in his hand, staring at Lila, looking dopey. "Yeah, gorgeous."

Will laughed. Lila stroked Hector's arm. She'd been doing that a lot.

Kenzie shook her head. "Pathetic. Ladies, we need to be *killing* these guys, not just winning by a few points. Rachel, stop holding Will's hand. Lila, stop teasing Hector. Let's bowl, people." She paused and shot Evan a glare. "Just as soon as Evan throws his gutter ball."

Kenzie didn't like feeling so awkward about Evan's boss, but dang it, had Evan come to chat with the leggy blond or play with them?

It felt like he took forever schmoozing. Did he not see that the woman had a baby with her as well as a gorgeous husband and a ton of her own friends?

Did Evan's boss really need to be monopolizing his time?

While the others had relaxed and taken Evan's departure as a cue to chow down, Daniel had grown impatient. Like her, he threw his all into a game. And like her, he played to win.

"Gutter ball?" Evan's tone was smug, sickeningly so. "When it means I might lose to Kenzie and her team of female vipers?"

"Hey." Lila frowned.

Rachel shrugged. "I'm good with it."

"Watch and learn, ladies." Evan stepped up to the lane, wiggled his fine ass—and it was everything she could do not to stare since her brother watched *her* every time Evan's turn came—then bowled a strike. The jerk.

"Ha," Kenzie barked. "Lucky bowl."

"It's skill, plain and simple." The look he shot her mouth had her belly fluttering because she knew he meant he had *other* skills, like the kind he'd showed her with that kiss.

She'd done her best to try to forget about it, but it wasn't easy. She hadn't been kissed in more than a year, and she'd for sure never been kissed like that.

Bryce had been a kind lover, and they'd had good if not great times. Nothing so passionate that she'd lose herself in a man's touch. Or push her so far beyond her control she'd forget her brother being near.

She grabbed her ball, and Evan stepped closer. In a low voice, he said, "I tell you what. I'll make you a side bet. We'll go double or nothing, winner of the next game wins the whole thing."

"Fine." That took a little pressure off her, but not much,

because she stood way too close to the man. And he smelled just as good as he had the other day.

"Winner gets whatever he or she wants."

Her heart raced because he kept glancing at her mouth.

"What do you want?"

"Hey, what are you two whispering about?" Will asked.

Evan leaned closer. "If we win, I want you to bring me a chocolate mint sundae, to my place, and serve it up fancy. Whipped cream, fudge, a big old glass dish, long silver spoon, the works."

She grinned. She could do that. "Okay." She thought for a second. "If I win, I get you to play handyman at my house for a few hours." A few? Heck, she'd have to pick the most important broken items for him. "Are you 'handy' enough to do it?"

"Are you kidding? Who do you think has kept my mom's forty-year-old house in working order for the past six years?" He held out his hand.

She took it and shook, her gaze glued to his. Her heart pounded, and the warmth of his palm messed with her brain.

"Quit distracting her with your testosterone," Rachel complained. "And step away. You smell too good."

Will raised a brow.

"He's not as good-smelling as *you,* love muffin. And I didn't say anything at all about his amazing gray eyes."

"Amazing? I'd have gone with mesmerizing," Lila added. "If I wasn't into brown all of a sudden. Like honey-brown," she amended, leaning closer to Hector.

Daniel made gagging noises. "I think I'm going to be sick. Can we please stop with…whatever you guys are doing and just bowl?"

Evan sat back down and whispered something to Daniel that had him staring in shock. "Seriously?"

"Yep. But we have to win first."

"Oh man. We are so winning." Daniel grinned, his excitement palpable, and Kenzie had an odd pang. Her brother used to be that uninhibited, free to express his laughter and joy with an adult, back when Bryce had been around.

It was nice to see him acting like his old self again. She refused to attribute that emotional freedom to Evan and instead considered how long it had been since she'd had some fun with her friends doing anything besides working or complaining about work.

"Well? You're up, Kenzie." Evan sat back, his arms linked behind his head, and waited. "Don't choke."

She wanted to choke *him*.

They lost by twenty points through no fault of her own.

Lila hadn't helped, distracted by Hector, his huge biceps, and his silly jokes which, okay, she found funny as heck. But it was Daniel who'd really won the guys the game. Her brother was on fire, everything he bowled knocking down pins.

The guys rubbed it in by ordering another pitcher of beer and a super large Icee for Daniel. The girls took it in stride, playing off the loss as if they'd let the boys win.

Kenzie's stomach balled in knots, in both dread and excitement. She refused to look at Evan then couldn't help herself and peeked before looking away again.

Her phone pinged, and she checked her message. Evan's address appeared.

I'll see you tomorrow at two. Don't be late.
And don't forget my cherry on top.

He high-fived her brother and the guys, and he smirked at her.

Unable to help it, she flipped him the bird when her brother wasn't looking.

He laughed hard, and she wished his smile didn't make him so irresistible.

As they left the alley, she saw his boss having a good time with her family. The man Evan had addressed waved, and Evan waved back. Then he curled an arm around Kenzie's waist, guiding her past the crowd. A subtle cue of possession or manners? She didn't know, but she wished she could turn off her perpetual hum of desire around him.

Once at her car, he waited while Lila flirted with Hector. Daniel hovered by Evan's car a few spaces down, peering through the windows with excitement.

She frowned. "What did you say to my brother to make him play that way? Because he was *inspired.*"

"Nah. It's a male pride thing. That's all." After putting Daniel's ball bag next to hers, he closed her trunk for her. "You're pretty competitive."

"So are you."

He smiled. "You noticed. Seems like we have some things in common."

"I guess." She rubbed her arms, nervous and feeling foolish for being so.

"You cold?"

"No. I'm just…" …*a doofus because being near you gives me goose bumps.*

"Allergic to losing?"

He startled a laugh out of her. "Yeah, that's it."

A sudden breeze pushed her hair into her face, and Evan slid it behind her ear and sighed. "Man, I've been wanting to touch your hair forever. It's really soft."

"Good shampoo." Stupid response, but aside from plastering herself to him, it was all she had.

He stepped away and rocked back on his heels. "Guess I should go before Lila and Rachel make me."

Kenzie looked around to see her friends staring at him.

He made a sign of the cross at them, and they laughed. "Vipers, vampires, lions. Why is it I envision deadly predators when I think of your friends?"

"Well, I kind of think of them the same way, so you're not far off."

Will walked up to Evan and patted him on the back. "You're a pretty decent bowler. How do you feel about soccer? 'Cause we have a coed league, the Legal Eagles, and could use another guy. Man, thanks to you and Daniel I managed to get out of doing chores for a week! And Rachel has to wear a sexy costume to dust our room. I'm going with barely there French maid."

Kenzie cringed. "Thanks for putting that image in my head, Will."

Will leaned in to kiss her on the cheek. "No problem. Let me know about the soccer league, Evan. Just tell Kenzie and she'll get word to me." He walked away with Rachel, holding hands.

"Sure I will," Kenzie muttered. "And thanks for asking me if I mind being your go-between."

Evan, in a low voice, said, "Guess I'd better leave before I try to kiss you again. You make it tough to be good, Kenzie."

"Evan."

"Don't forget my extra fudge sauce, whipped cream, and cherry." He winked and left. He bumped fists with Daniel before getting into his car and driving away.

On the ride home, she listened to Lila wax on and on about Hector and the date they had lined up later in the week. Daniel talked about Evan's car as if he owned it. Lexus this, torque that.

"May I remind you, you're only thirteen. You can't drive for another three years."

"Two until I can get a permit," Daniel answered quickly.

She shuddered. "I can't even…"

Lila grinned. "Don't worry, Kenzie. I'll show him what to do. And maybe Mr. Richards can help."

"One of your brothers?" Kenzie could have sworn all of Lila's family lived in California.

"That would be Hector Richards."

Daniel frowned. "I thought his name was Hector Jackson."

"It is now." Lila gave them a wide smile.

"Doesn't the woman usually take the guy's last name?" Daniel asked.

"Not this time. Hector Richards, my future husband, will give us whatever we need."

Kenzie chuckled. "Moving a little fast, aren't you? You only met him yesterday."

"I should warn the poor guy." Daniel gave a mock shudder at Kenzie in the rearview. "For he has no idea the horror that awaits."

"Do it and die," Lila warned. "Kenzie, what did I tell you about letting him watch horror movies without me? 'Horror that awaits'? I know that line."

While Lila and Daniel compared likes and dislikes about their recent horror faves, Kenzie took note of the time.

The countdown had started. Less than twenty-four hours until she met Evan, alone, at his home.

What would she do? Would she kiss him? Let him kiss her? Would they just talk or turn into holding-hands buddies? Or would they do…more? God, she wanted to, but was she ready to make that leap?

Even more troubling—what would she wear?

CHAPTER 10

Breakfast at his mother's did not go according to plan.

Evan had woken up late, cranky and distracted by his dreams involving Kenzie and the whipped topping from a chocolate-mint sundae. He'd beaten off in the shower and felt pathetic that he couldn't help himself. He liked a hell of a lot more than Kenzie's body. Evan had always been attracted to style over substance. His problem was that Kenzie had glorious helpings of both.

Thoughts of Kenzie's warm smile always brought to mind those ripe lips…which would look perfect wrapped around any number of Evan's body parts. So not good to be thinking about in mixed company.

Especially *this* mixed company.

"Evan, Son, I thought you were going to bring sweets?"

"I'm sorry. I forgot since I was running late."

"But it's tradition." Jane Griffith scowled. "I was really looking forward to an apple fritter today." She wore jeans and a USMC sweatshirt, the one he'd gotten her two Christmases ago. To his surprise, she looked young and vibrant. Perhaps anger agreed with her?

He would have said so but didn't want her jumping down his throat for it. He sighed and hit her with a skewed confrontation, hoping to shock a confession out of her by attacking her mood sideways. "Mom, are we ever going to talk about why you've been avoiding me?" Wasn't it the kid who needed less "mom time"? How had his mother turned from hovering to barely there? "What are you doing about all these appointments and errands I normally take you to? You don't drive."

She hadn't gotten behind the wheel since getting in a motor vehicle accident more than ten years ago. It hadn't been a problem when his dad had ferried her around. But since Dad's death six years ago, Evan had stepped in to take up the slack. She hadn't really needed him until a few months ago, when she'd gotten sick.

"There is such a thing as Uber, honey. Or a taxi. I think Lyft is a thing too." She frowned, checking her watch. "You know, it's not too late. Sofa's might not be out of apple fritters yet."

He had no intention of waiting in a huge-ass line at the popular bakery on a Sunday morning. The crowd would be ridiculous, especially since he'd be right smack in the middle of the Sunday-morning rush. "Mom, it won't kill you to go without. Now how about we talk about something important."

"Like my apple fritter?"

He bit back a curse. "This isn't about me being late or you not getting sweets you don't need." Her addiction to sugar was always a battle, one he liked to bring up to deflect from himself when he got in trouble.

"I know what I need." The militant gleam in her eyes didn't bode well.

"You're being weird. Talk to me."

"I'd been hoping to avoid this." She sighed. "I don't want to hurt your feelings, Evan. But you're… Well, there's no way to put it nicely. You've become clingy."

He blinked. "What?"

"Ever since we found out I might have cancer, you've been all over me all the time."

"That's not true. The cancer scare is real, and it sucks, but it's not why I'm always over here." He'd been spending more time with her since Rita had passed a few years ago, but not that much. Clingy? Really? "Mom, I hate to remind you, but you're seventy-one. There are things you can't do."

She huffed and poured them both cups of coffee. Pushing his toward him, she said, "That's a load of horseshit."

"*Mom?*" His mother *never* swore.

"I'm seventy-one, not dead. My knees are good, my hips work just fine, and my heart is in tip-top shape. I'm biking every day, and I swim. Yes, I get tired faster, but that's true of anyone who's not in great shape. And I know I'm older. I can count, Evan. Seventy-one is older than seventy, which is older than sixty-nine and sixty-eight, etcetera, etcetera. But my age is not why you've been so intolerable lately."

He gaped. "Me? Intolerable? What?"

"I'm a grown woman entering the second great love affair of my life. I don't need or want your permission."

He just stared, unsure of where her animosity was coming from. "Mom, this isn't about Jerome." *Whom he hadn't met yet.* "I don't disapprove, I just—"

"Just what? Think I need a nursemaid? I'm older but not in my dotage, and you are most certainly *not* my father. I don't need your approval, Evan. I'll date who I want when I want. And you can't tell me what to do."

"Um, okay." Was she getting senile? He hadn't said a bad word against Jerome. "Do I ever get to meet this paragon?" Whoops, and he'd been doing so well…

"Not with that attitude."

"You're not making sense. This isn't about Jerome."

"You're right." She wore the same mutinous expression he'd often seen in the mirror.

He blew out a breath. "Are you at least going to your doctors' appointments?" Even if she'd blown off the checkup yesterday morning, she should have had an important one last week involving some blood work. He only knew because he'd snooped on his way out of the bathroom earlier and checked her day planner.

"Evan, dear, I don't want to fight."

"Then don't."

She smiled. "I'm also not willing to let you run over me like a steamroller if I don't answer your questions fast enough. This isn't the Marine Corps, you know."

He snorted. "Trust me, I know."

"I'd like to share breakfast with you." She sighed. "Sadly, I can't because my favorite foods are absent. Not even an apple fritter, honey roll, or breakfast cookie to make an old woman feel young again."

"Now you're just playing for sympathy."

She made a sad face, her mouth turned down, her blue eyes cloudy with regret. She just stared at him.

A minute later, he threw up his hands. "Christ. Fine. I'll go get them. Don't expect me back for a few hours." He stomped out of the house and drove to the crowded bakery, groaning at how long it took to find a place to park. Then he waited in line, mindful of how masterfully she'd played him. And how they still hadn't talked about her doctors' appointments or her new beau.

He shifted on his feet, made small talk with the people standing around him, politely informed two of the women his girlfriend was waiting on him—*Kenzie, I wish*—to avoid any awkwardness, and picked up his mom's pastries and a half-dozen cookies, unable to stop from hoping he might win a kiss later from a woman he wanted like no other.

By the time he returned to his mother, she'd forgotten her odd pique and accepted him—and the sweets—with a hug. They ate, talked, and laughed as if nothing had happened.

But before he left, she arranged for him to meet Jerome next week.

A date and time he committed to memory.

———————————

At two o'clock, Evan stood in the middle of his living room, surveying the posh condo with pride. He wanted to impress Kenzie, so he'd pulled out all the stops. His high-end apartment, normally clean but a little dusty, gleamed. Chrome, white walls, leather, and dark woods decorated his manly bachelor pad.

Yet as he looked around at it, he found himself preferring Kenzie's colorful mishmash of home.

He wiped his palms on his pants, annoyed with himself for being so nervous. He'd gone over and over today in his mind, coming to the decision that he'd let Kenzie lead the way their relationship progressed. They both knew their chemistry was something special, off-the-charts hot.

As much as he wanted to make love to her, she was skittish. She would feel better if she set the pace. Or so he kept telling himself so he wouldn't ruin the day.

Having her all to himself was a treat. He knew she came with a ton of responsibilities; he also thought she deserved some pampering. When was the last time Kenzie had someone take care of her problems for her?

He spotted the hidden bouquet of flowers he intended to give her in addition to a small box of fine chocolates, confident she'd like them. And he had a brand-new box of condoms in his bedside table, top drawer. *That I'm not going to use today, not even if she begs. Well, maybe then…*

Despite his desire to keep things light between them, he'd dressed to impress in a long-sleeved button-down shirt he'd left untucked along with jeans. Seattle's weather veered from hot to cold with the passing of clouds. A cool front, and the fact he looked good in blue, had settled him on his choice of wardrobe.

He'd rolled each sleeve precisely, ending at mid-forearm. He hadn't bothered with socks or shoes, and he'd done his best not to be too heavy-handed with the cologne he knew she liked.

Damn, he was half hard thinking about her, so he calmed himself by straightening the house for the fifth time that hour. He adjusted the volume of classic rock in the living room, giving the house some much-needed noise.

Everything had to be just right for Kenzie. Would she like their date? The house? Him?

The doorbell rang, and he started then cursed himself for acting like an idiot and went to let her in.

"Hi." She stood in the doorway looking sweet, nervous, and sexy as hell in a pair of jeans and a blue short-sleeved sweater.

Great. They were twins.

He stepped back, hoping he appeared calmer than he was. "I can't wait for my dessert."

"Don't be a sore winner." She hefted two bags that he quickly took from her.

"Hey, I'm willing to share."

"You're darned right you will. I brought enough for two people."

"Then what are you having?"

She laughed and followed him inside. Kenzie whistled. "Man, and I thought the location was nice. This place is amazing."

A modern-style townhome in Phinney Ridge, his house was close enough to his old workplace and to Vets on the Go! that he had no intention of moving. Evan liked the neighborhood too. His rent wasn't cheap, but he didn't worry about leaving his car in the secured garage out back.

"Oh, I love your kitchen." She slid her hand along the marble countertop.

He placed the bags on the counter and watched her take things out. Tubs of mint-chocolate-chip, vanilla, and chocolate ice cream, hot fudge, marshmallow topping, and, of course, maraschino cherries.

She glanced over the kitchen counter to the dining area, set with two crystal candle holders and two large porcelain bowls for ice cream. "Fancy."

He flushed. "They're my good stuff. Leftovers from a past…ah, from a long time ago." Rita had been picky about what she ate off of, though he'd never cared. "I'm sure I have some paper bowls somewhere if you'd rather use them."

"No, no. I'll try to adjust to bowls that aren't chipped."

"Ha ha."

She gifted him with a grin. "The sad thing is you think I'm joking."

He leaned against the counter and watched her work, wishing the kitchen were smaller so he'd have an excuse to brush against her as she moved. In the background, Joe Cocker's gritty voice crooned.

"You look a little nervous," he said to needle her, hoping he wasn't the only one feeling as if ready to leap out of his skin. This was the first time, since that devastating kiss, that they'd been alone together.

She blushed. "Maybe if you weren't looking at me like that, I'd be better."

Hell. Busted. "How am I looking at you?"

―――――――――

Like you want to eat me? "Never mind."

He chuckled and crossed his arms, and the sight of his broad chest under that shirt made Kenzie want to undo each and every button. "I'm surprised Daniel let you come without him."

"Well, I had to lie and say I had shopping to do. Or I'd never hear the end of it from him or the girls."

"The girls too, huh?"

"My social life is an endless source of entertainment for Lila, Rachel, and Daniel." She frowned as she opened the ice cream. "Bring me those bowls, would you? And you do have an ice cream scoop, I hope. I forgot mine."

"Third drawer to the right of the sink."

He returned with the bowls, and she did her best to handle them with care. Geez, his entire home looked like something out of a magazine. For darned sure no kid had ever dirtied his or her hands in the place. It was too neat, too sterile. Well, not sterile, but not colorful. The wood should have warmed the place up, yet the cool gray and white tones all over the place, in addition to the chrome, made her feel as if she'd stepped into a futuristic party pad that had made the mistake of landing on a few trees.

"I'm a little worried about getting anything dirty. Please don't tell me your hand towels are white too." She was joking, yet the white towel he handed her didn't help.

He sighed. "I rarely do dishes."

"God, Evan. Do you ever make a mess?" Even the kitchen sponge, in its ceramic drain stand, looked fresh.

"If I admit I cleaned up, *a lot*, for you today, would that relieve you?"

"Not really, no."

"I don't like to clean. So when I make a small mess, I wipe it up right after. Besides, it's just me." He stared at her with accusation. "And don't try acting like you're any better. I saw your kitchen. It was spotless. I live with dust. You didn't have dust, clutter, or one microbe out of place."

"Okay. I don't like a mess. And living with a teenage boy, I'm always cleaning."

He grinned. "I like your brother. Once I could see past the phone prank, I realized he'd be pretty handy to have around when dealing with my friends. Plus he's a funny guy."

She smiled. "I love him. But then, I have to."

He watched her, his scrutiny intense. Evan seemed to observe quietly before commenting. His words always studied, never rash. What did he see when he looked at her right now? She hated not knowing.

"Would you please go in the other room? You're freaking me out."

"Hey, I just want to make sure you don't skimp on the fixings."

She pointed. "Go."

"I'll just watch you from a table five feet away."

"At least you won't be hovering."

He sat away from her, a frown darkening his handsome face.

"I was kidding."

"I know." He sighed. "Will it ruin the mood if I bounce a question or two off you about my mother?"

Please ruin the mood. Because I'm stuck between wanting to jump your bones or run screaming from the house, afraid for my born-again-virgin self.

"Hit me." She worked at the ice cream then decided to let it soften as she listened to Evan, who looked upset. He made her want to throw caution to the wind and offer comfort, hugs. *Then jump his bones.* "I can be a good friend," she said as much to herself as to him.

His ghost of a smile made her feel as if she'd accomplished something wonderful. "My mother is getting...I don't want to say old, but she's been acting strangely."

"Oh, that's sad."

"No, it's weird." He glared at the smooth wooden table, nary a blemish in sight.

Her dining table at home had been passed down from her grandparents to her parents and had scars and dings all over the place, many of them a result of Daniel's youthful obsession with racing toy cars over everything.

"I'm listening."

"My whole family used to be close. I'm an only child, and my parents had me in their forties. My mom always wanted kids, but I'm the only one they had. Since I was kind of a miracle baby to them, they poured a lot of love on me. They were pretty protective, and they always knew where I was and what I was doing. After college, I was in the Marine Corps when my dad passed away, and two years later I resigned my commission and came home. Mom and I have stayed close. She's always been there for me, and I love her. We can talk about anything. Or at least, we used to be able to."

He grew quiet, and she waited.

"But now she's got this new guy, Jerome, she's been keeping from me. My cousin saw her kissing him in public."

He sounded outraged, so she smothered a smile. Good for his mom for finding romance at her age.

"And you know, I've been the one taking her to doctors' appointments and grocery shopping and anything else she needs."

"Is she that bad off?"

"What? Oh, no. She was in a car accident years ago and hasn't driven since, not in ten years. My dad used to take her everywhere; now she walks, takes the bus or taxi, or goes shopping with friends. But normally I'm the guy she leans on. Except I'm not anymore." He looked baffled.

"It's got to be hard with her moving on. I take it she hasn't dated anyone since your dad passed?"

He shook his head. "I've thought about it. I'm not jealous or feeling replaced by Jerome. I can't say I don't worry about this man I've never met, but I don't begrudge my mom happiness."

Evan was so sweet.

"I just don't understand why she's pulling away so hard. I mean, can't we at least talk about it? She keeps not going to treatment."

"What's wrong with her, if you don't mind me asking?"

"She might have cancer." He swallowed. "It's not definite, and we're waiting on her results to come back. But she has a lot of the same symptoms my fiancée had."

She did her best not to visibly react. "Your fiancée had cancer?"

He nodded. "Rita passed away two years ago. I loved her, and she got sick. She ignored her symptoms for way too long, and then it was too late." He didn't look teary-eyed or overly emotional, but his eyes were sad when he said, "Rita was amazing. You would have liked her." He laughed. "She would have fit right in with you, Lila, and Rachel.

"I don't think my mom realizes how bad the disease can be. She saw me with Rita, and she helped a lot, but I tried to shield her from the worst of it. Rita didn't want anyone to see her when it got bad. She didn't even want me there, but hey, I wasn't going anywhere."

He paused, meeting her gaze. "I didn't mean to tell you all that."

"I'm a good listener." She winked, and he smiled back at her. "But it does help to get a fuller picture. Your mom and you were always close. You're an only child. You talk and share things. Then she gets sick, starts pulling away, finds someone else, and suddenly she won't talk to you."

"Exactly." He huffed. "She called me *clingy*. I mean, what the hell? I'm only doing what I've always been doing—being a good son. How is that clingy?"

"Interesting. So she's pulling away. But why? What's she hiding?" Kenzie tried scooping the ice cream and found it had softened enough, finally. "Is she feeling bad about dragging you into her medical problems, knowing what you went through already with your fiancée? Is she scared and not wanting to show you how scared she really is? Or maybe she's pulling away because you really are clingy and you just haven't realized it." She glanced up and noted his expression. "Hey, don't get mad at me. You asked me to bounce ideas."

"So I did."

Evan stood when she came around the counter with two fully loaded bowls of ice cream, fudge, whipped cream, and cherries on top.

"Oh my God. I'm in heaven."

She smiled. "Chocolate is my favorite thing in the world."

"Milk or dark?"

"Milk, of course. I'm not sophisticated enough for dark."

"And mint? Better than peanut butter or better than caramel?"

"Oh, that's a tough one." She handed him a spoon then dug into her bowl. "I think mint is right between a lower-ranking caramel and the top tier, peanut butter." She licked her spoon, saw him staring at her, and ducked her head down.

"Sorry. I just really, really wish I was a spoon right now."

"Evan."

He laughed. "Yeah, I'll eat and shut up."

After some time enjoying her sundae, she said, "We didn't exactly come to any resolution on your mom."

"No, but you did make me think of her behavior differently. What if she's trying to protect me because she knows it's cancer? Rita's death wasn't easy."

"I'm so sorry."

"Hey, it happens. But you know about loss, don't you? You lost your parents young."

"They were in a freak car accident and died when I was eighteen." She sighed. "It was rough. I was close to graduating high school, and bam. I'm left with a baby brother, a house, and some money—but not much—to pay the bills. Heck, I barely knew how to use my own checking account. It wasn't easy, but I made it through.

"Now I'm just trying to keep Daniel out of jail and get him to finish high school. That in itself is a full-time job."

"I'll bet." He grinned and ate more ice cream. "So can I ask you something?"

"Sure."

"How come you don't date? From some of the things you've said, you don't seem to go out much. I get the sense it's about more than just having to keep up with your brother."

She toyed with her ice cream, trying to figure out how much to tell him. Then she figured she might as well tell him the truth. "I was very much in love more than a year ago. And then one day, he just left. I had no idea he was leaving. He'd just had enough of being part of a family and needed to go."

Evan ate, watching her. "How long had you been together?"

"Two and a half years. I... It's hard for me to talk about Bryce. I never saw it coming."

"That's rough." He shook his head. "But he's obviously a moron for leaving you."

"Thanks. That's what Lila and Rachel say."

"Oh, come on. I'm sure they used more creative words than *moron*."

She laughed. "You're right. They did."

"Eat your ice cream," he ordered. "If I'm gaining five pounds of sugar, you're gaining it with me."

"Hey, you asked for this."

"I earned it, you mean."

"Whatever. Daniel won you guys the game."

He looked as if he meant to respond then surprised her with "I bet that guy leaving hurt Daniel too, didn't it?"

"Um, yeah." Thankfully, she didn't feel the need to tear up talking about Bryce. To her surprise, she wanted to punch him for being so thoughtless. "I've never dated all that much, not with having to raise Daniel. I never had the time or energy. But Bryce swept me off my feet. Then he was a part of my family, a kind of older brother slash father figure to Daniel, and my partner in every sense. So when he left, it hurt me, but it ripped Daniel apart too. It was awful."

"Did Daniel screw with Bryce's phone?"

Startled out of a downward spiral, she blinked. "You know, I never asked."

"Don't. You probably don't want to know. I mean, if I got ABBA, your ex probably got hit with Justin Bieber or Insane Clown Posse."

The thought made her laugh.

"And I can only imagine his screen name. Something like Idiot Who Has No Idea What He Lost. Jackass. Blind and Stupid. Something like that, but I'd put money on it that Daniel got creative."

His compliments warmed her. "You're good for my ego."

"Yeah? Well, you're bad for my belly." He patted his flat stomach.

Heck, she could bounce a quarter off those abs. "I'm full."

"I'm not, but I can pause to let you get your second wind." He stood, and she looked up at a man who had shown her compassion, made her laugh, and made her feel beautiful when he looked at her. "How about a tour? I promise, this is not an excuse to show you my etchings."

"Too bad." Oh hell. Had she said that *out loud?*

CHAPTER 11

EVAN LOVED THAT HER FACE TURNED BEET RED. ELATED that she felt what he did yet nervous because one of them should slow them down, he gave her an out.

"What did you say?"

"I said let's get started. On the tour, I mean. Not the etchings part." She blew out a breath, and he stifled a laugh. "God, I'm *so* not good at dating. And you can say what you want, but this bet was a date in disguise."

While he decided how to answer her, she added in a hesitant voice, "Wasn't it?"

He wanted to kiss her, right then and there. Instead, he kept a healthy distance from her as he waved her away from the table into the attached living room. "So what you're saying is my attempt to be slick about getting you all alone in my clutches was lame because you saw right through it."

She gave him a small smile. "Yeah, that's exactly what I'm saying."

"Well, damn. Don't tell Hector or word will spread that I suck at seduction."

She chuckled and relaxed, as he'd meant her to, and he showed her around his townhome.

"And before you ask, I cleaned a lot. Okay? I'm not that anal-retentive about how I live." He totally was but didn't want her to see his love of cleanliness as obsessive or anything.

"Good, because normal people don't live like this."

He smiled to show he understood her teasing and mentally reminded himself to mess up the space a little next time. "Well, it helps that I'm rarely home. Now I'm finding more time to enjoy life. You have no idea how stressful my CPA job was."

"I bet. Especially around April 15th."

He shuddered. She laughed and followed him around, taking in the office and half bathroom before moving upstairs.

She glanced around with wide eyes. "This place is huge. Three bedrooms *and* two bathrooms upstairs? Wow."

"I figured it would be nice if I ever had company. But I just don't. You're the exception." He sighed. "Now I sound lame again."

"No." She put a hand on his arm, and he treasured the comfort. "There's nothing wrong with being alone, you know. Just because you're a guy doesn't mean you have to have a steady stream of women coming in and out or you lose your man card."

"Are you sure? Because my oldest cousin calls me the anti-Casanova."

She chuckled. "Better than the anti-Christ."

"That's what my other cousin calls me. I'm not kidding. I control our budget for Vets on the Go!, and that doesn't make me Mr. Popular."

She laughed harder. "They sound funny."

"They're a laugh riot." He pushed open the door to his bedroom, watching her look around. He made sure he stayed well away from her, keeping his attention firmly off the nightstand, where those pesky, available condoms lay in the top drawer. "I love them though. I always wanted a big family, especially brothers. But it was just me."

"Yeah, me too. No cousins, aunts, uncles, or grandparents. My parents came from rough childhoods and cut off contact with family, not that they had that much to begin with. And now it's just Daniel and me left." She paused, and her joyful smile took his breath away. "And Lila and Rachel. And I guess Will. Family is what you make of it, isn't it?"

"It is." If he spent one more second seeing her smile he'd kiss her. So he hurried out of the bedroom, heading downstairs. "You ready for ice cream again?"

"I, ah, sure."

Kenzie didn't know why Evan seemed so determined to get out of the bedroom, but she thought it the smart move to make. Everything she learned about him made her like him more. Unless... Was he putting on a show for her? Trying to act all sensitive and nice when in reality he just wanted sex?

But then, why waste a moment in the bedroom? His eyes had seemed to darken, his attraction obvious. And he liked her, or at least he seemed to. So why rush her away from his bedroom? She studied him, wondering at his strategy.

They sat again at his dining table, where his sundae had melted, but it didn't slow him down.

She picked at her treat, a little full of chocolate mint. That and her nerves made it difficult to eat when she really wanted to kiss Evan again. Every time she remembered that kiss, she felt tingly. Then she'd tell herself she'd exaggerated how great it had been.

So great she'd wanted to have sex with him in her kitchen, where anyone could have seen them. God, when had she ever felt that kind of passion? The forget-the-world-exists kind?

"You're looking at me strangely," he said into the silence. "Should I be scared?"

She shook her head. "I don't know. Are you lying to me about anything?"

He stilled, lowered his spoon, and looked her dead in the eye. "No. I'm not big on lies. The truth always comes out, and then it's a big old shit sandwich—excuse the expression. Why would you think I'm lying?"

She waved a hand around. "Let's get real. You're super cute. You have a great house, a great job, and you apparently don't live with your mother."

He sat back, looking pleased. "Only super cute? How about I look like an Adonis?"

Kenzie rolled her eyes. "Okay, so there is a little bit of ego there."

He snorted.

"But nothing any number of women wouldn't jump all over. So why me?"

"Huh?"

Angry that she had to explain herself, she stood and crossed to him, looking down into his wide gray eyes. "Look, I'm attracted. I'm also still dealing with the fact that a man I loved left me behind. I have a teenage delinquent brother I'm raising. A money pit of a house falling apart piece by piece that I'm solely responsible for as well as trying to run a business to pay for a ton of different expenses.

"I'm not rich. I'm not stacked to here." She held out her hand far from her chest. "I can't drop everything to fawn over you whenever you want. And I'm not easy. There's no way

sex with me wouldn't be complicated and probably messy."
She was breathing hard, her adrenaline raised, prepared for
a confrontation.

She wasn't prepared when he scooted back and yanked
her down onto his lap. She squirmed until he had her straddling his thighs then stared at him in shock. Man, Evan could
move.

"First of all, don't panic. I just wanted us to be at eye
level for this conversation. You can leave at any time." He
held up his hands to show her he meant business. "Second,
you're fucking insane if you think you're not worth more
than uncomplicated sex. When I look at you, I have a hard
time catching my breath. I think you're perfect, in a slightly
neurotic kind of way."

She frowned. "What does that mean?"

"I want to be with you, in any way you'll have me. I have
my own share of baggage, from dealing with a dead fiancée
to a mother who calls me 'clingy.'" His self-deprecating laugh
set the butterflies in her belly to fluttering. "I think you're
beautiful, even with a hint of whipped cream on your lip."

Before she could wipe it off, he grabbed her hand to
stop her. Then he slowly neared and kissed the corner of her
mouth. Her breath came hard and fast, and her body locked
up tight.

"There, all gone." His voice deepened. "I want nothing
more than to see you smile, and I'd have cheated if we hadn't
won at bowling. Anything to get you to spend time with me.
But today has been really hard."

"Oh?" She stared at his face, mesmerized by the need
in his eyes.

"Because every time I'm near you, I want you. And I

don't want you to think I'm just after sex. I'm not, but…" He took her hand and put it over his heart. "You feel this? My heart is pounding like crazy. I'm tense all over." He blew out a soft breath, and a hint of mint and chocolate washed over her. "I mean, *all over.*"

She couldn't help looking down, between them, to see the bulge in his jeans. *Oh, wow.*

"I understand taking time to build a relationship. And I like to think I'm a gentleman." He swallowed. "But I'm also a guy, and knowing how you taste, what you feel like in my arms, has stayed with me."

Being desired was its own kind of aphrodisiac. Evan's honest attraction compounded the effect of truth in his words.

"I'm not playing you, Kenzie. I want you, but I want all of you."

"There's a lot of me to take." She meant her brother, her emotional turmoil, her responsibilities.

Evan's wicked grin made her blush. "Not more than I can handle." He stared at her chest and down her belly. "Baby, I could deal with every luscious inch of you right now." He closed his eyes and opened them again. "But I won't. I want to see you again. As in, date you. I feel something special with you, and I want to see where it goes. But that can only happen if you feel it too."

Was he blind? She was panting, her nipples hard, her entire body quivering as she straddled him. She'd swear she could see a cloud of lust over them both. How the hell was he holding off?

Kenzie had always been more tentative in what few relationships she'd had, moving so slowly glaciers had no trouble keeping up—something Bryce had once teased.

But with Evan, she suddenly wanted to throw caution to the wind. "Will you kiss me?"

His eyes glazed over. "Kiss you?" he asked, his voice hoarse.

"Yes." She scooted closer, settling herself right over his rock-hard erection. It was all she could do to hold in a moan at the feel of him against her. "Kiss me."

"Damn it. I was trying so hard to be good," he muttered then yanked her close and planted a doozy on her.

His lips devoured. This was no soft, gentle embrace but the desperation of a man in lust. And like called to like, because she couldn't think of anything better than being surrounded by Evan Griffith.

She put her hands on his shoulders then snaked a hand down his chest, teasing at the waistline of his jeans. The touch of her hand against his warm abdomen did the trick because Evan groaned and changed the angle of his lips, sliding his tongue through her mouth and flooding her with need.

Everywhere. She squirmed over his cock, riding him as he slid his hands under her shirt to cup her breasts.

She gasped, loving the feel of his fingers stroking through her bra, finding the ridges of her nipples and gliding back and forth.

"Fuck," he swore against her mouth. He pulled back, watching her ride him, frustrated by the clothing between them. "You're so beautiful."

"Evan." She toyed with his hair, teasing the strands licking his nape.

He pulled her close to kiss her again, and then one of his hands moved, so slowly, but in the right direction.

Their kisses grew rougher, the desire richer. He

unsnapped her jeans and parted them then pushed his hand under her panties. She raised her hips to allow him better access. Then his finger slid inside her, the intrusion shocking her into a ferocious need.

"You're so wet," he breathed, kissing his way down her neck. "You feel fucking *amazing*."

The thickness of his voice echoed the thickness of his cock, too hindered by clothing.

"I want you to come." He found her mouth and slipped his tongue between her lips, mimicking the actions of his finger. When he added thumb strokes against her clit, she knew the end was closer than she might have expected.

Moaning, trying to get closer, she grabbed his shoulders and pulled. He put another finger inside her, thrusting faster.

And it hit. An explosion that rocked her body, world, brain, everything.

She cried out and kept coming, so hard, while he kissed his way to her ear, leaving love bites against her neck.

"So sexy. You're drenching my fingers, Kenzie. Yeah, baby. That's it." His soft words made it worse and better, because he shifted his thumb and another spear of pleasure shook her.

He slowly removed his hand from between her legs and kissed her again.

Thankful, sated, and in shock, she kissed him back, wanting to eat him up.

He pulled back to stare at her.

Not sure what to expect, Kenzie eased at the warmth of his smile, which erased any possible awkwardness.

"Have I mentioned how pretty you are?"

She had to clear her throat to answer. "I believe you said 'beautiful' earlier."

His smile deepened. "Well, you're even prettier when you come."

She couldn't help it. She buried her head against his chest so he wouldn't see her blushing. "I can't believe I did that."

"I can. You're so hot. I knew you would be."

He shifted, and she felt him still hard beneath her.

"But you didn't…"

"But you did. That's what counts." He nudged her, and she stood on trembling legs until he rose and steadied her.

"Oh, Evan. That was so… I mean, I haven't, not with someone else, in…" Realizing what she'd admitted to, she blushed harder.

"Your face is what they call fire-engine red, I'd say."

"Shut up."

He chuckled. "And still beautiful. How about that?"

"You didn't feel what I did." She motioned to his prominent erection. "Do you want me to—"

He took her hand and kissed it. "Today was for you. And to make you feel so guilty for leaving me in this state that you go out with me again."

She had to laugh at the sly look he shot her from beneath his lashes. "Well, what's in it for me?"

"Hmm. How about a bribe? I'll help you fix your broken-down hovel of a house."

She frowned. "Hovel?"

"Hey, I like your place. You're the one saying it's got so many problems." When she didn't respond, not sure what to say, he added, "I want to date you. There. I said it. Is that so bad?"

"Evan, I like you. And I love what we just did, but—"

He put a finger over her lips, one that hadn't been inside her. She wanted to be more in awe of what they'd just done, and she would be when she thought about it later, but right now she was still in that state of pleasure overload.

"Kenzie, I just want a chance to get to know you. No agenda, no promises you think I'll break later. And I know this isn't easy for you. We can date, just you and me, without everyone knowing. That way there's no pressure on you to affect your family. What do you say? When's the last time you did something you wanted to do for you? And yes, I am something you want. Admit it."

"Well, I don't know…" She placed her hands on his chest, thrilled when he tensed and swallowed audibly. She'd never had so much power before. Evan had pretty much laid it out on the line. He wanted her, and he wanted to date her. But he wasn't pressuring her for anything more than a chance to…what? Give her more orgasms?

Was she stupid? Of course not.

"Okay. You and I can go out, date, I guess. But privately. Our business is no one else's. I'm not trying to hide you, but—"

"Kenzie, I get it." He pushed her hair behind her ear, looking so happy.

His joy, because she'd agreed to just date him, broke something inside her. That huge wall holding any possibility of a relationship at bay started to crumble. And yeah, he'd softened her with sex. But it had been *soooo* good. And he hadn't asked for anything in return.

"I think you should go." He gestured her toward the door. "Before you change your mind or I mess this up."

She laughed. "You just want me to leave remembering how good it was."

"Yep."

She stared at his bulge between his legs. "But Evan, how do I know you're not hiding something?" Feeling playful with a man and not nervous or worried about failing future relationships was new. And thrilling.

"Kind of hard to hide how I'm feeling right now." He glanced down at himself.

"But what if you're too small?"

He blinked. "Are you seriously asking about the size of my dick?"

"I should see it to be sure, shouldn't I?" She had no idea where this brazen, sexy woman was coming from, but she loved it.

His eyes widened, comically so. "Kenzie, today was for you. Trust me when I say I'm hung like a horse. You keep teasing me and you'll see a lot more than you want to."

"Oh?" She put a hand over his crotch, and he swore. She tingled with the need to give him as much bliss as he'd given her.

He covered her hand. "Yeah. I'll come like a geyser. Not pretty."

"I don't know. I think that might be pretty amazing." She stared into his eyes while she unbuttoned his jeans, amazed at her own sexual aggression. It felt so good to take what *she* wanted for once.

He swallowed. "You sure? Because I am so fucking hard right now."

"Shy? No problem." She smiled and slid her hand under his underwear to grip him.

He swore and rocked into her fist, throwing his head back. "Oh shit. Kenzie, honey, I won't last long."

"Good." She pumped him, fixated on his strong throat and his growled warning to slow down. "Do you really want me to let you go?" she asked, loving the softness of his skin covering that hot, hard shaft. He hadn't been exaggerating. The man was hung.

"*Fuck no.* I mean, no." He looked down at her, his eyes crazed. "Kenzie, I'm so close…"

"Wouldn't it be so much better inside me?" She nibbled her lip, wanting another kiss. "Or in my mouth?"

As if he'd read her mind, he took her face between his palms and kissed her, groaning when she squeezed him tighter and he climaxed, spilling over her hand.

Evan hadn't been lying about coming hard. He soaked his underwear, and the scent of his passion only added to his heady cologne that made her a little crazed herself.

As he calmed down, kissing and thanking her, half his words impossible to understand, she felt like she'd accomplished the impossible.

"Oh my God." Evan pulled back, holding her with gentle hands. "Kenzie, I… I feel dizzy. All the blood just rushed from my head to my cock. Hell. I am so damn out of my head."

"Now you know how I feel." She kissed him once more then pulled away to clean up. She returned to find him buttoned up and slumped on his couch, staring at a blank wall.

"I can't move." He blinked up at her, his slow smile warm. "Kenzie. Just…thanks." He groaned and got to his feet. "Now you have to go."

The abrupt change from welcoming to dismissive threw her. "What?"

He walked her to the front door. "You wait right here."

He left only to return with a bouquet of flowers and a box of chocolates he handed her.

She stared at the gifts, trying to remember the last time she'd received flowers. And chocolates? The gesture had her blinking back tears. Such a small thing to make her feel so emotional.

"These are for you." He kissed her cheek, sighed, then kissed her lips. "You need to go before I forget myself and try talking you into bed. Don't even act like you'll resist this— us—whatever we have here. I tried, and I failed."

"Oh, well." She flushed. "I wasn't much better."

"I know. You're weak, like me." He chuckled. "All I wanted was for you to feel special."

She stared at his gifts then at the man who'd played her body like he owned it. "You did make me feel special."

"Yes, but today wasn't supposed to be about me."

"It wasn't," she tried to assure him.

"Sorry, but I'm pretty sure my clothes are still sticking to me because you blew my head clean off."

She chuckled. "Stop. I'm trying to say I enjoyed everything we did today." Surprised to realize it was true, she couldn't help being glad she'd done everything she wanted. Well, almost. Making love to Evan would be spectacular. But the closeness that might create unnerved her. "I loved everything about today, Evan." She clutched the colorful bouquet in her hand. "So thank you."

"If you're sure." He studied her, then, seeming satisfied, hugged her. "God, you feel good." He sniffed her hair. "Smell good too." He seemed reluctant when he stepped back.

He no doubt spent a fortune for that rich scent he wore. Kenzie used an herbal shampoo for six bucks a bottle. *That's me. Sophisticated Target shopper.* "I didn't come over here for this. But I had a feeling it might happen," she admitted. "You're right. We do click in that way."

"Do we ever." He ran a hand through his hair. "I didn't mean for this to happen either. I mean, I've fantasized about it since I first saw you, but I didn't want to rush you."

And he hadn't. "No one made me do anything."

"Oh, come on. My clean house, amazing shirt, and spectacular forearms didn't seduce you into some hot chair sex?"

She shook her head. "It wasn't exactly sex."

"Hmm. You're right. But since we both got our *oh God oh God* on, we're halfway there."

"Evan." Laughter filled her, the joy of being with him taking away her inhibitions. "So do you want to do this again?"

He gave her a look that questioned her intelligence. "Are you kidding? Yes. But before you can throw up a bazillion reasons why we should never see each other again or invite Rachel to our next dinner because it's suddenly *her* birthday, we can take it slow. As slow as you want."

"Well, maybe I want to go a little faster." He was starting to annoy her, trying so hard not to scare her away he made her feel like a church mouse afraid of her own shadow.

"And now you're annoyed. See? This is why you have to go. Right now. Before I say something that pisses you off so much you won't want to talk to me again." He gently scooted her out the door and shut it. Through the door he yelled, "Call or text me and I'll come over to fix whatever needs fixing. Our next date is your call. I'll be there!"

"Evan?" She stood holding flowers and chocolates, no purse or keys to get her home.

Two seconds later, the door opened, and holding her purse and the bags she'd initially brought, full once more with tubs of ice cream and fixings, he hustled her to her car and opened the door for her. He put her bags and purse in the back seat and took her flowers and chocolates from her, dumping them in the passenger seat. Then he kissed her quickly, put the keys in her hand, and hurried to the door, shutting himself inside again.

She stared at the door. "What a strange man."

But on the drive home, she had to admit that strange man had given her one hell of an orgasm. One that still tingled her toes.

CHAPTER 12

EVAN HADN'T SMILED SO MUCH IN A LONG TIME. BY Tuesday, he'd been so pleasant on the job that Smith had stopped talking to him.

He whistled as he finished boxing up the clients' desk contents, his thoughts, as usual, on Kenzie.

He'd almost screwed it up on Sunday. As he'd predicted. Evan had no problem landing women. He could wine, dine, and flirt with the best of them. But closing the deal after sex? Well, a guy couldn't be good at everything.

With a bad habit of saying the wrong thing, he'd spent plenty of sorrowful day-afters making amends. Hell, he'd annoyed Rita about an hour after they'd first made love and had spent a week begging her to forgive him. Could he help it that he often grew awkward, unsure of what to say or do after an emotional encounter? Honesty, which he swore by, often annoyed his bedmates.

Apparently, even if a woman only wanted a friends-with-benefits relationship, asking her to leave a few minutes after you'd slept together was a faux pas. But the few times he'd tried to ease his way into separating, cuddling, making small talk until he thought he could say goodbye, his partners had accused him of wanting too much affection.

So he'd needed to get Kenzie to leave before he screwed up. And bingo. It had worked. They had a date planned for tonight after work, a get-together for dinner, her treat. He didn't like the thought of her paying for his meal, especially after hearing how she had financial trouble. But he also knew all about pride, and he didn't want to step on hers.

"Oh my God. Quit smiling so loud," Smith growled and grabbed the box from Evan's hands.

He chortled, Smith's upset making his day even better. Ever since that night at the bar, Smith had been a little stand-offish with Evan. But since Reid kept pairing them together on assignments, there was little the big guy could do to keep Evan at a distance. Because, yes, Evan did have the gift of gab. He could talk to anyone about anything and put them at ease.

Well, when it didn't involve a romantic relationship.

Evan followed him out to the moving van. "So what's the deal with you and Reid? You seem to be getting along."

Smith groaned. "Do I have to talk?"

"No, you can just watch me smile. I'm happy and in a new relationship. She's so special. Would you like to know what I like most about her?"

"Kill me now," Smith muttered.

"Her smile is what really makes my heart race." Evan poured it on thick. "She's funny, and when she's enjoying herself, her eyes sparkle. The green is more prominent than the brown, which is more like a honey-gold than—"

"Reid's okay," Smith interrupted, loudly. "He's actually not too bad to deal with. Much better than Cash, who's a dick."

Evan hid a smile. "He is a dick, that's true. But he's got a good heart."

Smith moved the boxes into the back. "What's your hard-on for feelings, man? Can't we just work?"

"Sure. But the silence gets old. At least it does for me. I know Martin feels the same way."

"But not Tim. He never talks."

Evan and Smith had worked with Martin and Tim the previous day, turning the Hillford job over to them. Tim had a lot in common with Smith. Both were large and quiet and worked like machines. Unlike Martin, who never shut up.

"Then there's Jordan." Evan liked Cash's girlfriend. Cute, smart, an ex-Army MP who didn't take anyone's nonsense, she was a favorite among the crew.

"She's cool." Smith shook his head. "Don't know what she sees in Cash."

Evan walked out of the truck, Smith behind him. They went inside the house and started moving the larger pieces.

As they carried out a sofa, made of concrete apparently, Evan said, "Cash is okay. He seems surly, obnoxious, and rough around the edges if you don't know him."

Smith grunted as they set the couch down in the truck then wrapped it. "And if you do know him?"

"He's surly, obnoxious, and rough around the edges." Evan grinned. "A lot like someone else I know."

"Asshole." But Smith's lips curled. "So I'll bite. Why are you so fuckin' happy lately? Is it really because you finally got laid?"

"There's more to life than sex, Smith."

"Yep, got laid. Who's the poor girl? Or guy? Not judging, man, but with you it could probably go either way."

Evan cocked his head, bemused. He had no problem with his sexuality, so he'd never been bothered by what other people thought. "I seem gay to you?"

"It's how you dress."

"How is that?"

"Fancy."

In Smith's world, apparently two plus two equaled seventeen. "So only gay people dress nicely?"

"Mostly, yeah."

"That's a stereotype."

"Tell me it's not true."

Evan tried, but all the gay friends he had did care what they wore. "Reid dresses nice. So do a million other professionals."

"Yeah, but Reid has Naomi. And she is *all* woman."

"I dare you to say that to her face."

"I would, but she'd probably stick one of those spiked heels through me just for breathing her air. Woman doesn't play."

Which Evan could tell Smith respected. "Well, what about you?"

"What about me?"

"What do you dress like when you're not here?"

Smith looked confused. "I dress the same. Jeans, T-shirts, sweats. Just normal clothes, and I drive a normal truck, not some jacked-up Lexus piece-of-rich-guy crap."

"Ah, I see. So the car and nice clothes make me gay."

Smith glared. "I was being an asshole. I thought saying you look gay might make you mad. It didn't. Let it go."

"I'm telling Lafayette." Who was gay and proud of it. "And Heidi." Heidi said little, but she didn't take anyone's shit. And she couldn't care less what others thought of her. Like Lafayette, she was a part of the team. One Smith claimed to want to belong to, no matter how much he bitched.

"Go ahead. Heidi's cool. She's like me, doesn't like chatter or people. But Lafayette's a pain. I've been trying to get a rise out of him for weeks. I get nothing. He's way too nice."

"A *rise* out of him?" Evan couldn't resist.

Smith flushed. "Fuck off." He stomped back into the house.

Evan laughed and followed him back inside. He continued to taunt Smith for the rest of the day, finally getting some genuine laughter out of the man. Surprisingly, Evan liked Smith the more he came to know him.

Though Smith pretended to be nothing more than a prejudiced, stereotypical redneck, he was anything but. Quick-witted and sarcastic, he actually did remind Evan a lot of Cash, except Smith was shockingly well read. Not that Cash was stupid, but he made no effort to even try to pretend to be educated.

Smith, it seemed, read everything from political thrillers and biographies to history. He also enjoyed loud discussions about his point of view with those who were wrong—aka those who didn't agree with him.

Hours later, having finished the job, Evan sat next to Smith in the truck as they drove back to the warehouse. "So when are you going to come clean on why you took a job with Vets on the Go!?"

Smith didn't blink. "Not sure what you're talking about."

Evan sighed. He'd give Reid another few weeks, then he was taking charge and getting all this secret brother bull out of the way. "So I noticed you're pretty interested in my social life."

"Not really. I just wanted to shut you up."

"Funny for a guy who doesn't date."

"Who says? Just because I don't talk all the fucking time about every fucking thing doesn't mean I don't have a social life."

"But you're always either at the office, working, or at the gym, from what I hear."

Smith colored. "I have a life."

"The same gym Cash and Reid belong to." Evan had checked the place out once but liked his better. And since working with Vets on the Go! on actual moves, he hadn't needed to hit the gym to get a workout.

"What? Are you writing a book? Why so interested in my life, Evan?"

"I'm making what civilized people call 'small talk.'"

"Yeah, you're small, all right." Smith chuckled.

"Another one who thinks life revolves around being huge." Evan rolled his eyes. "I'm six feet. That's not tiny."

"So that's why you talk so much. Compensating, eh?"

Evan smiled. He had nothing to compensate for. Not for Kenzie. He grew plenty big for his girl, as he'd secretly taken to thinking of her.

"Ew. Just stop. You look way too happy with yourself."

"I am. Life is good, and I have a hot date with a sexy friend tonight. What are you going to do?"

"Hit the gym." Smith paused at his automatic response and tried to cover up by saying he'd been joking.

"Now who's pathetic?" Evan laughed because Smith's face stayed red. "So who are you currently dating? A thirty-five-pound plate?"

"Asshole."

Their discussion turned to sports and the NBA, and Smith expressed firm opinions about whom he considered the top point guard currently playing.

Evan shook his head. "Curry? Come on, Smith. Drinking the same Kool-Aid as everyone else? I thought you were more than a sheep. What about Damian Lillard?"

"Please. The Trail Blazers suck. It's a proven fact Steph

Curry runs rings around them. Then I'd put Russell Westbrook, but no way Lillard…"

The conversation devolved into personal insults and four-letter words, yet Smith looked alive.

They pulled into the warehouse and locked everything up. They were the last on the roster today. Just as Evan finished signing out, Cash entered the spacious warehouse, checking on the trucks.

Smith and he locked gazes, sighting in on each other like two bulls about to charge.

"I'll leave you two to it," Evan told Smith. "Hey, Cash. Be nice. We had a busy day today."

"Sure thing." Cash crossed his arms over his chest, his cast standing out. It must have been killing him to have to stand by while everyone else worked.

Cash, like Smith, was a machine. Cash always did more than his fair share, and he never asked anyone to do anything he wouldn't do first. He didn't want a desk job, but without being able to lift anything for another few weeks, Evan had no idea what Cash might be doing.

Whatever it was hadn't helped his mood. "Hey, you." A familiar Cash greeting. "Get anything worthwhile done today?"

Oh boy.

Smith's eyes narrowed. "Some of us actually work instead of whining about lame injuries. Did you really need that cast, or are you using it to get Jordan to kiss it all better?"

"Look, dickhead—"

"That's my cue to leave." Evan rushed away as the argument grew louder. He figured they'd either yell it out or fight it out. Normally he'd soothe everyone and send them to their respective corners. Not tonight.

He had a date with Kenzie, and no way would he do anything to ruin that.

An hour later, he frowned. Evan stood on a soccer field under the lights as grown men and women kicked a ball around, warming up for a game.

Rachel waved at him from next to Kenzie, who looked embarrassed and irritated.

He sighed. He'd been kidding when he'd suggested she'd put another friend between them to slow things down. But if she felt so hesitant to be with him without a buffer, maybe they *should* take a break, as much as it killed him to think that.

She made a beeline for him, and he slowed his pace.

Just as she reached him, she latched onto an arm— to keep him from bolting?—and said, rushed and in a low voice, "Look, just go with this, okay? I tried texting you to tell you about our slight change of plans. But I don't have time to explain just now. Smile and nod."

Rachel joined them. "I'm so glad you came, Evan."

"Happy birthday," he said drolly.

Kenzie squeezed his arm and forced a laugh. "Ha. He's joking. Rachel, I told you like I told Will, that Evan wasn't sure he could fit soccer into his schedule. But he did me the favor of coming to check things out."

"Okay. But I'm pretty sure he'll make it work." She winked at him. "Especially if you ask him to. Hold on. I'll go get Will."

The moment Rachel stepped away, Kenzie yanked

Evan toward her and explained. "I was supposed to get you to come play tonight. But I forgot to text you, and Will and Rachel have been bugging me about it since we went bowling. So an hour and a half ago, when Rachel cornered me, I lied and said I'd texted you and you'd be here. I tried to tell you, but you weren't picking up."

She looked disgruntled as she said it, as if this mess were his problem.

Oddly enough, he found it humorous and gratifying that she acted as if he'd solve everything. And he wanted to make it better, just to see her smile.

"I do this, you'll owe me."

"Fine, fine."

"And," he drew out, "we still go out to dinner. Alone."

She nodded. "I'm really not trying to get out of anything. This was unexpected."

He heard the ring of truth in her words. "Okay then. I mean, I know I can be intimidating. I played you like a fiddle Sunday, and then you got to behold my magnificence, seeing my glorious manhood in all its splendor."

"Um, technically I didn't see it. I just held it."

He laughed. "Well, aren't you red."

"You like making me blush."

"I really do."

"Aw," Rachel said, having returned with Will. "Aren't you guys too cute."

"Yeah, yeah." Will put a hand over Rachel's mouth. "Look, man, we're short a guy. I don't suppose you could hop in and play tonight? We're the Legal Eagles, I think I told you before."

"I would, but I don't have any gear." He stopped himself.

"Actually, I have some gym gear in my car. But no cleats or shin guards."

"You don't need cleats to play, and we have extra shin guards you can use."

Will and Rachel looked so hopeful.

Kenzie sighed. "It's just a game, Will. I'm sure you'll survive."

"No." Will glared at her. "How many times do I have to tell you? This is *not* just a game. This is the future at stake, woman."

"What future?" Evan asked.

"It's about our reputation. And bragging rights. And shoving their snotty, arrogant, prick faces into the dirt." Will glared at a few guys on the other team, who sneered and shot him the bird.

"Friends of yours?"

A woman wearing a blue County Kings jersey shook her head. "Fucking lawyers."

Will said something uncomplimentary back then shrugged when Rachel told him to calm down. "What?"

Rachel shook her head. "It's a long-standing rivalry that continues through every sport season. We start with soccer, go through basketball, come back to softball, and every now and then throw flag football in the mix. But it gets pretty rough, so they've been cutting that out." She waved at a pretty woman in a gray-striped jersey similar to Will's. "It's a King County thing. We've got cops, firefighters, lawyers, corrections, animal control, you name it. That's Jemma over there. We like her."

"She's a great player." Will waved as well. "Married to a buddy of mine."

"An assistant DA," Rachel added.

Will turned to Evan, so earnest. "Come on, man. We

need some fresh blood. The other team was talking smack about me. We can't let Parks & Wreck beat us."

"But I'm not a county employee."

"So what? You were military. That counts."

"It does?" Rachel raised a brow.

"Hush, woman. We'll call him a potential witness. That's close enough."

"Witness?" Evan asked while Will nagged him to go get his gym clothes.

"I'm an assistant DA for the county. You're in the white-collar league tonight, buddy."

Evan blinked. "You're a lawyer?" Will looked more like a buff blue-collar guy. He seemed so down to earth. And heck, he was dating Rachel.

"I know." Will grinned. "Everyone's always stunned when I'm out of the office and out of my suit and tie. This is the real me." He motioned to his shorts and gray jersey. "I'm a T-shirt kind of guy."

"Great. So if I play tonight, you'll leave me alone?"

"Sure, sure. Just this one game." He gave his teammates on the field a thumbs-up, and they cheered. "Now, college pro, make us look good."

Evan didn't get the impression Will would leave him alone after just one game.

But for Kenzie's friend, he'd sacrifice his shins. "Fine. Just don't blame me if we lose."

Evan didn't realize how much he'd missed playing sports, but running around a soccer field avoiding illegal tackles and kicking the crap out of a small black-and-white ball had been well worth borrowed shin guards that didn't fit right.

And Kenzie stared at him as if he could do no wrong. He had to admit, he'd been working harder to impress her than he had to impress his teammates. Yet he'd done well enough, scoring three of their five goals and assisting with two others.

Will and the rest of the team plied him with compliments and bribes, while the other team demanded to know what connection Evan, a soccer ringer, had with those "cheating lawyers."

Will yelled at the Parks & Wreck team and ended by saying, "Our player has nothing to say to you. He's pleading the fifth. Bring all complaints before the board, you freakin' whiners."

Evan was confused. "You have a board for this?"

"We had to. Parks & Wreck complains at the drop of a hat, and they're not nearly as bad as the Adminis-traitors." Will made a face. "All the departments volunteer someone to sit on the sports board to hear issues once every two weeks. Personally, I find it ironic we can't all get along, but whatever. If it keeps the cops from cheating like a mother during softball season, I'm game."

He dragged Evan away from the team's many congratulations and demands that he return when they faced off against the Top Cops and Station 8. Everyone bitched about the firefighters, in particular, playing dirty.

He found Kenzie chatting with Rachel and a few other women, standing around a huge cooler.

She had a cup in hand and gave him a big grin. "My hero."

He bowed. "For you, *ma chere.*"

"Do you speak French?"

"Not really. No."

Rachel hugged Will. "Way to try hard, honey."

"Hey. I was good. Wasn't I, Evan?"

"Well, you did block that one shot with your head."

"See? I use my entire body when I play." Will kissed her. "Kenzie, can you believe how good your boy is? I mean, Evan said he played in college, but that was inspired."

Evan shrugged, feeling tired but happy. "I did go on a soccer scholarship."

"You have to play next week against the Top Cops." Will sobered. "I'm serious. If you don't, I'll end up getting stuck working traffic cases."

Evan chuckled. "Will, I'd like to, but I don't think I can. I'm not a county employee."

"But you're an accountant," Kenzie said. "Maybe you could do some consulting work for Will's office or something."

Will perked up. "We can work with that."

"Don't you have an accounting manager?" Evan asked, bemused. "What exactly are my tax dollars paying for?"

"I'll talk to some people. Expect a call." Then he darted away with Rachel under his arm.

Kenzie bit her lip. "Uh, sorry?"

He sighed. "This was fun and all, but not how I expected spending my night with you." He wiped the sweat off his forehead with his shirt, feeling sticky and smelly. "Don't get too close. I'm a little rank."

"So sexy." She laughed. "Evan, you were amazing. I had no idea you could move like that."

"Oh, you should see my moves." He gave her a lecherous

grin that had her blushing. "Sunday I was caught off guard. But when I'm on my game, I'm unforgettable."

"I don't know. You were pretty unforgettable on Sunday." She cleared her throat. "I think we should go before that annoyed-looking parks director comes over here. Hurry. He's looking right at you."

They walked quickly to the parking lot and dove into Evan's car, managing to avoid three of the opposing team's oncoming players.

"That was lucky." Kenzie buckled herself in. "But my car's back there."

"We'll go back for it. How about you let me take you to dinner? After I clean up."

"Um, I'm supposed to be treating you. And I really owe you now since you did Will a favor."

"I did it for you," he told her, not wanting any confusion.

"Well, thanks."

"Anytime." He grinned. "I will say it felt pretty good when I scored on that trash-talking goalie. And the cheating! The short girl on defense was all elbows and shoving. You have no idea how competitive those people were."

"Well, you showed her."

"She's lucky I didn't slide tackle her," he muttered, saw Kenzie's amusement, and laughed. "I can get a little competitive. I'm just glad you were there. Who knows who I might have clotheslined if you weren't watching?"

"Good to know." She put her hand on his knee and squeezed. "You've earned a special treat."

His entire body heated up. "Oh?"

"Yep. Let's head back to your place and I'll order us the most amazing pizza on the planet."

"It's a deal." He turned toward his home.

"But no more kissing. I don't think I could handle that on top of seeing your strong thighs in the same night. My head may explode."

"Your head, my dick," he said under his breath.

"*Evan.*"

"Sorry." He grinned. "Now tell me again how amazing I am, and I'll do my best to forget about how you suckered me into another non-date."

"Fine." She sighed. "You're the most talented soccer player I've ever seen." She glanced down. "With the absolute sexiest legs. And that first goal? Poetry in motion…"

CHAPTER 13

AFTER HE'D CLEANED UP AND THEY'D SHARED A PIZZA—extra cheese and pepperoni, Evan's absolute favorite—he drove Kenzie back to her car. The hour had reached nearly ten, and the park had cleared. One lone car sat some distance from hers. The streetlight overhead had burned out, leaving her vehicle in a spooky shadow. Outside, the night seemed still.

Evan parked his car next to hers, the engine running, and turned to her. "This is the part where you get out and walk to your car. I leave you and never look in my rearview. Meanwhile, something jumps out at you from the dark. The next full moon, you turn furry, and I'm full of regret for not having watched you safely drive off."

Kenzie just stared at him. "Where did that come from?"

"Netflix." Evan grinned. His hair was still damp from the shower, and even dressed in loose lounge pants and a T-shirt, he was the sexiest man alive. He smelled of soap and beer, thanks to the ale he'd contributed to dinner.

Kenzie suddenly had a hankering to taste the flavor from his lips. "Netflix? You need to get out more," she teased and did her best to not notice all the virility that sat so close.

"I did try, tonight in fact. And found myself playing soccer with a bunch of whiny parks and recreation county employees."

"Don't forget your whiny Legal Eagles. I don't think any team's ever had that many penalties for arguing with the refs."

"Oh yeah. Them too." He laughed. "I did have fun, you know. You didn't have to apologize with a pizza."

"Well, what if I apologized with a kiss?"

He paused, watching her with sharp eyes. "That might not be a great idea."

"Evan, why do you act like you like me then don't want to be around me?" She knew that wasn't the case, but every time he put distance between them, it...hurt. There was no other word for it. She really liked him, more than she had anyone in a long time.

But he kept trying to put the brakes on their progressing. While she appreciated his trying to act like a gentleman, it also made her wonder if he hadn't been as excited by their time together as she had.

Evan stared at her. "Are you nuts?"

"Well? I know you want me." His pants looked decidedly lumpy, though she'd been doing her best to pretend not to see it, not wanting to embarrass him.

"Of course I want you. But I'm not an animal. My body says yes, but until you say it, I'm not putting the moves on you. Period." Great. Now he sounded angry.

"I'm not asking for sex. I'm asking for a kiss," she growled and surprised herself. It was so unlike her to be aggressive with a man. Counting Bryce, she'd had a total of four boyfriends in her lifetime. With her job, with her friends, or just out and about in town, she stood up for herself, no question. But with guys, she'd always been on the shy side.

Not so with Evan. And she didn't know why she kept pushing him. Maybe to see if he'd get sick of her and leave her now, sooner than later? A terrible thing to think, especially if it was true.

Evan continued to stare at her. "You're kidding, right?"

She huffed out a breath. "Evan, I like you. You're the first guy I've been into since Bryce, but I'm not sure what's between us other than that we almost had sex before. You act so nice, like you like me, and then you turn cold. I've told you I wanted more. But you keep holding back. So what—"

He yanked her head close and kissed her until she couldn't think. It was like déjà vu from the first time in her kitchen. When he let her up for air, he cupped her cheeks, staring into her eyes. "We don't kiss. We try to kiss, then your hands are on me and mine are on you, and I can't think of anything but getting inside you."

"Oh." He had a point.

"Kenzie, listen to me. I like you. A lot. I don't want to ruin a good thing."

She didn't understand how they'd reversed their roles. "Isn't that my line?" she asked, her breath short.

He gave an exasperated laugh and leaned his head back, exposing his throat. "Fuck. I'm so confused. I don't want you to take off on me, and I have a bad feeling if we make love, you'll regret it."

"I appreciate that. I do." Her panties were damp, her body needy and way too receptive, especially seeing that thick bar in his pants. "But Evan, I want to make up my own mind. I don't want you making it up for me."

"I'm sorry, okay?" He seemed flustered as he ran an unsteady hand through his hair. "I don't want to lose you."

"Evan, it's just sex." Wow. Talk about overthinking it. She thought she was bad, but he seemed to be trying to look into the future to fix problems before they could start.

"I wanted our first time to be special."

She blinked. "You did?"

He stared at her then seemed to come back to himself. "You ever have car sex?"

"What? Um, no." She shifted, wanting to feel that erection so intimately against her, ready to have it now.

"Well, I have. It's awkward and uncomfortable."

"Oh." So much for a little adventure. Disappointment hit her hard.

"If you do it wrong."

She froze.

"Take off your pants."

"Here?" she squeaked.

He raised a brow. "You want sex, this is the way it works."

She'd never been very adventurous. But she could be now that she held the reins in her personal relationship. She toed off her shoes and pulled down her pants, moving in small measures, cramped by the car.

Evan gaped. "Holy shit. You're really doing it."

"And underwear, I assume?"

"Yeah." He swore. "Hell. I don't have any condoms."

"I do."

He just stared.

"What? Lila keeps sticking them in my purse. I must have twenty of them in there."

He grabbed her purse, opened it, and took out four. "Lila is *such* a good friend." He gazed hungrily at her naked legs. Her jeans and panties lay on the floor of his car. "Kenzie, are you sure about this?"

She nodded. "Unless you don't want to?"

He pushed his seat back as far as it would go and lowered it then raised his hips to pull down his pants.

She was in awe. "Oh my God. You're not wearing underwear."

"Yeah. And I'm aching. So what are you going to do about it?"

She felt like the star of her own movie. She'd initiated this. And her body liked it all too well. She'd always wanted to take control, and now she could. "Evan, can I ask you something?"

"Anything." He didn't seem at all embarrassed about exposing himself. Her shirt at least covered everything from her shoulders to the tops of her thighs. She still felt an odd mixture of shy and sexy.

"You're experienced, I'm assuming. More than I am."

"I'm not a player or anything, but I've dated some. Had a few girlfriends before and after I was engaged."

"Lately?"

"It's been six months," he said bluntly and gave a half smile. "No man card for me."

"Oh, right." She smiled back. "It's been over a year for me, and before then, there was just Bryce and one or two other guys I dated." No, there were three other guys. And Bryce. A whopping four lovers in her entire life.

"So…?"

"So can I kiss you?"

He opened his arms to her. "Hell yeah. Come here, you… *Kenzie.*"

She knelt over the console, her face over his lap, and breathed in the scent of warm, soapy male. Evan was large, thick, and definitely aroused. She ran a finger over his cock-head and heard him hiss in response. Then she kissed him there.

"*Jesus.* Kenzie, honey…" He tangled his fingers in her hair. "Again."

She smiled and drew the tip of him into her mouth, sucking just a bit. Bryce had loved her going down on him, but only after he'd gone down on her and never for too long. She'd loved him, and he'd appreciated it, but he'd always been the one to initiate everything.

But now, with Evan, she felt in control. He *really* liked what she was doing, and having such a powerful man at her whim aroused her unbearably. Knowing he was as helpless to their connection as she was evened the playing field between his experience and her desire.

She slid down his shaft, taking him deeper, and his fingers clenched in her hair.

"Fuck. Kenzie, honey, put the condom on me. Now."

She moved up and down over him, his rocking hips heady acknowledgment of how much he wanted her.

"Unless you want a mouthful, let me go."

She reluctantly sat up and licked her lips. Evan looked on the verge of a meltdown, his eyes wild, his breathing ragged. "You taste salty."

"*God.*" He grabbed a condom from the dash, tore the packet open, and put it on himself. Then he straddled her over him.

But instead of pulling her down, he kissed her, sliding his tongue between her lips while his fingers moved like silk between her folds and into her body. Evan sucked and teased, penetrating with his tongue and fingers until she shoved his hands out of the way, took his cock in hand, and slammed down hard.

She swallowed his groan. Then she rode him, uncaring

of anything but her frantic need for something so close yet still out of reach.

He gripped her hips and ground up into her on a hiss. "Oh yeah, take it." He pumped deeper into her and put his fingers to good use again, sliding over her clit until she shattered, Evan following with a muffled roar.

He continued kissing her, his affection warm, his caresses tender.

She calmed, still shivering, and reveled in the fullness inside her. "Car sex is amazing."

He groaned. "With you, yeah. I came too fast. Sorry."

"Nothing to be sorry about." She kissed him again, leisurely now, no longer in a hurry to reach an orgasm. "Wow. It's so much better with you inside me."

"Sure is." He kissed her back and hugged her. "I hate to ruin the mood, but a car has circled past the park twice. And if it's a cop, it would be best if we weren't caught with our pants down."

She gasped. "No, that wouldn't be good." She hustled off him and put her clothing to rights, grimacing at her sodden panties.

"I really filled this up," he said with a touch of humor as he removed the condom and tied it off then set it on the floor. He pulled his pants back up. "Thanks for christening the Lexus."

She grinned, feeling adventurous. Sex in a car. Check. One more item off her bucket list. "Now you'll never forget me."

He leaned close to kiss her again. "Not a chance." His bright smile shifted something inside her, her heart alight with happiness.

When he turned off the car, she had a sudden thought he meant to make love to her again in the back seat. It looked cramped, and she wondered how they'd fit. She couldn't wait to see.

Instead, he left the car, came around to her side, and opened the door. "I'm escorting you safely to your car. No way I'm letting you get turned into a werewolf. Not on my watch."

"You are so weird."

He laughed. "Back at ya, Ms. Car Sex."

She flushed. "That's weird?"

"Not really. That you haven't done it in a car before now is weird to me. If I'd known you in my teens, I'd have had those panties off and those ankles around my ears in the back seat of my dad's Dodge, for sure."

"So romantic, Evan." Ankles around his ears, hmm? Something else to aspire to.

"Now drive home safely and text me when you get there, okay?"

"Evan."

"Please, Kenzie. I'll worry."

She softened at the affection she clearly heard. "Fine. You do the same."

He grinned at that. "I will. And see you Thursday. Just because you gave me another orgasm doesn't mean you don't owe me a proper date."

"Whatever." She was still smiling when she arrived home.

Thursday night, Kenzie continued to feel bad about Tuesday's date, even though it *had* ended on a spectacular note.

Who knew a little white lie to Will and Rachel would turn into a soccer commitment from Evan? Apparently Will had gotten Evan a small job consulting on a case for the DA, and Evan could now be considered an official employee of the county. So, hello to Soccer Saturdays.

Kenzie rang Evan's doorbell.

He opened the door and stood back, waiting for her to enter. "Did you bring everything?"

She nodded and handed him a stack of papers and a flash drive. "All that I could think to bring. I really do appreciate you looking into this for me. I'll pay you—"

He held his hand out. "What did I say? You offer to pay me one more time and I'll do something drastic."

She didn't want to ask what that might be.

Kenzie liked Evan. *A lot.* More than she should. The way he kept protecting her both annoyed and tickled her because he clearly cared. Most men would lunge at a woman offering sex. Evan kept making sure it was what she wanted.

Man, going down on him had been sexy. She wondered what he thought about it. Did he revisit their time together over and over in his mind? Or was she the one too fixated on simple pleasure?

Being forward seemed to please him. He had said he'd gone without for six months, but she knew that wasn't because he hadn't had any offers. At the soccer game, she'd overheard more than one woman talking about him.

She'd been jealous.

But why shouldn't she be? Had she ever had a sexier accountant? Evan wore a pair of reading glasses, another button-down, untucked shirt, and faded jeans. He looked like a cover model advertising casual chic.

And he was ignoring her.

Focused on her paperwork, he frowned. "Hey, Kenzie? I'm going to head into my office for a little bit to look this over. You can set up on my dining room table if you want to work. I won't be long. I swear."

"No problem. Thanks." She forced herself to sound chipper, but Kenzie was a mess. Did he not feel the pull between them anymore? Because she couldn't think of anything but getting him naked and inside her again.

She'd turned into a nymphomaniac, apparently. Having gone so long in her life without sex, the first few times she'd had it, she'd liked it. The first boy had been a little clumsy but sweet. Her second and third lovers pleasant but forgettable, sadly. Bryce had been her best when they'd developed a rhythm that worked for them both. But not like this. With Bryce, the emotional connection had made the sex better.

But with Evan, the sex was amazing from the get-go, and her feelings for him continued to deepen even more because of it. She didn't know him all that well, but she feared she'd started to fall hard for the man. She thought about him all the time, and when she wasn't thinking about him, she was dreaming about him.

Kenzie had been wondering how to handle tonight, to let him lead or to once again take charge. She liked giving the orders. She did what she wanted and didn't hold back. But Evan didn't seem too eager for more than her paperwork. He'd barely glanced at her before disappearing into his office. Perhaps he'd had enough. Some guys just needed to get off with whomever they had at their disposal, and then the passion slowed. Or so Lila and Rachel complained.

The sexual times had slowed with Bryce, but they'd had

so much more to deal with than just doing the deed. They'd had their jobs and Daniel and their friends. Bryce's family, a new job. Then a trial separation when he'd been traveling for said job. Sex hadn't been important, and Bryce had found it easy to ignore her.

Oh my God. Evan is not Bryce. Evan loved sex with you. He came. You came. Stop overanalyzing.

Neurotic and wishing she could turn off her brain, she did her best to focus on Rob Talon's proposal. He'd given her a few ideas of what he was looking for by phone conference the other day, and she had two more weeks to put a professional package together.

Working on her laptop, she'd finally lost herself in her project when Evan called her name. To her surprise, almost two hours had gone by. She'd need to get home soon. Daniel had no problem with her being gone. He was a teenager, after all, and Lila had stayed home tonight to work, so she'd be in and out of the house.

But Kenzie liked letting her brother know where she was because they took comfort from each other. And though he'd never admit it, she knew he worried about being left alone. With their parents gone, it really was just down to him and her.

"Kenzie? Can you come here for a minute?" Evan called from his office.

"Sure." She saved her work and tracked him down. The moving man was gone, and in his place sat a professional brainiac. Evan had rolled up his sleeves. His glasses framed his already masculine face, giving him that sexy smart guy look, and the light gray of his eyes gleamed with intelligence.

Kenzie had never been more attracted to a man.

"Can you look over this and let me know if I have it right?" He had pulled up a chair next to him at his desk.

Disappointed that her libido needed to take a back seat to her brain, she spent the next half hour reviewing her forms with Evan.

"Okay, so you'll pay a small penalty for not filing extensions, but I reviewed some of your write-offs and deductions and balanced what I thought looked off. You should be good now."

"Thanks so much."

"Don't thank me yet. I'd suggest a thorough audit to figure out where things stand for your company, but that takes time." He took off his glasses, and she fought the urge to ask him to put them back on. "Kenzie, we need to talk."

She swallowed, nervous. "Okay. Talk."

"The other night... I feel like maybe I came on too strong. And I wanted to apologize for that."

She felt poleaxed. "For the sex?"

"What? Hell no. That was perfect, and I want to do it again."

She relaxed. "Oh. Good. Okay then."

"I meant I thought about what you said, and I'm sorry if I keep sounding like I don't trust your judgment. I do. I mean, you're a grown woman. If you want to have sex in my car, we can go out there right now and do it again."

She grinned. "Really?"

She wanted to crow with glee. Though she appreciated his apology, she'd rather they kissed and solved their differences with tongue.

Oh yeah. She'd definitely become a horndog. So did that mean Evan had become the shy girlfriend she needed to seduce into bed? Too funny.

"Why do you look like you're trying not to laugh at me?" he asked, wary.

"Sorry. It's not you. I'm happy to be with you."

He relaxed. "Good. It's just, I'm not saying this right. I should probably show you."

He just watched her.

"Okay. Show me."

His wicked grin turned her to jelly. "I was hoping you'd say that." He lifted her in his arms then tossed her over his shoulder as if she weighed nothing.

"Evan. What are you *doing?*" she asked, breathless, as he raced upstairs.

"Getting ready to show you what you've been missing. Because car sex ain't got nothing on bed sex."

CHAPTER 14

ALL THAT TALK IN THE CAR TUESDAY NIGHT ABOUT NOT wanting to lose her then acting standoffish had almost lost him the girl. Ironic.

Evan needed to get his head on straight. More, he needed to show Kenzie that he was a man who could make her melt. His only excuses in coming so fast both times were that, one, it had been a while, and two, Kenzie had shocked him with those moves in the car. In both cases he hadn't had time to mentally prepare himself.

But he wanted to show her she really should hold onto him. He'd helped with her books. He was a handy guy around the house and planned to fix whatever had broken. He had money, more than he needed, and he'd show her in some non-grandstanding way she could count on him financially.

She needed to see that he was a keeper. Because fool that he was, he'd fallen in love with the woman. At first sight, if that didn't beat all.

As she'd come through the door earlier, his heart had stopped. Seeing her smile started it again, feeling her warmth in every part of his body.

Her happiness mattered more than anything, he realized. Crazy as he knew it to be. Kenzie had baggage she'd clearly claimed, as well as a hurt he suspected had yet to heal. And he had his own issues, his mother's health notwithstanding.

But when he stood next to Kenzie, nothing else seemed to matter.

And that sex in the car… He'd never forget it. *Ever*. Because the memory of her mouth over him, her vulnerability when she'd asked if she could kiss him, had been seared into his brain.

He could only be thankful that Bryce guy hadn't realized what a gem he'd had in Kenzie. Now Evan just had to convince her to take a chance on him and not come across as a lovesick fool in the process.

"Where are you taking me, you crazy person?" she asked, laughing, over his shoulder. She slapped his butt a few times. "Oh, so firm."

He grinned. "You seem to like being in charge."

"I do."

He set her down on her feet and steadied her when she wavered.

"Sorry. Blood rushing from my head."

"Right. Now, I think I need to show you what you've been missing. Don't get me wrong. I like you telling me what to do. And I for sure loved your kissing me in the car." Fuck, he was hard. "But I think it's time for me to make you mindless for a bit. What do you say?"

Her pupils looked impossibly large. Her eyes dark, her lips a rosy pink he wanted to kiss all night long. "So, you want to make love here?"

"Yeah. I really do."

She stared up at him and nibbled on her lower lip.

He paused, seeing a hesitance he hadn't anticipated. "Kenzie?"

"Evan, I… I want us to be together. I really do." She blushed. "And I want you to come inside me. No condom."

He blinked, not sure he wasn't hearing what he

wanted to hear. To feel Kenzie, skin to skin? A definite dream come true.

At his silence, she blurted, "I'm on birth control. And I'm clean. I trust you." She sighed. "Am I freaking you out? I just like not having anything between us."

"You had me at no condom," he said with all honesty, relieved at her smile. "I'm clean, and I trust you too. But honey, are you sure? I'm only comfortable with it if you are. I need you with me all the way." He tapped the side of his head. "In here."

He wanted to tap his heart too because that's where he really felt her. But confessing his love would send her running. It should have been too soon for him too. Yet he felt it all the same.

She sat back on his bed and looked up at him. Her smile was slow in coming, but it brightened the whole room. "I don't know why or how it happened, but I really trust you. You're a good man, Evan."

He scoffed, teasing. "I don't know if I'd go that far. But I'm clean, I respect the hell out of you, and I want you all the time. I'd never do anything to hurt you, Kenzie."

She nodded. "I believe you."

Her trust meant more than he could say.

"And I think it would be sexy without it." She let out a breath. "So let's—"

"No. That's the other part of this. You just lie back and enjoy."

"I—oh. Okay."

Evan unbuttoned his shirt and jeans but kept them on. He knew Kenzie liked his body, especially draped in a collared shirt, and he wanted to use that desire to his advantage.

He pulled her to her feet and took her shirt off. Evan looked her over, intoxicated by the soft curves and toned belly and that lacy white bra. *Jesus.*

"I love how you look," he whispered, trailing his hands over her arms, shoulders, breasts. She sucked in a breath as he caressed her belly and toyed with the snap of her jeans. "I love how you taste." He kissed from her cheek to her throat, stroking with his hands as he followed with kisses up and down her skin. He knelt before her, kissing her belly, and slowly unzipped the fly of her jeans.

He eased them down and left her in matching white-lace panties. Oh, just…wow. He could only stare, enthralled.

Taking a deep breath, he slowly let it out and stroked her from ankle to thigh. The outside of her legs then the inside.

Kenzie's breath sawed faster, her hands gripping his shoulders then toying with his hair.

He nuzzled her belly, then lower, pressing his face against her mound. She smelled incredible, sexy and sweet. And he kissed her through her panties, wanting his mouth on her in the worst way.

He glanced up at her and saw an answering passion regarding him.

"You good?"

"Yes." She stroked his hair, her fingernails grazing his scalp. "You're so sexy, Evan. I love you in that shirt. Especially when it's unbuttoned."

"I know," he said smugly, startling a laugh out of her.

That joy, her sincere pleasure, drew him more than anything. An innocent zest for life and happiness. He wanted more.

Evan pulled down her panties, staring at the trimmed light-brown hair covering her pussy. "Beautiful," he murmured and stood to remove her bra, pushing her hands down when she would have helped him. "No, let me."

He tossed her clothes to the floor then lowered her to the bed and stared his fill.

"You are without a doubt the most beautiful thing I've ever seen," he confessed, in awe. Her breasts would fit his hands perfectly, not too large or too small. She had a flat belly and trim hips, her waist defined, and her legs long and toned. The creamy richness of her skin so fine beneath his darker hands that had been tanned from the sun and roughened from hard work.

He knelt over her, absorbing everything from her fluttering pulse to the blush covering her cheeks, as well as the rose-colored nipples standing firm.

Evan couldn't stop himself from kissing her, just a soft press of his lips over hers, catching her sigh of pleasure. Then he moved lower, wanting to taste those nipples, to suck and indulge.

He cupped one breast while he kissed the other, gratified by her gasp and the way she tugged at his head, pulling him closer.

"Oh, yes. Yes." She writhed, arching her hips, and he knew she'd be wet, ready. Wanting him.

"You're so sexy," he whispered then kissed the other breast, loving how much she shared with him. She was so open in her responses.

Evan kept moving down, kissing his way past her ribs and belly toward the musky heat of her. "This would have been too hard to do in the Lexus," he teased, taken with her heavy-lidded stare.

"Evan, I want you inside me."

The words he'd been dying to hear.

"Not yet." He'd rushed both times before, lost to his lust when he should have been focused on her. "Spread wide for me, baby."

He parted her legs with her help then leaned in and kissed her there, taking the hard nub into his mouth as he licked up her sweet need.

She cried out, and he moaned, lost in her, a perfect harmony of sound. He slid his fingers along her folds, toying with parting her, then slowly slid his finger into her while he sucked and teethed the taut bud.

"Oh God. God, Evan. Please." She tugged his shoulders, but he refused to be rushed.

Kenzie deserved to be worshipped, loved, and he wanted her to feel it all.

He continued to kiss her, riding her clit with his tongue, his fingers buried deep in her body.

Her gyrations moved them faster, and he felt himself unable to resist pumping his hips, his body knowing what it wanted, as he drove his mouth against her.

When she screamed and jerked against him, he licked up her cream, gentling his strokes, in love and in lust and ready to show her.

Evan moved back and stood, taken by the woman who'd manage to make him fall in love all over again. She looked like a goddess, sated and lush on the bed.

His bed.

His woman.

He slid the shirt off his shoulders, pleased when she stared at him.

"God, Evan. I can't move."

He smiled. "That's not all."

"Oh, there's more?" She eased up on her elbows, thrusting her breasts forward, and he wanted to fall on her, fuck her hard and fast, and fill her up.

So he deliberately slowed himself, unbuttoning and unzipping his fly and easing his pants and underwear down. His cock sprang free, thick and heavy. She stared at it, her eyes narrowed, and parted her lips.

The urge to fuck her mouth hit him hard, and he had to stop for a moment and get a grip on his discipline.

"You were right. You *are* hung." She winked at him. "I bet you'll feel even better inside me tonight."

"Stop talking, woman," he rasped. "I'm trying to make this last."

She nodded. "Okay." Then she eased onto her back and stretched out, her body beckoning his.

He kicked his jeans free and joined her on the bed, and the feel of her body against his was like heaven.

"Oh, you're warm. And solid." She stroked his shoulders, her breasts pressed against his chest. She parted her legs, splaying them wide. "I want you in me."

"God, yes." He angled his shaft to brush her wet warmth. Then so very, very slowly, he eased inside her, staring into her eyes while he thrust.

Her eyes, more green than brown, widened, and she arched up into him as he pushed as deep as he could go. Evan remained there, breathing hard, the need to take her drowned by the need to share his pleasure.

He withdrew slowly, inch by inch, then slid back inside. Slow, deliberate thrusts, all of him out then in, until he was rocking faster. She'd wrapped her legs around him, her ankles locked behind his back.

The feel of her flesh gloving him, enhanced by the friction of his chest against her breasts, had him ready to burst. The sight of her open and accepting made a memory he'd never forget. The lovemaking felt almost spiritual, and he never wanted it to end.

"Kenzie, yes, baby. Oh yes," he moaned as he quickened the snap of his hips. He'd held off as long as he could, and now he had to come.

She was with him, grinding into his pelvis, when she moaned and clamped down on him, her body like a vise.

He closed his eyes and poured into her, jetting with a moan. Colors flashed behind his lids, and he grew lightheaded, the pleasure intense. He continued to spend, his orgasm unearthly, never-ending.

Until it ceased. He was left on shaky arms, their bodies locked. A bead of sweat ran down his temple. Evan felt as if he'd run a race and won, gliding through the finish line.

Then there was nothing left. He let himself down and shifted, taking her with him as he rolled them onto his back, still joined.

"Fuck me," he whispered, totally done in.

"I think I just did."

He blinked up at a smiling Kenzie, her hair falling over his shoulders. She kissed him then drew back, breathing heavily. "That was... I can't even... You're even better than coffee and chocolate, Evan. You're that good."

He hugged her, nuzzling that spot at the crook of her neck that smelled of Kenzie, all woman and softness, covering a core of strength.

"I can't believe we did that. Pinch me so I know I'm not dreaming."

She kissed him and rubbed his nose with hers. "I wish I had the energy to do that again, but I think I'm tapped."

"I know I am." He groaned. "I'm really not a one-hit wonder. I can go again, I just need a little time." Hell, Evan wasn't sure he had anything left. He'd given it all to Kenzie.

"No, no more." She groaned when he laughed. "I hate to do this, Evan, because I feel like an insensitive clod, but it's nearly eleven. I have to go. Daniel has a dentist appointment tomorrow morning, and I just know I'm going to sleep like the dead tonight."

Evan tightened his arms around her, loath to let her go, but he eased off. "I guess I have to say good night."

"For now." She smiled.

He was totally, absolutely in love. And she'd be horrified to know it. Evan sighed. "Using and abusing me. I see how it is."

"Evan?" Her smile faded. "I'm not using you. Daniel really does have a dentist appointment in the morning."

He chuckled. "I'm messing with you. So serious. Maybe you need more sex to mellow you out."

"I wish I had the energy."

"A day or two will fix that." He smiled. "Come on, let's get you home to your brother."

They parted, and she gasped and raced to the bathroom. Evan said, "That's all your fault, you know. I think I let you have it with both barrels."

"I'd say so," she called out. "Geez."

He used his underwear to wipe himself clean and donned his jeans. She joined him, still naked, and he felt himself stir. "Just...wow." Her blush made him feel protective, and he kissed her again and again as he helped her dress.

"I can zip my own jeans, you know."

"But I want my hands on you."

She kissed him. "I like them on me."

"Good. Because this is just the beginning."

"Okay." She grew quiet. "I feel like this changes things between us."

"It does." He deliberately grew serious. "Now that you've seen me naked, you have to marry me. It's the law."

She rolled her eyes. "Please."

"That or you have to pay me for my skills. That'll be a billion dollars for services rendered. What can I say? I was one of our firm's top accountants." Good. He'd relaxed her with humor. Meanwhile, he felt as tense as a bow, praying he wouldn't snap and say the wrong thing. *God, Evan. You're better than this! Stop being such a spaz.*

"I'll bet." She shook her head, flouncing her hair. "Evan, you were amazing. I want to be with you again."

He could feel a *but* coming and stopped it before she could speak. "Me too. But we should be careful, right? Take our time getting to know each other."

She nodded but gave him a closer look. "We're dating now."

"I'd say so." He stretched, pleased that she followed the constriction of muscle in his arms and chest.

"So it's just you and me. I mean, we had sex without protection. I won't do that if you're going to be with someone else."

"Fine. I'll cancel my two o'clock tomorrow." When she didn't laugh, he tilted her chin up to see her eyes. "Hey, I'm joking. Kenzie, I take fidelity to heart." *You're it for me. Nope. That's too soon.* "When I'm with someone, I'm only with her.

No one else. That's how I hope you feel too. You and I are exclusive, right?"

"Exactly." She sighed. "It's just… It's been a while for me. And before Bryce, there weren't that many guys, like I told you. I'm not good at relationships."

"I think you're just fine. You've been open and honest with me, and that's exactly the way I try to be when I'm dating." He scratched his head. "Though it's been a while, so I could be rusty."

"Not rusty at all." She turned her head to kiss his palm. "Evan, you made me so happy tonight."

"Back at ya, hot stuff. I swear, it's a miracle my legs work."

"Ha." She turned red, as she always did.

"You know we have to do this again. Next time, you're in charge."

"I don't know. You did pretty good tonight." She crossed her eyes. "I can't see straight."

"Funny girl." He kissed her and walked her downstairs, arm in arm. They gathered her things then went out to her car. Once she'd buckled herself in, he leaned through the window and kissed her. "Man. When will I see you again?"

"Um, how about this weekend?"

"I know you need some work done at the house. How about I pop by to fix a few things? With Daniel probably at home, it won't be a date or anything. But we're friends. Maybe you, me, and Daniel could bowl again or hang out. I have to tell you I had a blast at bowling night. And I'd love a chance to beat your brother."

She studied him, for what he didn't know. But then she nodded. "That would be nice. I just… I don't want Daniel to get too attached to you too fast in case we—" She cut herself off.

It hurt, especially after their incredible coming together, but he understood. He cupped her cheek. "Sweetheart, you set the pace with us, okay? I'm happy to be 'friend Evan' for as long as it takes."

"Thanks, Evan." She seemed torn, and he didn't want her leaving unhappy.

"Just remember, we're only dating each other. And hey, if I'm good on Saturday, maybe you can come over again on Sunday and let me eat you up all over again." He leered at her.

She flushed. "Stop. You're giving me tingles. One more orgasm and I'll have a heart attack."

He laughed. "Bye, Kenzie. Go home and dream of me."

Because he'd be dreaming about her and the future he only hoped they might one day get to...if she'd let him into her life.

CHAPTER 15

EVAN HAD A TOUGH TIME CONCENTRATING ON HIS mother as they sat at her favorite place to eat breakfast in Ballard, the Señor Moose Diner, waiting for Jerome to show. Distracted by memories of Kenzie, he nodded and smiled absently at her chitchat about Reid and Naomi until she smacked him with a menu.

"Whoa, Mom. What's up?"

"Are you listening to anything I'm saying?" Her phone rang, saving him. "Hold on." She took the call, obviously from Jerome because her smile warmed and she told her caller not to worry about anything and that she'd miss him. After she hung up, she said, "Jerome had to cancel. Before you try making some smart remarks, he's helping a friend who had to go to the hospital. The neighbor broke his leg, and Jerome is watching his grandson while he's getting fixed up."

"Hope the guy's okay."

She seemed to relax when he didn't make any comment about Jerome ditching them. "Apparently Harvey, the neighbor, was up on a stepladder painting the living room— they have a cathedral ceiling—and he fell. But he'll be okay. He had his grandson with him, though, babysitting for his daughter, who's at work. So while Harvey's in the hospital, no one's around to watch the baby."

More detail than Evan needed or wanted to know. "Mom, it's okay. Stuff happens, and it sounds like it's a good thing Jerome"—*was late*—"hadn't left his house yet." More like her inconsiderate beau had been a stroke of luck for the unfortunate neighbor.

"Oh, it is a good thing. But Jerome was sincerely sorry for holding us up and missing out on meeting you. He really took to Reid and Naomi."

"Good." *I can't believe she introduced her boyfriend to Reid before me. What the hell?*

"What has you so distracted today? You've barely touched your coffee."

They paused while the waiter came by to take their breakfast order, since they no longer had to wait on Jerome. After he left, Evan said, "I met a woman who's really nice. And I'm getting to know Smith much better. A lot going on."

"Oh? Tell me."

This he knew and welcomed. Breakfast with his mom, where they shared the important parts of their lives. A mutual respect for each other and each other's situations.

Evan did his best to remain blasé about Kenzie. Show too much interest and his mother would be all over her. Show too little and she'd wonder why he'd mentioned her at all. He also steered clear of asking her for any information on her doctor visits.

Having pondered Kenzie's take on his mom, he'd started to think he might have been sharing stress over her condition without being aware of it. Which would make her feel a need to shelter him, keeping him far from her health scare. No matter what, he'd be there for her, but cancer took such a toll. She didn't need his crap on top of her own.

"You look good, Mom." She did.

"Thanks. I've stopped swimming, but I'm doing yoga now with Jerome. I'm pretty good at it too."

"I'll bet. You've always been pretty limber."

"Because I was a top gymnast in my day."

"I know. I love those old pictures." The ones in the spare room at the house.

"I was going through some photos the other day and thought you might like them. I found some family pictures of the three of us."

"I'd like to see them." He smiled.

She narrowed her eyes on him. "You seem different. Happier."

Before she could interrogate him, he told her about soccer. "Mom, it was so much fun. I hadn't realized how much I missed playing." Not entirely a lie, though his good mood had more to do with a certain hazel-eyed angel.

"How nice. Honey, you were so good. It was a shame when you stopped playing. I always thought you'd go pro."

"Well, I wanted to. But the Marine Corps drew me. I'm not sorry I signed up."

"I'm just glad you stayed out of the worry zones. Your cousins weren't so lucky."

"I know. Must be why Reid is so messed up now. Oh wait. No. He was always a bossy kid."

"Evan." His mother laughed. "He's such a cutie. I really like his girlfriend. Naomi was sweet but not a pushover."

He snorted. "Wait until you meet Jordan. She keeps Cash in line."

"That I have to see to believe."

"I know. All of us still watch and wait for him to revert to the way he used to be. But it's like he's a different man with her."

She nodded. "Love will do that." She clasped her hands on the table and glanced down.

"Mom?"

"Evan, I—"

"Your order is ready." The waiter handed them their plates.

Evan waited for him to leave.

"Oh, this is lovely." She dug into her eggs Benedict while Evan studied her.

"What were you about to say?" *Finally. Just tell me what's bothering you, Mom.*

"Just that I think it's wonderful your cousins have found someone special." He didn't believe for a minute she'd wanted to talk more about Reid or Cash. "You had that with Rita, and I know you can have it again."

"So can you."

She nearly knocked her coffee over. "Whoops. Silly me."

"Mom? What's wrong?"

"Nothing. I'm just a clumsy old woman."

"Who does yoga, bikes fifty miles a week, and has no problem telling me where to stick it for calling her 'old,' so try again. What's got you so nervous?"

"Oh heck. I'm no good at subterfuge. Jerome and I are thinking about getting married."

He hadn't expected that. Evan sat there, not sure what she wanted him to say. Though he knew "congratulations" normally followed one of those announcements, she didn't look happy about the admission.

"Um, are you happy about that?"

"Why wouldn't I be?" she snapped.

"Mom, I'm not judging you. I'm happy if you are."

"Are you really?"

Puzzled and concerned, he put his hands over hers.

"Mom, stop. I'm not sure what's wrong, but whatever it is, we can fix it together."

She stared at him, started to smile, then burst into tears.

"Mom?"

A few other customers looked over at them.

"I'm so sorry. I, you... I'm so emotional lately." She stood. "I'll just freshen up in the bathroom." She took her purse and went down the hall toward the restroom.

Evan sat and picked at his eggs, barely tasting them. Had he somehow lost his mojo with the opposite sex? He used to be good talking to his mom, but now she cried instead of opening up to him. He had Kenzie hooked on sex, but he worried about the past she hadn't quite gotten over, unsure if he'd do or say something to send her running in the opposite direction. And now that he'd found her, he couldn't imagine life without her.

Kenzie had jump-started his heart after it being cold for so long. It was as if he saw the life he could have, a perfect amalgam of family and friends and purpose. If only he didn't step wrong and topple the whole damn applecart.

He'd been loopy about Rita too, and he'd been fortunate to share two wonderful years with her. Not all of the time happy, of course, but every second with her had been worth the pain. Evan knew true love didn't come around that often. He'd dated a lot, but only Rita, and now Kenzie, had ever left him breathless, heartsick, and agonizing over time spent apart.

He should talk to someone, Reid maybe, and hear out loud that he was going to ruin a good thing by worrying it to death. But he didn't want Reid to know he was such a basket case. Evan knew he came across as a guy who had his shit together. Sure, he used to stress when working for Peterman & Campbell Accounting. But for the most part, he'd been a success in life.

He shook his head, not used to being so anxious all the time. At least if this thing with his mother would settle, he'd feel better. But not having their relationship on an even keel bothered him more than he could say.

She returned, dry-eyed and smiling.

He flat-out asked, "Mom, are you on medication?"

She sat next to him and burst out laughing. "God, you'd think so, wouldn't you? Or that I need some. But no. Just a ton of vitamins, Evan." She frowned. "Oh, now my eggs are cold."

"We can get them warmed up."

They signaled, and the waiter took her plate, poured them both more coffee, then discreetly left.

His mother sighed. "I owe you some explanations."

"Please."

"This has to do with your father."

"Um, okay." He had no idea where this was going.

"When he passed away six years ago, I thought I'd follow him. My life wasn't worth living."

He sat back and nodded. "I know how that feels. And I know it was awful for you because you and Dad had been together so long." He swallowed. "I still miss him."

She reached for his hand across the table, and he warmed when she clasped it tightly. "I know you do. I do too." She sniffed. "See? This is why I've got the waterworks. I have feelings for Jerome. They came on suddenly, and they stayed. I never thought I'd find anyone else after your father. Heck, I wasn't looking. Jerome and I just found each other, and it's been magical. He wants to get married, have us live together."

"And what do you want?"

She teared up. "I want that too, and it makes me feel awful."

He handed her a napkin, and she blew her nose. "Mom, I hate to laugh, but did you hear what you just said?"

She smiled through tears. "I know. I'm messed up."

"Tell me why being with Jerome makes you feel awful."

"Because I feel disloyal to your father, that's why."

"That's silly. Dad's gone. He'd want you to be happy." That was if this Jerome fellow turned out to be a decent man. Evan had yet to determine that.

"I know. At first, I resisted feeling anything for Jerome. But he's kind and funny. He makes me laugh. And he's not old. I mean, he's sixty-seven, so he's not young. But he doesn't make me feel ancient. We do things together that make me feel young again."

"That's what life is about. Living."

"I know. It just… It really hit me when he mentioned moving in together." She paused. "He wants me to sell the house and move into his home. His summer home in Bainbridge Island. He's been planning to sell his house in Magnolia for some time. But he wants me with him, for us to get married and live there year-round."

"Do you trust him?"

"I know what you're thinking, but he doesn't want me for my money. Jerome is loaded. He has two other homes he's signing over to his kids now so there's no squabbling after he passes."

Bainbridge Island wasn't far, but it took a ferry to get there from the city unless one was feeling adventurous and took a two-and-a-half-hour drive around to get there. No thank you.

Evan had never thought about what it would be like to not have easy access to his mom. But if she moved to the island, he knew he wouldn't see her as much.

She gripped his hand once more. "It's been just you and me for a while, hasn't it?" She smiled.

"Yeah." He felt…weird. A little emotional himself. "I guess it has."

"Don't get me wrong, I love your cousins. But they're pretty self-contained. Not unexpected when you consider Aunt Angela and Uncle Charles."

He cringed. "No."

"But you and I have always been close. And after Rita, we became even closer." She reached out to wipe his cheek, and to his horror he realized a tear had slipped out. "I don't want to lose you, sweetie."

"Mom." He hastily rubbed his eyes. "Don't worry about me. I love you no matter where you live." Oh wow. She'd been feeling guilty about leaving *him* behind? Her grown-ass son who apparently had no life without her? "But what about your illness?" he asked as gently as he could. "Is Jerome okay with that?"

She nodded. "I've been going to the doctor a lot without you. At first, I was scared I might have cancer. I know how difficult that was for you with Rita, and I didn't want to drag you down again. It took you a while to get right after her, and while I know how much you loved her, that last year you spent taking care of her about broke my heart."

Mine too. "When you love someone, you stay with them through the good and the bad, Mom."

"I know." She wiped her eyes. "You're such a good man, Evan. Your dad would be so proud."

He smiled. "Yes, I'm awesome."

She chuckled. "But you've been such a good son that I worry about you. You seem to have time for everyone but yourself. So I distanced myself, trying to keep you from my prognosis. Only it turns out I don't have cancer. I found out a few weeks ago but had secondary tests to be sure, and the doctor confirmed this morning that it's just some exhaustion and low hormone levels, but nothing some pills won't cure."

"Mom, that's great." He felt lighter than air at her news.

"Yes, it is. And it was the last barrier holding me back from making some important decisions. Jerome and I actually met at the hospital, you know. He was helping his son-in-law through some medical problems, and we met and talked. Then we started meeting for coffee, a lunch here and there, the movies. He invited himself to my book club and stayed, and that was it for me. A man who likes to read? What a keeper." She grinned, her bright blue eyes full of joy. "But every time I see you, I see your father, the Evan I married."

"Mom, I—"

"No, no, don't you dare feel guilty about that. This is all my problem. Remembering your father made me feel bad about wanting to be with Jerome. Especially because you're always taking care of me, the way your father used to. I don't want to seem ungrateful, but—"

"But I was clingy." He sighed. "I'm so sorry. I guess I never saw it that way."

"You were *not* clingy. I misspoke," she said fiercely, defending him.

"No, I think the cancer threat made me realize I could

lose you too, and I didn't give you space to breathe. I'm sorry, Mom."

"Don't ever be sorry for loving your mother."

He huffed. "Right. Please just don't tell Reid and Cash I really am a mama's boy. I'll never hear the end of it."

She laughed. "No problem." She paused and added, "None of this hit me until I thought about seriously selling the house. You grew up there, Evan. I wanted to see what you thought about all of it, but I didn't have the courage to ask. What with the cancer scare, you working so hard and taking care of me, and dealing with my feelings about Jerome, I kept avoiding this big talk. But when I saw those photos the other day, something in me gave. I knew I couldn't keep this in.

"If I move in with Jerome, I won't be a simple fifteen-minute drive away. And if we live together, we'll likely marry. Both he and I aren't into shacking up like your generation."

"Mom."

"But it's important to me what you think of him. I want you two to meet, especially now that you know how I feel. He's a good man, Son. I know your dad would like him." She blew her nose and wiped her eyes. "It's the thought of no longer having that house, that anchor to your dad and you, that makes it all so overwhelming."

He thought about it, studying her. "It is overwhelming, isn't it? Falling in love." He exhaled. "I didn't want to tell you this yet, but I might as well. I met a woman I really like. A lot."

"Not just soccer putting a bloom in your cheeks, is it?" Her smile was knowing. "I didn't think so."

He flushed. "I'm pretty much gone for her. I was from the moment I first saw her. It's weird, Mom. But I just know."

"Sometimes you do. It was like that for your father. He said the minute he first saw me, he fell in love. Took me a little longer to warm up to him, but he won over my mom and dad, and that was no easy feat. Your granddad was a cantankerous old man, but he sure did like your dad. They were always doing projects together." She gave a tremulous smile. "Part of me feels guilty for loving Jerome. But all of me feels the love I still have for your dad. It's there every time I look at you and see what a miracle we made."

"Come on, Mom." Evan tried to laugh away the well of emotion causing his eyes to burn. "This conversation is way too deep for Señor Moose."

She laughed. "It is. I just feel so much better getting all that off my chest."

"You should have told me this before." He paused. "Did Jerome really have to miss today, or did you tell him not to come?"

"Oh no. That accident really happened. He's been on me to introduce the two of you for months."

"How long have you been dating, exactly?"

His mother blushed. "We met back in April, but he didn't really put the moves on me until last month."

"Huh. And you love him."

"I do." No hesitation.

"And you're going to sell the house and marry him."

"Well, maybe. I need you to meet him."

"You don't *need* me to. You *want* me to."

"Yes, yes. Semantics. It would make me feel better if my son, whom I love, met the man of my heart."

He leaned back and laced his hands behind his head. "Ah now. That feels good. This honesty between us."

"Evan."

He grinned. "Fine. And I'll even let it go that Reid and Naomi got to meet him before I did."

"I *knew* that would bother you. But I was afraid for you to meet him. I thought maybe if Reid liked him, you'd like him too. Reid was the litmus test, and Jerome passed. Reid thought he was terrific." She paused. "But Reid's not you."

"That's obvious. I'm much better looking."

"And smarter too," she teased. "Now tell me about this girl that has you blushing."

His cheeks heated on command. "Her name is Kenzie Sykes. She's been raising her brother all on her own for the past, ah"—he did quick math—"thirteen years. She's smart, funny, beautiful, and runs her own business. She makes me nervous, Mom."

"When a woman makes my unflinching son nervous, she's the one."

"The problem is we just met a few weeks ago. I know it's sudden, but—"

"When you know, you know."

"Yeah. She makes me feel the way Rita did. But with Kenzie, it's…more. Probably because I know how precious love can be."

"Losing what's important shows you how much it matters." She took a sip of her coffee and grimaced. "This is cold." She frowned in thought. "And the waiter never did come back with my eggs."

"Come on, Mom. Let's go visit Jerome."

"At the hospital?"

"Yeah. It's time he passed muster."

She shook her head. "Channeling your father with

all that bossy talk." His mother grabbed the bill before he could. "Fine. But I'm paying today. And after we're done with Jerome, I want to meet this Kenzie. We'll see if she's good enough for my boy."

"Yes, Mom." He smiled, feeling better than he had in a long while.

"Come on, mama's boy."

He groaned.

"Or should I call you my dancing queen?" She laughed harder.

And he laughed with her.

CHAPTER 16

Saturday morning, Daniel stood with his sister and Rachel, up at a god-awful hour—it was an *early* ten-thirty—to watch Will and Evan play soccer. The day looked grim, the clouds content to blanket the sun. A persistent drizzle came and went, bringing with it a wet cold. But with any luck, heavier rains would hold.

Since Daniel was trying out for the high school soccer team, Kenzie thought it might be a good idea for him to watch grown men fumble around a ball, wishing for the golden days of their youth. Not exactly how she'd put it, but that's exactly what he expected to see today. Now if she'd taken him to a Sounders game, he might have been a heck of a lot more enthused.

Ten minutes into the first half, Daniel started to pay attention. The Legal Eagles—Will and Evan's team—battled the Top Cops. He'd joked to Kenzie, "Three guesses as to who makes up a team called the Top Cops," and laughed. Yet despite the cheesy team names, there was some real skill work on the field. The Top Cops were brawnier and more aggressive. Especially the women, which Rachel seemed to love. The Legal Eagles used more finesse, though Will and the lady next to him kept knocking into people and getting super close to illegal tackles.

Evan played up as a central midfielder. He clearly had the ability to lead the team, even as the new guy, as he set up passes and stole the ball time and time again from the

Top Cops' lame forwards. He had some fancy footwork. Actually, the guy was pretty damn good.

The game went back and forth until Will yelled at Evan to stop playing around. Up until that point, Evan had been playing to support the team rather than taking the ball and running it himself. A mistake, Daniel had thought, agreeing with Will's assessment. The Legal Eagles' coach shouted a few commands, and the team positioned itself around Evan.

The score suddenly changed from 0–2 to a tied game. And then 3–2, Legal Eagles in the lead. They scored again. And again.

Halftime came and went, and the game grew even more exciting as tension on the field increased. The Legal Eagles couldn't seem to believe their success. The Top Cops looked angry, and boy, could they run. They weren't the best with the ball, but they were fast and mean. And pissy.

Daniel cheered with Kenzie when Evan dribbled past two defenders, took a fake shot, then passed the ball to his open teammate. Had the idiot not been offside, they'd have had a goal.

"I'm confused. Why didn't that count?" she asked.

Rachel groaned. "I'll tell you why. Because Will's boss had her eyes on Evan's ass and not on the other team's defense."

"Yep, that," Daniel agreed.

Personally, he didn't know why so many people seemed fixated on guys' butts, but whatever. He could admit to being interested in the differences between girls and boys, so he didn't think too hard on it. Or at least he pretended not to listen. But he watched his sister, saw how intently she watched Evan—not Will—and how much she didn't like the thought of other people looking at Evan.

Her "friend."

He snorted. Yeah right. Evan was a nice enough guy, and he had a sweet car for sure, but from what Daniel could tell, adult men and women didn't have friendly kinds of relationships. They either dated or they didn't. Then again, he only had Kenzie, Lila, and Rachel as examples to go by.

His sister was lamer than lame when it came to the opposite sex, not that he could blame her. It had taken him until just recently to let memories of Bryce go, not letting the douche sour him on life. Because while Kenzie had lost a fiancé, he'd lost a big-brother-almost-dad.

Lila seemed to be a more realistic version of a regular girl who had a normal social life. She dated a lot, no one seriously, and she complained about every dude she met. Except for Hector, but the new guy was, well, new. Yet Lila claimed he had the biggest muscles of all of her dates, and Daniel knew for a fact a lot of girls liked buff guys.

Which had helped convince him to switch his PE class from team sports to weight training.

Then there was Rachel. She had been dating Will for more than a year, and she really loved the guy. It had taken Daniel a while to deal, having just been dumped by Bryce, but he had to admit Will had stones. Anyone who could handle Rachel's high energy and constant drama but still treated her like gold couldn't be all bad.

His sister's friends had normal dating lives but no great guy friends. Just men they dated. They didn't hang out with guys, not the way they interacted with one another, always spending time after work together, having movie nights and sleepovers.

He would never tell Kenzie this, but he loved Lila and Rachel being close, and he missed Rachel since she'd moved. He'd known them both since he was just a kid, and they felt like family. Lila sure the heck nagged like she was his mother.

A shout brought his attention back to the game, and he watched Evan on a breakaway, just him bearing down on the goalie. Damn, the dude could run, and that was while dribbling a soccer ball. He faked like he was going to shoot, pulled the ball back and around his left foot, then let fly with a solid left shot that hit the upper corner of the goal.

The crowd went wild. Well, he, Kenzie, and Rachel went wild. The rest of the team supporters clapped and gave a few tame hoots. The other side booed and hissed.

"Screw off, coppers!" Rachel flipped someone the bird, and Kenzie and Daniel hurried to hide her infamous finger before someone ticketed them on the way home "just because."

Rachel laughed so hard she started snorting. "S-sorry. But Lee had it coming."

Oh, that explained it.

She stuck out her tongue at her ex-boyfriend, who wore a sour expression. "Especially since his new girlfriend totally screwed up the last pass Evan intercepted. Oh my God. Today is the best day ever!" She waved to Will, who grinned and waved back.

Meanwhile, two of the other team's players converged on Evan, getting right up in his face.

Daniel watched, fascinated, to see what Evan would do.

Thus far, he liked what he knew of the guy. But he always found it enlightening to see how grown-ups acted around other grown-ups, especially people they weren't friends with.

Evan rolled his eyes and tried to push past the smaller guy, who had a thick neck and really wide shoulders. He looked like a mini battering ram. His buddy stood behind him, hands on his hips, fists clenched.

"Will, help Evan!" Rachel shouted, pointing at the far end of the field.

The Legal Eagles turned as one and watched, assessing. The Top Cops laughed and pointed, waiting for their bully defenders to do something.

Well, the short guy shoved Evan in the wet grass, and the bigger guy stuck out a foot for Evan to trip over. Evan landed on his ass in the mud.

Everyone grew quiet, and the lone ref watched, a whistle in his mouth, clearly entertained.

Evan laughed. "Ha. Too bad you didn't do that three goals ago."

The Legal Eagles started mocking their opponents. Oh, nice. Daniel grinned.

Evan stood and looked down at his shorts, brushing at the dirt.

The tall guy said something and made a move, probably planning to shove Evan down again. But Evan spun and ended up kicking the guy in the ass. With cleats.

The big dude went down, face first, in the mud.

Evan huffed. "Don't be a dick. It's just a game."

"Uh-oh." Rachel cringed. "That's not going to end well."

The smaller buff guy grabbed Evan in a bear hug.

Will started running for the far end, a few of his teammates joining him. The cops looked at each other and clamored en masse. Which caused the rest of the legal team to join Evan and his attackers.

In the meantime, Evan did some funky maneuver awfully fast and reversed the hold then used his weight to send them both crashing down, Evan on top of the shorter guy, both of them now muddy.

Then Evan started wrestling with both guys, swearing and laughing. Daniel couldn't tell if they'd initially meant to have fun or if the fight had been serious before turning into a mock brawl.

"Close your ears," Kenzie warned him, seeming torn between grinning and grimacing.

"Wow. Evan's sure creative." Daniel heard more than a few curses, his favorites being *thunderfuck*, *fucknugget*, and *bonerbreath*, which was just funny.

Rachel clapped. "Evan's holding his own, Kenzie."

He had some nice moves. Evan got punched a few times but just rolled with it and returned with some jabs and knees of his own.

All in all, it was a pretty tame fight, busted up in minutes. But those minutes had entertained, for sure. Especially when the ref called the game in favor of the Legal Eagles, citing the Top Cops for poor sportsmanship, not to mention they plain lost the game 5–2.

Evan and Will returned to the stands, covered in mud.

"What a game." Evan bro-hugged Will then leaned in as if to hug Kenzie, who shrieked.

Instead, he laughed. "Kidding. Hey, man, I didn't realize you were here." Evan bumped fists with Daniel.

"Nice moves, bonerbreath."

"*Daniel.*"

Will and Rachel found that hilarious. Evan flushed. "Oh, sorry. But that guy was asking for it. He can barely kick his own ass around, let alone a ball, and he and his dickless friend think they can take me on? Forget that." Geez, Evan was oozing testosterone, obviously hopped up from his tussle with the po-po.

Daniel's estimation of him went way up. Evan could play like a soccer ninja *and* kick ass. Awesome.

"Wow." Kenzie stared. "I had no idea you could be so... mean!"

Everyone looked at her, hearing the same breathy exclamation he did.

Gross. She was flirting. At a sporting event.

"Kenzie." Daniel glared at her then pulled Evan away. "Ignore her. She's being all girlie. Hey, um, do you think you could show me some of those moves? I'm trying out for the school team."

"Sure. Will, kick me a ball, would you?"

The rain started again, but Daniel didn't care about getting wet. His sister had been right about making him come this morning. Because Evan was running rings around him with the ball, attracting a bunch of players to watch. An inside touch and scissor. An elastico, which was a kind of outside-inside move, very fast and very effective to elude players. And a friggin' Maradona—a 360-degree spin around the defender. Damn.

Laughing, having fallen and gotten back up and now as muddy and wet as Evan, Daniel listened and watched as Evan showed him step by step how to move the ball, controlling it with precision. Then he taught him the best way to practice. Putting a foot on top of the ball for balance and speed in agility drills. Really helpful stuff.

It was like having Superman teach a guy how to fly. Amaze-balls.

"Okay, guys, I'm drenched, and we can't spend all day playing soccer," Kenzie reminded them.

Will and a few stragglers complained, but they eventually broke up and headed back to their cars. Evan walked with Daniel and Kenzie, and Rachel and Will promised to come over later for dinner as they headed to their vehicle.

"Hey, Evan, do you want to come too?" Daniel asked, though he probably should have checked with his sister first.

"Sure. Kenzie already told me I had to stay for dinner if I was going to fix all the stuff around the house I promised."

"Oh, cool." Daniel hadn't heard about the plan, but it worked for him. "Where are you going now?"

Evan grinned. "Your place. I owe your sister a few favors, and she insisted I pay up. She's pretty tough for a cute chick."

"Oh, the compliments." Kenzie made a face at Evan, and to Daniel's pleased surprise, Evan made one back.

Kenzie laughed. "That was one ugly face."

"You should talk."

Daniel liked their banter. It felt real, not all flirty but that of two people who enjoyed each other. And Evan didn't ignore him the way Bryce sometimes used to toward the end. As if pretending Daniel wasn't around.

"Hey Daniel, what do you think?" Evan made the same face at Daniel.

"She's right. That's hideous."

"Dude, I'm a mirror. That's yourself you're looking at."

Daniel frowned. "That made no sense."

"If we were in the twilight zone, it would."

"Huh?"

"Oh my God. You have no idea what that is, do you? Today's youth." Evan shook his head.

"Hold on. Let's get back to you owing Kenzie some favors. For what, exactly?" This should be good. Did his sister and Evan really think he couldn't see they had something going on between them? Hell, it was so obvious.

And Rachel and Will talking about how cute a couple they made didn't help, no matter how many times Kenzie denied it.

She liked the guy, and Evan had a tough time keeping his eyes off Kenzie whenever she was around.

"Um, well, Evan got a few more clients because of me."

"Right. She introduced me to more people."

"Sure she did." Daniel contained a snort, barely. "I guess we'll meet you back at the house." He coveted Evan's car, big-time. "Or I could drive back with you and meet Kenzie at home."

Evan glanced at her. "Fine with me."

She frowned at them. "Okay. But Daniel, behave."

"Hey, I wasn't the one throwing elbows and punches and calling people fucknugget."

"*Daniel Sykes.* Watch your mouth." She glared.

Daniel pointed at Evan, hiding his laughter behind a fake cough. "It was him."

"And you." She poked Evan in the chest. "Be a good role model."

"Yes, ma'am." Evan gave her a mock salute. "You'd have made a good Marine."

She smiled, and Evan got a stupid look on his face.

Oh brother.

"See you at home." She left, and the rain that had turned back into a light drizzle finally stopped.

Evan sighed. "Of course it stops. Now that we're

leaving." He dug in the back of his car and fished out two towels. "Unless you want to ride on the roof, towel off." He wiped the muck off his face and stripped off his shirt.

Daniel tried not to stare, but Evan had surprising muscle on his frame. In his clothes, the guy looked tall and streamlined, but without a shirt, his pecs and biceps looked huge.

But not to be a gazer, Daniel dried off as best he could and didn't look back at Evan until he put on a clean sweatshirt.

"Okay, towels on the seats. And before you tell me I'm being anal-retentive about my car, I know. But can you blame me?"

Daniel agreed. "No problem on my end. If I had a car this nice, no way I'd let it get dirty."

"Good man."

The praise was a platitude, but it still made Daniel feel proud to have earned it.

As they drove back to his house, Daniel watched Evan handle the car. Assured, confident, manly. Yeah, Evan was a guy's guy without being all macho. And he didn't have a weak chin. Bryce had had a weak chin. Not good.

"So you and my sister…"

Evan sighed. "Go ahead and ask your questions."

"I just did."

"That's not a question."

Daniel spaced out each word. "Are you having sex with my sister?" He didn't get the awkward reaction he'd anticipated.

Evan laughed. "This is my punishment for cussing on the field. Your sister made sure you'd harass me all the way to your place."

Daniel started to disagree then realized Kenzie had been awfully easy about letting Daniel drive off with Evan in his killer sports car. "Hmm. You may be right. But you still didn't answer the question."

"I like your sister a lot. But she's a tough nut to crack. I'm on my best behavior, so don't go getting me in trouble at your house."

"Hey, I'm no narc."

"Good to know." Evan turned and gave the car some gas. Nice. "So what's the deal with your house?"

Not what Daniel had been expecting. He'd been waiting for Evan to ask him for dirt on Kenzie. And if the guy knew Kenzie as well as Daniel thought he did, for dirt on Bryce. "The house?"

Evan nodded. "Your sister seems to think there's a lot wrong with it. Tell me what you think. You're the man of the house."

Daniel shot him a sharp look, but Evan didn't seem to be poking fun at him. And technically, he was right. Daniel *was* the man of the house.

Feeling okay about that, Daniel answered, "Well, you helped fix up the water heater. So that's good now. But the garbage disposal keeps breaking, so we just dump all the food in the trash. A few of our overhead lights in the kitchen don't work. The bathroom tile is cracked. If water flows over onto the counter, it spills behind the cabinets. But I think Kenzie said that was easy to fix with chalking."

"Caulking," Evan corrected. "I bet you need sealant."

Daniel shrugged. "And I think the vacuum is clogged."

"Huh. That's a lot of problems. How old's the house?"

"I don't know. It was built before Kenzie was born

though, and she's thirty-one." Daniel looked Evan over. "How old are you?"

"Thirty-one." Evan grinned. "I'm single, have all my teeth, earned a bachelor's in accounting, am a CPA and have a master's, also in accounting, served six years in the Marine Corps as an officer, have one mom and two cousins, and work part-time at a moving company when not working for myself. Anything else?"

"Um, what are your hobbies?"

"Well, I like soccer. I played in college and loved it. I pretty much don't have any other hobbies." Evan sounded surprised by that. "I used to work too much, and when I'm not working, I help my mom with stuff."

"That's nice." The guy took care of his mom. Daniel was starting to really like Evan. "Ever been married?"

"I was engaged once." A sad smile crossed his face. "But I haven't had time to date in a while."

"How long is a while?"

Evan snorted. "You writing a book?"

"Maybe."

"Over six months. Happy now?"

"Why didn't you get married?" Had Evan left his fiancée like Bryce had?

"She got sick and passed away. It was pretty rough. But I got through it. She was an awesome lady."

"Oh. Sorry." Daniel flushed. "I gotta look out for my sister, you know." He was quiet as they crossed the Fremont Bridge. "She was really into Bryce, her ex-boyfriend. And it wasn't easy for her to date him. She has me, and she's always put me first. I don't think she's been with too many guys. Not that I ever met, anyway. Then Bryce came, and he was nice.

She loved him a lot." *I did too.* "But he couldn't take always having me around." Daniel looked out the window at the buildings they passed. "And Kenzie and I are always going to be together." He glanced back at Evan, who hadn't reacted. "She and I are a team. We're family."

Evan nodded at him, met his gaze, then looked back at the road. "That's how it should be. Your sister is a good person, Daniel. She cares about you. It couldn't have been easy for an eighteen-year-old to take responsibility for a baby. But she did it. And she did a pretty good job, except for that hint of smart-ass there on your forehead."

Daniel rubbed his face before he realized what Evan had said. He chuckled. "Jerk."

"Yeah, I've been called worse. My point is I respect the heck out of your sister. She does what's right. And where I come from, we put family first too. Like my mom, my cousins. They're important. Money and girls come after that."

"Huh. That's good."

"Yep." He paused. "I know what you're going through, looking out for your sister. My mom has a boyfriend. I met him yesterday. Freaked me out, to be honest. I mean, she's my mom, and she's dating. But he was a super nice guy. I liked him."

"What about your dad?"

"He died a few years ago. It's past time my mom went out and had a life." Evan pulled into the driveway. "My cousins have their own girls, starting new pockets of family. It's cool because we just add more people to the mix. Well, one of my cousins is pretty much alone. He's a definite work in progress." Evan rubbed his chin, and Daniel noticed the stubble there.

He wondered what it was like to shave your face. When he'd have to start.

Evan saw him staring. "You shave yet?"

Daniel blinked. "Uh, not yet."

"Don't worry. It'll come. I was fifteen when I started. My macho cousins were younger, I'm sure." He sighed. "I always wanted brothers, but my parents only had me."

"Me too. I mean, I'm the only boy. Kenzie's old enough to be my mom."

"Yep." Evan smiled. "Make sure you tell her how good-looking she is for a woman her age. Women *love* to hear that."

"Yeah, right." Daniel chuckled.

"Daniel?"

"What?"

"Your sister is lucky to have you looking out for her. Don't ever stop."

Daniel felt warm and fuzzy inside. Bryce had often told him to relax and let go, that *he'd* be the man and Daniel could just be a kid. And look how that had turned out.

"But don't be afraid to ask for help, either. Seems to me you have Lila and Rachel. Will, too. I envy you."

"You do?"

"Yep. You have a family you built. That's golden, man." He slapped Daniel on the shoulder. "And now you have me here to show you how to fix some basic things. Kenzie says you're a criminal genius. So pay attention. I've been fixing things in my mom's old house for years and saved her a ton in repair costs."

"Yeah, that's what I need to do." Daniel nodded. "I'm handy with tools. I can do it if I know how. I usually Google things, and we watch a lot of YouTube."

"So do I. But you have to know when to let a pro fix something, especially when electricity is involved."

"That's what Kenzie says."

The front door opened, and Kenzie waved at them to come in.

"Well, I guess we'd better do what else she says." Evan smacked his lips. "I for one want some cookies. She promised to bake peanut butter chocolate chip if I do a good job."

"Oh, nice. Those are my favorite."

"So you're not just a delinquent, but a delinquent with good taste."

"Ha."

Evan grabbed a duffel bag from the back seat. "Come on. Tell your sister how great a catch I am, will you? And how responsible I am behind the wheel. And speaking of, I haven't forgotten your spectacular bowling. Next weekend, it's you, me, and a large parking lot. I'll give you some lessons. But this is a manly thing, so don't be blabbing to your sister."

Daniel nodded, more than excited at the prospect of getting behind the wheel of such a cherry car. "Deal." He held out his hand, and Evan shook it.

"Deal."

After they'd both taken showers and used up a good bit of hot water, Kenzie put them to work. But, Daniel noticed, she spent a lot of time checking up on Evan. And Evan spent a lot of time checking out Kenzie.

Daniel still didn't know how to feel about that.

Then Evan distracted him by daring Daniel to come up with even better cuss words than he'd used at the game.

Three hours later, between fixing things and running back and forth from the home improvement store together, he and Evan were rolling in laughter, and Kenzie looked baffled.

"What's so funny?" she asked after she stuck her head in the kitchen.

"Guy stuff," Evan said when she asked.

"Guy stuff," Daniel agreed. "You wouldn't understand."

They smiled at each other as she stomped away, muttering about idiot men.

"Okay."

Evan looked puzzled. "Okay what?"

"Okay, dick-for-brains. You've got the green light to date my sister. But one wrong move and I'll make ABBA look cool."

"ABBA *is* cool, fartnozzle. Just not as a ringtone."

"And I thought you had game."

"Please. I kicked your scrawny butt on the soccer field, didn't I? And let's not forget how I made Will look like a teen virgin at her first after-prom party. Boy looked about as scared as you could—"

"Ahem."

They both jumped. Evan took his time turning around. "Oh, ah, hey Kenzie."

She glared at the pair, but Daniel saw her biting back a grin. "Well, when you and fartnozzle are through fixing the garbage disposal, I have a reward for you."

And then Kenzie put them both to work...eating cookies.

CHAPTER 17

KENZIE HADN'T HAD SO MUCH FUN IN A LONG TIME. Sure, bowling had been a treat with the gang and soccer fun to watch, but seeing Daniel blossom with Evan, smiling and laughing and trying to act all manly, made her heart happy.

He hadn't bonded with Will the way he'd once befriended Bryce. And while she knew and respected his need to keep a part of himself distant, she'd been worried Bryce had done damage that might never heal.

No matter what she and Evan might become together, he'd done wonders to bring her brother out of his antisocial shell. For a long time his only friends had been Lila, Rachel, her, and his school buddy, Rafael. Too smart for his own good and too accustomed to scaring people off, Daniel could too easily go through life alone.

It was great for him to have a man to emulate, and Kenzie loved that Evan seemed to genuinely like her brother.

Yet…warnings flashed that she might be getting too attached to him too soon.

Watching them laugh as they all played Clue, along with Rachel and Will, brought to mind the mistakes she'd made with Bryce. Mistakes she still didn't understand.

"You coming?" Evan called. "We're waiting on you, Miss Scarlet."

"She's always Miss Scarlet," Rachel complained. "It's a little annoying."

"Well, I'm always Professor Plum." Will shrugged. "I dig the pipe he smokes on the card."

"You mean the card I can see because you keep your hand too low?" Daniel said with glee.

"Ah. Thanks." Evan turned to hide his game paper and marked off the professor as a possible murderer.

"Thanks a lot, Mr. Green." Will glared at Daniel.

Rachel glared at him too. "Not nice, Daniel." She leaned back and grinned, giving him a thumbs-up.

Will shook his head. "It's like she thinks I can't see her or something."

Evan chuckled.

Kenzie swallowed a sigh. Evan was so freakin' handsome, and he fit in so well with her friends. Watching his sexy moves on the soccer field. Just…wow. Then he'd turned aggressive and she'd felt lightheaded, totally in lust with the man. She'd had no idea she could be so attracted to the fighting type.

He raised a brow. "Should we wait?"

"Yes, yes. I'll be right there." Dinner had been Chinese takeout, and she'd learned Evan loved all food except Mexican. He couldn't stand tacos or burritos and loathed nachos. Except for that bizarre palate—*didn't like tacos?*—she could find no fault with him.

And she'd been trying.

She finished wiping down the kitchen counter. "Okay, okay. Coffee's on. And we have more beer, wine, and lemonade in the fridge."

Daniel groaned. "Lemonade? Come on, Kenzie. Can't I have a beer? It's just us."

"You should let him," Evan said.

She stared at him, as did Rachel, but Will agreed, "Yeah."

"Really?" Daniel gaped.

"Yep." Evan nodded. "Drink as much as you want. Then when you vomit all over yourself, your bed, and your shoes—"

"Don't forget him pissing all over himself," Will said.

"Oh right. And after you've peed yourself, and we take the pictures to prove it, you'll never want another drink."

"You're drinking." Daniel didn't look so pleased with Evan now, but Kenzie wanted to kiss him.

"Well, sure. I'm trying to be manly to impress Will."

Will grinned. "Color me impressed."

Evan clinked beers with Will. "Of course, it took me five years from my first beer to get an urge to drink again. It was awful. Trust me."

"Oh." Daniel looked disappointed, and Rachel hid her face so he wouldn't see her laughing at him.

Will, however, added his own horror story as well as those of a few of his fraternity brothers.

Evan pushed his beer away. "Ech."

"Can I just have a sip then?" Daniel asked. He looked at Evan, who looked to Kenzie.

She joined them at the table with a glass of water for herself. "Sure. One sip."

Evan offered his. "After Will's last story, I'm done for the night. Maybe for the next month."

Will grimaced. "Seriously, man. All that pilsner, it came out of every orifice."

"Gah. Stop." Rachel slugged him on the arm.

"Sorry, hon. It's true." Didn't stop Will from chugging his bottle though.

Daniel took a sip from Evan's beer and gagged. "This stuff is gross."

"Yep. The price of being a man. Pretending you like beer." Evan sighed. "Now if you're done delaying your sister's eventual demise, can she roll the dice or what?"

"Please, Kenzie. Roll. I need some cake to wash out this taste."

"Oh." Evan perked up. "What kind of cake?"

Evan's kryptonite, apparently, was a love of all things sugar. He loved her cookies and seemed enamored with the idea she'd baked them from scratch.

"What kind of cake?" Kenzie pointed to the pan Daniel was cutting into. "Chocolate, of course."

"Daniel, the pan." Rachel ordered him over. "Bring it."

The rest of the evening passed in a blur, and before Kenzie knew it, everyone was leaving. Rachel promised to see her Monday morning, early. Will left after getting Evan's agreement to meet Wednesday night for their next soccer game, but only after committing to help Daniel at his school. Apparently they needed a few parents to assist while they worked out some coaching issues.

"Hey, Evan, will you come too? You're good at soccer, and my team could use the help."

Evan glanced at Kenzie before answering. As if to ask if that was okay? She shrugged, leaving it up to him.

"Ah, I think that'll work. We can warm up on teenagers, right?" Evan gave Will and Daniel a thumbs-up. "Now I guess I should go too. It's getting late."

Kenzie realized Evan had spent the day with them. The *entire* day. Except for a few moments that felt unreal, Kenzie hadn't minded sharing her brother or her house with him.

She kept waiting to feel déjà vu, waiting for the dread to build and Evan to pull a Bryce.

But he didn't. He'd seemed to enjoy himself working alongside her brother. Evan hadn't made a wrong move in her direction all day either. Oh, he'd looked, because she'd caught him a time or two when she'd snuck a peek. But he hadn't given one hint he and she might be doing more than acting friendly.

Will and Rachel left, and Evan cleared the table before moving to get his duffel bag.

"I'll walk him out," Daniel offered.

She blinked. "Ah, okay."

Evan returned with his bag. "Thanks, Kenzie. I had a lot of fun today." He smiled at her, his heart in his eyes.

Her pulse raced. He seemed so enamored, and she wanted so badly to believe a future might be possible. But she'd been down that road before, so she tucked the fantasy away and came back to earth, where Evan, a man she was dating, had enjoyed her company and her cake. Period.

"I had fun too. Talk to you later."

"Sure. Text me when you want to pick up your tax stuff." He walked out, Daniel behind him.

She gave them a moment before hustling to follow, keeping quiet and in the shadows.

"Nice game. Too bad you cheated." Daniel snickered.

"Oh please. Rachel had two extra cards. Will kept feeding them to her. Those two are awful." Evan chuckled. "You're a lucky guy, Daniel. You have one heck of a family."

Daniel's sincere smile meant so much to her. "Thanks. I know."

"Cocky much?" Evan muttered and got into his car. "Later, dickweasel."

"See you, buttmunch."

They laughed, and Evan left. She snuck back inside before her brother noticed and busied herself loading the dishwasher.

"So." Daniel popped onto the counter near her.

"So what?"

"Evan's cool. Will too, actually."

"I told you that a while ago."

"Yeah, well, I'd been giving him time to get used to me before I sprang my frightening intelligence on him. He held up pretty well tonight."

"Uh-huh." *Buttmunch?* She fought laughter.

"Evan's a pretty good guy too. Man, he can *move* with that soccer ball."

"I heard you ask him to help your team out."

Daniel shrugged, as if asking someone to help him out wasn't a big deal.

It was *huge.*

"He knows the game, clearly. And he's good. It's just to help us out while they figure out who's going to be head coach. Will and Evan can have us run drills. I'm going to keep practicing. They announce first string and make cuts on Friday."

She'd make sure to get Evan and Will on the approved parental list at school to avoid any hassle with their volunteering.

"Right." She finished with the dishes, suddenly dog-tired. The stress of the day, of having Evan in her home, so close to all that she prized in her life, had taken its toll. "I'm heading for bed. Lock up, will you?"

Daniel nodded. "Good night…Mom."

"Little punk."

He laughed. "Kenzie, seriously, I like Evan. He's cool."

"Oh?"

"So, like, if you wanted to date him, that would be okay."

She waited for his gaze to meet hers. "Daniel, just because he's good at soccer and he's fun to be around doesn't mean he'll be around forever."

"I know." He sounded defensive, and she hadn't meant to ruin his good mood. "But he's a nice guy, and he's helping me learn how to help more around the house. He's my friend too."

"Oh. Okay." She was glad and scared, because she didn't want Daniel to get attached only to be hurt again. So hurt and lonely. "Well, good night." She kissed him on the forehead, as she'd been doing since he was a baby, then she went upstairs to bed.

And made a decision. One that would give her a little buffer and time to think about where things might be going with Evan. If they even had room to go anywhere at all.

Evan had no idea what he'd done wrong, but by Wednesday, as he and Will stood around the high school parking lot, trying to find the soccer field, he knew he needed to figure it out.

Kenzie had been nice but distant since Saturday. He'd had a blast and wanted to hang out again. Being with her, Daniel, and her friends had been what he'd always wanted. A tight group, people who teased and had fun and cared for one another.

Yet since that day, she'd shut him out with excuses of being too busy at work to spend time together.

And he'd been dying to make love to her, having hinted more than once about having her come over on Sunday.

Nada. Nothing happening.

"There it is." Will pointed to the north end of the school. "I tell you, Evan. You must have really impressed Daniel. I've been dating Rachel for over a year, and the kid has never asked me for help on anything."

"Really?"

"Yeah. You guys seemed to get along pretty well the other night. Don't get me wrong. Daniel's a great kid. But he's been standoffish. Not that I blame him after what I heard about Bryce Tillman. Rachel is *not* a fan."

"Tell me about him."

Will shrugged, his broad shoulders impressive. "All I know is that the guy lived with Kenzie and Daniel. I guess he dated Kenzie for a while. Then they got engaged. She was always up front about Daniel being a huge part of her life. I mean, dude, she's raised the kid since he was a baby.

"Bryce seemed fine with it. Lila said she always sensed something off about the guy, but Rachel said she's full of shit. Neither of them, nor Kenzie, had any idea he'd just up and take off one day."

"Damn." Evan had known he'd have an uphill battle getting through Kenzie's shields, but abandonment was a tough road. "So he just took off? No warning?"

"They were engaged. The wedding was planned. Would have happened back in February, I think. Anyhow, he packed up his stuff and told her he just couldn't do it anymore. He was out, not ready to be a dad to someone else's kid. Dumped Kenzie and Daniel and never looked back."

"That's terrible." And sad.

"Yeah. As bad on Daniel as it was on Kenzie. The kid thought Bryce could do no wrong." Will scowled. "I've been working my ass off to make friends. Rachel's like Kenzie's sister. Lila too, and they think of Daniel as theirs. You're lucky. You're coming into this a year after it all went down. I started dating Rachel right when it happened, and I took the brunt of hurt emotions for a long time because Bryce was a dick. But I know how it works. If I take on Rachel, I take on her people, which includes her sisters and parents, who think I'm barely good enough for their daughter, in addition to Lila, Kenzie, and Daniel. But I'm good with all that."

"You're a brave guy."

Will grinned. "That woman is perfect for me. Besides, she tolerates my wacky family, so it's all good. And I'm learning Korean. Now I know when I'm being insulted at least."

"Ouch."

"I meant by Rachel, not her family."

"Double ouch."

Will laughed.

He'd given Evan a lot to think about.

The soccer team reminded Evan of his youth, the passion for the sport and the will to soak up any and all expertise a familiar draw. He gave Daniel special attention, using the boy to demonstrate warm-ups and a few defensive moves. Seeing Daniel around a bunch of other teenage boys proved what Evan had thought, that the kid stood out.

Good-looking in a young, needs-a-haircut kind of way, he had a lanky grace and a surprising quickness for someone his size. But he lacked the bulk that was part of the game. At this level, he'd need to get stronger to hold his ground when the opposition tried pushing him around.

Will proved a good sport, allowing Evan to dribble around him while also showing how tenacity and strength helped wear a guy down.

Will pulled him to his feet after a particularly rough defense, and Evan dusted off his shorts. "Yo, Evan, I hate to tell you, but we have to go. Game starts in half an hour, and we need to move to get there in time."

"They can play without us if we're late."

"Ah, not exactly. After word about the brawl got out, we lost two players, and Netsinger's out with the crud."

"Well, crap." Evan wasn't ready to leave yet.

Fortunately the coach and a few assistants had already arrived and taken over.

"Thanks for helping. Can we call on you again?" the coach asked after shaking their hands. "You guys were a real help."

"Fine by me," Evan answered. "Daniel knows how to reach us."

The coach nodded and left.

"A little free with volunteering *us*," Will emphasized.

"Oh? Was I? I mean, I'm not even part of the legal department, yet I'm somehow now a part of your team, *and* I have a job with you guys."

Will scratched his head. "Eh. You have a point."

Evan waved the kid over. "We have to go, Daniel. Wish us luck. We're up against Food for Life today."

Daniel rolled his eyes. "Someone really needs to help with the team names. Later, scrotumbreath."

Will's eyes grew wide. "What did you call him?"

"Good luck, numbnuts." Evan saw Daniel's look of disappointment and sighed. "Sorry, I blanked. I'll try to come up with something better next time, assface."

"Meh." Yet Daniel was smiling and said to Will, "See ya, compensator."

He turned and yelled at some teammates then took off to join the coach for more drills.

Will looked puzzled while Evan laughed.

"Oh, we made up nicknames for each other, kind of a contest to see who has the best insult." Even as he saw the comprehension on Will's face, he had to add, "Compensator is because he's saying you have a small dick."

"You know what, Evan? I figured that out." Will slapped a big hand on Evan's back.

Evan whooshed out a breath.

"You'd better hope we win tonight, or I'm telling Kenzie her kid brother has a potty mouth."

"Narc."

"Yep, that's me. All law and order." Will nodded to the parking lot. "Now move that fine ass, Mr. Moving Man. We have a game to win and shit to start. But I'm warning you now. Those health services chicks don't mess around. Watch out for the small one. She plays sweeper. She's maybe five two and as scary as Rachel."

"Thanks for the warning."

"Besides, if anything happens to you, the girls will kill me. They like you hanging around Kenzie to look at your pretty face."

"As they should. I'm gorgeous."

"And so humble. Come on." Will checked his phone. "Oh, and don't leave right after the game. Lila's coming, and she wants to talk to you." Will smirked. "Rachel is nothing compared to a pissed-off Lila. But you didn't hear that from me."

Evan groaned. "Well, at least we're not playing Top Cops again. I had no idea cops had such bad attitudes."

"You poor kid. You think they were bad? Wait until you see what the health services team does to fresh meat."

The Legal Eagles won 4–3, but Will hadn't been kidding. The sweeper, who actually did resemble Rachel, had left bruises behind his shin guards. And the things that had come out of that mouth…

She waved and smiled as she left, looking not much older than Daniel, portraying an innocence he hadn't seen once during the game. "Tell Rachel she owes me ten bucks, Will."

"Sure thing, Caroline." He waved back. In a low voice to Evan, he said, "Rachel's cousin."

"Red Card Caroline is Rachel's cousin?" When he'd heard her nickname, he knew it fit. Especially since Caroline had earned not two but *three* yellow penalty cards and a final red one—which normally would eject a player from the game. But that sweet grin she turned on the older male ref, and her diminutive stature compared with his much larger one, had swayed him from booting her.

"Yep."

"Ah, I see the resemblance."

Will left him by Lila, who'd been cheering so loudly he couldn't help but hear her over everyone. "Good luck, brother. You're gonna need it."

Evan sat on the nearby bleachers as the next team warmed up. He carefully removed his shin guards and winced at his sore legs.

"That's gonna leave marks," Lila said, empathizing. "Never tangle with Caroline in a soccer game. Why do you think everyone usually lets Will lead? She attacks him and leaves everyone else alone."

"Apparently Will forgot to clue me in to that strategy."

"I guess so." She cleared her throat. "Okay, I'm here to make a bargain."

"Said the devil," he muttered.

She laughed, purposefully cackling, then held out a hand. "How's this for a deal? You help me with Hector, I help you with Kenzie, who I know for a fact has been avoiding you."

"Oh, okay. Deal." They shook on it.

"So when are you planning on marrying her?"

CHAPTER 18

"MARRIAGE?" EVAN'S HEART FLUTTERED. HE WASN'T SURE he'd heard right. Lila couldn't possibly know about the engagement ring he'd already picked out and put a deposit on downtown.

"Yep. You love her. We can tell. So what's the deal?"

"Hold on." Evan draped his long legs over the lower bench and groaned. "Man, my legs are killing me. Now try again."

"Evan, I like to think big. The future is ours for the taking, am I right?"

"Maybe."

"When we see a company in need, Sykes Designs incorporates all facets of that company into a design. Now, if I was designing you, I'd make sure to put an immovable force on your page somewhere."

"Uh-huh."

"A knight in shining armor. A protector, a man with romance in his heart and soul and—"

"Why is Kenzie avoiding me? How about you start with that?"

She sighed and twirled one of her braids. "Kenzie is neurotic, and she's got a right to be. You know about Bryce, right?"

Never one to turn down useful information, he shrugged. "I know what Daniel and Will thought of him. What did you think?"

"I thought he was nice. At first. He was a good guy until the end. And I think he did genuinely love Kenzie."

He didn't like hearing that, but he nodded for her to continue.

"The problem was Bryce heard what he wanted to hear. She was straight with him from the jump. Daniel was just a kid, and he needed someone to look out for him. Bryce liked Daniel and was kind. But you could tell he was only nice to the kid for Kenzie's sake. I'm not saying he wasn't genuine with Daniel, but he never went out of his way to help the kid unless Kenzie could see him helping."

"I see."

"And it wasn't actually all Bryce's fault. Daniel had a tough time with Bryce at the beginning. Bryce was the first guy Kenzie brought home to live with them. She hasn't been with a lot of guys, Evan. I mean, she had a few boyfriends before Bryce, but no one serious." She sounded as if there was something lacking in Kenzie because of that.

"That doesn't matter to me. I like her the way she is just fine."

Lila studied him. "She was just fine for Bryce too. You ask me, she was too nice to him. He helped take care of her, but she bent over backwards to make him feel good. Why the hell didn't they vacation where *she* wanted to go? Or eat out at *her* favorite restaurants? Oh, Bryce would pay for them all, and he had manners. He wasn't abusive or anything. He was a nice guy. But he was a little selfish."

Evan listened and made note of all she said. "Where did Kenzie want to vacation? Where does she like to eat? I know she likes flowers, but what's her favorite?"

"See? Bryce should have asked those questions. He didn't. He just did what he wanted to be nice, and she accepted it. I mean, that's cool and all, but still. Why not do what *she* wanted instead of what he wanted for her? See the difference?"

"I think so." Evan studied Lila. "But none of that explains why she's avoiding me. You weren't there, but we all had such a good time Saturday. Ask Rachel."

"She told me." Lila sighed. "Come on, Evan. You're a smart guy. Obviously Kenzie likes you. I know my girl, and she's way too emphatic about how you two are 'just friends.'" Lila snorted. "Please. Even Daniel sees through that. Kenzie really likes you, and you're the first guy since Bryce she's dated. You're not a rebound guy, but she's understandably gun-shy. What if she likes you a ton and you dump her like Bryce did? And now it's worse because she introduced you to Daniel and the kid likes you too. I heard how he watched you play soccer and how he asked you and Will to help him out today.

"That boy doesn't ask for anything. Even with Rachel and me, he's not grabby or demanding. And we're his aunts!"

"So Kenzie's afraid I'll ditch her."

"That's what Rachel and I think."

"But that's a problem because I can't prove I won't. Couples grow together, in love or out. I can only show her, day by day, that I'm here." He decided to share a truth the others would come to see eventually. "I care for her. A lot. She's amazing."

"Yeah, she is." Lila smiled at him. "Evan, I like you. And not just because you introduced me to Hector. Kenzie's happier now. And I know it's because of you. But you have to be careful with her, okay?" Though she didn't add *or I'll break your legs,* it was a given.

"That's all I want. But I can't do that if she avoids me.

I'm not going to harass her. She should *want* to be with me. I shouldn't have to guilt her into spending time with me."

"I know. Look. Let me ask you something."

"What?"

She leaned closer. "What do you really think about Daniel?"

"Daniel?" He shrugged. "He's a smart-ass, a pretty decent soccer player, and a nice kid." Evan had enjoyed showing Daniel how to fix things Saturday. Spending time with the boy filled that need for male companionship, but more, for that missing sibling he'd always wanted but never had.

Cash and Reid had each other, and though they tried, that closeness just didn't extend far enough to him to make him feel a solid part of their unit. Oh, they would do anything for him. But he wasn't the first guy they looked to if going to hang out.

Daniel had seemed to soak up Evan's coaching, and he'd paid close attention to everything Evan said on Saturday about the house. For his part, Evan had liked teaching Daniel things. And being a part of Daniel and Kenzie's world felt perfect, as if Evan fit.

But he also wanted Kenzie to himself. Had that been part of what had pushed Bryce away? Always having to share the woman he loved?

"You take on Kenzie, you take on Daniel." Lila nodded. "So maybe you should think about that."

"I will."

He still missed her, but Lila had a point. Maybe Evan should see if he could handle Daniel, one on one and for more than a few days. Perhaps Evan got a kick out of game nights because they were so new. Would soccer games and quiet nights with just Kenzie and Daniel grow boring? Having a young teenager underfoot would interfere…

Evan didn't hit the bars, wasn't into the party scene, and liked the quiet after a hard day's work. What was he clinging to, exactly?

Lila tapped him on the shoulder. "Kenzie loves the food from Pecado Bueno. That's a go-to for when she doesn't want to cook. Dinner at Manolin will get you big points, and I know she's been dying to go to Tarsan i Jane, but that place is pricey. She really wants to go to Hawaii for a vacation, just because she's never been anywhere tropical. And she likes flowers of all kinds, though she's partial to tulips, which I think is weird, but that's Kenzie. My turn now."

Lila had been *more* than helpful.

"Thanks, Lila. A lot. So what can I tell you about Hector? We're friends, but not best friends or anything."

"Ah, Hector." She sighed. "I think I said something that annoyed him last night, but I can't tell what it was. I know about his time in the Navy. That he has a twin brother—*hubba hubba*—and that he has family in New Orleans. He said he plans to stick with the moving company and go back to school for a business degree. Maybe. But in any case, Hector has plans."

"Sounds about right. Hector is one of the nicest guys I know. He gets along with everyone, and I know Reid thinks of him as second in charge of the company, well, after Cash."

"Not you?"

"Nah. I only recently left my accounting firm, and I'm usually just a silent partner when it comes to Vets on the Go! I'm the magic money man who runs the budget. I don't want to be in management." Just imagining trying to herd the vets who he'd worked alongside gave him hives.

"Oh. Well, do you know anything else about Hector?"

"I think someone said he was taking ballroom dance classes. He volunteers at a local animal shelter, and he's a genuinely nice guy."

"I know all that." She sighed. "I wish I knew why he turned all cold on me."

"Hector's usually pretty straightforward. What were you talking about when you noticed his attitude?"

"Nothing. I mean, I don't know what triggered it. I just know we were walking together downtown, and after a while I noticed him being really quiet."

"Huh."

She bit her lip in thought, and he had to admit, Lila was one tall, gorgeous drink of water. "Do you think he got offended when I mentioned a threesome with twins? Like, that's every girl's fantasy."

Evan grinned. "Every guy's too."

"Right? But that shouldn't make him mad. I was teasing."

"And Lafayette is gay, so not possible anyway."

She paused. "Uh-oh."

"You don't like gay people? Yeah, that's not going to work with Hector."

"No, no. But I was on the phone teasing a friend of mine, who happens to be gay. We talk trash all the time. I wonder if he overheard something and took it the wrong way."

"Why not ask him?"

"Maybe I will." She wore a militant expression that told Evan Hector would be in serious trouble soon. "I mean, if he had a problem, why get all quiet on me? Why not ask me what I was thinking?"

"Not being Hector, I have no idea."

"Because if that man doesn't have the balls to be up-front with me, I have no time for him."

"I wish more women were like you," he said, thinking of Kenzie. "Just be honest and open about what you think. You avoid a lot of problems that way."

"Yeah." She walked down the bleachers and motioned for him to join her. "Come on. You can drive me home. I came with Will earlier. My car's in the shop."

"Yes, milady. Anything you wish."

"See? Now if you're saying stuff like that to Kenzie, she won't be ditching your ass."

He chuckled. "I'll keep that in mind."

"Good. Now you set me up with a time to talk to Hector where he can't avoid me. And I'll make sure Kenzie comes to your place, alone, and lets you say your piece."

"I'm game." He opened the door for her to get into his car, and she gave him a sweet smile of thanks.

"A gentleman. No wonder she's so gone for you."

"Not gone enough, but I can fix that. Thanks, Lila."

"You can thank me by getting that skittish man to stay in place long enough to hear me out."

"You got it. Plug your number into my phone, and we'll make magic happen." He handed her his cell and waggled his brows up and down, loving her deep laugh.

"You know, if Hector weren't around, you'd be just my type."

"That's what I told him about you," Evan said. "That if Kenzie weren't around, I'd be asking you out."

"See? A man with good taste. Kenzie needs you in her corner, Evan."

"I know. Now let me think... Can you get Kenzie to my place Friday evening?"

"Sure."

"Good. Now if I can make a suggestion about dealing with Hector, just be yourself. You're a beautiful schemer. Use that gift God gave you."

"Schemer?"

"Hey, I call 'em like I see 'em." He paused. "But because I like you, gimme a day or two to see what Hector says about you. I'll play it casual. You do the same for me with Kenzie. Then we'll share notes."

"Oh, it's like we're back in high school, which sounds pathetic, but I like it." She grinned. "Now drop me at the corner and turn around. Don't go past her house. Keep yourself distant for a while. Let her stew in missing you."

"Whatever you say."

"I know how to play the game, Evan. But sometimes the right information makes all the difference between winning and losing."

"Yes, sensei."

She laughed. "Idiot."

"At your service."

Kenzie, Lila, and Rachel spent the rest of the week brainstorming. With the Talon account needing work, Ellie's branding nearly done, and two new clients they'd started working on, they didn't have time to waste.

Thursday afternoon, Lila was giving Kenzie a headache. All that talk about the men in their lives, and she and Rachel kept harping on her about Evan and asking why they hadn't seen him around lately.

"Look, butt out," she finally said, crabby enough to get angry.

Lila and Rachel looked at each other, looked back at her, then burst out laughing.

She groaned. "I mean it."

Rachel wiped an imaginary tear. "Sure you do."

"And of course we'll respect your 'boundaries,'" Lila said while drawing a square in the air. "Now we want to know. Why have we not seen sexy Evan around? What did he do? Should I kick his ass?"

Rachel frowned. "He was here all day Saturday. He helped fix half the house and was a ton of fun at game night. Daniel told me—ah, I mean, it seems like he's been helping Daniel with soccer and doing guy stuff."

"Wait. What guy stuff?" Kenzie knew Evan and Will had stopped by soccer practice and that they'd been a hit with the boys and the coaching staff. But nothing else.

"I don't know. You'd have to ask Daniel."

"Or Evan," Lila suggested.

Kenzie shrugged. "Daniel hasn't acted different than usual. Except for being nervy about soccer cuts tomorrow, he's been the same." Although he had seemed more excited about school lately, which surprised her. He started back next week, and she had to admit she could use the extra quiet.

Between the girls and her brother, she never had a moment's peace to just sit by herself. Or be with Evan.

She hated that he crept into her thoughts constantly. And now with her blabbermouth friends infatuated with the man, he once again invaded her working hours, though she'd been doing her best to keep him out.

"Kenzie, what's the deal?" Rachel asked, her smile kind. "We know you like him."

"Heck, *we* like him." Lila nodded. "I asked Hector all about him, and he said Evan is steady, a super nice guy, and you can trust him. He's not a serial dater, a thief, or a mama's boy." She frowned. "He was pretty clear about that, and I get the sense there's an inside joke there, but he only said the guy loves his mom, so that proves he can't be all bad."

"My parents would agree with that," Rachel added. "They secretly love Will, not only because he's so good to me but because he's learning Korean to impress them. He respects their culture, but he's also really into pleasing my mom. She digs that."

"Your mom would." Lila snorted. "If I don't bow and tell her how amazingly young and beautiful she is every time I see her, she swears at me in Korean. Don't tell me I'm making that up. Your sister told me she put a hex on me."

"Dude, we're Korean. Not witches." At Lila's raised brow, Rachel conceded, "Though my mom is pretty superstitious."

"See?"

Good. They'd gotten distracted. Kenzie focused on her design.

"But we're off topic." Rachel glared Lila into silence.

Kenzie groaned.

"Come on, we're your best friends. Tell us what's going on."

Kenzie glanced up to see concern, not fun, on her friends' faces. "It's nothing bad."

"Well?" Rachel waited.

"It's…well…I really like him. A lot. It feels like way more than a crush, and it scares me."

"I knew it." Lila nodded. "You can pay me later."

Rachel rolled her eyes and slapped a five-dollar bill in Lila's hand. "Here."

"Seriously?" Kenzie glared at her friends.

"Keep talking or we'll bet on something else," Rachel advised. "You know we love you. We just want you happy."

Lila agreed. "It's been too long since Bryce, but you're finally not flinching at his name." She gave a smug smile. "My aversion therapy worked, didn't it?"

Kenzie grudgingly laughed. "You're such a pain in the ass. But it helped, yes. Guys, Evan scares me. He's sweet, kind, so smart. And God, he's hot."

"He so is." Rachel fanned herself. "If it helps, and don't tell Evan this, but Will has the bro-hots for him. He thinks Evan is awesome, and he's crushing on your man's soccer skills. I focus on Evan's powerful thighs. Will can't get over what the guy can do with his feet. And Will's been getting huge kudos at work for finding the team a ringer. The Legal Eagles now have bragging rights over both the cops and health services. It's epic."

Kenzie grinned. "Well, with that kind of endorsement, I should propose to the man." The notion that she didn't necessarily mind the thought of that scared her even more.

"Oh, marriage." Lila looked positively gleeful.

Kenzie scoffed. "I barely know the guy."

"Honey, you know Evan," Rachel said. "But you could know more about him if you'd give him a chance to show you what he's capable of."

"I did that with Bryce, and he ruined me for months."

"Oh my." Lila put the back of her hand to her forehead and turned on a Southern accent. "Oh my, oh my. That man ruined me. I'll nevah, evah be the same again."

"Not sure why the accent, but you nailed the drama for sure." Rachel turned a sneer on Kenzie. "Sac up. Bryce does not define you."

"I know." Kenzie knew she was being overly dramatic. Maybe not as much as Lila, but still… "I just don't know if I can go down that road again. Daniel was so hurt, it still breaks my heart to think about it." She grew teary remembering how hard he'd cried, how he'd been despondent for months afterward.

"Oh, Kenzie, we know." Rachel left her desk to give Kenzie a hug, and Lila followed. "And we know it hurt you so much more. But that's life. You can't bury yourself in work just so you'll never get hurt again. I got lucky with Will after a string of bad dating *years*. And Lila is still floundering."

"Hey. We're talking about Kenzie."

"You're being smart, and that's good. But honey, it's been over a year since Bryce. You need to move on. Evan's a good choice. You didn't rush into anything."

"Well, it *has* only been a few weeks," Lila murmured but shut up when Rachel glared at her.

"The point is you're not committing to anything but seeing where this goes. Yeah, you and Daniel got hurt. Badly. But you both learned from that. It's not the last time Daniel's going to be disappointed or heartsick."

"Because women can be such bitches." Lila nodded. "But we'll be there when his first girlfriend breaks his heart."

Kenzie smiled through tears. "Yeah, we'll all be there."

"And we'll be here for you if Evan breaks your heart."

"Just thinking about it stresses me out." She wasn't kidding. Her stomach cramped, and she felt a headache creeping on.

"Don't borrow trouble, as my mom likes to say," Lila said. "Stop worrying about what you can't control. Sure, you can dump Evan now. Be a pussy and ghost him." Kenzie knew Lila hated that disappearing-breakup practice. "But you might be throwing away a guy you'll be sharing morning breath and bad hair with fifty years from now."

"You're so romantic." Rachel grinned. "She's right, though. If I had ditched Will at the beginning, I'd be missing out on an amazing man. I was so man-hater-mad back when Bryce broke it off with you. I tried to make Will leave in so many ways. But he stuck to me."

Lila nodded. "Like a bad rash."

Rachel ignored her. "It's really up to you. We'll support you either way, but by not even giving yourself a chance to love Evan, you're kind of hurting yourself. Not just him."

"And Daniel," Lila pointed out. "Don't teach him it's okay to be scared and retreat from life. He's finally starting to show signs of his old self again. Show him you might be afraid, but you're still getting yourself out there."

Rachel handed her a tissue.

Kenzie blew her nose. "Thanks, guys. I guess I should stop being such a wimp about it and face Evan. He hasn't done anything wrong."

"Yet. He's a man. He'll do something stupid at some point," Rachel helpfully pointed out.

"True." Kenzie laughed. "But I don't need to worry about stuff that hasn't happened. Things are actually good, so of course that's when I worry. And I shouldn't. I mean, Evan actually fixed a lot of broken things in the house. And he's teaching Daniel." She thought about that, then she thought about Evan in that unbuttoned shirt. "Sex with Evan was better than anything I've ever had."

Lila hooted. "I told you they hooked up. You see the way he looks at her."

Rachel sighed and pulled out another bill to put in Lila's hand. "You know, Kenzie, you could have held out a little. Such a ho."

"Seriously?" Kenzie knew Rachel was messing with her, and the familiar banter helped settle her nerves. "You slept with Will on the first date. I at least held out until our third."

This time Lila put the dollar back in Rachel's hand. "Damn it." Lila excused herself to use the bathroom, and Kenzie gave Rachel a bigger hug.

"Thanks for always being there for me. I feel silly for being scared about falling in love. But I can't help it."

"You be as scared as you need to be. Sometimes I worry Will and I will fall apart too. But nobody knows the future." Rachel pulled back. "Heck, if I did, I'd be losing a lot less money to that penis worshipper in the bathroom."

Kenzie grinned and, seeing Lila still gone, whispered, "Five bucks says she hasn't slept with Hector yet. That's why she's been so crabby."

"No way. She hit it with the big man, then he pulled back." Rachel eyeballed Kenzie and held out a hand. "You're on."

Lila returned, and they watched her. "Out with it."

"So, ah, have you and Hector been...close?" Kenzie asked.

Lila sighed. "He's playing hard to get, and it's killing me."

"Yes." Kenzie threw her fist in the air. She almost never won their bets, but she'd been keeping an eye on Lila since the woman had fallen head over heels for Hector. Recognizing a fellow heartsick soul, she felt for her friend. But not bad enough to ignore taking advantage of Rachel.

Rachel threw a crumpled bill at Kenzie. "Damn it. This is *so* not my day."

CHAPTER 19

EVAN SPENT FRIDAY WITH SMITH, ALONE, MOVING MRS. Rassom, an older woman who'd lost her husband two months ago. She reminded him of his mother, and he'd done the best he could to help, from talking to her when she sat for a spell to assisting her in packing up her things.

Smith acted like he had places to be, dancing around and grumbling under his breath while they waited for the older woman to show them what to do and what to pack where.

But he remained quiet and seemingly patient in her presence.

"I swear, my Andy was a packrat."

Behind her, Smith was nodding, and Evan thought he read *No shit* from the man's big mouth.

"But he always liked to surround himself with things that mattered. See this?" She held up a jar of pebbles. "These are from every vacation we ever took together. I wanted refrigerator magnets. Andy collected pebbles. He swore he could feel each one and recall the exact memory of our time together."

She pointed to a few boxes of newspapers. "And those are from when friends and family made the news. Our daughters have done some amazing things during our lifetime."

"Where are they, if you don't mind me asking?" Evan handed the newspaper boxes to Smith.

"Oh, they wanted to come help, but I told them not to bother. I knew it would get too emotional with them here.

I'm moving out to be with them as soon as we get these items to my sister's."

Smith spoke up. "How are you shipping your stuff to your new place?"

"Well, my daughters all live in New Jersey, so once I settle out there, I'll have to figure out how to get my things there." Mrs. Rassom looked so frail, her eyes teary. "Andy had always planned to go with me, you know. That was our dream, to move out and be with our daughters and grand-children together. But he had to finish putting our things in order here." She gave a watery laugh. "Worked his last day on a Friday. Died conveniently on a Saturday morning. Never missed a day of work in all his seventy-two years."

Smith frowned. "He was still working? Man, that sucks."

Mrs. Rassom chuckled. "He used to say that too."

Smith shifted the box in his arms. "Well, when you're ready to move your stuff to New Jersey, you call and let me know. Vets on the Go! just does local moves, but I know a guy who's good and cheap, and he'll make sure all your stuff gets to where you want it in one piece."

"Thank you, young man. That's sweet of you."

Smith nodded and walked away.

The rest of the move went smoothly, and Evan enjoyed spending his time with Mrs. Rassom. Though the lady and his mom had to be close in age, his mother seemed worlds younger.

She also wasn't dealing with the recent tragic loss of her husband and had a new love to put some spring in her step. He smiled, remembering how impressed he'd been by Jerome and how his mother had blushed and stammered in her new boyfriend's presence.

"Hey, slacker, hurry the hell up. I know you're weak and all, but this table's getting heavy."

Evan ignored Smith's insults and helped him with the solid-oak table. Mrs. Rassom's possessions, while not exactly high-class, were of exceptional quality. Solid woodworking and attention to detail seemed crafted in every piece of furniture. When Evan had learned her husband had made all their stuff, he'd been beyond impressed.

"Careful," Smith cautioned before he could. "Her old man made this. We don't want to mess it up, Einstein."

Evan grinned. Smith could say and do all he wanted, but at heart he was a softie. He had imaginary teatime, comforted old guys when no one was watching—though Evan had seen Smith hand the homeless man ten bucks and walk quickly away to escape the man's heartfelt thanks—and offered to help out an old woman because he cared.

They grunted with the effort to lift the table up into the van despite the loading ramp. Because no way two guys could lift her furniture if they had to hand it up to someone to pull in the truck.

Panting, Evan asked, "So who's this coast-to-coast mover you know?"

Smith let out a loud breath. "Fuck, that was heavy. Eh? Oh, some dude I met when I came back. He owns his own truck, moves crap for people on the side when not making deliveries for some company. He's solid and has a heart. He'll move her for cheap because he owes me a favor."

So instead of calling on the favor for himself, Smith would use it to help out a sweet old lady who'd just lost her husband.

"You know, for a huge dick, you're not that bad."

Smith cracked a rare smile. "Well, you're not lying. You did say huge."

"Boys," Mrs. Rassom called. "I have cookies and tea for you."

Smith jumped down from the truck. "Come on, Evan. Don't make Mrs. Rassom wait."

Evan joined them for tea and cookies, astounded to see Smith pouring on the charm and being sincere about it.

On the drive to Mrs. Rassom's sister's house, he couldn't help trying to solve the puzzle that was Smith Ramsey.

"Quit staring at me," Smith barked, his gaze glued to the road. "What?"

"You're...*human*." Evan mock-gasped. "I just..." He reached over and punched Smith lightly on the arm. Solid muscle.

"Hey. What the fuck, man?"

"Nope. Human flesh, not robot metal."

Smith frowned. "What are you talking about?"

"Your ability to charm that lovely woman. You smiled. Willingly. And you were polite. I was just checking to verify that you're not, in fact, the robotic asshole you normally are."

Smith reddened. "She was nice. And sad. Gimme a break."

"Yeah." Evan nodded. "You're a Griffith, all right."

The van swerved before Smith righted it. "What did you say?"

Tired of being jerked around by people dancing around their feelings—his mother, his cousins, Kenzie—Evan confronted this one truth he was sick of hiding. "Look. Your name is Smith Ramsey. We all know that. Just as we know you and Cash could almost be twins. You have a hate-on for him that's beyond normal. And sometimes when you look at Cash and Reid, there's this longing besides the hate and anger."

"You're full of shit." But Smith didn't sound so much angry as nervous.

"Why are you hiding it? You obviously came to Vets on the Go! with an agenda. And the guys…" Evan paused. He'd started this, but should he pursue it? Granted, he was Cash and Reid's cousin, but he could claim no blood tie to Smith. And hell, to be honest, he couldn't claim a blood tie to Cash. Not now that he knew Cash's father, Evan's father's brother, wasn't a Griffith, but the same guy Angela Griffith had gotten pregnant with when she'd had Smith.

"And the guys what?" Smith pulled off the road into an empty lot and turned to glare at Evan. "Don't stop now. Say what you gotta say."

Evan wouldn't lie. Being the recipient of Smith's ire, in a small, enclosed space, was discomfiting, to say the least. He cleared his throat. "Fine. Look, the guys are planning to talk to you about this." *I am so overstepping.* "But you have to understand. Cash and Reid, their mom, she wasn't all there."

"She seemed there to me." Smith snorted. "So there she abandoned me without a thought. Just dumped me with my aunt, a bitter old woman who fucking hated me. Oh, and I grew up thinking she was my mom because that's what I was told. I only found out a few months ago that she was actually my aunt—Angela Griffith's sister."

"Damn." Evan rubbed his chin, now understanding Smith's animosity.

"Yeah. That bitch who gave birth to me kept her sweet little boys, the ones she really loved, but threw me away. My whole life I heard how my 'cousins' were so much better than me. So special, but I was trash and would never be anything like them. That their dad had made a bad choice and married the wrong sister. Fuck, man. I got out of that house as soon as I could. Imagine my surprise when I came home and she told me to never come back because I wasn't even her son anyway."

Evan heard the buried hurt and knew the abuse Smith had suffered would make a reconciliation with his brothers even harder. "I'm so sorry, Smith."

"I don't want your pity. I want to know why you think this will have a happy ending."

"I don't." That took Smith aback. Evan continued, "I only know they were stunned to find out they had a brother. Their mother never told them. Hell, she never told them anything. Aunt Angela wasn't all there."

"What do you mean?"

"I mean she treated her sons as if they didn't exist for most of their lives. Uncle Charles used to treat Cash like shit. He beat him, yelled at him, criticized him for everything, even existing. But Reid could do no wrong. And through it all, Aunt Angela holed up in her house watching soap operas, reading books, and binging on TV. The woman lived in a fantasy world while her husband and sons were stuck with each other. And it was hell. Cash left home at sixteen, I think. So I'm sorry about your life because it sounds shitty. But they didn't have it much better."

Smith frowned, and damn but he looked exactly like Cash. It was eerie.

"Why are you here, Smith?" Evan tried again.

"I—I thought I could see why she was so into keeping

them and not me. These Marine Corps hometown heroes." The bite that normally accompanied any mention of the Griffiths wasn't there. "So she sucked at being a mom, huh?"

"You have no idea. She really messed them up. And so did their dad." Evan was about to overstep again. "They found a secret journal, going through the house after she died."

Smith's eyes narrowed.

"That's when Cash learned he wasn't Charles's son. I guess she gave you away because her husband had found out she'd cheated and that Cash wasn't his kid. They made up and had Reid a few years later. But when she got back together with Cash's—and your—real dad and got pregnant with you, she knew she couldn't keep you."

"This is so fucking bizarre." Smith barked an angry laugh. "Are you serious? How could the guy not know she was pregnant?"

"I have no idea, though I know she was always on the thin side. Maybe she hid it. Maybe he was traveling when she gave birth. All I know is Cash and Reid had no idea you even existed. You came here, all angry, resembling Cash, and it's not like they didn't wonder. But they found the journal, and it's turned their lives upside down."

Evan took a brave step and reached out to put a hand on Smith's shoulder. "Look. You and Cash share the same mom and dad. You and Reid have the same mom. I'm related to the guys through our dads being brothers. But the biological ties don't matter, Smith. Family is what you make of it. If you want them, you have two brothers and a cousin. And an aunt, because my mom is dying to meet you."

Smith's eyes widened. "Your mom knows about me?"

He nodded. "I told her about you when you first arrived, not even knowing about the journal and Aunt Angela. My mom always suspected something wasn't right about their marriage. But there was nothing she or my dad could do. She's a great mom, by the way. And she'd be a great aunt to have if you'd realize not everyone is out to get you. Some of us, me at least, would love having another guy to hang with, call family."

Smith looked so confused it hurt. Evan felt for the guy.

"Look, just sit with this. Cash and Reid are trying to figure out the best way to talk to you about it all. It would help if you didn't look like you want to strangle them every time you talk to them."

"But I do."

They both grinned at the bald confession.

"Well, Cash at least," Smith admitted. "He's such an asshole."

Evan thought it amusing neither Cash nor Smith realized how alike they were, though everyone else saw it.

"Reid isn't so bad," Smith said. "He's more...I don't know, he's smoother than Cash. Easier to talk to."

"Yeah. And think about this. They both know who you are, and they haven't said anything because they don't want to make more mistakes where you're concerned. You've been an outright dick, to *your bosses*, and you still have a job."

Smith frowned.

"With anyone else, you'd have been fired, and you know it."

Smith sighed. "I kind of wanted to see how far I could push them. Reid just backs off. Cash looks like he wants to slug me then storms away after calling me names." Smith shrugged. "Sometimes I can't help myself with him."

"Trust me, I know Cash." Evan couldn't help a chuckle.

"But Smith, you have an opportunity to get to know another side of family you never had. Quit being a fuckhead for two seconds and think about it."

"Fuckhead? Really?"

Evan just looked at him.

"Okay, fine. Look, I'll think on this. I mean, if I didn't want to talk to them at some point, I'd already have left. But I...I just don't know."

"Now you have something to think about."

"I guess."

"But you could start small."

"What do you mean?"

Evan knew his mother wanted to meet Smith. "Why don't you come to dinner with me and my mom? You can visit, ask any questions you want, and get a free meal out of it."

Smith glanced out the window. "I don't know."

"Well, the invitation's there. Think about it."

"I will."

"And do me a favor, don't tell my cousins we talked about this. You need to talk to them and work through this on your own. But now you know a little more about what you're getting into." And Evan didn't feel bad about that. Smith had had a crappy childhood, yeah. But Cash's and Reid's hadn't been much better, and Smith needed to know that.

"Fine. We never talked about any of this." Smith started up the truck and drove again. "But this doesn't mean we're best girlfriends or anything, you get me?"

Evan rested his head against the side window. "Whatever. I have more important things to worry about than how much you like or don't like me."

Smith grunted. "Gotta be a chick problem."

"You got that right. And no, I don't want to talk about it."

Smith snickered. "Like I was gonna offer." He turned on the radio. Alternative rock played a low hum. "But Evan, if you're serious about being all family-like, it wouldn't hurt if you picked up donuts and coffee now and then. Like Jordan sometimes does. And Hector. They try to buy my love."

"More like your silence," Evan grumbled.

"Yeah, 'cause they're smart like that. Learn and grow, my man. And for the record, I like 'em glazed. I can eat about six at a stretch. Just sayin'."

Evan glanced at Smith. "So you're saying I can bribe you into being a decent human being?"

"Never said anything about being decent, but if that's what helps you sleep at night, sure."

"Oh my God. You are just like Cash."

For once Smith didn't growl at the name. His evil laughter wasn't much better, but Evan had hopes for the guy.

"Six glazed donuts, huh?"

"Yep. But I'd never say no to seven."

Hours later, as Evan finished at Vets on the Go! and started his car, his phone rang. He hit the hands-free button and pulled out, more than ready to celebrate his first free weekend from work in weeks. Of course, with his luck he'd be bored to tears because Kenzie would no doubt still be ignoring him.

He groaned. Lila hadn't told him much, only that she'd been putting a good word in for him. He hadn't had much to say to her about Hector. He hadn't seen the guy in days. On a big job with his brother, Finley, and Martin, Hector had been working out in Tacoma from sunup to sundown.

"Hello?"

"Um, Evan?" Daniel's voice brightened Evan's whole day.

"Yo, Daniel. How'd the tryouts go?"

He'd been thinking about the boy since his discussion with Lila. Every time he tried to imagine a future with Kenzie, he saw the kid in it. And it didn't bother him in the slightest.

"I made the team!"

Evan cheered. "That's incredible. Way to go, man! I knew you could do it."

"Yeah. I've been practicing those moves of yours and working really hard. And…I won't lie. I kind of told the coach you were working with me, like, giving me extra coaching and that you'd help out if he needed it, no problem."

"So, you lied."

"Hell, yeah. Dude, I made the team."

Evan laughed to himself. "Daniel, it doesn't have to be a lie. I'm happy to help you practice if you want."

A pause. "Kenzie's working, so she probably won't be around after school or anything."

"Does your sister play soccer?"

"No."

"Then why would she be at your soccer field? Look, I love the sport, and you're growing on me. Like a fungus, but you know, it's not so bad."

The boy laughed.

"I can't make it every day, depending on my schedule, but I'll have a lot more time once my cousin is working again.

Should be another week and I'll go back to being behind a desk a lot more." Which bothered him, to his surprise. "So I'd welcome the chance to get on my feet."

"Yeah? Cool."

Warmed by the boy's amusement, Evan asked, "I'm sure you're celebrating tonight."

"Well, that's the other thing. I've been waiting to tell Kenzie and the girls. Kenzie's going to want to make a big deal out of it."

"It *is* a big deal."

"I know." Daniel sounded so proud, and Evan couldn't have been happier for him. "But the guys on the team planned to get together instead. I want to go, but I don't want to hurt Kenzie's feelings. We always celebrate big things together. So I was thinking maybe you could go over there and, like, distract her. Be all manly or something and make her want to be with you instead of me."

"All manly? Look, cockalorum, I *am* manly. And I've been trying…" No, best not to drag Daniel into his issues with Kenzie. "I'll deal with your sister. Tell her I was bugging you about returning some tax documents. And that I was bugging you because she's been too busy to return my calls."

"Oh, blowing you off, is she? And hey, what's a cocka— that thing you said?"

"Believe it or not, *cockalorum* is a real word meaning a self-important dickhead." *I've had to resort to Google to keep up with a thirteen-year-old. I'm embarrassed at myself. Still, it's a great word.* "It applies to you, trust me."

"Hmm. I think someone has been using the dictionary. So lame, asshat."

Evan groaned. "I know." He talked over Daniel's laughter.

"And for the record, your sister is not blowing me off." *She's totally blowing me off.* "We're both busy people."

"Sure thing, slick."

"Do you want this favor or not?" he growled.

"Sure, sure. Kidding, man. So I'll tell her to text you. And maybe you can let me know when you guys are together, and then I'll drop the news I made the team."

"That works. Of course, that's if your sister takes the bait."

"Oh, she'll take it. Thanks, Evan. About the soccer and everything."

"No problem. It's been fun, you know, me running rings around you pathetic teenagers." He laughed with Daniel. "Have you talked to Will, or would you rather I—"

"No thanks. I mean, I really do like Will. He's a great guy, but he's more into football than *fútbol*, you know? You can tell he played linebacker in high school. And he's a little clumsy on the field."

"Oh, you noticed."

"Yeah. But he's been nice, so don't tell him I said that. Besides, he's a lawyer so he's probably busy. Later, man. And thanks."

"Will's busy, but I'm not?" Evan asked himself since Daniel had disconnected.

But the realization he might have Kenzie all to himself that night made him drive faster. Time to go home, shower, and plan. And maybe he'd stop by the market on the way and grab a few things. With Kenzie, he planned on pulling out all the stops.

CHAPTER 20

KENZIE GLARED AT EVAN'S DOOR AS SHE POUNDED ON IT. He'd better get ready to change his plans because she had no intention of hurrying away while he got ready to head out for a night on the town with "his bros, looking for a good time," according to her brother. Her initial plan to apologize for avoiding him had turned into a need for a confrontation.

How could she think herself falling in love with someone who had plans to troll around town looking for a hookup?

Evan opened the door, freshly showered by the look of him, and like clockwork her body flooded with endorphins and those blasted take-me-I'm-yours hormones. Even in jeans and a T-shirt, the man made her drool.

"Well, well, look who finally showed at my door."

"Oh, sorry. Am I ruining your plans?" She stomped inside, trying to ignore the fact that Evan politely stood aside, always the gentleman. He gently closed the door behind her.

Evan looked her over, his warm eyes approving. "Want something to drink? Or did you just want to grab your paperwork and go?"

"What?"

He sighed. "I told Daniel I could have easily dropped off your files whenever it's more convenient for you."

"I'm sorry," she said, trying to be as polite and calm as he acted. "Am I interrupting something? Getting ready to go out with your bros?"

He frowned. "Ah, no. Hold on." He went into his office

and returned with a stack of papers and her thumb drive, which she'd forgotten to take with her last time. "It's all there. I also listed a few things I think you could do to save yourselves more money in the long run."

"Oh, um, thanks."

She looked him over, missing him when she'd done her best to ignore how he made her feel.

"What's this about me going somewhere with my 'bros'?"

"Something Daniel said." She frowned. Her brother hadn't mentioned the soccer tryouts, but he didn't seem depressed, so she didn't think he'd been booted from the team. Then again, he hadn't announced he'd made it either. She wanted to know but also didn't want to stir up bad feelings. He'd tell her what was going on when he wanted her to know.

"How is he?" Evan crossed his arms over his chest, making his biceps bulge.

She swallowed and forced herself not to look below his eyes. "He's good. He's been practicing hard for soccer. But you and Will helped him out this week, didn't you?"

"Yeah. It was a lot of fun." Evan smiled, his gray eyes bright. Inviting. "I hadn't realized how much I missed the sport until Will dragged me onto the team. And helping out Daniel and his guys was great. I can't thank you enough for starting it all."

"Oh, well, sure." She studied him, looked around, and realized he had a fresh bouquet of pink tulips on the dining table. "Who are the flowers from?"

He blinked. "You think someone sent me flowers?"

"Well, that or you bought them for yourself." Not

something she'd attribute to a guy like Evan, who had such a cold, white-and-chrome kind of bachelor pad. "Did you?"

"No, I didn't buy them for myself." He smiled.

Annoyed he seemed to like her jealousy, she put her hands on her hips then straightened, pulling back on her hostility. The man hadn't done anything to earn it. Not really. That she knew of.

God, I am better than this. She cleared her throat and offered in a polite voice, "Oh. Right. Well, thanks for the files."

"So you don't want anything to drink? Or eat?"

"Eat?"

"You know. Dinner. I ordered some food from Pecado Bueno because I didn't want to cook. Want some?"

She frowned. "I thought you didn't like Mexican food."

He shrugged. "It's not all bad. I like some places." He glanced away for a moment. "Here. Give me those." He took the files from her and sat her down at the table, right in front of those beautiful tulips.

"I like your flowers."

He grinned and returned with two plates. One full of a taco platter she normally ordered when she went there, the other with egg rolls and rice noodles on it.

"Oh, I usually order myself more than one thing, in case I change my mind."

She saw the flush on his cheeks and marveled that she'd been such an idiot. "You got me Mexican food. And the flowers." *You did my taxes. You treat me like you really care for me.* Her nerves fluttered.

"Do you like them?" He tried to pretend like it was no big deal.

"Evan, did you lure me over here to feed me?"

"Maybe." He winked. "And maybe I just wanted to see you again. You know, since you've been too busy to see, talk, or breathe my same air all week." He lifted a brow.

She sighed. "I like you so much it scares me. Happy?"

"Actually, yeah." He took a big bite of his egg roll. "Eat. You look too skinny."

"Flattery will get you nowhere." She dug into her plate but could only get a few bites before she had to tell him. "I'm sorry. So sorry I didn't talk to you. I was just nervous and weirded out."

He didn't seem to have any problem eating, she noticed, a little annoyed. "Continue."

When she just looked at him, he nodded to the flowers. "Yes, pink. I got you a dozen pink tulips, and there are a dozen more red ones in the kitchen, in case I got the color wrong. And yes, I really did order the Mexican food just for you. I *hate* tacos." He looked at her like he loved her. And that freaked her out even more. "So please, continue with your apology. And feel free to grovel if you want."

She couldn't help laughing. "You're such a cute jerk. I want to smack you and kiss you at the same time."

He opened his arms wide. "I won't hit you back, but be warned, I will kiss you."

Just as she planned to knock him a good one, her phone rang. "Hold that thought."

"Hey, Kenzie," her brother said. "Where are you? Are you at home?"

She frowned. "I'm at Evan's. Where are you?" Because if he was at home, he'd know she wasn't there.

"Oh, okay. Hey, good news. I made the team!"

"Daniel! That's so awesome! I'm proud of you." She said to Evan, "He made the team."

"Great news." Evan looked happy for her brother. "That's because the douchenozzle has skills," he said loudly enough to be heard.

She laughed and to her brother said, "Ignore him, Daniel."

"No, he's right. About my skills, I mean. Um, would it be okay if I went out with some of my new teammates?"

Since she'd been on the verge of dropping everything to return home and celebrate with him, it took her a moment to process. "You want to go out with friends?" Her antisocial criminal hacker brother now had more than one friend?

"Rafi's coming too. He's going to be the team manager. So is it okay if I go out?"

She'd had some issues with Rafael in the past because the boy had been getting into trouble at school. But he'd also been kind to her brother, so she'd let it slide. "Oh, um, sure."

"We can celebrate tomorrow. Maybe we could have everyone over, like, the girls and their guys. And Evan could come. Ask him."

"You want me to ask Evan if he wants to come over for dinner tomorrow night to celebrate you making the team?" Evan's wide smile was all the answer she needed. "He said yes."

Daniel whooped. "Tonight is so great. Okay, I gotta go. I'll be back by eleven, I swear. We're hanging at Sean's house and partying. No drugs or alcohol, I promise. His dad's the coach, and both his parents will be there," he said with exaggerated patience.

"Fine. How are you getting there?"

"Lila said she'd take me. Hold on." She heard him yell his request to Lila and rolled her eyes. "Yeah, she'll take me. Text her if you don't believe me."

"I believe you. Have fun."

"You too, and be safe."

A text came in from Lila: Daniel made team! Hector & me tkg dork 2 & fm soccer pty. Hv fn LOVE SLAVE. Trust Lila to spell out the important parts.

Kenzie texted back, Thx and back at ya, penis wrshpr, and absently asked her brother, "Be safe?"

In a lower voice, he said, "Use birth control, okay?"

"*Daniel.*" He disconnected on laughter.

"What's wrong?" Evan asked.

"N-nothing." Kenzie cleared her throat, now unable to think of anything but kissing Evan again. "So, um, what were we talking about before?"

"You were about to throw yourself in my arms, apologize for grievously wounding my fragile male ego, tell me how much you can't live without me, then have your wicked way with me. But you can go in any order you want."

She made up her mind and stood. "You, come with me." She marched through the living area to the stairs, went up without looking behind her, then entered his bedroom and waited for him.

He was a little slower than she'd have thought, but desire shone from his eyes, no question.

"Get naked and get on the bed."

She left him to use his bathroom, taking off her clothes and giving herself a quick finger-brush of toothpaste, not wanting to gross him out by tasting like hated tacos.

And what mutant didn't like Mexican food?

She smiled at the thought then joined Evan in the bedroom. He lay back on his bed, completely naked, aroused, and waiting for her. At the sight of her, he leaned up on his elbows. "So you're going to grovel now?"

Kenzie laughed. "I'm so sorry, Evan. I shouldn't have ignored you, but who knew your fragile ego would take such a beating?" She crawled over him, saw him swallow, and felt powerful.

"I'm a weak man where you're concerned," he admitted, his voice gravelly. "I'm trying really hard to think about soccer, football, my new cousin, anything so I don't come too fast."

"Is that a problem for you?" It hadn't been the last time they'd made love.

"It is when I'm around you and unable to kiss you. Or be with you. Or fuck you nice and slow."

She shivered, loving the sound of his need. "I missed you, Evan."

"God, I missed you too." When she kissed his chest, he hissed his pleasure. "Slower, baby. Man, I missed you. And not just for sex."

She paused then caressed his chest, teasing his nipples and loving the way he shifted under her. He liked that. So she kissed him there, the way he did to her.

A large hand palmed her lower back, pulling her body in to graze his erection.

"Fuck. You drive me crazy. I could come so easily right now."

"Did you touch yourself and think about me?" She couldn't believe she'd asked that, but the thought of Evan masturbating turned her way on.

"Oh yeah. But it's not the same."

She sat back on her thighs, straddling him. "Show me."

He watched her as he fisted himself, his hand swallowing up his cock. And he dragged it up and down while staring at her, the moisture at his tip a testament to his arousal.

"Sit over me, Kenzie, I want to come inside you."

"But you'll come too soon, you said."

"I probably will. But I'll make sure you come with me."

Granted, it wouldn't take her long. But she wanted to make things right between them. The man was so thoughtful. He bought her flowers and dinner, messaged, and called. He'd done her freakin' taxes.

"We'll come together. Don't you worry about that." She moved his hand away and replaced it with hers.

"Oh yeah. That's it." He moaned. "Be with me, Kenzie."

So beautiful, that honest desire. But instead of straddling his hips, she leaned down and put her mouth over him.

He swore, and she loved him, sucking him deep to the back of her throat then gloving him with her mouth. She drew faster, harder, and cupped his velvety sac, not surprised to find him so hard.

His sexy moans had her wet and ready for him, but she wanted to feel him come first.

"Kenzie, honey, I'm so close."

The last warning she figured she'd get. But she didn't want to pull away.

Kenzie drew down, rubbing faster, and felt the burst of seed hit her tongue as he moaned and came, jerking into her mouth.

She sucked him down, touching him everywhere she could reach, until he pulled her away, breathing hard.

Kenzie couldn't get over how sexy it felt to be with him, how right.

But she didn't have long to ponder because he turned her so that she lay under him and kissed her.

Hungry to feel him, she drew him into her mouth, wondering if tasting himself might turn him off.

If anything, his moans deepened, and she was soon squirming under him, wanting more.

He pulled back to look down at her and brushed her hair from her face. "You don't want to hear this. I know that. But I can't help it."

The emotion in his eyes held her spellbound. "Evan?"

He cupped her face, watching her with so much affection. "I love you, Kenzie."

Shocked, pleased, and scared all over again, she didn't know how to respond, but Evan didn't let her. He kissed her with so much passion, she felt lightheaded. Then he proceeded to show her. With every kiss and caress, he stirred her to a fevered arousal.

He teased her nipples, sucked them into hard points, and trailed down her body, kissing her belly, her hips, then moved straight between her legs. He drew her clit into his mouth and slid his finger inside her, fucking her while licking her up.

And just when she neared orgasm, he backed away, leaving her frustrated and lost. Then he started again, kissing her legs, the insides of her thighs, and moving back up to her breasts.

He brought her up and down so many times, leaving her impossibly wet, her body screaming for release.

He'd ignored her swearing and pleading, until she'd had

enough. She maneuvered him onto his back and bore down on his once-again stiff cock. The satisfaction of finally being filled eased her frustration and started her on a quick climb toward satisfaction.

"Finally. Took you long enough," he teased, though his expression was strained. "That's it, baby. I want to feel you come all over me." He put his fingers between her legs, and she rode him hard.

On fire to feel him, to have him reach that pinnacle with her, she leaned down and kissed him when she came.

He moaned into her mouth, snapping his hips up and gripping her to hold her still.

She tore her mouth away, gasping for breath, lost in the taste and smell of him. Like heaven, if only she could get her heart to stop racing.

"What do you wear that makes you smell so damn good?" she asked when she could catch a breath.

His low chuckle vibrated through her. "I call it Eau de Kenzie."

"Funny."

He hugged her and rotated his hips, pushing inside her still. "God, you feel so good. I missed this, Kenzie. I missed you."

I love you, he'd said.

She wanted to talk about that, but not yet. Not until she'd wrapped her mind around it. It was one thing to think she might be falling for him, another to know he'd already fallen for her. It would be Bryce 2.0, except this time the man had said it first.

And Evan isn't Bryce.

After they'd managed to clean up and come back to

bed together, Evan held her in his arms. "Now, before that brain makes a mess of everything between us, I wanted to be honest. I don't expect anything from you. I love you."

Damn it. He'd said it again. Her heart wouldn't stop racing.

"I like being with you. I like being with Daniel. I can't prove I'll never leave you, I can only show you that I won't."

She thought about him sticking by his sick fiancée, seeing her through her cancer. About how he helped his mother and felt it important to be there for his cousins. How he'd helped her when she needed it, and even after they'd had sex he wanted to do more for her.

"I—"

"Shh." He put a hand over her mouth. "Don't talk and ruin my moment."

She laughed against his hand. Then she licked it.

"You're so gross." He wiped his hand over her face. "My feelings are my responsibility, not yours. I just wanted you to know. Kenzie, I don't fall in and out of love at the drop of a hat. I also don't date indiscriminately. I'm not with you for sex or money or your incredibly high-maintenance friends."

"Incredibly high?" What had they done to him she didn't know about?

"Or for your talented brother, who really is good at soccer, by the way. I'm impressed with that as much as I am his phone skills."

"You're never going to let that go, are you?"

"Nope. And I'm also not with you for that hot piece of property on Fremont. And I'm not teasing you about that. The house is old and has problems, but your property value is high, and you have to know that.

"I make my own money, drive a hot car, and have no problem getting a girl." He let out a gasp when she yanked on a few of his chest hairs. "I'm not bragging, I'm being honest. The simple truth is I love you."

She tensed again.

"And now I'm done talking about it until you want to discuss how you feel. Or we might never talk about it. I'm okay with that."

She had to see his face, so she leaned up and saw a smile so beautiful, so real, it brought tears to her eyes.

"I'd like you and I to just take our relationship—because that's what this is, two people exclusively dating who like being together—day by day. You know how I feel. Now I'd like you to set the pace about what we do and how we go from here."

"I... You do?"

"Yes. I'm good with what I have with you. Would I like more? Sure. But if you don't want that, what's the point of talking about it? My feelings happened pretty soon for me. You're not sure what you feel."

I love you, you big dope. And it scares me spitless.

"You know all this, do you?"

"Yes." He grinned. "I also know how it annoys you when I tell you what you think. So maybe you're less weirded out by my confession and more aggravated by me. Yes?"

"I"—she blew out a breath—"yes."

He laughed and hugged her tight. Then he sat her up over him. "Let's talk, okay? I want to tell you about meeting my mom's boyfriend. And I want to know what you've been up to without me this past week."

"Okay."

"And I really just want to look at your breasts, so if I zone out while you're talking, know it's your boobs taking my attention."

"Evan."

He sighed. "You're so pretty." He cupped a breast, and her body heated up. "Man, I could make love to you for days and not get tired."

Make love. Not *fuck* or *do* or *take.*

Evan was a romantic, one who confused her on a level beyond comprehension. He had to be too good to be true.

"Are you a serial killer?"

He paused then reached for her other breast. "Ah, not that I know of."

"Married? Have a bunch of children by tons of women?"

"Nope and nope." He grinned.

"Are you deeply in debt?" She brightened. "Or a career criminal? Like, you owe the IRS tons of money under fake names?"

"Sorry, but no." He rubbed her nipple back and forth, and her body stirred. "Have I told you how much I love touching you?"

She knocked his hand away so she could think. "Stop that."

"Sorry. Look, if you want to get even, you can touch my nipples. Or my dick. Dealer's choice."

She bit back a laugh. "Evan, focus."

"What?"

"And don't try looking innocent with me, buddy. You're naked and getting hard again. I can feel you against my leg."

"It's your fault. Those breasts… I love your body."

There went that L word again.

She cleared her throat. "You were going to tell me about your mom's new boyfriend while I try not to feel strange about being naked while we talk."

He blinked. "Is that weird for you? Why should it be? You're beautiful."

She blushed. "Thanks. But yes, it's weird. I've never talked while naked with anyone."

He watched her and asked slowly, "Not even with Bryce?"

CHAPTER 21

EVAN KNEW HE'D TAKEN A HUGE RISK TONIGHT. BUT damn if he could hold it in any longer. He loved Kenzie, and she needed to know that. Oh, he'd seen the panic on her face when he'd said it, but then they'd been swept away by a feeling they both knew well. Her orgasms were fucking hot. Besides, watching her come, which had to be the most amazing thing on the planet, made him feel good for giving her such pleasure.

He'd taken a chance telling her everything up front, not waiting to see if she felt anything back. But Evan truly believed what he'd said. He didn't expect or want her to repeat words of love to make him feel better. But she should know what came from him and that he wanted nothing but to make her happy.

Bringing up Bryce had to be done. He needed to see if she'd talk about him or if she'd ever get over the loser.

"Bryce? You want to talk about Bryce while I'm naked? While *you're* naked?"

"For the record, you said his name twice, so technically you're already doing it."

"You should probably slap me," she muttered.

"Huh?"

"Nothing." She blushed. "Fine. You want to talk about him?"

"No. I want you to talk about him. I'm just here to listen."

She frowned. "Don't try to be all mature and sensible on me. I've heard you call my brother fartnozzle."

"True." He grinned. "Fine. Tell me about the fuckhead loser you used to date. The one that broke your heart and turned you against all men. Except not all men, because you've turned into, and I quote, 'a love slave and penis worshipper.' Although penis worshipper sounds like a pretty good thing to me."

"Stop." She laughed. "I don't think I can handle talking about Lila and Rachel while I'm sitting on your penis."

"Would it help if it was inside you?" Oh yeah, that got him hard.

"Evan, shut up." She shifted, and he closed his eyes and sucked in a breath. "Finally. Yappy, aren't you?"

He blinked his eyes open, happy to see her looking calmer and not so terrified of her ex's name.

"I met Bryce after breaking up with a guy I'd dated for a few months. The guy I broke up with was boring, to be honest. Bryce wasn't. He was nice, he made me laugh, and he was nice to Daniel. We met at a coffee shop and hit it off.

"He was an engineer and made nice money. I'm a graphic designer and not rolling in dough. He told friends about me, and I got some jobs that helped the business at a low point. I'm a contractor, and we have good times and lean times. So if you're dating me for my money, think again." She glanced around her. "I'm pretty sure you're paying three times what I am for your rent."

He nodded. "And let's not forget how crappy your car is compared to mine."

Her eyes narrowed. He bit back a grin. "Anyway, Bryce and I started dating. But because Daniel had met him when I did, Bryce was in both our lives from the beginning. At first, Bryce was nice to Daniel, probably to impress me. But then he seemed to take to my brother. Daniel isn't clingy, but he and I are a team."

Evan still winced every time he heard the word "clingy," thinking of his mother's accusation.

"I always put Daniel first. And I've been accused of hiding behind my brother when it comes to men. I'm sorry, but it's not fear that has me taking care of him or putting him first, it's love."

He had to say something. "I understand. I've had a few similar conversations about my devotion to my mother."

Kenzie lost a bit of her tension. "Right. You understand." That seemed to settle her. "Bryce moved in a year and a half after we'd started dating. He also started looking at moving, expanding his career. I had told him from the beginning my life was here with Daniel. My career is established, my friends—who are my family—are here. I have roots."

"Like a wise old tree."

"I'm sorry. Old?"

"Ignore me."

"I would if you'd stop talking." She wiggled again, arousing him, and smirked. "I have roots, yes. And I have yet to meet a man who'd make me want to uproot my roots for him."

"Ouch. Put in my place." He twisted an invisible key over his lips then ruined it by saying, "I'm going to be quiet now." Plus he didn't mind the "roots" comments because he had no intention of moving anytime soon either.

"Anyway, Bryce kept mentioning possibilities of starting his own company somewhere else. Or taking time off to travel and see the world and get new ideas. A lot of pie-in-the-sky nonsense. Well, not nonsense, but not something a person with a ten-year-old can do."

He stroked her legs, feeling for her.

"It wasn't that I didn't want to go. I couldn't. But Bryce couldn't see that. And he'd complain I never had enough time for him."

"You had Daniel." Easy enough to understand. Yet how could Evan judge, when he'd only been with Kenzie for so short a time? Still, he liked Daniel and couldn't see begrudging a boy his mother—which Kenzie was, for all intents and purposes—out of a sense of jealousy.

"I had, and have, Daniel." At her warning, he nodded. "Bryce and I talked about his ideas, but eventually he realized my stance. He stopped mentioning it, and I thought he'd gotten used to the idea that I couldn't move. Yet. Maybe once Daniel finished high school in another few years. Then Daniel got into some trouble hacking the school's computer. And a few companies. And then that incident with the bank."

"What?"

She flushed. "Will helped us deal with that. Anyway, Daniel's been keeping himself out of trouble. Mostly. But Bryce... We were engaged. Happy, I thought. Then one day he told me he was leaving." Her brows drew close. "He didn't want to talk about it. Hadn't given me any warning he was still having issues. I thought about it a lot, Evan." She looked sad more than angry. "Bryce never showed me anything but that we were happy, in love. He took Daniel to soccer games, to the movies. Bryce and I had date nights. Not a lot, but enough for me. Rachel and Lila liked him. It felt like a real family.

"We weren't perfect, and we both had things that meant more to one of us than the other. But he just left. One day he was there. The next day he and his things were gone."

She paused, quiet. "He didn't even say goodbye to Daniel."

A teardrop hit his chest, and Evan swore. "Aw, baby. Come here." He drew her down for a hug, feeling so bad for her. "That sucks. He was a fucking coward, and he didn't deserve you."

She hugged him, and he let her cry it out.

Muffled against his shoulder, she said, "Lila has been using aversion therapy on me. Anytime I say his name, she slaps me."

Evan laughed. "Lila's a smart one. I guess I owe you a few slaps. More if you wipe your nose against me again. Not all body fluids are sexy, Kenzie."

She smashed her face against him. "I'm so embarrassed right now from crying all over you. Don't rub it in."

"Shouldn't that be my line?" earned a hiccup and a laugh from her. He set her aside gently. "Stay right here."

He returned with some tissues. "Blow. Not me, blow your nose."

She'd tucked herself under his blanket and sat up with it covering her breasts. She stuck out her tongue at him, and he sat next to her, relieved to see her no longer so sad.

"I'm going to tell you something I never told anyone, not even my mom, okay?"

She nodded and wiped her face.

"When Rita was sick, I didn't know what to do. At first. I really loved her, Kenzie. The way you loved Bryce. It was real, and it meant something. It was a part of me. Just because she died doesn't meant the love died. So don't feel sorry for loving Bryce. It was real at the time."

She leaned forward to kiss his cheek. But even with red, puffy eyes and a snotty nose, she was beautiful to him. "Thank you. No one's ever told me that."

"Sure. Just don't love him now."

She smiled. "I don't. If he came back tomorrow and begged me to marry him, I wouldn't. We're over, and I've moved on."

"You're crying."

"Hey, you said the love is still there. I can cry for what I had. Not have. Had."

That sounded healthy to him. "True. So back to Rita. She was sick for a while, and anytime I tried to get her to see a doctor, she put me off. See, Rita's parents were doctors, her dad an oncologist, if that doesn't beat all." So ironic, still. "She knew her symptoms could have been cancerous, but she didn't want to believe. And she was estranged from her parents, so maybe that's why she put it off too. By the time she finally went in for a diagnosis—because I made her—it was too late to do anything about it.

"We were happy together, and we'd probably still be happy if she hadn't died." He'd cried all the tears he could over her. And now when he remembered her, he thought of her with love and not sadness. Well, not all sadness. "She was messy and snippy and a morning person. She loved tacos and a snarky sense of humor. She'd have loved you."

Kenzie looked taken aback for a moment then gave him a gentle smile.

"Being with her that last year, when she was so sick, was so hard. At times I almost hated her for putting me through it. Oh, not for anything she did to make me stay by her side. She did everything she could to make me leave her to die. But I wouldn't."

Kenzie reached for his hand, and Evan gripped it as he continued, "But she made me mad because she might have been able to live longer, maybe even beat her cancer if she hadn't waited. By the time they caught it, it had spread through her body. And she…" He still had a difficult time thinking about it.

"She what, Evan?" Kenzie stroked his hand.

"She tried to kill herself. I understand why she tried, but I thought, if I can stand by you through all this, why can't you stand by me?" Oh hell, his eyes were watering.

Kenzie sniffled and offered him a tissue.

"I'm not crying," he growled.

"No, of course not."

He blinked the offending tears that weren't tears away. "I cried myself dry a long time ago, and I came to peace with what happened. Losing her didn't turn me off to loving again or assuming that the next person I love might get sick and die. We all die in the end. Now I'm not saying I dove right back into the dating pool. It took me a while. Over a year and a half before I tried. But I haven't tried that hard.

"So my point with all of this is that I understand pain and betrayal. You weren't expecting him to leave. I wasn't expecting her to either. It happened. And it's okay to feel angry or sad, you know." He pushed Kenzie's hair back behind her ear, loving the fact he could do that. Touch her and see her smile. "I never want you to pretend with me. About anything."

She watched him. "Evan, do you love me?"

He didn't hesitate. "I do."

"And Daniel? What do you feel for him?"

"Honestly? I've wondered what it would be like to always have him around, because when I think of you, I think of him. Two halves, one whole. A family. He's a great kid. I always wanted a brother, and I used to pretend my cousins were mine. But a younger brother would work for me too.

"Relationships take time, I know. What I feel for you happened fast, and I'm still confused by it. But I accept it all the same." He put a hand over her heart. "You need to process all that. And by all that's holy, stop ignoring me. If you don't want to talk, just tell me you need time."

"Isn't that the same thing?" she asked.

"No. It's not." He knew the emotional crisis had passed, and now he wanted to remind her of what else they had in common. He pushed all the spent tissues to the floor and tugged the blanket down, exposing her breasts.

"Evan?" Her eyes were wide, brown flecks of desire swimming in the green depths.

"For instance, there's a difference between making love and fucking."

She licked her lips, and he could see her feeling that undeniable sexual chemistry between them. "Oh?"

"Yeah. What we did here, taking our time, feeling all that romance and a slow burn to orgasm? That's making love."

He pulled her off the bed to her feet and kissed her, showing her how much he wanted her. Wanted to imprint onto her so that she always knew she belonged with him. "But that need, the hunger that gets your pussy wet and my dick hard, that's how our bodies come together. For a good, hard fucking."

He cupped her breast and squeezed her nipple, not too hard but enough to get her attention.

She gasped, and he thrust his tongue into her mouth. Then he began mimicking what he soon planned to do with his cock.

She grabbed his dick, not one to stand by while he had all the fun.

He kissed down her throat, and she surprised him by yanking him by the hair so she could whisper, "I know. It's just feeling and fueling that need." She pushed him farther down, to kneel between her legs, and she spread her feet wider.

Evan shoved his face between her legs and ate her in earnest, letting himself take what he needed and letting her demand what she desired.

As she cried out and came against his mouth, he shoved his tongue deeper, and then, lost in her taste, he hurriedly stood and turned her to face the bed. He bent her, positioned himself behind her, and thrust deep into her as she continued to come.

She cried out, her breathy moans making him lose all sense. He was pounding into her, gripping her hips so tight, and then he was coming, shouting as he filled her up, his dick so far inside her he felt as if they'd joined as one.

"Never letting go," he murmured as he sawed in and out, the aftershocks of passion jolting him into new pleasure.

"Oh, Evan." Kenzie sounded dreamy, not upset, thank God. "I love when you do that dirty talk thing and get a little mean."

He groaned as he withdrew, loving that some of him trickled down her leg. Because he'd spent inside her. A part of her now. And maybe, someday, if he were very, very lucky, he'd plant a little someone inside her.

The love he felt bloomed anew.

"Fuck. You drained me dry, penis worshipper."

Still bent over the bed, she pressed her face into it and groaned. "Stupid Lila." Before she could rise, he put a hand on the small of her back.

"No, stay there a minute. I'm committing this picture to memory. That sweet ass, those spread thighs, and my come down your leg. Now if you could somehow turn so I'd get a shot of your breasts too, that would be perfect."

She raised her head off the mattress. "Not physically possible."

"Too bad. I hear people pay big money for pictures like that."

A moment of silence. Then she flipped around and glared. "If you ever take a picture of me, I'll... Oh, no phone?"

"What? No way. You naked is for my eyes only. God, what are you? Some kind of exhibitionist?" He pretended to be horrified and backed away. "A...love slave? That's what you are, isn't it?"

"Whatever, fucknugget. Now are you going to help me clean up or what?"

He laughed. "Come on. If you're good, I'll let you clean me. With your mouth."

"Evan, we just fucked *and* made love. How can you think about doing it again?"

He just looked at her.

"Well?" she asked.

"Duh. I'm a guy."

They spent the next week together. If not every day, every other day. Daniel had told her they looked good together, even if Evan was a little "too dopey with all the smiling." Kenzie had laughed, though she agreed Evan smiled and laughed a lot when with her. Heck, he always seemed happy, and his buoyant mood lifted her own.

He still slept at his house, and she slept at hers. For all that he'd admitted he loved her, he hadn't said it again. And she hadn't asked to hear it. It lay between them, that love. Or at least, it felt that way to her.

She sat with Lila, Hector, Rachel, and Will at Daniel's first soccer game of the season. School had started the past Wednesday, and to kick off the weekend, the freshman team had a soccer game directly after school that Friday, followed by the football team's game in a few hours.

"Am I getting overtime for this?" Lila asked. She sat awfully close to Hector.

Kenzie looked over at Rachel and nodded at her friend. She mouthed "did she or didn't she?"

"I see you talking behind my back," Lila said.

Hector put an arm around her shoulders. "Lila, if it's behind your back, how can you see anything?"

"I see all, I know all. Don't forget it."

"Told you she was mean," he said to his brother, who sat behind him with his boyfriend. "Isn't she great?"

"I think he's got a screw loose," Lafayette said to Simon. "No way my brother can keep up with a chick as hot as Lila."

"I really like your brother," Lila said to Hector.

"He's mine, woman. Hands off," teased Simon, the boyfriend.

Kenzie had liked Hector off the bat, but meeting his brother and knowing they'd come out to support Daniel just because Lila had asked them to made her like them all even more.

Kenzie looked at the field, where Evan stood saying something to Daniel, who seemed to be absorbing every word. Evan helped Daniel every day with soccer, apparently. Even if he couldn't make practice to help the team, he'd show up and take Daniel to a nearby field to work on his moves.

To her astonishment, her brother had latched onto soccer and let go of his bad hacker habits. Or so he said.

"I could help if they wanted," Will offered. He glared at the head coach on the field. "But no one asked."

Kenzie met Rachel's gaze, ready to offer an apology on Daniel's behalf, though the offer wasn't his to make.

Rachel shook her head. "Will, you can't teach the kids to tackle each other like it's football. That's why you aren't down there giving advice. Because they're not allowed to clothesline each other."

"I was just saying not to take any crap. A nudge here or there is expected."

"That's what my cousin thinks," Rachel said dryly. "You remember Red Card Caroline."

"Hey, aren't red cards bad?" Hector asked.

"Yeah." Will sighed. "But I meant well. I can teach kids what they need to know. What does Evan have that I don't?"

"Um, skills?" Lila offered.

Lafayette muffled his laughter, but Simon let loose.

Hector cleared his throat, trying to keep the peace. "You play?" He pointed to the field.

"I play on our county league team. I brought Evan into the game. He's actually pretty good."

"Cash told us Evan played in college. I'd like to see you guys sometime." Hector shared a sly glance with Lafayette that piqued Kenzie's interest.

"Sure. We have a bye next week, but our next game is two Sundays after that. You should come." He sighed, looking glum as he stared at the field. "They like my advice on the Legal Eagles."

Evan clapped Daniel on the back, then they bumped fists. Evan returned to the stands after waving to a few friendly parents.

"Hmm." Rachel leaned close to murmur, "Is it just me, or are there a lot of single soccer moms staring at your man?"

"I thought it was just me."

"Oh good. You're jealous. You should be," Lila said.

"He is fine," Lafayette said.

"I'd do him," Simon agreed.

Hector cringed. "Please, stop."

Lila laughed and kissed him on the cheek. "You're so cute." Then she leaned forward and yelled, "Take 'em out, Daniel! Kick some soccer ass, boys!"

Fans around them stared, not used to such loud, vehement cheering. Rachel and Kenzie didn't bat an eye.

"Oh, I really like her," Simon told Hector. "Lila, if things don't work out with Hector, you remember Lafayette and me, okay? Because honey, I play competitive rugby, and I would *love* to have you cheering for my team."

Lafayette grinned. "Yep. You really need to come to his next game. They're brutal. Last week one of the guys broke a collarbone."

"Oh, a death sport. I'm in."

Hector sighed. Lila leaned into him.

Will expressed some interest in watching and learning the sport as Evan sat down and asked, "What did I miss?"

Rachel ticked off her fingers. "Lila's going to watch

Simon's next rugby game, Will is fuming because the coach no longer wants him to teach the boys to tackle each other—"

"That's not what I said."

"And Kenzie's jealous of all the soccer moms staring at your fine ass."

Evan grinned and said to Lafayette, "Did you know I'm an MMFA? A Moving Man with a Fine Ass. It's a thing."

Hector turned to Lila. "What about me?"

"Oh, honey. Your ass is just fine, but there are so many other parts I could worship just as well."

Kenzie smirked, and Rachel handed over the five bucks they'd bet just yesterday and swore.

"What's that about?" Evan asked.

"I'll tell you later."

The whistle blew, and Daniel's team got possession of the ball.

Kenzie grabbed Evan's hand when Daniel nearly scored, but the goalie caught it.

She liked the feel of Evan holding her. She looked down at their interlaced fingers then caught his warm smile.

"I love this."

She could see he meant it, and that joy in just being a part of her world moved something in her. Another brick guarding her heart crumbled. "Me too."

Lila screamed. Daniel was open and running down the left side of the field with the ball.

They all cheered, the noise deafening from Kenzie's section in the bleachers.

Her small family that seemed to get bigger—and better—with each new addition.

And the game was on.

CHAPTER 22

EVAN COULDN'T BELIEVE DANIEL HAD SCORED TWICE IN his first game. The celebration they were having back at Kenzie's house was epic.

Jokes, teasing, laughter, and more competition, where Hector and Lafayette tried to beat each other throwing a stupid beanbag through a hole in a wooden board, took up a good portion of the evening.

He laughed as Will tried to put Rachel in a headlock, only to watch her climb him the way she'd done Lila not too long ago.

"Hey, Evan." Daniel joined him on the back porch and watched the wackiness in the backyard.

"Mouthbreather." He'd been dying to use that one since Smith had called him that the other day.

Daniel grinned. "Not bad. So, you enjoying the party?"

"You mean, sharing the greatness that is you and your magic foot? Yes, I am, thanks."

Daniel took a bow, and Evan laughed. "The game was hard. I still can't believe we won."

"By your teammate's last-minute goal. Nice assist, by the way."

"You going to tell me everything I did wrong?"

"Not tonight. Tonight you celebrate. Tomorrow... tomorrow I need a favor."

"Sure, what?"

"I think it's time I took Kenzie to meet my mom."

"Yeah?" Daniel didn't look upset about that. Which made Evan realize the kid had adapted to having him around. A good thing.

"Yeah. I told her all about you guys. She thinks Lila and Rachel are funny. And that maybe Lila has serial-killer tendencies we should all be aware of."

"Dude, that's a given." Daniel laughed. "But she's pretty gone over Hector. I can't believe he lets her talk to him like that."

"Lets her?"

They watched Lila put her hands on her hips and taunt Hector, who took it for a solid minute. Once he'd tossed his beanbag, he dragged Lila close and shut her up with a kiss.

The crowd around them went wild, and Lila, though embarrassed, wore a goofy grin.

"He's the man. But with those muscles, it's easy to see." Daniel gave Evan a less-than-impressed once-over. And Evan had to admit no one did scorn quite like a thirteen-year-old.

"I know you did not just mock my manliness." Evan flexed to impress, but Daniel yawned.

"Whatever, stick man."

"Oh? Let's see your guns."

Daniel did a few poses, none of which showed him to be anything but a skinny kid. He finished, looking proud of himself.

And Evan laughed out loud. "Oh man, I feel like I'm looking at myself eighteen years ago."

"So you're all I have to look forward to?" Daniel's dismissive stare made Evan laugh even harder.

"You are so like your sister. Obnoxious yet oddly charming."

"You think Kenzie's obnoxious?" Daniel blinked. "And I'm charming?"

"Well, she thinks she's better than me at math, sometimes. And I have to remind her I'm the accountant."

Daniel cocked his head, looking puzzled.

"What?"

He glanced around him then asked, "But if you insult her, doesn't that make her not want to like you? I mean, if I liked a girl, I'd probably compliment her a lot. Or maybe, I don't know, pretend I liked stuff she liked. Or something."

"Ah. I see." The boy had a crush on someone. "Well, the thing with girls is—"

"Yes? What is the thing with girls?" Kenzie asked from behind him.

Evan and Daniel jumped, not having heard her approach.

"Kenzie, Daniel and I are talking."

She frowned. "But I'm a girl."

"Yes, a very pretty one. Who bakes the best cookies and is ignoring her guests." Just as she started scowling, he added, "Rachel was talking smack about you. I tried to defend you, but—"

"Hey, you. Yeah, Rachel, I'm talking to you." She stormed over to the group.

Daniel was in awe. "You totally deflected that."

"It's a gift." Evan sipped his soda, not drinking beer tonight since he'd said he planned on driving home soon.

Daniel kept waiting for him to sleep over, but so far, Evan and Kenzie weren't doing much more than kissing or holding hands in front of him, staying nights at their respective houses. And the kisses were short. Not that Daniel wanted to see any tongue action, but he would have liked to see them moving toward being a real couple.

He liked Evan. A lot. Evan was real with him, not trying to be his best friend or anything but not ignoring him or trying to get Kenzie all to himself. Kenzie had shared a few things Evan had told her, about how much it had hurt Evan to lose his fiancée to cancer. About how he still loved and took care of his mom. About how he worked hard and had plenty of money, to somehow ease Daniel's conscience in case Daniel might think Evan was out to steal from them.

He didn't know. He only knew Evan had become his friend, and not just because of Kenzie.

"So you were saying about girls…?"

"Oh, right." Evan put the soda down. He looked dressed up even when he wasn't. Daniel wondered if he could be like that. "Girls, under all their illogical weirdness, are people too. But you need to be straight with them. Pretending you like something some girl does, just to get her attention, is one thing. But then you have to keep pretending you like it when you're dating, and then it's lying. Lying and relationships don't work."

"Well, I get that. But what if you, say, liked a girl but she didn't know you existed? I mean, how would you get her to talk to you if you say she's obnoxious? Besides, even if she is, you might still like her." Because Pam Webber was totally cute and sarcastic, and she loved computers. Sometimes she snorted when she laughed, which always made him smile. Plus she'd changed over the summer, looking more grown-up. Which he liked a lot too.

"What would I do? Find what you have in common and try to talk to her about it. I know girls like to travel in packs, which makes it tough to get one alone."

"Well, typically in nature, the hunter separates the weak one from the herd and takes it down. Should I do that?"

"You lost me."

Daniel felt stupid. "Well, that's what they showed on the nature channel. This awesome lion took down a wildebeest and didn't get trampled or anything."

"Unless you want to date a wildebeest, I don't suggest taking her down. Tiger." Evan snickered.

Daniel tried not to blush.

"I'm messing with you. No. You like a girl, you talk to her when she's alone, in between classes or at her locker. Or in a club. And you talk about the things you have in common. What does she like that you like? Do you know?"

"Computers."

"Perfect. So you talk about computers, and then you segue into asking her favorite drink or food. She tells you, and you ask her if she'd like to get that food or drink and talk more about computers. See, the key is to *talk to her*. To be honest and be yourself. Because there's no point trying to get a girl to like you just because she's pretty but as smart as a doorknob or as mean as a drunken Lila."

"Oh, too true."

"You want her to be someone you can think about being with for more than just kissing…or whatever."

Daniel felt his cheeks catch on fire.

"That stuff is nice too. But it's nicer with someone you like a lot, or love."

"Like you love Kenzie?" Daniel pressed.

"Yep."

Daniel couldn't believe the guy had admitted it. Holy crap, that was *huge*. He waited. "Does she know?"

Evan shook his head. "Uh-uh. That's between me and your sister. But my point is that girls like compliments, sure. Everyone does. But you want to be real. And another thing. Most girls like to be complimented about more than how pretty they are. Try to see beyond the superficial."

"Yeah, yeah. More than T&A, I get it." At Evan's raised brow, Daniel muttered, "I know about sex stuff."

"Good." Evan watched the party, still smiling.

"Hey, Evan. You wanted a favor?"

"What? Oh, right. My mom wants to meet Kenzie."

"Cool. So you want me to occupy myself while she's gone. Dude, I do that all the time. I—"

"And you. My mom wants to meet Kenzie and you, so do you think you could join us for brunch tomorrow morning? I know it's a lot to ask, and my mom's kind of old and probably boring to a teenager, but it would mean a lot to me."

Daniel just stared, puzzled and...happy. Warmth unfurled because, just, wow. "You sure?"

Evan frowned. "Did I stutter? Look, I know it's an imposition, but—"

"No, no. It's all cool. Gotta be there for your mom, right?" *So stupid to feel giddy about Evan asking to introduce me to his mom.*

Evan nodded. "Yeah. I appreciate it. I haven't told Kenzie yet, though. She's still a little weird about dating me."

"A little?"

Evan laughed. "Okay, a lot. So let me break it to her. But I'll pick you guys up at eleven. Be ready."

"So do I need to wear a tie or anything?"

Evan put an arm around him and squeezed, and Daniel felt that hug all the way to his feet, grounding him to this moment he'd never forget.

"Nah. But if your clothes were clean and didn't have any holes, that would be cool."

"S-sure." Daniel coughed and quickly excused himself. "See you tomorrow!" He raced inside, feeling edgy and teary and plain excited for no reason that he could think of but that he'd found something in Evan's companionship. Something that might have a shot at growing, if Kenzie would just deal with her feelings for the guy.

Daniel sighed. He'd have to keep an eye on his sister and hope she didn't mess this up. Because Evan was the closet thing to a father—well, older brother—he'd had that felt genuine in forever. Bryce not included. And he didn't want that to change.

Kenzie had changed her clothes four times. The fact that her brother wore a collared shirt and jeans instead of a T-shirt and shorts had at first unnerved her. Now it terrified her. Daniel had fallen. She had seen him last night standing with Evan, a bad case of hero worship on his face. He talked about nothing but his soccer game or Evan all night and all morning, and her nerves were shot.

God, why did Evan want her and Daniel to meet his mother?

From her bed, where Daniel lounged, waiting, he said, "So Evan told me his mom likes apple fritters from Sofa's Bakery. Is that why you got up so early and bought a bunch?"

She'd also had them add some other sugary treats so it wouldn't seem like she was trying to impress his mom. Which she wasn't. Not really. She was just being a thoughtful guest.

She came out dressed in a simple floral sundress with a cornflower-blue cardigan in case it got cold.

"Wow. You look nice."

Kenzie froze. "Too nice? Too dressy? I should change."

Daniel groaned. "Why are girls so weird?"

A car horn beeped from outside, and he shot off the bed. "Finally. Hurry up, Kenzie. I'm taking the bakery box to the car."

She had to go in what she had on, so she added a spritz of perfume, patted her hair, and forced herself to calm down. She grabbed her purse and keys, locked the door behind her, then joined Evan and Daniel in the car.

Evan didn't comment on her attire, though he did smile at her, so she didn't feel overdressed. To Daniel, he said, "Nice shirt. I have one like it somewhere. I can't find it, and I swear I left it hanging up at work, then my cousin wore an identical shirt to work a week later. I see him wearing it, I'm stealing it back."

"Yeah, can't let him get away with that."

He glanced in the rearview and gave her brother a sly smile. "Remember that phone trick you played on me?"

"No," Kenzie said before her brother could answer. "He is not getting into trouble again."

"No, you're right. I just meant he could teach me how to do it."

"Ha." She didn't believe that for a second but pretended not to see Evan and Daniel both grinning. She loved the fact that the pair had bonded. It made her feel so good inside. Because when it came to her feelings for Evan, she was still all over the place. Ecstatic, scared, unsure.

Take your pick.

"Um, something I need to tell you guys," Evan said. "I didn't know until earlier today, and I hope it's okay."

"What? What is it?" She must have sounded odd because both Evan and Daniel were looking at her strangely.

"Nothing major. I just wanted to let you know we won't be the only guests there today."

Thank God. Feeling a load of pressure off her shoulders, she let out a silent breath of relief. "No problem, Evan."

"Yeah, no problem. Who else is coming?" Daniel asked.

"Jerome, my mom's boyfriend, and maybe my cousin, Smith."

Daniel asked, "Smith? That's his first name?"

"Yep. He's big and loud, curses a lot, and can look pretty mean. But he's a nice guy inside."

"Oh, sure." Kenzie wondered if this was the secret cousin she'd heard about.

"He's new to the family." So it was.

Then she realized Jerome would be there. "You never did tell me about Jerome," she said to Evan and was instantly reminded of why they'd been so distracted. Telling each other of their buried pain, then going at it like rabbits.

A heated gaze met her own. "Yeah. Well, you'll meet him this morning and can make your own judgment. And remember, this is my mom. Not my grandmother. She has white hair and is older than me by a lot. But she's my *mom*."

"Evan, I see you looking at me in the mirror." Daniel fiddled with his collar as they pulled into the driveway of an older but very nice house in Queen Anne. "I'm not deaf. I swear not to call her your grandma."

They walked to the door, Kenzie's men—Evan and Daniel—wearing nice collared shirts and jeans. Daniel even wore boat shoes, not the ratty sneakers he normally wore everywhere.

She caught Evan's knowing grin and smiled.

He grabbed her hand and squeezed just as the door opened and a pretty older lady with Evan's smile stared at them.

"Hey, Mom." He leaned in to kiss her on the cheek but kept hold of Kenzie's hand. "This is Kenzie, and this is Daniel."

"Hello." Kenzie tugged, but he wouldn't let her go.

Daniel nodded. "Hi, Mrs. Griffith." He held out the box. "These are for you from us."

"Call me Jane, dear. Oh, that's so sweet." She took Daniel by the arm and gently pulled him inside. "You're a tall one, aren't you? It's so nice to meet you. I've heard all about your soccer skills, young man."

"Yeah?" Daniel sounded pleasantly surprised.

"Oh, yes. Evan's told me how good you are. I hear you scored two goals at your first game too."

Daniel gave her a shy smile. "I did."

"Well, then you have to tell Jerome all about it. He's a big Sounders fan, you know."

She led them inside, and Kenzie was pulled back into a warm body then felt a kiss at her temple. "Relax. You already have an in with my mom. It's me. I'm your in."

She laughed and let go of the tension she hadn't realize she'd been carrying.

His mother was so sweet and pretty and had so many mannerisms similar to Evan's. It just felt so important that she like Kenzie.

Jerome seemed as different from Jane Griffith as he could be. Dark where she was light. Bald, handsome, and so masculine. He had some kind of Mediterranean or Middle Eastern ancestry. His dark eyes gleamed when he caught sight of Evan.

"Hey, Evan. So good to see you again." He stood behind Jane, his hands on her shoulders.

Kenzie noticed the tight grip and wondered if Jerome was nervous and, if so, if Evan had given him a hard time.

But Evan didn't act as if he noticed. He stepped forward.

Jerome watched Jane set the box on the counter then accepted a big hug from Evan. He seemed to ease into the embrace and moved back after a moment looking much more relaxed.

"Well, that's all right." Jerome's wide smile moved to Daniel. "Is this the soccer star?"

Daniel's clear pride eased all of Kenzie's fears. Her brother would do just fine here. "Yes, sir. I'm Daniel."

Where the hell had her brother picked up *sir*? She gaped, and Evan closed her jaw with a low laugh.

"And your pretty sister. Kenzie, is it?" Jerome held out a hand to her.

She took it, and he clasped it in both of his. "It's so nice to meet you."

"I hope so. Your man there can be a little intimidating."

Evan puffed up. "See? I am a man, Kenzie. No need for any more confusion."

Daniel laughed.

"Man?" His mother chuckled. "More like a strutting

peacock. Now who's ready for some coffee and sweets? I thought we'd wait until Smith arrives to eat breakfast, but it's okay if we nibble."

"That's fine by me," Jerome said. He engaged Kenzie in conversation, and she learned he'd made his money as a geologist who'd transitioned into the oil business. Some profitable work in Colombia and Nigeria had allowed him to eventually buy his way out of his oil company to go back and teach geology at the university level.

"And now I'm retired and loving life. My kids are grown and living abroad, so I don't see them much. But I found Jane, and I'm consolidating. Moving into the house on Bainbridge. Have you been to the island?"

"Oh, not in a long time." She blew on the cup of coffee Evan had refreshed for her. A sip showed he'd put in the right amount of cream and sugar. Just one of many small things he seemed to know or remember about her. "Thanks, Evan."

He smiled and left her with Jerome. Evan joined his mom and Daniel by the sweets, eating as much as her brother, who was actually on his best behavior and not gobbling down everything in sight. In fact, he seemed to be paying particular attention to Evan, doing what Evan did.

"You know, Evan thinks the world of you," Jerome said, his voice pitched low. "I can't tell you how often his mother hears your name coming up in conversation. I'm so pleased you came today. She—and I—have really been wanting to meet you."

Kenzie blushed. "Oh, it's my pleasure. I know how much Evan loves his mom. I was pretty intimidated to come, to be honest."

"Bah. Why? Jane is a sweetheart. I'm just her humble servant."

Her love slave? slipped into Kenzie's mind, and she coughed as she choked on a sip. "Sorry. Hot coffee."

He patted her back. "Good coffee, good food, good company. Though if we don't start eating soon, my stomach might crawl out of me and start eating on its own. I don't know if this Smith fella is coming."

She agreed. She had to eat, and she'd been doing her best to avoid the carbs her stomach and thighs craved but that she didn't need. "Evan wasn't sure he'd show either. I gather there's some family drama connected to Smith."

Jerome sighed. "A lot, yes."

The doorbell rang.

Everyone froze. Then Evan moved before his mother could.

"I said I'd come, dickbag," she clearly heard Smith rumble.

Daniel laughed then coughed when Jane gave him a look. "Sorry." But that didn't stop Jerome, who clearly found Smith's choice of words amusing.

Jane shook her head and yelled in a booming voice Kenzie wouldn't have expected from a woman so petite, "Evan, bring him in."

Smith entered behind Evan, and Kenzie gaped at the muscular giant, recognizing him from that day she'd followed her brother to the Vets on the Go! warehouse. No, she definitely wouldn't want to meet Smith in a dark alley. For all that he was good-looking, with short dark hair, green eyes, and a chiseled chin, he looked mean.

"Dude. You are way bigger than Evan." Daniel didn't seem perturbed.

The big man gave Evan a look. "Yeah. I am."

"But not as fast on the soccer field," Evan reminded the room. "And that's important."

"True." Jerome grinned. "Unless you're not playing soccer."

"'Dickbag,' huh? That's a good one."

"Daniel," Kenzie said, horrified.

"What? *He* said it." He pointed to Smith.

"I did," Smith admitted.

"He did," Evan agreed.

"Boys." Jane sighed then gave Smith a big smile. "Looks like you'll fit right in. Welcome to the family. I'm your Aunt Jane. This is Jerome, that's Kenzie, and that's Daniel. And you obviously know Evan..."

CHAPTER 23

FIVE DAYS HAD PASSED SINCE THEY'D SHARED BRUNCH at his mother's. Five days of backbreaking work at the job, followed by soccer, helping around Kenzie's place, and trying to steal moments when the two of them could make love.

Or fuck, as had become Kenzie's favorite thing to do. The woman was insatiable. Evan loved that about her because she made him the same way. He had a healthy sex drive, but he'd never been more ready for sex than with Kenzie.

He groaned as he came, spending inside her delightful body. He had her turned around and pressed against the back of his front door, her pants down to her knees, slightly bent over, her hips jutting out. He hadn't undressed except to unzip his pants and thrust up into her.

The hottest sex they'd had to date.

Life was just about perfect lately. Every time with her just got better.

He and Daniel were tight, the little brother he'd always wanted his good friend. Evan helped him with soccer when he had time. With Cash coming back to work in a few days, Evan would soon have more time to spend with Kenzie. As it was, he'd been working from a few clients' homes and from his home, as well as doing time on the moving jobs. He felt spread thin. It might have helped if he could have stayed a few nights at Kenzie's so he wasn't always rushing around in the wee hours, but she hadn't seemed keen on him broaching the subject.

She sighed as he withdrew, pliant and replete. He turned her in his arms even as he put a cloth between her legs to clean her up. He kissed her, loving how she responded. She put her head on his chest and let him fix her clothes before holding her.

Every second spent with her felt like a gift. He loved her so much.

Lila and Rachel approved. Daniel had hinted more than once that he'd like Evan to move in. And the guys at work, Smith in particular, teased him—nicely—about finding a woman way too good for him.

But when not coming down off an orgasm, Kenzie seemed distant. He felt her withdrawing, and he didn't like it. At all.

"Hmm." She sighed. "I want to do that all over again, but I'm too tired."

"Well, you could leave your car here and I could drive you home."

She nuzzled his chest and breathed in. "I need my car for a big meeting tomorrow."

"Oh, right. The Talon account. You'll smash it."

"I hope so." She sounded stressed.

He had wanted to ask about her financial situation more than once, but that was another line he knew not to cross.

"About needing your car… I could drive you home in your car, so you'd have it for tomorrow. I can grab an Uber to bring me back here."

She tensed and pushed him back a space. "Evan, I—"

"Kenzie, I don't want to pressure you. I sincerely don't. But baby, I'd like to sleep with you in my arms. And I know you can't leave Daniel alone. I'm not asking you to," he said quickly, in case she went there with him. "I know letting me in is hard because of what happened with Bryce." *That prick.* "But I"—he didn't say *love you*, not wanting to pressure more than he already was—"miss you when we're not together."

"Oh, Evan. I miss you too."

He at least had that going for him. "Then why can't we sleep together? I don't like sneaking around."

"I know. I just, well…" She looked at her feet. "Okay."

"I don't know why—okay?" He blinked. She'd said *yes*? At her nod, he dragged her into his arms and spun her around. Kenzie laughed, breathless, until he set her down. "God, Kenzie. I've been waiting forever to hear you say yes. Let's go before you change your mind."

He quickly packed a duffel bag and locked up then headed toward her car.

"Might as well bring both cars so you can get to work in the morning without having to hassle about transportation."

He stopped, trying to read her expression. Closed? Resigned? Not happy. "Kenzie, I don't have to come. I just wanted to be with you."

"I know." She threw herself into his arms. "Sometimes I don't like myself very much."

"Why?"

"Because you're so perfect, and I'm still having trouble with us."

"I don't have to stay over."

"No, you do. And it's not like we need to hide it from my brother." She looked up at him, chagrined. "He left a box of condoms on my bed and told me to use them until I'm ready to ask you to marry me, to do it right."

Evan tried not to laugh. What a great kid. "Um, are you

afraid I'll say no?" Because he'd found her, he loved her, and he had no intention of letting go. But he also knew she needed to realize she could trust him with her heart. And no amount of sleepovers could cure that. She had to feel it and *know* it.

"I'm afraid you'll say yes. No, don't ask me any more questions. And no sex at my place. Just sleeping."

"Yes, ma'am."

She sighed. "I'll meet you at home." She left.

He followed, wondering how she'd react when he gave both her and Daniel a key to his place. Wondering how he felt when she said "home." Because he no longer thought of his condo as where he hung his hat, but at Kenzie's—where his heart was.

Kenzie could feel herself breaking into tiny, stressed-out pieces.

They hadn't landed the Talon account, and she didn't know how to tell Lila or Rachel because they needed the money. She'd been banking on that business, and she shouldn't have. She still didn't know why Rob had rejected them. She'd nailed everything he'd said he wanted.

Of course, when she'd politely put his hand back on his own knee, that might have had something to do with it. Not exactly something she could tell her business partners, who would go psycho on his ass. Or Evan, who she could easily see beating Rob Talon's pretty face into a pulp. Satisfying, but it would only hurt Evan when Rob decided to sue.

She groaned. To make matters worse, Daniel was on

cloud nine because his new "big brother" Evan now lived with them. He didn't, but try telling Daniel that. Just because Evan had been staying over each night didn't mean he'd moved in.

And Evan symbolically giving them the keys to his townhome—one for her and one for Daniel—made it harder to remember why she shouldn't cave and go for broke. Ask him to stay, to make a family.

So he could one day decide he'd changed his mind and leave?

Stupid thoughts stuck in her mind, a pervasive fear that everything was too good to last.

Evan coached Daniel in soccer without fail. He helped out around the house, continuing to fix everything she'd been putting off forever. And Daniel clung to his every word and action like gospel.

Evan this and Evan that. She couldn't believe she'd been worried her boyfriend might not take to her brother. Sometimes she wondered who Evan liked better.

Then she'd feel terrible because she knew she was at fault for not being closer to him. She didn't mean to, but she kept pushing him away. She hadn't given him a key to her house, though he knew where the spare one lay, under the mat out back.

He saw Lila and Rachel in the evenings and practiced with Will and the Legal Eagles. And he'd invited Smith over once, this past weekend, and they'd had a blast playing horseshoes, of all things. The giant had left after giving her a kiss on the lips Evan hadn't liked. At all. But it still warmed her that Evan cared so much.

And shouldn't.

Because he deserved so much more than what she'd been giving him.

Sometimes she wished he'd never told her how much he loved her.

And yet, he hadn't said it since. Just that one night, but she knew he still felt it.

One week to the day since Evan had first slept over, she sat in her basement, staring morosely at a concept for the new recycling facility job Rachel had landed, thanks to a connection Will had to someone Evan had introduced him to. Evan again. God. He kept making her life so much better, so why did she feel so much dread?

"You going to stare us into a new template or what?" Lila asked, chomping on some gum. She had her hair up in a complicated twist and looked like a goddess. Kenzie wanted to smack her for being so happy and together. Lila and Hector were a hot thing, so now Kenzie had to see Evan laughing it up over at Lila's house, hanging with his buddy and Kenzie's best friend…when he wasn't chilling with Will.

God, Evan was taking over her life! Her friends, her job, her brother.

"Ack." She got up from her desk and started pacing laps, her brainstorming pattern a clutter-free circle on the floor so she could think around creative blockages.

Lila looked as if she meant to say something more, but Rachel shook her head, and Lila returned her attention to her computer.

Five minutes of internal swearing, some sweat, and much walking, and Kenzie still had no idea how to handle Evan. She wanted so badly to love and trust him. But something still held her back, and she feared a buried sense of intuition was telling her he wasn't as good as he appeared to be.

He sure wasn't perfect. For all that he could be romantic or sexy or thoughtful, he left the toilet seat up, which drove her nuts. He hated Mexican food, and Taco Tuesday was a home staple. And he had a habit of pausing before he spoke to her, as if weighing every word. Which totally pissed her off. He should feel free to speak his mind, for fuck's sake.

She came back to her desk and plonked in the seat.

The entire room remained silent. A glance at the clock showed it had reached two thirty. God. This day sucked so much ass. The last time she'd looked, the clock had read two twenty-six.

It was Rachel who broke the silence. "We got the Talon account."

Kenzie started and answered before she could think to prevaricate. "No, we didn't."

"We did." Rachel was somber, concerned. "Kayla called me earlier today, told me what happened and how sorry she was. Her brother is taking a short break and apparently had a mental breakdown shortly before meeting with you."

"That's the story they're sticking to," Lila said dryly. "I want to know why you didn't tell us."

"I'm confused. How do you know any of this? Okay, he put his hand on my knee. I moved it back. He apologized for being thoughtless. We didn't get the account. End of story."

"Apparently not, because Kayla heard about what happened from Evan then she heard it from her beat-up brother. She's so sorry and furious with Rob because she's all woman power, blah, blah, blah," Lila said. "I still want to beat the shit out of him for coming on to you, but I guess Evan handled that." She gave a lethal grin. "Good man."

"Hold on. How did Evan know?"

Rachel answered, "I don't know, exactly. Somehow Evan got Rob to tell him the whole truth. Then he beat the crap out of him for it."

Great. Now Evan would land in huge trouble with the wealthy Talons. "God. It was just a hand on a knee." At Rachel's raised brow, she flushed. "Okay, it made me uncomfortable. But they're rich, and they have the money to hire lawyers who will say it never happened." And would sue Evan's sexy butt for all he had. Her anxiety spiked.

"But it did, and it has happened before, apparently." Rachel frowned. "You should have told us."

"I was going to." Kenzie felt miserable. "I'm sorry. I know we need the money, and I was so sure we'd get the account. I had everything Rob passed on from Kayla. We nailed it."

"She thought so too." Rachel nodded. "Which is why she gave us the account."

"But I still don't understand why Evan got involved." Kenzie wanted to know, her blood pressure rising at thoughts of Evan once again interfering where he had no business being.

Lila answered, "I heard him talking to Hector about it. He saw Rob in town and asked about the job. Rob made up some bullshit excuse that Evan saw right through. And when Evan called him on it, Rob trash-talked you before admitting what he'd done. I guess that pissed Evan off because Kayla said she wasn't sorry about what Evan had done to Rob and not to worry about it."

"Oh, that ass."

Rachel and Lila exchanged a look. "Rob, right?"

"No, Evan."

Lila blinked. "Um, he did us a solid. Also helped with what Rachel's working on."

"That's not the point. He's too involved in everything." Kenzie reached and crested her boiling point between one breath and the next.

She screamed, and her friends stared at her in horror. Especially when she started sobbing.

Kenzie was so out of control, so scared, and she didn't know what to do.

Evan started at the sound of Kenzie's shriek. He'd swung by to pick up Daniel, who'd forgotten his cleats and shin guards and needed a quick ride home and back to practice. It wasn't a problem because Evan had intended to talk to Kenzie today. He wanted to clear the air and let her know his intentions. He'd wondered if maybe he'd been too vague and wrong in not being completely open.

The ring he'd picked up a few days ago was in his duffel bag upstairs. Every time he looked at it, he wanted to give it to her. But he knew rushing things wouldn't help. Kenzie needed time.

Yet another part of him insisted he loved her. He wanted to marry her. She should know, right?

But that scream terrified him.

He and Daniel had been halfway to the car when they heard her, and they raced to the outside entrance, down the stairs, and into the hallway past the boiler to see the girls in a huddle on the floor, Kenzie crying her eyes out in a group hug.

Lila spotted him and subtly shook her head, so he stayed back with Daniel and put a finger over his lips.

Daniel nodded, and they listened from the hallway, the women easy enough to hear.

"I'm sorry. I'm so sorry." Kenzie sounded awful, and his heart broke for her.

"Kenzie, honey, talk to us. We're your best friends. What's going on? You keep complaining about Evan."

He blinked, confused, and met Daniel's equally baffled gaze. What had Evan done but help her?

"It's all his fault." Kenzie cried harder. "I have real feelings for him, but I'm so scared, Lila. I'm so afraid to be wrong again."

"Oh, honey. It's okay." Rachel kissed her on top of her head, rocking her friend.

"He has all the answers all the time. And he's taking everyone. Daniel, you guys, our business."

Lila glanced at the hallway once but said nothing.

"Everyone loves him. He's smart and nice. He makes me laugh. He works really hard, and he's always paying for stuff. Yeah, he's a fucking paragon."

Evan hadn't expected the vitriol, and it shook him. Especially because Kenzie had "feelings" for him. Not love.

"He's all over me, and I feel like I can't breathe."

Rachel asked, "Did you tell him you need some space?"

"No. Because that would hurt him." Kenzie cried again. "I don't want to hurt him. I want to love him, but I don't know how."

She didn't want him around. She didn't love him. A fist of hurt squeezed his chest, and he put a hand over his heart, in literal pain.

Next to him, Daniel patted his shoulder, but Evan

couldn't look at him. He'd worried he might be moving too fast. And apparently for Kenzie he was. He'd pushed her to a meltdown. But why hadn't she been able to tell him she needed space or time?

Because you all but invited yourself to live with her, maybe? He felt terrible because he still loved her and he'd hurt her. And she didn't love him.

"You should have told him," Lila said. "He's a big boy. He'd get over it. And if he really loved you, he'd understand."

Thanks a lot, Lila. I do love her, but I apparently don't understand her as well as I thought I did. All the while he'd felt as if he'd been growing into a family, finally surrounded by a brother and a woman he loved like no other, she'd been feeling pressured. *God, I'm so clingy. Mom was right.*

"Yeah, because he's sweet and nice and kind," Kenzie spat. "And rich, and athletic, and sexy, and *perfect.*" She cried harder. "He's everything I'm not. Hell, without the Talon account, we'll end up back in debt and going without paychecks for the next two months. And Evan's driving a Lexus and paying for a condo he's never in! I'm bad at my job, and I found another gray hair yesterday," she wailed. "I feel like I've gained ten pounds." Evan thought she looked like she'd lost ten. "I make killer tacos, and he hates Mexican food. Why does he want to be with me?"

"Kenzie, where is this coming from?" Rachel asked, sounding upset. "You're not making sense."

"He gave us his keys, Rachel. He has a ring in his bag, an *engagement ring.*"

Shit. He knew he should have kept the thing at home. But no, he had to keep toting it around with him. He didn't look at Daniel, who gripped his arm.

"She doesn't mean it, Evan. She loves you," the boy whispered.

Evan felt like a complete heel for forcing Kenzie into a situation she wasn't ready for. And worse for getting so attached to Daniel and now needing to leave.

"Go give her a hug," he whispered to the boy. "But Daniel, don't let her know I was here. I don't want her hurting anymore."

Daniel's eyes filled. "Don't leave, Evan. She really does love you."

Evan forced himself not to cry and smiled instead. "I know she does. But she's been hurt, and she needs time to heal. Let's give her that time, okay? Don't be mad at her, Bro." He pulled Daniel in for a hug. "Remember, don't tell her I was here. She'll just feel worse."

Daniel nodded and wiped his eyes with the back of his hand.

"I'll see you at your game tomorrow. But I might not be where she can see me, okay?"

"O-okay."

Evan turned to leave, but Daniel grabbed his sleeve. "I love you, Evan."

Evan's eyes *burned*. "I love you too, Daniel. That hasn't changed." He looked beyond the hallway. "And I love your sister. But she needs time."

He hurried to his car as the tears streamed down his cheeks. And he drove home, sat in his colorless house, and stared out at the empty backyard, wondering how easily he'd lost something he'd never hoped to have again.

CHAPTER 24

KENZIE'S CRYING JAGS MADE NO SENSE, BUT AFTER LET-
ting go of that initial stress, she did feel much better. That
and realizing she'd caught the same crud Daniel had suffered
from the past three days. You had to love high school, a living
petri dish of germs.

It also explained why she'd been so sick to her stomach. Hers and Daniel's bouts of nausea had been coming
and going for two days straight. Stress was a terrible thing,
and she'd been wrestling with so much lately. She hated that
Daniel had seen her at such a low point, but she was relieved
Evan hadn't been able to join her for the past two days, an
emergency with his mom and Jerome taking precedence.

At least Daniel had recovered enough that he'd been
able to go out again.

"I'm still mad at you," Lila said Sunday night. She, Rachel,
and Kenzie were spending their evening at Lila's while Hector,
Will, and Daniel did guy things over at Kenzie's house.

Kenzie needed girl time, so she'd been fine with her
brother spending the evening with the guys. She only wished
Evan could have joined them. "I'm so glad Evan wasn't there.
I mean, I was freaking out. I feel like an idiot for it."

Rachel shrugged. "Hey, stress will do weird things. My
mom once cut off all her sister's hair when she was planning
the wedding to my dad."

"Yeah, but wasn't that because she found out said sister
put the moves on your dad?" Lila asked.

"Well, yeah. Stress."

The three laughed. Kenzie kept thinking about Evan, wondering why he hadn't called or texted in a while.

"He hasn't called," she said an hour later while they watched the latest Tarzan movie for the fifth time, giving a loving critique of Alexander Skarsgård's body. And no, no one found anything wrong with the film except the actor wore too many clothes for the better part of the movie.

"What?" Lila paused the movie right when he swung wide, showing off his pecs. "Oh, now that is nice, even for a white boy."

"You're just spoiled because Hector's so massive."

Lila waggled her eyebrows. "Is he ever."

Rachel and Kenzie laughed, then Kenzie frowned. "He hasn't texted either. I think Evan might be mad at me."

Rachel and Lila said nothing. Kenzie knew she'd missed something.

"What? What's going on?"

"Well, Kenzie…" Rachel paused.

"You see…" Lila paused.

They didn't speak.

And she knew.

"No. No way. He wasn't there. He couldn't have heard me losing it."

"He was, actually. I'm so sorry." Lila moved next to her to hug her. "He and Daniel heard you yell, and they were by the hallway near the back door. I guess he stayed to make sure you were okay and heard enough."

"Oh God." She tried to recall everything she'd said, and what she remembered was bad. The tears fell, as they did so easily since she'd caught that crud Daniel had brought home from school. And speaking of crud, her stomach rumbled. She darted into the bathroom and heaved until she had nothing left.

Then, feeling spent, she washed out her mouth and dried her eyes. "I'm still sick, and my life sucks."

"Now, now." Rachel covered the lower half of her face with her sweatshirt, protecting herself from Kenzie's germs though she sat on a chair a few feet away. "Look, Evan loves you. He said it himself. If I was him, I'd be mad and upset."

"And hurt."

"You're not helping, Lila." Rachel glared her friend to silence. "And hurt, yes. But he also loves you, Kenzie, enough that he bought you a ring."

"It was pretty. And big. And he loved me." Kenzie sniffed.

"Loves, with an *s*." Rachel nodded. "Look, you said yourself you felt rushed and pressured. So he owns some of that too."

"But I said yes."

Lila nodded. "Yes, you did. So you own a good portion of the crapfest that is now your life."

Rachel rolled her eyes.

"No, Rach." Kenzie wiped her eyes. "Let her tell it to me straight. That's Lila's specialty."

"You're damn right." Lila sat next to Kenzie, uncaring of her illness, and poked her in the chest.

"Ow."

"You, shut it and listen. You have friends, family, and a kickass job that, yes, occasionally requires creative spending. True?"

"Yes."

"You got shit on all over by a man who said he loved you and ditched. And he hurt Daniel. True?"

"Yes." Ouch.

"But you're here now. You're healthy. You can hear, see, smell, breathe, walk, run. I mean, in the big scheme of things, what are you really complaining about? You got your heart broken big-time. But you're still alive and kicking. Your life could be much worse. You could be homeless. You could have cancer. Or you could—"

"Cancer. Evan's fiancée died of cancer. He went through something horrible."

"And he stayed with her until the end," Lila stated, having heard the story. "So your pathetic I-feel-sorry-for-my-broken-heart shit is nothing compared to that."

Kenzie's nausea rose again, but Lila must have seen it because she covered her face with the bottom of her shirt.

Rachel's eyes narrowed. "Nice, Lila."

"Yeah? Well, I don't see you sitting next to the Black Death here."

Kenzie darted for the bathroom and returned moments later. "Sorry. Just dry heaves."

Lila shrugged and through her shirt said, "Hey, I've been there. Felt like my life was ending. Then I watched the news and realized I can handle my shit because it's not nearly as bad as half of what the world suffers."

Rachel shook her head. "You're so worldly yet such a moron." She lowered the sweatshirt from her face slowly. "Kenzie, you've been dealing with a ton of stress from your new boyfriend and work. You needed the stress relief. Now you've got it. And you're bothered because Evan hasn't texted or called."

"Yeah." She sighed.

"So imagine him never coming back. Imagine he went away. Or he died. Or he's just gone. Now how do you feel? Not relieved, because you're crying."

"I love him." She wiped her nose on her sleeve.

Lila cringed. "You are so gross."

"Watch it or I'll vomit all over you."

"Yeah, Daniel tried that two days ago. Good luck with that."

Kenzie gave her friends a weak grin. "I just said I love him, and nothing in me wanted to puke."

"Well, you're cured."

"No, I mean, the stress isn't there. I've been thinking about Evan a lot. All the time before and since the Incident."

"Your spaz attack?" Rachel asked.

"Psychotic break?" Lila offered.

"Oh, I like that better." Rachel nodded.

Kenzie glared. "I'm calling it *the Incident*. Anyway, I think at that moment I allowed myself to just be angry with Bryce."

Lila hit her.

"Stop it!"

"Sorry, habit."

"And to be angry at Evan for making me move past He Who Shall Not Be Named." Kenzie kept an eye on her slap-happy friend. "Evan woke me up again. He forced me to deal with my feelings, and that made me mad, deep down. I resented him." She mentally pored through her feelings. "But it also made me realize he's not the type to cut and run. He won't just quit on me. He's been there, being my rock even though I didn't lean on him. He was there."

"This is such a moment." Lila gazed, wide-eyed. "I wish I had popcorn."

Rachel snickered then laughed louder when Kenzie glared at them both.

Lila chuckled. "Well, it is, dipshit. We've been telling you this since 'the Incident,'" she emphasized, using finger quotes. "And now he's all alone and feeling unloved. But he's Evan, so instead of tying one on and getting a BJ from some hottie downtown at a singles bar, he's probably moping at home and listening to emo music, missing you."

Rachel kicked at Kenzie with her funky toe socks. "So what are you waiting for? Go get your man."

"What if he's mad at me or won't talk to me?"

Lila frowned "Then work it and *make him* talk to you. Hell, kiss him and get him sick, then just 'be there' to nurse his helpless ass—"

Rachel interrupted. "Sexy ass."

"—sexy ass through it all."

"But I'm sick." Kenzie stood when Lila shoved her to her feet then stupidly waited for Rachel to return from a trip to Kenzie's house holding her purse, her keys, and Evan's ring. The little box had been haunting her ever since she'd shown it to Lila, who'd taken it from Evan's duffel and insisted it remain on Kenzie's dresser as a reminder of her man.

"Here." Rachel dumped it all in her hands. "And take this. Chew several." A pack of mint gum.

Lila grabbed everything from Kenzie and said, "Eh, maybe use my toothpaste and gargle some mouthwash before you go. Then feel free to chew ten pieces of gum at once."

Kenzie did what she was told and returned to gather her

things then chewed only one piece of gum. Embarrassingly, everyone gathered in Kenzie's driveway—the guys and the girls—to watch her get into her car. Daniel appeared beyond thrilled.

Will pointed at her then put a finger across his throat. "We need him for Monday night's game against the Burning Embers. So help me, you put his head on right, woman, or I'm taking you out!"

Rachel said wryly, "Such respect for love."

"Screw love." Will glared. "I bet on our team to win."

Kenzie scared up a grin. Her brother raced over to her and kissed her cheek through the open window of the car.

Daniel nodded. "He's at home."

"And you know this because you texted him?"

"No, I know this because I initiated 'Track My iPhone' on his phone when I borrowed it." At her shocked look, he nodded. "I mean, yes, I texted him. Go get my soccer coach back. I miss him."

She ran a hand over her brother's cheek and prayed Evan could forgive her stupidity. "Wish me luck."

The crowd cheered and waved her away.

And her heart raced the long drive to Evan's.

———————————

Evan had binge-watched Marvel's *The Punisher*, just so he could see people get hurt and get back up. Then he forced himself to watch some Hallmark movies, where people fell in love and stayed in love, and he yelled at them to stop dreaming, criticizing the guys in each film as being too easy and wimpy.

He wasn't proud of it, but he'd cried himself to sleep Thursday night and drank himself to sleep Friday. By Sunday, he'd recovered enough to work all day, catching up on his accounting.

He was due to work at Vets on the Go! in the morning, on a moving crew as backup in case Cash couldn't make it. He texted Cash that he was sick and wouldn't be in.

Then Cash asked why Evan was due to work when Cash had been assigned that job, apparently all healed up.

Evan left him a one-word answer. Reid. And he knew that would be a discussion best happening between brothers.

He flicked through the channels as he lay on his couch in his living room. He'd bought a purple-and-red-striped pillow as well as a blue-and-yellow-polka-dotted one then added a green throw. So now his living room looked as though the color gods had puked all over his professionally decorated sophistication. He'd bought cookies and cake from a nearby bakery but couldn't force himself to eat anything Kenzie hadn't made for him.

And he felt pathetic for being so downtrodden. It wasn't as if his life had ended. So the woman he loved didn't love him back? So what? She could grow to love him.

Or he could leave her alone and find some self-respect.

She'd texted him a bit today, but he hated the thought she pitied him or worried she'd hurt his feelings.

Because yeah, he had pride—maybe a single ounce of it, but he had some left.

Someone knocked at the door. Then they rang the doorbell. He didn't want to see anyone, so he figured they'd soon go away.

He forgot he'd given Kenzie a key.

She let herself in, but he didn't stir himself to greet her. She'd probably just come to return his stuff to him.

"Evan?"

He lay on the couch covered in green. He probably looked like one long, unshaved, slovenly cucumber. And he didn't care.

Or he told himself not to care, wishing his heart didn't pound so hard.

"Oh, are you sick?"

Fuck. She looked good, and he was so hungry to just see her. Her hair was pulled back into a ponytail, her face thin but so darn pretty. She looked clean, scrubbed, and innocent. And the sweats she wore only accented her natural beauty.

He closed his eyes. "Yeah, I'm sick." *Of loving you.* "You should go."

Instead, she sat next to him on the couch, scooting him over when he refused to move. Then she put a hand on his forehead.

"You're not warm."

"I'm not a lot of things" slipped out before he could help it.

"Oh, Evan." She just had to hug him, didn't she? He'd been slowly trying to get over her massive rejection, raging at Hallmark, enjoying a streaming bunch of bad guys getting death and dismemberment, empathizing with a hero who'd lost his wife and kids. And then she had to show up and hug him.

"Go away." He refused to look at her again, miserable. He waited for her to leave.

"I'm so sorry you saw me freaked out. Evan, my only excuse is I was under a lot of stress, and I was sick."

He opened his eyes. "You were sick?"

Come to think of it, she really was much thinner than she'd been. And paler.

"I caught Daniel's crud. He was sick too. It's been going around the high school." She leaned down and kissed him on the mouth, and he was too stunned to stop her. She tasted minty. Very minty.

"Did you eat a peppermint plant or what?" His mouth was burning. He tried to sit up, feeling ridiculous as she loomed over him. But she lay on top of him, keeping him in place.

"No. You're going to let me finish."

He sighed. "Fine."

"I wish you hadn't caught me when I was so low. But I'm glad you did. You claim you love me. But I said some awful things. I meant some, and I didn't mean some. Do you still love me?"

"Damn you. Yes." He hated that he couldn't stop himself.

Except her joyful smile took his breath away. "Oh, Evan. Say it."

"No."

She tried to tickle him, even found a few of his sensitive spots, but he grabbed her hands to hold her still. "Say it, please?" she asked.

"No." It hurt too much.

"Will it help if I say it first?"

"No. Don't lie to me."

She kissed him, and when he tried to move away from her, she wouldn't let him.

His body, predictably, didn't care that he was hurting. It only cared that the woman who smelled so damn good, the woman who made him insane with lust, had returned. And she was moving against him in that way she had, stirring him past sense.

She leaned up, and he released her hands. She cupped his face and kissed him again.

Fool that he was, he let her. When she looked into his eyes, hers looked shiny. "I love you, Evan. From the bottom of my heart. I'm only sorry it took the thought of losing you to realize it."

That…that sounded sincere. He stopped trying to free himself and waited.

"Knowing I'd lost the Talon account killed me. Then realizing you knew that Rob had been a jerk and you'd fixed things when I couldn't, it hurt my pride. My brother loves you. My friends love you. You're patient and understanding, and I love you. But I'm afraid. What I feel for you is so much more than anything I ever felt for Bryce.

"You're kind, even when I don't say I love you back. Even when I push you away, when I gripe at you about the toilet seat or Taco Tuesday. You smile and tease and make me fall for you all over again." She blinked, and a tear spilled down her cheek to land on his.

"Don't cry." He hated her tears. "Please."

"And so polite." She wiped her eyes. "You're so self-assured, and I'm not. Evan, you're intimidating."

He couldn't believe she'd say that. "God, Kenzie. I'd never hurt you."

"Oh, stop. Not physically, although you're muscular and could crush me if you wanted to. I mean you're intimidating because you're so honest and giving. And I've been living a big lie because I'm afraid. Evan, I love you. And if you ever left me, I don't know what I'd do. Bryce broke my trust, and he broke my heart.

"You feel like everything I've ever wanted. Do you understand how immense that is?"

"I really do." He drew her down, pouring all he felt into his kiss.

When she pulled back, she had stars in her eyes. "Oh my God. You're it for me, Evan. You."

"I love you."

Her eyes teared again. But this time she ignored them and kissed him for all she was worth.

Her clothes joined his on the floor. The blanket no longer between them, they came together in a rush of motion. No words, just a promise of feeling as they crested into a tangle of love and need that lasted forever and wasn't long enough.

Sometime later, Kenzie stared down into his eyes, and he realized he'd left some stubble marks on her cheeks. "Sorry if I was too scratchy." He stroked her face. "I haven't felt like doing much of anything for a few days."

"Please don't shave until you've gone down on me at least once. I have to know what that feels like."

He laughed, his world bright and perfect once more. "You know, that's better than any apology for breaking my heart."

She kissed him over his once broken heart, and he sighed with happiness. "Evan, I'm so, so sorry. When I think of all the bad things that could really separate us, knowing I did it because I was scared and super emotional, I feel so ashamed. I'm so sorry."

"Stop it." He threaded his hands through her hair, forcing her to look at him. "Damn it. You had your reasons. Yes, they were insane, stupid, ridiculous, barbaric, and asinine, but they were real to you."

Somewhere around ridiculous, she'd started smiling. "And maybe foolish, silly, impractical, and unintelligent?"

"Maybe, yeah." He kissed her. "But you had the courage

to see past them. Kenzie, I want you. I want Daniel. I want to live in your old house, or you can live in this one or one we pick out together. I'll even let you drive my car."

"Oh wow. True love."

"Um, and you might as well know I kind of let your brother drive it last week, as part of a bet."

"Oh, I know. I saw his texts to his friend Rafi. He bragged about it."

He hesitated. "You're not mad?"

"Actually, I thought it was cute and kind of funny you two thought you could hide something from me."

"Huh." He didn't know how to take that, but she didn't look upset. "Anyway, I love you. So will you marry me? I know I should be kneeling on the floor to propose, but you're on top of me, and I'm still inside you, and I can't think of a place I'd rather be."

She wiggled her hips. "Do you think if I give you a little time we can go again? And I can shout my 'yes, God yes' and make you a happy man?" She kissed him. "Because you know I'm still neurotic, and I don't understand how you hate tacos, and we'll always have Lila and Rachel in our lives."

"I know all that. Will you marry me?"

"Yes, Evan. I will. But only if you promise to take on me and Daniel because we're a set. Let us love you for the rest of your life."

"Fuck, Kenzie. Cut it out." He wiped at his eyes. "No one must ever know I cried."

"And we don't tell them you proposed while making love to me."

"Deal." He smiled. "Now how about we have some hot shower sex and you scream my name?"

The shower sex sealed it. He shouted; she shouted; they both came. Twice. Then he put the ring she'd brought with her onto her finger. It fit her perfectly.

Just as he was tucking her into bed with him, messages arrived from Rachel and Lila confirming no one had expected her to come home tonight, or at least they'd hoped she wouldn't, and Daniel would be taken care of.

He grinned. "Hey Kenzie, Ra—"

Kenzie bolted out of bed.

He heard her throwing up and grimaced, hoping she didn't feel as bad as she sounded.

But a strange, crazy thought struck and made him dizzy with want.

He hurried into the bathroom to see her draped over the toilet. "Ah, so lovely."

"Shut up." She shot him the finger. "Oh man. I feel good one minute, sick the next." She teared up. "Evan, I wanted to get you sick so you'd be stuck with me taking care of you. That's not very nice, is it?"

He helped her rinse out her mouth, though she hadn't thrown up anything. He drew her with him back to bed and pulled a trash can next to it. Then he sat her up and looked into her lovely face. "Kenzie, I need to ask you something important."

"I already said yes, Evan." She stared down at her hand with loving adoration. "I love this ring."

The flawless marquise-cut, colorless diamond was perfect for Kenzie. And something he'd very much hoped she'd like.

"Kenzie, when's the last time you had your period?"

She blinked, stared at him in shock, then looked down, twisting her ring. "Wait. Wait. It was…"

He leaped from the bed and returned with a calendar from the other room.

She frowned at it. "I should have had it last week, I think. But Evan, I'm on birth control. I swear. I can show you my pills at home."

"I believe you. But you've been sick and, let's face it, emotional lately."

"Yes, but...but...Daniel had the same virus."

"Daniel had it for one day. He and I have been texting. He's just been bummed about you and me and pretending to still be sick to skip school."

"Oh." She swallowed. "Do you think I could be pregnant?"

"We should get a pregnancy test and find out."

She gripped his hand tightly. "Is it bad that I hope I am?" The dawning joy on her face made him love her even more.

"Is it bad that I'm thrilled I might have knocked you up? Then you're stuck with me for good."

"Evan. I'm stuck with you with or without a baby. You have my heart."

He held her close. "We should get some rest. Then we'll go tomorrow and get a few tests for you to take. But, I mean, you probably just have the flu. It's just me wishing for something we should take our time thinking about."

"Sure. Yes. Plenty of time for us to think about a child."

He turned out the light. They got under the blankets. Five minutes had passed before Evan turned on the light. "Should I get the car?"

"Yes, let's get dressed. I need to know."

CHAPTER 25

TUESDAY EVENING, SMITH RAMSEY STOOD ON THE SIDE-lines next to Hector and his mouthy girlfriend. She had an amazing body and a face that could have been in magazines. She also had a very direct way of looking at a man. She'd taken a good hard look at him and winked.

"Hello, man candy." Then she'd turned to Hector. "He's fine as shit, but he has nothing on you, baby."

"Of course not." Hector shot Smith look.

Smith held up his hands in surrender. "Hey, I can't help that I'm good-looking."

Next to him, Lafayette and his boyfriend nodded. "Mm-hmm. You surely are. But you're on the wrong team, Smith." Simon sighed and hugged Lafayette, who had an arm around him. "I'm just lucky I found you, Lafayette. You know what they say. All the good ones are either taken or asshole straight boys."

"Yes, that is what they say." The pair laughed, and Hector and Lila joined them.

Rachel and Kenzie returned from wherever the hell they'd gone, holding a bag of sodas. Smith reached for one and had his hand slapped.

Next to them, Kenzie's younger brother, Daniel, grinned.

"Hands off, MMFA #2." The petite Korean chick unnerved him almost as much as Lila. He glared but took a step back.

She harrumphed. "Good. Now let's cheer on Will and Evan. Oh, here they go!"

Not two seconds after the whistle blew, Evan's team was racing after the ball. A bunch of huge-ass dudes in fire-engine red, aptly named the Burning Embers, shoved Evan on his ass and raced after the ball.

"Uh-oh." Evan looked pissed. The guy didn't get mad that often, but when he did, look out.

Smith had come to know Evan a lot more, and he liked the guy. Evan was genuine, nice, and a sarcastic ass. But he teased with such politeness it made Smith laugh instead of wanting to pound his face in—the exact opposite of what he normally felt when around Cash.

Then he noticed the newcomers heading their way. "Shit."

"Dude, language." Hector frowned. When he spotted the bruisers and their ladies approaching, he groaned. "Oh boy. Look, man, be easy, okay? The guys are just here to root for their cousin."

My cousin too, he wanted to say but didn't. Evan acted excited that Smith was now part of his family. He didn't care who was related to whom, only that Smith belonged. And Aunt Jane—she'd insisted Smith call her that—was beyond awesome.

Smith had tried to remain aloof, but the blasted woman kissed him and begged him to help her and Jerome every five seconds. Except instead of helping with her supposed chores, he'd been to dinner or breakfast a bunch of times the past week and a half.

And he'd liked it.

Smith had never belonged, had never had softness or

acceptance. And suddenly he had Evan, Evan's friends, and Aunt Jane.

He had no idea how to handle it, so he kept retreating to good old silence.

Unfortunately, now Reid and Cash were trying to act all buddy-buddy with him, and it was all Smith could do not to pound the pair into tomorrow—even Reid, whom he normally liked.

Cash, that asshole, was intolerable. Even Jordan was complaining about him because Cash had had his cast removed and thought he could move anvils again.

It had taken Smith and Jordan to stop him, and suddenly Smith was the bad guy once more.

Jordan spotted him first and waved. He waved back, mostly to annoy Cash, who looked like he'd swallowed something bitter.

Naomi and Reid looked pleased to see him.

The newcomers joined Kenzie and the gang. Hector made introductions. Daniel stood by Smith, surprising him.

He tugged at Smith's arm and, when Smith lowered his head, whispered, "Don't worry, man. They screw with you, I'll have their bank accounts empty by dawn."

Smith blinked at the kid. "You're a little scary."

Daniel smiled. "You have no idea."

Did Evan have any idea of the family he was marrying into?

The game progressed, and Evan was kicking ass...and getting his ass handed to him by the firefighters.

Reid and Cash shared a glance. Jordan saw it. "No way. Uh-uh."

Cash blinked. "What?"

"Nice try. But no fights. This is a family event."

Smith had to disagree. "The Burning Embers are booing our team, and one of the dudes' girlfriends almost tripped Will when he got too close to the sideline." Smith frowned at a guy on the red team, who scowled at him. "Cheat much, you prick?" he yelled.

The Legal Eagle fans laughed. The other side booed.

"Bring it, shithead." The dude flipped him off.

"Oh, nice one, jackass," Jordan yelled back then turned and apologized. "So sorry. But that's uncalled for."

"Yeah, this is *the* game of the season," Rachel said, excited. "Will couldn't wait to play them. I hear they got into a free-for-all last year with Top Cops."

Kenzie said dryly, "This is not the best example of soccer I want my impressionable brother seeing."

"It's awesome," Daniel gushed. "I freakin' love this sport."

Smith had to admit it had it's charm. Another bruiser in a red shirt glared at him.

"Bring it, asshole," Cash said before Smith could.

He glared at his…brother. "Hey, I had that."

"Whatever." Cash ignored him.

Before Smith could tear into him, halftime sounded, and Evan and Will raced over to join them.

Evan wore a dopey grin, grabbed Kenzie from the stands, and kissed the breath out of her. "We're getting married," he told everyone.

Kenzie flashed the hand she'd been hiding.

Her friends freaked out, and Daniel cheered, though he didn't look surprised. Smith figured he'd already gotten the news. But the kid still wheezed when Evan hugged the breath out of him before passing him to Reid and Cash.

"Welcome, little cousin," Reid said with a big grin. "Congrats, guys."

Kenzie was breathless and so dang pretty. She hugged everyone, even Smith, and he felt… Damn it, he felt *good*.

"And one other thing. I, um, I might be pregnant. It's soon to tell, but—"

Her girlfriends went nuts. And even Jordan and Naomi looked taken aback by all the estrogen-laden tears and laughter.

"You move fast, Evan." Smith gave him a hug, lost in the moment.

"Life moves fast. You gotta hop on before you miss the ride." Evan and his nuggets of wisdom. He moved to Daniel. "I hope the baby thing is okay with you. It kind of just happened."

Daniel sighed. "I left her a box of condoms, Evan. Geez." Then the kid high-fived him while everyone laughed.

The whistle blew, and Will nudged Evan to return. To the group, he said, "After we beat these assholes, you guys want to go celebrate?"

"Heck yeah." Cash grinned. "Ringo's?" He glanced at Daniel then changed his mind. "Nah, they suck on Tuesdays. How about you guys come over to our place? Jordan actually cleaned up today."

Jordan frowned at him. Smith still didn't know what she saw in the blowhard. "Really? You want to talk about cleanliness?"

"Ah, no. Not really." Cash gave her a wide smile. "My bad."

"You're damn right, your bad." She ignored the guys grinning at her and looked at Smith. "What do you say? Feel like putting down a few brews to celebrate Evan's baby and engagement?"

Will looked pained. "And the *win*, lady. We're going to *win*."

"You poor sap. Good luck with that," Jordan murmured.

Reid laughed, as did Cash, but Naomi hushed them both and wished the Legal Eagles luck.

Will and Evan left for the field, but not before Evan planted a huge kiss on Kenzie's lips. "I love you."

Her silly smile hit Smith right in the feels. So he said to Jordan, not looking at Cash, who seemed totally uninvolved in the conversation anyway, "Sure, I'll come. Why not?" Then he leaned down to Daniel and whispered, "I get you both their phones, you work your magic?"

Daniel gave an evil little laugh and whispered back, "'Ice, Ice, Baby,' it's *so* on."

The Legal Eagles won 3–2. The after-fight was glorious, but the Burning Embers kicked serious ass.

Kenzie learned weeks later she was indeed pregnant.

And Smith agreed to be the kid's godfather in a mistaken round of good cheer and a lot of beer.

What the hell had he done?

ACKNOWLEDGMENTS

Thanks to the folks at Sourcebooks for helping me to put this book together. I couldn't do it without you!

ABOUT THE AUTHOR

Caffeine addict, boy referee, and romance aficionado, *New York Times* and *USA Today* bestseller Marie Harte is a confessed bibliophile and devotee of action movies. Whether biking around town, hiking, or hanging at the local tea shop, she's constantly plotting to give everyone a happily ever after. Visit marieharte.com and fall in love.